# LOVING LYDIA

## RESCUED HEARTS OF THE CIVIL WAR ~ BOOK 2

## SUSAN POPE SLOAN

WILD HEART
BOOKS

ISBN-13: 978-1-942265-63-4

## PRAISE FOR LOVING LYDIA

"The action-packed plot is fueled by complex characters with rich backstories and no shortage of secrets to hide. Fans will eagerly await the next in the series."

— PUBLISHERS WEEKLY

*To my people:*
*Word Weavers Columbus and Word Weavers International, ACFW*
*NW Georgia, ACFW critique scribes, my local Toastmasters clubs,*
*friends, and family near and far.*
*How can I thank you enough?*

*"The Lord Himself goes before you and will be with you; He will never leave you nor forsake you. Do not be afraid; do not be discouraged."*

*Deuteronomy 31:8 (NIV)*

# CHAPTER 1

*H*undreds of Union soldiers camped outside the village, their mere presence enough to set the locals on edge. The anxiety increased when small groups of them ventured into the outlying homes to seize food or whatever appealed to them.

Fear pushed Lydia Gibson to the hilltop, where she could see the farm below. Rumors at the mill had whirred as noisily as the wooden shuttles clacking back and forth in the weaving room. Stories were spreading of Union soldiers preying on helpless women.

*I should've stayed home with Millie instead of going to work this morning.* Their lack of funds had seemed the more immediate need. Lydia's job was their only source of income, and she needed to keep it, but not at the cost of Millie's safety. With all the family members she'd lost over the years, Lydia couldn't face losing another.

Although the mill was running again, it hobbled along like

1

an injured bird after the soldiers had paid their visit last Saturday. Overgrown boys bent on devilment, they'd scattered cloth and thread across the floor, then ripped the belts from the machines to halt production. Shock had paralyzed the workers until the intruders left.

The enemy had arrived in their little corner of Georgia.

After hearing the reports, she'd pleaded illness and left her station early. Lydia skirted the white oak on the downward side.

She caught sight of two soldiers loitering near her front door and quickly ducked back behind the tree.

Her *open* front door. Each man held a burlap sack. She'd heard enough rumors to know those sacks would collect any property that took their fancy. Those scavengers were no better than the vultures that circled dying critters, waiting to pick them clean.

Before she could think what to do, one man yelled toward the house. "C'mon, Harris, we don't have time to dally with the girls."

A third soldier staggered out the door, holding a kerchief to his bloody nose, a limp sack dangling from the other hand.

Behind the tree, Lydia gasped, but the sound went unheeded as the soldiers snorted with laughter.

"Serves you right, Private. You'll learn your looks don't sway 'em all."

The younger man muttered an indistinct reply as the three tramped down the road.

Lydia released the breath she'd been holding, waiting until they disappeared from sight before she left the shadows that shielded her.

Running on shaky legs, she rushed up the steps and halted at the entrance. "Millie? Millie, are you unharmed?"

Her blond stepdaughter ran to her, weeping. "Oh, Lydia, that awful soldier. Did you see him? Am I in trouble for hitting him? What will they do to me?"

"I don't expect you're in trouble." She stroked the girl's hair that rippled to her waist.

Millie pulled back from Lydia's shoulder. "Are you sure? Did you talk to him?"

"They were leaving when I arrived. I saw his bloody nose and figured you'd given him what for."

Millie nodded, her face flushing. "I hit him when he tried to grab me. He said..." She sniffled.

"Never mind that now. His friends laughed at him and said he got what he deserved. So I don't think you're in trouble. He's probably too embarrassed to tell anyone a girl hit him, especially one he was trying to sweeten up."

Millie scoffed. "Don't know why he'd even try, since my condition is obvious now. I can't get into any of my dresses but this one. Guess we'll have to let out the seams in the others." She patted her thickening waist.

Lydia wanted to wallop the man who'd weaseled his way into Millie's bed. It seemed life was as hard for a pretty girl as for a plain one. One had to ward off the men while the other could barely get them to notice her. Millie's bright hair and perfect complexion drew all eyes her way. Lydia often felt like a little brown wren next to the brilliant bluebird that was Millie, especially since she'd blossomed in the last couple of years.

Millie swiped her tears with her hands. "Why are you home early? Machines break down again?"

Lydia shrugged. "I wanted to be sure you were all right. Motherly worries, I guess. Now go wash your face, and let's see what we can find for supper."

Millie padded into the kitchen, absently placing a hand at her lower back. She must be six months along now. Was she spreading in the rear? Didn't that mean a girl? *Oh, dear God, what are we going to do with a baby?*

Pain pierced her heart. She'd felt it over the years as women all around her were bearing children while she was not. Her desire for children was a large part of the reason she'd said yes to Cal. She wanted babies, and Cal already had Millie—eight at the time they married. But year after year had passed with no babies of her own to rock.

Then the war came. Cal enlisted right away, sure that he and his cronies could knock the Yanks to kingdom come. She'd wondered if his real reason was to get away. Away from the mill, away from the responsibility of a family, away from her and her "constant carping," as he'd often complained. He'd gotten away all right, right into the fire of enemy cannons.

Putting aside her sense of failure, she replaced it with the heady anticipation of a baby in her life. A grandchild, though she was only twenty-eight herself. It would be much like having her own. That sweet baby smell, cuddles and kisses, and watching him or her grow.

But reality always elbowed its way back in. Dear Lord, how were they going to manage? Especially now. The mill barely limped along, the army camped at their doorstep. What was to become of them?

"God, if You're there, we could sure use some help here."

*Leave.*

The voice rang so real, Lydia whirled around to find its source. All she saw was worn furniture, the door firmly shutting out even a slight breeze.

Was she losing her mind?

Perhaps.

Shaking it off, Lydia started for the kitchen again.

*Pack and leave.*

She froze in the middle of the small room. Could it be? Did God answer so swiftly someone who rarely searched for Him? She certainly counted herself a believer, but life had been so hard, she struggled just to keep herself going.

Now jolted into action, she found Millie at the sink,

washing a couple of scrawny potatoes. A pot of water bubbled around three duck eggs.

"While I'm at work tomorrow, I want you to gather up our things and get ready to leave. We won't wait around here for the fighting to find us."

Millie dropped a potato and gaped. "But where will we go?"

"Dunno for sure. I think I have a distant cousin down near Columbus, where there's another mill. I'll see if I can find a name in Granny's Bible." She had brothers in Alabama, too, but she didn't want to be a burden. She'd have to think on which way to go. Farther south seemed the best direction, since all the fighting came from the north.

"But what about...what if someone comes looking for us? How will they know where to find us?"

Lydia pondered the question. She hadn't thought that far ahead. "I'll write to Pastor Bagley once we get settled, let him know where we are. I have a strong feeling we need to leave, not just sit around and wait for something to happen."

Later, she lay in bed and mulled over the day's events. Seeing the soldiers at her door had brought home the insecurity of their present situation. The Voice had only amplified it. Her faith had grown dusty with disuse over the years, but she had no doubt about Whose voice it had been.

Why would God speak to her? Her, Lydia Ruth McNeil Gibson. Oh, she attended church on Sunday and took part in each service. The music spoke to her weary soul, and she often gleaned a nugget of hope from Reverend Bagley's sermon. Even in that atmosphere, though, the cares of life seemed to press in, especially over the last few months.

Guilt weighed down her spirit. Despite repenting over and over, she figured forgiveness was out of reach. Her husband was likely lying in a common grave on the battlefield, a casualty of war. The official report was "missing" since the battle at

Chickamauga, but if Cal had survived, surely he would've contacted her somehow while he was so close to home.

Her fault because she had pushed him to go.

~

SATURDAY MORNING, JULY 9, 1864
GEORGIA-SOUTH CAROLINA BORDER

*W*akened from a restless slumber by violent vibrations and thundering hooves, Seth Morgan reached for his weapon. How had he not heard the call to battle? Could he be dreaming?

No weapon met his hand, only the rough wood of a wagon bed. He pushed aside the hat covering his eyes. Memories marched in swift succession before halting at the present. He'd stashed his Confederate-issued bayonet under the wagon seat at the request of his female companions.

Looking about, he breathed deeply until his heartbeat slowed and took in his surroundings. The noise and shaking emanated from the wagon rumbling across a rickety bridge. Water sparkled below, shimmering under a hazy sky. Though the sun still climbed in the east, it poured merciless heat on the people in the wagon.

"We's come to the Georgia line, folks. Y'all might get a bite to eat at the farmhouse over yonder." The driver pulled his tired nag to a halt and pointed toward a structure south of their position. "I reckon y'all might find another wagon willing to take you on a ways."

Seth grabbed his knapsack and jumped over the side of the buckboard. Robby joined him, and both turned to offer their assistance to the three women. The men retrieved their weapons, and Seth waved his hand toward the driver.

"Much obliged for the ride, Moses. Maybe the private and I will catch you on our way back."

"I'll be here, Sergeant Morgan, if the good Lawd wills and the crick don't rise." He turned forward. "Walk on, Daffodil." The mule leaned into the traces and made a circle to reverse directions. Moses sang in his rich baritone as the wagon lumbered over the bridge again. "*Swing low, sweet chariot, comin' for to carry me home.*"

Seth smiled, remembering how Moses's song had hampered the women's chatter earlier. Their grumbling about the wagon's discomfort had grated on Seth's nerves, but his upbringing had kept his mouth shut. His ploy to feign sleep had turned into blessed slumber. Heaven knows he'd had little of it lately.

He also had little patience for whiners. Two of the women had raged from one subject to the next. They castigated the State of South Carolina for not continuing the railroad beyond Greenville, which caused them their need to seek another means of travel. They reprimanded Moses for going too slowly and then protested when a faster gait bounced them off their seats. The older one, Mrs. Hobbs, had tried to stem the tide of the youngers' chatter, but her efforts had failed.

He could've told them about what their menfolk endured to the north. On top of the battles they fought, the conditions in camp tried the heartiest of soldiers. Lack of proper meals, combined with disease and the loss of limbs, eroded everyone's morale. Some men never returned from furlough. Others straggled at the rear of their units, disregarding orders about not plundering the towns and homes in their path, which incited the wrath and suspicion of civilians. What had started as a crusade for states' rights had denigrated to a vicious fight for survival.

Walking along the dusty road, Seth and Robby flanked the women to provide protection, slowing their longer strides to match the arthritic gait of Mrs. Hobbs. Oddly enough, she was the most cheerful of the group.

"Mrs. Hobbs, won't you take my arm and let me help you?" Robby extended his elbow.

Seth hid his smile, knowing the younger man chafed at the pace she'd set. Robby had always run, trying to keep up with Zeke, his older brother.

"No, thank you, Private Roland. I imagine you're as fatigued as I am since you've been traveling longer. We'll be able to rest in a few minutes when we reach that farm."

"Well, as to that, ma'am, our first day from Richmond was on the train, so it wasn't so bad. We stayed on it until we reached Greenville, with stops here and there. If it wasn't for the war, I expect the railroad would stretch all the way to Atlanta by now."

Somehow Robby had captured her arm to lend her his strength. She smiled up at him and patted his hand. "Yes, the war has put a halt to a good many things, I suspect. I've seen quite a few changes in my lifetime, and no doubt you will too. Sometimes I think we need to consider whether all those changes are for the better." She directed her attention to their destination. "Someone's coming from the house to greet us."

Seth looked over her head to verify the news. Indeed, a tall woman in a shapeless dress stepped from the porch to the yard. Her greeting fell short of hospitable. She clutched the handle of a pitchfork, its prongs pointed heavenward. Her stance indicated her readiness to fight the devil himself if he showed up at her door.

Seth took a step forward, and she flipped the pitchfork toward him. Surprised, he lifted his hands and stepped back.

Mrs. Hobbs pushed past him. "Good day, missus. I'm Elmira Hobbs, and these are my sisters, Daisy and Thelma. These here are Sergeant Morgan and Private Roland. They're on furlough from the army in Virginia. These gentlemen have graciously watched over us on our journey from Charlotte, and I can assure you they mean you no harm."

The tall woman's eyes darted from Seth to Robby and back, but she returned the tool to its original position. "I seen you get off the wagon at the bridge. The last soldiers who come that way took our food and tore up the house, looking for any valuables, so now I don't allow no weapons inside my house. If you're looking for a meal, I got stew and cornbread for two dollars apiece. I can put up the women in the house, but you men'll have to stay out here."

Mrs. Hobbs looked at Seth to speak for them.

"That's fine, missus," he said. "We'll be glad to pay you in advance. Is there a place where we can wash up?" He stepped sideways to lean his rifled bayonet against an overturned wheelbarrow and motioned Robby to do the same. Seth pulled several bills from his breast pocket, extending the peace offering to his reluctant hostess.

Setting aside the pitchfork, she gestured to the side of the house. "The well's around that way. I'll bring your food out soon's I serve up the plates."

"Much obliged, ma'am." Seth led the way to the well. They pulled up the bucket and made quick work of washing their faces and hands. By habit, Seth surveyed the land for any threat or indication of problems. The area around the house resembled a patchwork quilt, with blocks of grass sprouting in sections against the reddish dirt.

The call of a crow directed his gaze to the roof, where a couple of loose shingles curled in the heat. If he could persuade the woman of the house to trust him with a hammer and nails, he'd climb up there and fix the problem. Otherwise, she'd have trouble with a leaky roof whenever it stormed.

Like many of the places he'd seen in the last several months, an unnatural stillness brooded over it. No chickens pecked in the yard. No dogs served as sentries of protection. Only one gray cat prowled the area.

In too much of the South these days, the healthy, boisterous sounds of life had faded, succumbing to the silence of impending death.

# CHAPTER 2

SATURDAY AFTERNOON, JULY 9, 1864
NEW MANCHESTER, GEORGIA

*W*ith her spinning machine stopped, waiting on fresh cotton, Lydia grasped the chance to leave. She hurried to the stairs, past the loud clacking and shuttling of the looms in the weaving room. She passed the carding room and the door of overseer Henry Lovern's office.

She paused outside to gather her courage and mentally rehearse her speech. Lydia noted the desk littered with papers. He rifled through them, searching for something. A battered valise sat on the floor beside his chair. It appeared Mr. Lovern also prepared for a hasty retreat, following the example of the mill's superintendent, who'd reportedly taken the books and money with him.

She stepped into the room, and the overseer glanced up. His chair squeaked as he shifted his weight and peered over his glasses. "What's ailin' you, Miz Gibson? You comin' down with fever too?"

"I feel fine, thank you." She fingered the sides of her skirt to keep from displaying her nervousness. "I wanted to tell you I'm leaving, and I'd like to collect my pay today."

He stared at her. "Leavin'? Now?"

"I can finish out the day." She waffled, then firmed her resolve. "But I need to get my pay now, if you please. In bills, not company scrip, since I won't be here to use it."

"I don't know how you can—"

A sudden commotion near the front of the building halted his words. The noise intensified as a group of soldiers advanced through the aisles of machinery. Lydia moved deeper into the room, drawing her skirts to the side and shrinking into the shadows.

The tall leader filled the doorway, his gaze raking the man and the contents of the desk. Though the room was small, he never looked Lydia's way. "Are you the man in charge here? Everyone must clear the premises now. You and your people have fifteen minutes to gather your belongings and assemble at that bridge near the sawmill on the north side of town. This building and its contents will be fired."

"Who...who are you to tell us what to do?" Henry stammered. Sweat beaded on his brow. His hands hovered over the strewn papers, his fingers twitching.

"Major Haviland Tompkins, United States Army. I report directly to General W. T. Sherman, presently in command of Union troops in Marietta, Georgia." His eyes narrowed under bushy brows. "Do not think to question my authority or mistake my orders. This building will be destroyed, along with anything or anyone remaining inside."

Turning to the men who'd followed him, including a couple of harried weavers who'd joined the procession, the major issued orders to spread the word to the workers. The men scattered to comply, and the major turned away. Like a clear-day tornado, he left as suddenly as he'd arrived, sucking the air from the room and leaving chaos in his wake.

With frantic movements, Henry stuffed papers into the valise. Perspiration now coursed his cheeks, dripping onto his hands as he muttered under his breath. Whether oaths or prayers, it mattered not now.

Judgment day had arrived.

The motion shocked Lydia into action. Forgetting her earlier errand, she scurried up the aisle, gathered her dinner pail from her station, and joined the other mill hands already spilling into the bright sunshine.

By the time she reached her little farmhouse, smoke from the burning Sweetwater Mill rose behind her. It drifted upward, needing no breeze to carry the dark tendrils across the desecrated countryside.

Panic drove her. Would the Yankees burn the whole town, as they'd done in other places? She tried to plan a course of action, but her mind kept repeating the same phrase. *Get Millie and get out.* Every step rang with the order. *Get Millie and get out.*

She should've looked in the barn for the old vegetable wagon yesterday. Would it carry their trunk, or would they have to leave it behind and take only their hand luggage?

The house came into sight.

Millie stood in the yard next to the loaded cart, her face lifted to peer at the stain across the sky. Turning at Lydia's approach, she gestured to the smoke. "What happened?"

"The Union army's burning down the mill. I'm glad you're ready to leave, but you should've waited for me to put those things in the wagon. Is anything left inside?" Lydia surveyed the wagon's contents and wedged her lunch pail in a corner.

"Only your carpetbag. And you might grab Mama's old umbrella. It looks like rain's building to the west."

Lydia ran inside and snatched up the last items. "Let's go by Ferguson's first and see if he has anything better than this old wagon. We'll have to hurry, though, to get there before the army arrives at the sawmill. I don't care to run into that army major again." *Or anyone else who might threaten our safety.*

~

Saturday afternoon, July 9, 1864
Campbell County, Georgia

Lydia pushed another parcel into the crowded wagon in the line at Ferguson's bridge. Soldiers had been there when they arrived, blocking the road and directing everyone to the wagons.

When Lydia questioned a wagon driver, he pointed to the officer she'd seen yesterday. "Major's orders said to arrest every worker and take 'em to General Sherman in Marietta."

She considered her options. With no clear plan, she figured Marietta was as good as any place for the present. Surely, the Army would release them once they arrived, wouldn't they?

Lydia turned to hide her anxiety from Millie. What a mess. Smoke tainted the air, and heat still emanated from the burned ruins of the sawmill despite a late afternoon sprinkle. Steam rose where water puddled, dissipating in the July sunshine.

The odor of horses mingled with the pungent smell of charred wood as soldiers coaxed the geldings into a staggering column. Mud spatters decorated every boot and hoof, the slick substance hindering the efforts at order as much as the congestion of bodies.

Children and elderly people sat wedged between trunks and jumbled mounds of baggage in each wagon bed. Prodded by armed soldiers, the population of the little town swarmed the area east of the mill. Their anxiety over the upheaval was plain to see in furrowed brows and pinched lips. Dismay hunched shoulders and dragged at their steps.

In their haste to comply with orders and take advantage of

the rides offered, it looked as if folks had simply dumped all their belongings into sheets and tied the four corners together. A few others must have had the same idea—or Divine direction —as Lydia did. Cases and carpetbags sat piled on top of trunks.

She studied the space where she and Millie had arranged their few bags in one of the wagons. There must have been a dozen or more conveyances lined up. "Millie, you stay with our things. There should be enough room for you to sit here. I'm going to walk for a while."

Millie gripped her hand as if she would protest, but her energy flagged in the heat. "You'll stay right beside the wagon, won't you? Then we can switch whenever the wagons stop to rest the animals."

"Of course. I'll stay where you can see me. Try to take a nap. You need to recover your strength." Poor girl. Expectant mother she might be, but she was still a child in many ways.

Millie sank and leaned against one of the softer bags. Her eyes closed immediately.

Lydia climbed over the wheel hub. She leapt to the ground, but a tug on her skirt kept her from moving forward. The tail of her skirt had caught on a spoke. She twisted to clear it.

"Hold still or you'll tear it." The stranger's voice stopped her.

The auburn-haired woman untangled the cloth from the wheel. "There. It doesn't seem to be harmed."

"Thank you. This is my last one without patches. I seem to catch them regularly on mill machinery." Lydia adjusted her bonnet and tried to place the slightly familiar face. "I'm Lydia Gibson, by the way."

The other woman nodded her greeting. "Olivia Spencer. You worked in the spinning room, didn't you? I imagine you're not the only one to sport a few patches for that reason." She grimaced. "I have a few myself, but mostly because I don't watch where I'm walking. With only the open road, I should manage not to disgrace myself like that here."

"You're planning to walk rather than ride?"

"For a while at least." Olivia swept her hand toward the wagon behind them. "Though Major Tompkins wanted to keep the men separate, I convinced him my uncle wasn't up to such a long journey on foot and needed to be close to family. I volunteered to walk in his place, but it'll be more pleasant to share the time with someone, if you're agreeable."

Lydia's heart lifted. "I'd like that."

A soldier on a dun-colored horse rode up the line, giving instructions to his men and the townspeople along the way. "We're ready to move out now, folks. Everyone in the wagon needs to stay seated until we stop up the road in an hour or two. Those of you walking will have to keep pace. My men'll keep an eye in case of problems."

He urged his horse farther up the line to repeat those words to the next heavy-laden wagon. With the slow intensity of a prowling cat, the column inched forward. Around them, clusters of young women and older children matched the column's speed.

Olivia Spencer picked up their conversation. "Are you alone or with family?"

"It's just me and my stepdaughter. She's resting in the wagon for a bit."

"Oh, how old is she? My five-year-old stepson is hoping to find some children to tag along beside."

Lydia shook her head. "She's sixteen. Although she'd probably be glad to meet him, he might not care for a playmate so much older. Besides that, she's..." Lydia swallowed and decided she might as well get used to saying it. "She's in the family way."

"How wonderful! Although I suppose this journey must be taxing for her." Olivia's eyes shone with empathy. She gave a brisk nod. "And it's a good thing we've become acquainted. My husband is Dr. Evan Spencer. He's away, of course, with the army, but my aunt and a neighbor have often attended him with births."

"That's good to know. I have no experience in that area at all." A memory clicked into place, and she turned a puzzled expression to Olivia. "Dr. Spencer, you say? But I thought his wife..."

"His first wife, Anna, died nearly three years ago," Olivia said. "We married last October before he left to join the army."

"Ah, forgive my blunder, Mrs. Spencer." Lydia blushed at her error. She certainly didn't want to alienate this friendly woman.

Olivia waved away Lydia's concern. "No need to apologize, but please, call me Olivia. I'm still getting used to my new name. It doesn't seem real yet, with Evan so far away."

"I can imagine, and what little social life we once had has disappeared with the war. I hardly talk to anyone besides people at work and Millie at home. We don't even take time to visit after church anymore, except to hear about the latest battles."

Olivia nodded. "Is your husband with the army too?"

"He went missing last year at Chickamauga. That's the official word. I don't hold out much hope he survived. I've not had word from him since then."

"Oh, I'm sorry. And now here you are with a daughter and her baby on the way. Mrs. Gibson—"

"Lydia, please."

"Lydia, you must let my family adopt the two of you." She chuckled. "You may as well say yes, because Aunt Edith and Uncle Isaac will insist when they meet you."

Lydia grasped Olivia's arm. "You don't mean Edith and Isaac Wynn? Why, I lived near them when I was a girl. My brother Ellis was friends with their Thomas. My family thought so highly of them."

"Then you must know how they take in anyone who comes their way."

Another memory surfaced. "I seem to recall, about the time I married Cal, two nieces or young cousins coming from... Kentucky, wasn't it? That was you and your sister?"

"Yes, although my sister is no longer with us. We lost her to influenza last year. But now we have Wade—that's Evan's son—and Shiloh, who's from the coast near Sa..." She snapped her lips shut as if to stem the flow of words, then continued. "She's another niece of Uncle Isaac's. Aunt Edith says we're a patch-work family."

Olivia's smile slipped, and she turned her face to observe the road ahead. "Tell me about your childhood home. You mentioned one brother. Do you have other brothers or sisters?"

Lydia didn't miss the abrupt change of subject. Every family had a skeleton in the closet somewhere. Lydia hoped she could keep her own safely concealed. Talking about her girlhood was easy. It was her marriage that was difficult to discuss.

# CHAPTER 3

Saturday afternoon, July 9, 1864
Hall County, Georgia

"You plannin' on marrying again, Seth?" The question assaulted him without warning, and Seth stopped in his tracks to face his companion.

Robby looked up in surprise, no teasing glint or calculating expectancy noticeable in his eyes. He glanced around. "What? What is it? You hear something?"

Seth grunted and started walking again. "Just your idiotic question. No, I don't expect to remarry. I don't even think about it." The dull ache of an old wound restricted the area around his heart. "Losing somebody you love is too painful."

"I reckon you're right, but I don't see how any of us can avoid it."

"That don't mean we have to go looking for it, especially now with all the suffering around us. It's hard enough to lose men you're supposed to lead. Losing a family member…" Seth shook his head. Where was his cheerful companion, the babbling young man who spouted nonsense about nothing? What had sparked this serious conversation?

"What made you ask such a question anyway?"

Shrugging, Robby directed his gaze ahead. "You go out of your way to help the women we meet. You know, like fixin' that roof yesterday. Just wondered if you're thinking along the lines of finding another wife."

"We help our neighbors in times of trouble. In case you hadn't noticed, pretty much all that's left around here is women. They're carrying a heavy load now, with their men off fighting this fool war."

*Just like you are, Seth Thomas Morgan, only you're using the war to fight a personal battle.*

His long strides ate up the ground while he wrestled with his conscience. His grandpa would have quoted the verse about vengeance belonging to the Lord, but Seth pushed the reminder away. He hated the war, but he'd use it to accomplish his goal. Sooner or later, he'd run across the man who'd destroyed his family.

His mind mired in the pit of anger, he almost missed Robby's hiss of warning.

"Seth, stop! I don't like the looks of that animal headin' this way. Is it a dog or a wolf?"

Robby came up beside him as Seth slowed his steps and peered at the spectacle ahead.

The creature wobbled toward them on shaky legs, its speckled coat barely discernible under a layer of dirt. Drool dripped from its chin.

"Whatever it is, it's pure danger. Looks like rabies." With controlled movements, he raised his rifle and braced his feet. Robby did the same.

"You're a better shot than me," Robby said, "but I aim to be ready in case he lunges."

"Just wait for me to get off the first shot. We don't want him to charge."

Moisture collected on his back as Seth held his weapon at the ready, waiting for the animal to come close enough that he could be sure of his shot. For once, he was glad there was no breeze to cool his brow. He didn't need anything to play havoc with his aim.

"Come on, you sorry cur."

Finally, the animal moved toward them, and Seth fired.

Robby's shot followed.

The sounds echoed in the stillness of the countryside. The animal halted, then staggered and fell.

Robby's breath whooshed.

Seth wiped his brow and waited for his heartbeat to slow.

"We should move him off the road," Robby said.

"Yeah."

But they stood unmoving for long minutes.

*No matter where you go, there's death and danger. All the earth is a battlefield with little protection and few places of safety.*

Saturday afternoon, July 9, 1864
On the road between New Manchester and Marietta,
Georgia

*L*ydia stood with a couple dozen women in a jagged semi-circle, facing outward. Both ends of the arch met at a clump of bushes. Each woman took her turn in the middle of that protected area, two or three at a time, while the others visited amongst themselves. Even with fewer petticoats than they'd worn in earlier years, their skirts created a visible barrier and afforded a measure of privacy for those inside its enclosure.

That wasn't enough for some of the women, who grumbled about the situation. "I don't like having those soldiers just a few yards away. They know what we're about here," one woman said. "It ain't decent."

Lydia ducked her head to hide her grin.

"None of us like it, dear, but it's what we must endure, thanks to menfolk and this awful war. Both sides share the blame."

Others murmured their agreement.

"Does anyone have elderberry syrup with them?" one woman asked. "My bottle is near empty, and my little one has a cough."

Several of the women offered information about different remedies they had on hand. Lydia listened closely and mentally catalogued the answers for future reference. A body never knew when quick action might be needed if someone fell sick or got injured. When at last the wall of women disbanded, they made their way back to the waiting wagons.

As Lydia approached the place where Millie waited, she found Olivia there as well. "I've introduced myself to Millie," Olivia said. "And this is Shiloh." She put her arm around the younger woman with curly brown hair as she presented Lydia and Millie. "Lydia and I have been walking together while you tended Wade."

Lydia smiled at the olive-skinned woman. "Hello, Shiloh. I'm Millie's stepmother." Beyond the women, two familiar figures ambled their way holding the hands of a young boy. "Ah, here come your aunt and uncle, Olivia. I'd know them anywhere, though it's been years since I last saw them."

She greeted the older couple. Edith Wynn's energetic step and large frame contrasted with Mr. Isaac Wynn's slender build and slower gait. The only evidence of the elapsed years Lydia found was a greater quantity of white in their hair. She explained to the younger women about their earlier association.

Lydia then turned to the boy. "This must be young Mr. Spencer."

The boy negated the assumption with a shake of his head and serious eyes. "No, ma'am, I'm Wade," he said. "My Pa is Doctor Spencer, and this is my new Ma." He gripped Olivia's hand and beamed up at her. "Can I walk with you awhile, Ma? I'm big enough now."

Olivia pressed her hand to her heart and chuckled. "How can I refuse that smile? You'll have to stay right beside me, though, and not run ahead. These horses and mules aren't used to little boys getting close to them like Old Girl was."

"I'll stay with you." He turned to Lydia with the confident authority of a five-year-old. "Old Girl was our workhorse, but the soldiers said they needed her."

"Ah, I see." Lydia addressed Millie. "Did you want to walk now? I think I'll continue on as well, since I've rested up a bit."

Millie huffed. "It can't be any worse than bumpin' around in that wagon. Will you walk as well, Shiloh, or do you want to ride?"

"I'd be pleased to walk, if'n it's all right with y'all." Shiloh looked to Edith and Isaac for permission. Lydia understood her uncertainties. Thrown together by circumstances, everyone treaded unfamiliar territory.

Isaac waved them all away. "You young people go ahead since you're all bound to go a-foot. We'll mind the belongings, not that they're going anywhere, packed tight as they are."

Edith took his arm but divulged her husband's real reason to stay in the wagon. "He likely wants to keep talking to the young man driving and catch up on news from the other side." They climbed in and took their places just before it rolled forward.

Shiloh and Millie set off together, so different in appearance. Lydia hoped those two would become friends. Perhaps Millie would confide in someone nearer her age. Her usual sunny attitude had waned into melancholy, but she'd refused to share her troubling thoughts with Lydia. Having a friend might lift her out of the doldrums.

~

SATURDAY EVENING, JULY 9, 1864
HALL COUNTY, GEORGIA

*F*rom the sloping terrain and the distance they'd traveled, Seth figured they must be on the outskirts of Gainesville. At this pace, they might reach Marietta late tomorrow and have close to a week to spend with family before they had to head back to Virginia. And he'd have time to search for more information about his wife's murderer.

The prospect of a good meal cheered him. Even Robby's mood had suffered after their encounter with the rabid dog, mourning the need to kill any animal. How did the lad handle killing men on the battlefield?

Seth pointed out the houses on each side of the road ahead. "Looks like we're nearing the next town. More small farms around here."

A smile lit Robby's face. "Just in time, too. My stomach says it's about supper time."

"So, take your pick, boy. Right or left?"

Before Robby could respond, an older man stepped off the porch of the closest house on their left and waved them over. Robby grinned and waved back. "I guess that's our answer. Looks like we found a friendly welcome."

They veered toward the house where the man waited. Three black-and-white puppies danced around Seth's ankles, but he paid them no mind. An ancient rooster pecked in the dirt between the house and the barn. Perhaps this farm had been missed by the raiders who roamed the countryside.

Seth called out to alert anyone waiting inside the house of their arrival. "Good evening, sir. How fares your family this warm summer day?"

"We're fine as a fiddle, thankee." Short tufts of white hair poked in every direction from the man's head. His tanned skin showed a quantity of wrinkles, and his slanted smile pushed at the wad of tobacco inside one cheek. His watery blue gaze went to the chevrons on Seth's arm. "What're you two fellers doin' out this way?"

A glance reminded Robby to let Seth do the talking. "We're heading over to Marietta, going home for a few days on furlough." He stretched out his hand as they drew closer. "I'm Sergeant Seth Morgan, and this fine fellow is my neighbor, Private Robert Roland. Could you spare a drink of water and a place for us to rest our feet a while?"

"Rufus Spalding. Pleased to meet ya." The man met Seth's firm handshake, then reached to welcome Robby. "I expect we could do a mite better'n that for two fine soldiers. Supper's almost done."

Seth offered a polite protest. "We don't want to put you or your wife to any trouble, Mr. Spalding."

The older man stepped aside and spat a stream of brown liquid into the grass before he answered. "Between her and my son's boy foraging, we eat decent." He opened the door and motioned them inside. "Dottie, you got enough for two more? These fellers look like they could put away a panful of biscuits and gravy."

Dotty barely glanced their way as she added plates to the table.

Seth removed his kepi and slapped it against his leg. "Where could we wash up, ma'am? My mama'd have my hide if I sat down to her table looking like this."

Surprise lit the woman's plain features, but she spoke to the boy behind her. "Albert, show these men where the outside pump is, and mind you wash yourself too." She shot a meaningful glance at her father. "Pop, you could use with a scrub after digging in the garden."

The man started to protest, holding out his hands. He seemed to think better of it and joined the others headed outside.

Robby cut his eyes to Seth and whispered, "See? I told you. Always looking out for the women."

Seth could only shake his head.

They returned to a meal of biscuits and sausage gravy with a side of greens. Seth wasn't sure if the greens came from someone's garden or a wild patch, but any fresh vegetable was a treat. Conversation around the table centered on general topics about the war and the South's economic situation until Robby mentioned their incident earlier in the day.

Mr. Spalding leaned across the table with interest. "You're sure it was a dog, then? What'd it look like?"

Seth wondered at the interest. "It had a black-and-white coat, not spotted but mottled. I'm guessing it'd come up to my knees."

The older man looked at his grandson. "Could've been Checkers. It would explain why she never came back."

Sniffing back his emotion, the boy nodded. "She was protectin' her puppies and us too."

"You think it was your dog?" Robby asked.

"Sounds like it," the grandfather said. "She went tearin' out of here a couple weeks ago, chasing a fox who got too close to the henhouse. Her litter of pups was already weaned, but she would've come back if she could."

Dotty spoke up. "We thought she might've been snake-bit. Ah, well, it's better to know what happened than to worry over it. I'm glad you shot her and put her out of her misery."

Seth pushed away his plate. "You need to be on your guard, though. There might be other animals carrying the disease."

"The sergeant's right, Albert." Dotty picked up plates as she rose from the table, giving the boy a look. "No need to be goin' near stray animals, least not until Pop has had a look at 'em to make sure they're safe."

The boy's head drooped toward his chest. "Yes'm."

Mr. Spalding slapped his hands on his knees and pushed away from the table. "Well, young fellers, that old sun's a'wavin' goodbye. We'd be pleased to fix a place for you to stretch out if you've a mind to. We can throw a few quilts on the floor here. Dotty has a couple plants that help keep the skeeters away, so it's better'n bein' outside."

Seth patted his belly and grinned. "I'd say that's the second-best offer we've had all day. The first being Miss Dotty's fine meal, of course. We thank you kindly."

Seth refrained from looking Robby's way, lest the boy tease him again about his attention to the woman. Seth had promised himself to help women whenever he could, in any way he could, so they wouldn't fall prey to the kind of monster who'd attacked his sweet Meg.

Memories of his late wife drifted across his vision. Her angelic smile and sassy mouth, teasing him for his stubbornness, chiding him for his lack of faith in her, or daring him to explore the wonders of the world around them. Whenever he helped any woman, he did it for Meg and imagined her smiling down from heaven on him.

He wasn't on the hunt for a wife. Not ready to cross that bridge yet. He didn't know if he ever would be.

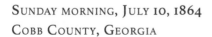

Sunday morning, July 10, 1864
Cobb County, Georgia

*L*ydia tamped down the alarm threatening to build as she watched the swift current flow past.

*Dear heavens, we'll all drown.*

"What happened to the bridge?" Millie asked.

"I don't know if there ever was a bridge," Olivia said. "Uncle Isaac said he never crossed here before. He always followed the Sweetwater Creek to where it joined the river. But he wasn't going to Marietta either."

Olivia didn't seem upset at all. She threaded the ends of an old shawl through the handles of her valise and secured it about her waist. That would leave her hands free to lift her skirts or grasp the saddle's pommel when one of those cavalrymen put her on his horse.

Lydia imitated her friend's movements.

The soldier who'd carried Wade across the stream guided his horse their way. With one arm, he helped Olivia mount behind him and guided the horse back into the creek. Another soldier reached for Millie while Lydia waited. When they'd understood the nature of their situation, she'd persuaded Millie to leave everything in the wagon. She'd hate to lose their few possessions if the wagon should be lost, but Millie was infinitely more valuable.

Though they weren't blood kin, Millie was her responsibility, her family to care for. As the youngest of her siblings, Lydia had never left their little corner of Georgia. The others had married, moved away, and started families of their own while she'd dealt with the loss of both parents and all her grandparents. Granny McNeil had pressed Lydia to marry Cal to be sure she'd have a home. Granny had died soon after her wedding. Of Lydia's brothers, only Ellis had come to mourn her passing.

Despite Lydia's fears, the crossing took only a few minutes. With the help of her escort, she slid off the horse with her dignity intact. She managed a wobbly smile for the soldier.

"Thank you." He nodded his acknowledgment and headed back to the other side and the remaining women.

A sudden commotion near the wagons diverted her attention.

Two soldiers tackled a man running toward the creek bank. As they grappled in the dirt, a crowd formed and blocked her view. Anxious for the safety of her friends, Lydia spun around, searching for familiar faces.

Lydia spotted Edith and Wade standing in the wagon beyond the creek. Isaac ambled away from the crowd. She caught up to him and clutched his arm. "What's happening? Who is that man and why did they grab him?"

Isaac patted her hand. "Army business. I don't know if the man is a Confederate or a shirker. Didn't see a uniform of any kind, but people tend to jump to their own conclusions."

*Well, that's just dandy, ain't it? We go from one upsetting event to another.*

One officer shouted an order to fetch Major Tompkins.

"Good, that man will take matters in hand, I've no doubt." Isaac led her to the wagon and took the bag she'd carried with her across the stream.

While he stowed it in the wagon, Lydia surveyed the disorder. "Do you know where Millie went? I hope we haven't lost each other in all the confusion."

"I believe she went with Olivia to the ladies' area over there." Edith pointed to where a group of women congregated. Lydia lifted her damp skirts an inch to examine the hem. "I could use some cleaning up myself. If I miss Millie, tell her to wait here please."

Shutting out the sounds coming from the group of men, she hurried toward the equally noisy women, ignoring the complaints and frustrated efforts to restore order. She found Olivia hovering over a weeping Millie. Alarm sizzled from her head to her toes. "What's wrong?"

Olivia patted Millie's shoulder and angled her head away to speak in a whisper. "Pregnancy doldrums, I believe. My husband has written reports about it. Somehow the baby inside upsets the body's humors so it takes very little to bring on a spate of crying."

Lydia knelt as best she could without further soiling her skirt. "Hey, honey. Is there anything I can do for you?"

Millie's blond hair poked from her drooping bonnet, and one side of her dress was dark from a spray of water. She shivered but straightened up and wiped the tears from her eyes. "I'll be fine in a minute. I just want to rest here a while."

Lydia interpreted that as a request to be left alone, so she rose and tended to her skirt. Shiloh joined them, and Olivia motioned to Millie. "Shiloh, will you stay with Millie until she's ready to go?"

Shiloh agreed, and Olivia nudged Lydia away. "I think she'll be fine. You should rest too."

How could she rest? Trouble kept sprouting up like weeds in a garden. She could only handle one problem at a time, and right now her priority was keeping Millie safe.

# CHAPTER 4

SUNDAY MORNING, JULY 10, 1864
HALL COUNTY, GEORGIA

Seth fumed. One trouble after another had followed them on this journey, and he was clean fed up. Arms akimbo, he pitched his voice low as he faced the old man who'd invited them to stay in his house. "Mr. Spalding, what happened to our weapons?"

The man's incredulity struck Seth as less than innocent. "What's that? You can't find your weapons? But I know you left them near the back door last night."

Robby watched the interchange from his spot on the floor as he pulled on his boots. Albert had gone outside to collect eggs, and Dotty hummed an off-key tune as she stirred a pot of grits on the stove.

Calling himself all kinds of a fool, Seth walked to the back door and peered out. There'd been soft noises during the night. Stealthy steps from the hallway to this door and outside. Figuring it was someone needing to relieve himself, Seth let the need for sleep overcome his wariness. The luxury

31

of a good meal and pleasant companions had dulled vigilance. Now he could pursue the matter and raise the ire of these good folks, or he could accept responsibility for the loss.

He swept his gaze around the yard as the sun spread its yellow glow across the fields. Besides the barn and outhouse, there didn't seem to be anything that might serve as a hiding place. Resigning himself to the obvious, he reined in his temper. "Would you mind if we searched the property?"

Spalding reared back with a snort of offense. "That's mighty poor payment for the hospitality we offered, but go ahead, if it'll set your mind at ease." He spun away and stomped to the front porch.

The words stung, but Seth was undeterred. He and Robby needed those weapons. The Confederate army would not be pleased about having to replace them.

Motioning Robby to take the barn, Seth braced himself to invade the family's private quarters. Ten minutes later, his anger still smoldering, he examined the floorboards and fireplace for secret latches. Dotty stepped aside as he surveyed her sparse kitchen, both fully aware it offered no niche big enough to hide a couple of rifles and cartridge boxes. Robby shambled in the door with a shake of his head.

Seth ran his hands over his face, his shoulders slumped. Someone on this homestead knew where that equipment was, but it would do no good to offend them further. He set his kepi on his head and picked up his knapsack. "Well, I guess there's no use in tarrying. Miss Dotty, thank you for the fine food." He turned to the boy who stood beside his aunt. "Nice to meet you, Albert. You take care of those puppies now."

The woman stepped forward with a bundle. "Here, Sergeant, take these few biscuits at least. I...I'm awful sorry about your weapons."

"Thank you, ma'am. Let's go, Robby." Seth pushed open the

front door and swallowed his ire. "Mr. Spalding, I appreciate your hospitality."

He held out his hand and waited to see if the man would take it. Spalding turned to him with a frown and lowered brows, but his eyes seemed to plead for understanding. "I got to look out for my family here, Sergeant. You'd be welcome if you come by this way again."

Seth nodded, a kernel of empathy softening his attitude as the man gripped his hand. "Maybe I'll do that. You never know what might happen."

~

SUNDAY, JULY 10, 1864
COBB COUNTY, GEORGIA

*Oh, heavens, why's this happening now?* Lydia stared at the young man held in the firm grip of two Union soldiers. His head drooped on his chest, still heaving from the exertion of running and wrestling with his captors. Blood dripped from his nose and bloomed at the corner of his mouth. Shaggy, light-brown hair covered his features now, but she'd seen them clear enough when the sergeant jerked him to his feet.

Troy McNeil. What in the world did Lydia's nephew think he was doing, sneaking around these parts in the midst of such a large contingent of Union soldiers? What had possessed him to get so close to their party? At eighteen, he ought to know he had to evade them, as well as the Confederates, if he valued his life.

The officer confronting him glared and slapped a riding crop across Troy's face. "Where'd you come from, boy? Are you a spy or a Rebel deserter? I'll tell you now, I despise both and will treat you accordingly."

"I'm neither."

Troy mumbled the words, but Lydia heard him well enough. The officer was either deaf or chose to disregard him. "Speak up, or I'll turn you back over to our welcoming committee." Another slap accompanied his shout.

Men's laughter echoed around the soldiers' ranks, then a feminine wail overwhelmed the other sounds. "No. No!"

Everyone's attention shifted. Shock waves rolled over Lydia as she watched Millie break through the crowd, headed for the center of the gathered crowd. *What in the world?*

Strong arms prevented Millie from reaching the officer in charge, but she thrashed and continued to wail. "Let me go. He's not a spy or a deserter. He's an innocent citizen."

The officer stepped away from Troy and confronted Millie. "You recognize this man?"

Millie's gaze settled on Troy, who regarded her with the same surprise that held Lydia immobile. "Yes, I know him." Her words were barely above a whisper but audible in the sudden quiet. Her features contorted in obvious distress. "He's avoided the war, refusing to fight his friends and family on both sides."

A snort of disbelief. "Then why is he here? Obviously, he had some reason for sneaking around our camp."

Millie's eyes darted between Troy and the captain. "I guess he hoped to go north or join up with y'all."

Troy stared ahead. He neither confirmed nor denied her statement. He stayed still, probably gathering his strength and waiting for a moment to break loose while his captors focused their attention elsewhere. Millie must have arrived at the same conclusion. She crushed his plans with a single statement.

"He likely came looking for me." She dipped her head to hide her flushed face but caressed her distended belly.

Stunned silence reigned for a few moments. Lydia glanced from Millie to Troy. How had she missed their developing relationship? Would Millie pretend an involvement to save Troy?

Major Tompkins had arrived but remained on the sidelines while his captain dealt with the intruder. Now he stepped forward. "Does anyone else here know this man?"

Murmurs rippled through the onlookers, either repeating the question or commenting on the spectacle playing out as they watched. Lydia forced her feet to move. Others slowly emerged from the crowd as well, making a total of four people willing to acknowledge an acquaintance with the accused. Troy had spent his summers there for years. Surely there were others who hung back out of fear. Not that she blamed them. Who knew what their admission might cost them?

Major Tompkins directed his question to those who'd stepped forward. "As far as any of you know, has this man been a member of the Rebel military in any capacity?"

The others gave a negative opinion, and she added, "No, sir."

The major addressed the gathered crowd. "All right, then, seeing as we have no proof of spying activities and only the hope of an amorous encounter by this young man, we'll treat him as one of the operatives arrested yesterday." He turned to his officers and ordered them to put Troy with the other male prisoners, with an extra guard assigned to watch him until they reached Marietta. That seemed to appease the suspicious-minded.

Keeping his head down, Troy didn't acknowledge anyone. Whether from shame or anger, Lydia couldn't tell. He appeared utterly unmoved. Why didn't he offer any defense, especially in view of Millie's powerful pleas on his behalf? And when had those two developed such a close relationship?

Soldiers hustled Troy to the edge of the crowd, and the spectators returned to their own affairs. Only Millie and Lydia remained to collect their emotions. Looking at the girl's slumped shoulders and bowed head, Lydia couldn't bring herself to chastise. She eased to Millie's side and wrapped her arms around her.

Hearing soft footsteps, Lydia glanced up to find Olivia. "I just heard what happened. I'm sorry I wasn't here."

Edith and Shiloh followed, and all three women gathered Lydia and Millie into their sympathetic embrace.

As tears trickled down her face, Lydia's gratitude swelled. Granny McNeil always said shared troubles made for strong friendships. If more trouble lay ahead, at least she wouldn't face it alone.

∿

SUNDAY, JULY 10, 1864
COBB COUNTY, GEORGIA

*L*ydia kept a furtive watch over Millie and Shiloh as they trudged along the road. Those two looked to be developing a close friendship. It would be good for them each to have someone close in age and circumstance to share this journey with. Perhaps a friend could have prevented Millie's current situation, if one had been around a few months ago.

The change in Millie was puzzling. She'd always been a sweet child, never selfish like some who had no siblings. Losing her mother at an early age had been hard on the girl, and she'd been glad when Lydia and Cal married. Probably relieved to have another female in the house.

Lydia viewed the situation now with the advantage of hindsight. Cal had never met Millie's needs as a father. He gave the impression that providing food and shelter was the extent of his duty. When Lydia joined the household, she and Millie bonded right away. Both had been hungry for the affection natural in a parent-child relationship.

Beside her, Olivia peeked around the edge of her straw bonnet. "Want to talk about it?"

Her friend must've seen something in her expression. "Sorry. I'm not used to having anyone to discuss matters with anymore."

Olivia waved off her apology. "No offense taken, and I don't mean to pry. I'm not one to hand out advice, especially when dealing with half-grown children. For that, you'd need to ask Aunt Edith, who's a fount of wisdom and good sense. However, I'm willing to listen if you want to talk."

"I guess I'm still in shock that she and Troy would even be friends, much less become intimate. I can't imagine how they found time and opportunity to grow so close, but it's even more amazing when you know they fairly detested each other as children."

A soft chuckle escaped Olivia. "The old folks say that when sparks fly, somebody gets burned. I guess that can go several ways. But if he's hiding out from both armies, how did he come to be so close now, as he evidently was, what, six months ago?"

Lydia twisted her handkerchief. "I have to take the blame for that. He's my nephew, you see. The son of my older brother, who moved to Alabama a while back. Troy's visited and stayed with us several times over the years."

Lydia paused to count on her fingers silently. "That started before the war. Must have been six or seven years ago, not long after I married Cal. Millie would have been ten or eleven and Troy probably thirteen. They nearly drove me crazy with their bickering."

Olivia raised her eyebrows. "A ten-year-old girl is vastly different from a sixteen-year-old young woman, especially to a young man, I would guess."

"You're right." Lydia sighed. "He visited us last winter... hiding out, really, trying to avoid conscription or arrest. I expected them to behave as they had before. Obviously, that

37

was a terrible mistake." They walked in silence for a while. "I guess I'm more disappointed that Millie didn't confide in me. And she still hasn't. I feel like I've failed her."

"She'll come around. Regardless of Troy's intentions, you're her family now. She knows she can rely on you, and I have a feeling all of us will be clinging to each other in the future. Only God knows what lies on the road ahead."

# CHAPTER 5

*M*arietta came into sight as the sun began its descent in the west. The weary travelers followed the guard to a place out of the heat. Grabbing their baggage from the wagon bed, Lydia and Millie followed the other Sweetwater operatives inside the brick building.

Disappointment swallowed up their joy. The room must have served as a classroom once. Desks lined the walls, stacked three high, pushed there to make room for the blankets where a couple dozen people sat or lay. None of those long faces looked familiar.

Four windows on two walls stood open to catch the breeze. The gatherings of sleeping pallets, trunks, and various types of baggage created a visual barrier, perhaps to provide the illusion of privacy for the occupants. Several blankets held only a stuffed pillowcase or small piece of furniture, doubtless to identify ownership.

Lydia's dismay was echoed in Millie's pitiful whine. "How

will we have room to sleep? There's already a bunch of folks here."

"As long as I can sit down, I'll sleep. My poor feet are worn out." Lydia dropped her carpetbag to the floor and sat, beckoning the others to join her.

Edith flapped her skirts around her feet. "I just want to change out of these clothes for a few hours. I wonder how far it is to the outhouse?"

Isaac gestured from his wife to the youngster pulling at his hand. "We'll go find out for Aunt Edith, shall we, Wade?"

Olivia chuckled. "I suspect Wade's real interest is the group of children we saw playing a game of tag."

Lydia surveyed the room with a critical eye. Did this indicate how the army would treat them? She picked up a discarded newspaper and plied it like a fan to cool Millie's brow. The poor girl slumped between Lydia and Shiloh, defeated by the afternoon heat and the long day of travel.

The officer who'd seen them arrive had promised to find other accommodations, if any were available. The look of disgust he'd thrown at the overcrowded room convinced Lydia he meant what he said.

Exhaustion took its toll. Lydia awoke from a light doze to hear voices near the door.

"These are the people Major Tompkins brought from the Sweetwater Mill. You say you got another place for them?"

"For some of them anyway." The deeper voice said. "Another train of wagons is on its way from Roswell and should arrive shortly. We've located several vacant houses on the outskirts, but it's going to be crowded everywhere."

"Ma'am?" The officer from earlier addressed Edith. "I'm Captain Griffin of the Seventh Pennsylvania, acting for Major Tompkins and Colonel Gleeson. If you folks can gather your things and come with me, we've a place where you might be more comfortable."

He offered a hand to a few of them and volunteered to carry whatever he could. Olivia gestured to the back door. "I just have to call my son and uncle from outside."

In short order, their little band loaded into wagons, watching others from New Manchester do the same. Captain Griffin waved a signal to the drivers as he paced back toward the building's entrance.

"For a Yankee officer, he sure seems interested in finding us a decent place," Lydia said. His concern surprised her.

The vehicle lumbered over streets rutted from recent rains and so much heavy passage. The ride smoothed out as they turned onto a less-traveled road lined by several large town-houses. Huge oak trees shaded the road on both sides, bringing blessed relief from the late afternoon heat. The wagon stopped before one house with stone steps and a wide porch, its front door standing open, its second-story windows raised halfway.

Well accustomed now to hasty exits, each woman grabbed her own bags and trudged up the steps and through the open door. The driver and lone guard assisted Isaac with the larger baggage, stacking everything in the front hallway. Promising to return with something for them to put together a meal, the driver spurred his horses back the way they'd come.

Edith took the lead. "Suppose we should have a look-see at what's here."

Lydia followed along with the others, but reluctance slowed her steps. "Do you reckon the owners are being forced to put us up?"

Olivia lifted her shoulders and gestured to the unkempt yard. "My guess is they abandoned it before the army arrived."

Lydia wagged her head. "That's not much better, is it?"

She wondered if her house would be invaded by uninvited visitors. Soldiers and vagrants would grab anything available. Other refugees might need a place to stay. Nothing of value was left there, nothing she would bemoan losing, but the thought of it made her uncomfortable.

Casting aside those depressing thoughts, she climbed the front porch steps with Olivia. As unlikely as it seemed, maybe better days lay ahead. One could only hope.

~

SUNDAY AFTERNOON, JULY 10, 1864
MILTON COUNTY, GEORGIA

Staying within the cover of close-growing pines, Seth climbed the gentle rise north of the river. He'd hoped to see where the Federals had pitched their tents. Better an enemy you can see than one you can't. At least then he'd know which direction to go to avoid them.

Wrapping his hand around his spy glass to cover the metal pieces, he rotated the barrel to adjust the magnification. Starting with the southern landscape, he began a careful sweep of the land. Far off to the west, he caught the glint of metal in the sun. Not just one, but a half-dozen at least. Beyond those points of light lay a stretch of white, a scar unnatural to the green expanse. If not for the July heat surrounding him, he'd think it was snow.

He shivered in response. "Cold, like the snow and the wind from the north," he said under his breath. "That's the Union army for sure."

He finished his survey, making mental notes of obstacles he and Robby might encounter on the way. The prospect of danger increased the oppressive heat, blocking his breath. "Dear Lord, what were we thinking?" Plotting their course back in Virginia, they'd been sure they could sneak past the enemy lines. It was just the two of them, after all.

Only one place to get help. Raising his eyes heavenward, he

stuttered out a disjointed prayer. "Lord, I know I've been like the Prodigal Son these last few years, running away from You since...since losing Meg. You don't owe me anything, the way I've been. I don't ask for myself, but for the family, please keep me safe until I can be sure Mama and the others are all right. Help me protect Robby, too, for his family."

Robby, waiting at the base of the hill, turned when he heard Seth coming. "See anything?"

"Tents spread out, close to Roswell, I think. We'll have to go south toward Atlanta. That'll bring us to your house first, which is good. I'm hoping your folks are far enough out of town that the patrols won't bother them."

"Zeke won't let 'em get close to the house. He already said he'd take the oath if he had to do it to keep Mama and the young'uns safe."

"I hope it won't come to that. Your folks built that storm shelter a few years back, after the tornado came so close. I reckon they could hide out in there for a while if need be." Seth repacked his spy glass and took a long draw on his canteen. "Well, let's get on our way. Maybe we'll get to your house in time for supper and tonight you can sleep in your own bed."

∾

SUNDAY AFTERNOON, JULY 10, 1864
COBB COUNTY, GEORGIA

*L*ydia and Olivia explored the second floor of the house while the others took the main floor. Peeking into the bedrooms, they found several beds with bare mattresses, bureaus, armoires, and lamps or lanterns in place. The owners must have left in a hurry, or else they expected to return shortly. She resisted the temptation to inspect the drawers and cedar robes. All they required for their stay was a place to sleep and food to eat. A bath would be welcome, but she didn't think such a treat would be offered.

Just as they returned to the first floor, several vehicles clattered down the street. Six wagons traveled to other houses.

Olivia and Lydia drifted to the front porch. She recognized Captain Griffin as he handed a boy from the saddle behind him. The officer then dismounted and strode to the nearest wagon to help the riders descend. Lydia counted four women, a young girl, an older man, and a boy. The captain kept pace with one of the young women as the two parties converged on the porch.

Flashing a brief smile, the captain offered a general introduction. "Ladies and gentlemen of Roswell, these folks are from the Sweetwater Mill in New Manchester. I regret you will have to share these living quarters for a day or two, but I think you'll find them more agreeable than the military academy, where your fellow workers are staying."

He turned to address the soldiers, who hefted large bags of foodstuff. "I believe the summer kitchen is accessible through the rear door."

The women stared as the men passed by, carrying more staples than Lydia had seen in months. *What a marvel. Someone in the Union army thought to bring us food.*

One of the new arrivals addressed the officer. "Captain Griffin, do you mean for all of us to occupy the same house until... until advised otherwise?" Her troubled gaze flitted over the assembled company. Though dressed no better than the rest of them, she carried herself like one accustomed to being indulged. Or maybe it was a defensive posture to cover her uneasiness.

The captain nodded curtly and moved from the porch to a lower step. He gave clear deference to the speaker. Irreverently, Lydia imagined him saluting the woman with the same respect as a superior officer. There was an undercurrent in their manner toward each other. Maybe old friends?

"That's right, Miss Carrigan. Temporarily. Well, I'll leave it to you ladies to complete the introductions and decide on sleeping arrangements." He gestured to the soldiers still unloading the wagon. "Private Jones and Private Allen here will assist you as needed. I'll try to check on you again tomorrow. Good day."

After the captain left, Lydia followed Olivia to meet the newcomers. Miss Carrigan introducer her sister Celeste, then pointed out the others in their party. "That's the Anderson family with us. The young woman is Emily, who worked in the mill with us. Those are her husband's parents, J.D. and Ada, and her children, John, Mark, and Sarah Grace."

~

SUNDAY, JULY 10, 1864
COBB COUNTY, GEORGIA

Seth buttoned his coat and picked up his knapsack. "It must be near midnight, folks. I'd best be leaving. I may have a long night ahead."

"I'll be praying for you to get home safely," Mrs. Roland said. She'd fussed over Seth as much as she had Robby since the two arrived at her door about dusk. The whole family had sat around the table, sharing news and stories as the travelers ate the cold supper set out for them. When Seth noticed Robby's younger sister yawn for the third time in as many minutes, he figured he should leave so the family could retire.

Zeke's warning about the Union guards on all the roads reinforced his decision to approach his house under cover of darkness. The Rolands lived outside the city boundaries, far enough away to elude the Union army's attention. If they kept to themselves, they should remain unmolested.

While Seth's family home boasted a prominent address a good distance from the town's center, he doubted it would escape the enemy's notice. He refused to contemplate how different it might look or what his family might have endured under Yankee occupation.

Fatigue pulled at him, slowing his movements, but his freedom, perhaps his very life, depended on his stealth and cunning now. Good thing he'd roamed these hills and woods since childhood. His path would need to be winding and circuitous to provide the best concealment. Stars in the inky black sky helped with direction as he passed through the dense areas. Movement of the pale crescent moon provided enough light to judge the time.

He figured it was past two in the morning when he squatted behind the summer kitchen on Morgan property. Not allowing his body the rest it craved, he used the discomfort to keep him awake. At this point, timing was everything.

With his eyes well-adjusted to the dimness, he studied the guard's movements. Only one marked the distance between the Morgan home and its neighbor to the east. Seth counted the seconds silently. Forty-eight seconds up the street, forty-nine seconds back. He counted it five times to be sure. On the sixth time, he plotted his course. He'd dash to the back porch while the guard walked east, wait a full minute to be sure the coast was clear, then crawl to the root cellar. The tricky part would be lifting the cellar door. He hoped Joshua had remembered to keep the hinges oiled as he'd been told.

A childhood memory surfaced, and he smiled at the irony. Like the biblical Joshua at Jericho, Seth would make his move on the seventh pass to breach the stronghold before him.

He eased off his haunches, ready to sprint. His breath

quickened as the guard pivoted away. One, two, three steps, and go!

Seth dared not look around until he reached the edge of the porch and slid to the ground. He forced himself to go through an entire verse of "Dixie" as if he were singing it, figuring that was a close approximation of one minute. Then he crawled to the cellar and peeked around to verify his timing. Good, the guard was headed up the street again.

Holding his breath, he grasped the door of the cellar. No squeaking. *Thank You, Lord.* He slipped inside and found the steps with his feet, pulling the door behind him. It closed with a soft *thump.* Seth froze, waited. When he heard no alarm raised, he groped beside the entrance and found the candle and flint in the crevice, just as he'd left them eighteen months before. After lighting the candle, he shuffled to the farthest corner behind the shelves he'd made as a lad.

He pinched the flame, dropped his knapsack, and stretched out on the floor. His body welcomed the hard-packed earth as though it were a featherbed. He fell asleep with one word on his lips. Home.

~

Monday morning, July 11, 1864
Marietta, Georgia

*L*ydia crept through the dark house with care. Amazed that she'd slept so well in these strange circumstances, she forced her sore muscles into action. She lit a brace of candles on the sideboard and found a slice of leftover cornbread. She dipped a cup of water from the covered bucket, then sat at the table, reviewing the events of the past week. So much turmoil in so few days. What surprises would the future hold?

A noise from the hall heralded an end to her solitude. One of the sisters from the Roswell mill—the one Captain Griffin paid particular attention to—entered the dining room. Lydia searched for the woman's name. Something romantic and delicate, like a flower…Rose? Yes, that was it. Lydia offered a smile. "Good morning. I see you also get up with the chickens."

Rose nodded. "A lifetime habit that's hard to break. Da used to say he had to rouse the sun and the roosters. Even if he'd been up late with a family at a wake or sitting with a sick parishioner, he was still the first one in the kitchen, putting on water for coffee or tea."

"Sounds like a wonderful father. So was mine, for as long as I had him." She motioned toward the sideboard. "There's still a bit of cornbread under that dish, if you're hungry."

Rose helped herself to the meager meal and pulled out a chair facing Lydia. "You lost your father at a young age, then?"

"When I was nine, but he was near sixty. My mother was his second wife, and I was the youngest of six. What I remember most is his gentle nature. And his distinctive laugh."

Edith and Shiloh entered the dining area. While they gathered portions of the leftovers, Edith repeated her amazement at their present situation.

"The soldiers who came to New Manchester were let loose to plunder," she told Rose. "They stripped all the crops from the field and even came into the houses to seize whatever they wanted. Finding this place in such good order is a miracle."

Rose looked perplexed. "They didn't burn down your mills, then? We didn't know they'd come so close until the soldiers burst into the mill and ordered us out."

"Not right away," Lydia said. "They must've been there a week or more before Major Tompkins announced he was going to burn it down."

The women polished off the last of the bread while they traded other observations about the Yankee invasion.

Edith brushed a few crumbs from the table into her hand. Her quiet voice carried the weight of elder authority. "Since we don't know how much longer we'll be here, I think we'd best cook up double portions of food we can carry with us. Biscuits and such."

Lydia studied Rose. "I don't know how much time you folks had to pack your things, but the soldiers rushed us out with hardly any notice. Even though they'd camped in the area for days, the order to move out was a hurried affair. If Millie and I hadn't started packing the day before, we wouldn't have as much as we do now."

"Why did you start packing beforehand?" Rose asked.

Lydia blushed and glanced at Edith, who answered for her. "The Good Lord told her to, just like He did my Isaac." Edith chuckled and wagged her index finger. "Only difference is that Isaac wrestled with the Lord for a few days. Lydia had the good sense to hop right on it."

Rose stared in wonder, and Lydia felt compelled to explain. "I can't claim to be one who's always done right, certainly not as good a person as you are, Edith, or your fine husband. The only reason I can figure why God would speak to me was that I was desperate for direction. Trying to protect Millie and the baby took priority. I guess it was my need that touched His heart, regardless of the fact that I didn't deserve anything from God."

Edith patted Lydia's shoulder. "I expect that's true for all of us, dear girl." She pushed away from the table. "Well, those biscuits won't make their selves, so we'd best get on it. You ready, Shiloh?"

The shy woman bobbed her head and followed Edith to the dining room door.

"Do you want some help?" Both Lydia and Rose volunteered to join them, but Edith waved them away. "No, the kitchen is a good size, but there're so many bags and barrels right now, we'd bump into each other. What you could do is check the root cellar and pantry to see what's in there we can use."

Rose glanced at Lydia. "Should we do that? I mean, surely the people who live here will return home sometime."

Bowing her head and planting her hands on her hips, Edith said, "I figure it this way. Those folks who lived here took all they wanted or could carry with them. Nobody knows how long they'll be gone or even if they'll make it back. We left most of our own possessions at home. I won't begrudge anyone who goes to my house and makes free use of what I left there. It's perilous times, ladies. So long as we only take what we need, I believe it's all right."

As Shiloh followed Edith out to the kitchen, Lydia turned to Rose. "I believe she has the right of it. If anyone in need happens to end up at my house, I'll be glad for them to take whatever they find, especially any food that might not keep. Truth to tell, there's a few things I wish they'd carry off, like my ugly kitchen rug." She grinned and gestured toward the door. "Let's get to that root cellar now."

Olivia came down the stairs as they passed. "I heard Aunt Edith order you to scout the cellar. I'll help with that." She snagged a lantern near the back door. "We might need this. Who knows what kind of creatures might be hiding down there?"

Lydia gestured for Olivia to lead the way. The cellar door opened noiselessly as they entered the dark space. Lydia moved with caution until her eyes adjusted. Several tall cases of shelving formed rows with an aisle between them. The lantern revealed a line of jars and crocks that might prove useful.

Lydia looked around for a basket or larger container. She hadn't bothered to don an apron this morning, but maybe Rose had. "Rose, are you wearing an apron?"

"No, but I found a basket here on the floor. Do you need it?" The answer sounded as if Rose hadn't moved far from the door.

Lydia wondered if the woman was afraid of close places like Granny McNeil had been.

Lifting her voice, Lydia called back. "Yes, there are several jars of honey or preserves here. We could—"

"Oh, my goodness!" Olivia's cry startled her. "Lydia, Rose, come here."

The urgency in Olivia's voice made Lydia swing around the shelf she'd been inspecting. Coming beside her friend, she followed Olivia's finger pointing downward to a bundle of blankets. No, not just a bundle. She could make out a boot and a hand. Her gaze traveled to the dark corner and found a face nestled in the folds. As the light spread over it, the man lunged toward them, brandishing a long knife.

# CHAPTER 6

*H*earing women's voices, Seth had wavered in the twilight between sleep and waking. Probably his mother and sister had come to disturb his rest. The women continued their chattering as they drew closer. One gasped before calling for the others, and his nerves sprang to life, registering the names.

Rose and Lydia? Who were they?

Finding the knife under his makeshift pillow, he sprang up with a warning. "Stay back!"

Alarmed, the women retreated several steps and huddled together. The one farthest away from him squeaked like a mouse caught in a trap. "We mean you no h-harm. We're only collecting some f-food."

Dropping the arm with the weapon, Seth ran the other hand over his face. "Sorry. I wouldn't hurt any woman, but you'uns gave me a scare, you did." He peered at each face in the dim light. "Who are you, and what are you doing at my house?"

"Your house?" The women exchanged looks of disbelief. "We thought the family had abandoned it." This one reminded

Seth of a little wren, small and plain, cocking her head as if to question the truth of his statement.

"The Federal army brought us here," the one with auburn hair said. "They took us prisoner at the mills they captured and burned."

Seth cursed under his breath and dropped to his knees. "The house, the whole town, is truly in Yankee hands then? I'd heard they were coming this way but had to come see for myself, see if my family was safe."

He paused to catch his breath, belatedly remembering his manners. He pushed to his feet again. "Begging your pardon. I'm Sergeant Seth Morgan, Eighteenth Georgia Infantry. Been walking for days, it seems, hardly sleeping at all. Got here about daybreak, hid in here until I knew how things stood. Thought maybe I'd catch my folks before they left town."

The little wren sank to the floor to face him, her skirt billowing around her. "I'm Mrs. Gibson. This is Mrs. Spencer and Miss Carrigan. We don't want to disturb you, but you'd best stay out of sight if you're wearing the gray or butternut. There's Federal guards all around here, and they'd jump on you like ticks on a hound dog."

The mouse stepped forward, motioning with her basket. "We'll just gather a few things and then leave you to rest, Sergeant. That is, if you don't mind us taking some of your stores."

He waved them away and lay down again. "Take whatever you need. If the family's gone, they won't mind it going to help fellow Southerners. If someone could come later and wake me up?"

"Yes, and we'll bring you something to eat as well." That was the red-haired one. What could he label her? A red fox? No, a squirrel perhaps. "Sleep a while now," she said. He didn't wait to hear more. Exhaustion pulled him back into the abyss of sleep.

~

MONDAY EVENING, JULY 11, 1864
MARIETTA, GEORGIA

*L*ydia glanced around the yard, wondering whether she should take advantage of the confusion to check on their slumbering visitor in the cellar. Shouting from the guard who'd seized someone stealing food had come at the end of the meal they'd warily shared with that Union officer. How unsettling that Captain Griffin had showed up again today. His gift of paper for the children's schooling had touched the women's hearts more than a bouquet of flowers from a suitor.

The noise probably would've wakened Sergeant Morgan, with everyone spilling out of the house to investigate the kitchen thief. The culprit turned out to be a runaway slave trying to make her way north to freedom.

Some folks might consider it strange, but all the women had rallied around the runaway, shielding her from the Union soldiers who could decide her fate. While Edith and Shiloh tended her in the summer kitchen, Captain Griffin followed the youngsters into the house to look at the Anderson boy's arrowhead.

Now only Rose and Olivia lingered in the yard. Lydia grabbed the covered plate set aside for Sergeant Morgan and made her way to the cellar.

She stood inside the entrance, letting her eyes adjust to the dark interior. Not wishing to startle him again, she called his name softly. "Sergeant Morgan? It's Lydia Gibson. I've brought your supper."

Rustling fabric suggested he was moving in her direction. The scratch of tinder and the acrid odor of a lit match preceded a faint light in the back corner. Stepping from the shadows, Sergeant Morgan held the candle aloft to lighten the area.

"Did you say supper?" At Lydia's nod, he scraped his face. "I've slept all day then, haven't I? And yet I think I could sleep another few hours."

Lydia located an empty spot on a shelf for the plate and utensils. "Travel does that to you, I hear. Not that I've traveled much myself. And you said you walked a long way to get here." She turned and gestured to the shelf. "I hope you've a taste for greens and potatoes and cornbread. It's all we had left tonight. Do you have a canteen? I brought a cup but was afraid I'd spill it dry on the way over."

She stilled and stopped chattering when the man touched her hand. His lopsided smile set her at ease. "It's fine. I thank you for bringing whatever y'all have. I'm sorry, but I don't remember your name."

"Lydia," she said out of habit, then blushed at her forwardness. "Lydia Gibson."

He sketched a playful bow. "Nice to make your acquaintance, Miss Lydia Gibson. I'm sure there's enough here for you as well." He gestured to the plate.

She waved away his generosity, impressed with his manners, though she figured he must be starving. "Oh, you go ahead. I already ate. And it's Mrs. Gibson, but most folks just call me Lydia, even my stepdaughter."

He swallowed the spoonful of potatoes and poured water from his canteen into the cup. Nodding politely, he picked up the conversation. "I suppose your husband joined the fight? Where's he serving?"

Lydia avoided eye contact, uncomfortable discussing Cal, and leaned over to straighten a jar on the far shelf. "He joined in sixty-one. According to all the reports, he was killed at Chickamauga."

After a pause, he repeated the customary phrase. "I'm sorry

55

for your loss, ma'am. This war has claimed too many lives already, both on the battlefield and off."

Lydia walked away, leaving him to finish his meal in peace. She'd have to wait until someone signaled it was safe to leave. She explored the underground space, inspecting the supplies and furnishings. "This is a mighty fine cellar, Sergeant. I believe it could hold enough food to last a year or more. Depending on how many mouths you had to feed, of course."

The sergeant paused in lifting the cup. "Mama believed in being ready for any crisis. She served on the relief committee here in town and tried to set an example of being prepared and giving generously in donations. How do things look upstairs?"

Crossing the aisle to where he stood, she finally looked him full in the face. "I'd guess nobody was here between the time your folks left and we arrived. We were astonished to find everything in order. Oh, it's clear your family took some stuff with 'em, but they left quite a lot too. We're doing our best to keep everything as clean and neat as we found it."

"I'm relieved to hear it. There're a few things I'd like to take with me when I leave if you think y'all could collect them. I can write a list if you'll bring me a pencil and paper. There should be some in Mama's bureau."

"Of course. I'll look for it and be sure somebody brings it to you tomorrow." Her gaze flitted around the room while she pleated her skirt between her fingers. Curiosity overcame her hesitation. "Do you...do you plan to leave right away then?"

He nodded. "I should get away before those guards get suspicious. I wouldn't want you ladies to get in trouble on account of me."

He used the napkin to wipe his mouth and handed her the empty plate. "I'm mighty grateful for the food, ma'am. That'll set me up for a good while."

"It's the least we could do, being as we're occupying your home." The candle had dwindled to a stub. "Where did you get the candle? I know the army provides its soldiers with matches, but I wouldn't think they'd hand out candles as well."

With a mischievous grin, he gestured toward the door. "I'll show you." When they reached the entrance, he pointed to a crevice in the side of the wall. "We always keep this ledge stocked with candles and lucifers, in case of storms that last longer than our lantern. My little brother did a good job of keeping it supplied, as well as oiling the door hinges. I'll have to reward him somehow when I see him...whenever that may be."

Without thinking, Lydia reached out to touch his arm before she yanked her hand back. "I'm sure you'll see him before long. This war has got to end soon. Do you know where your family was bound for?"

Seth frowned. "Mama's last letter mentioned the coast. I guess that'd be Savannah. She has old friends there. I wish I had time to make that trip and be sure they arrived safely. With only Joshua and old Jubal to guard three women and two children, I'll worry until I hear they made it safely."

Lydia pressed her lips together to keep from asking about the women and children. She didn't want him to think her overly curious. "Joshua is the brother you spoke of?"

"Yeah, he's fourteen, the baby of the family, although he'd trounce me for calling him that. Jubal's been with the family longer than I have. He's still capable, but he's getting on in years. He'll watch over them. But he wouldn't last five minutes in a fight. Pearl and Ruby—those are my sisters—they can handle a pistol well enough, but they're just as likely to forget the gun and jump on any attackers." He smiled.

"Who do the children belong to?"

"Pearl. She moved back home after losing her husband at Gettysburg. It was good for Mama to have them here." He paced away, curling his fists. "Ruby came home after Will, her brother-in-law, joined her husband's company out of Alabama. That was the same time as me. We figured between Will and me, we'd catch up with the no-good varmint who murdered Meg."

Lydia's breath caught. She ought to leave well enough alone, but she had to ask. "Who's Meg?"

He turned, his look making her blood run cold. "Will's sister. My wife. Murdered in our own home by a no-good straggler in a Confederate uniform. He's hiding in an army unit somewhere, but we'll find him eventually. From the neighbor's description, it was someone we know, a man with a grudge against me. You can see why I want to make sure the rest of my family is safe. They're my responsibility."

He'd gone pale and seemed to brace himself against the cellar's earthen wall. Was it thoughts of his loved ones, or had the journey worn down his resistance?

~

TUESDAY, JULY 12, 1864
MARIETTA, GEORGIA

Seth struggled to his knees, pausing as a wave of dizziness hit him. "I have to get back to camp, to my unit."

Was that where he needed to go? Savannah came to mind. Why was that? Oh, yeah, his mother and sisters had gone there, or so he thought. Confusion made his head hurt. His face burned like it was on fire, and his eyes refused to focus, but an urgency pressed him to get away.

"No, you don't. Not today." Several pairs of small hands clutched his upper body and pushed him back to the floor. Someone slapped a wet cloth against his neck, bringing a blessed cooling to his hot skin. He didn't have the strength to struggle against the restraints any longer.

Hovering at the edge of sleep, he could hear those voices

floating above him. Not his mother's or sisters' voices, though. He gave up trying to figure out who they belonged to.

"What do you think it is?" one woman said.

"I'm not sure. Could be influenza or pneumonia. With the heat and the recent rains, plus his exhausted state when he arrived, either is possible."

Seth forced his eyes open so he could focus on the women's conversation. Memories of the previous day surfaced. Yeah, there was the wren next to the red squirrel. He blinked when his gaze moved to the figures hovering in the background. He must have hit his head because he saw two of the mouse. That would be mice, wouldn't it?

The wren crossed her arms and leaned against the wall without shelves. "Well, one thing is sure. He's not able to leave now. It could be days before he can stay upright."

"So, what do we do? How can we help him?" One mouse glanced at the others, her voice soft with compassion.

The other mouse pursed her lips and sighed. "We'll have to take shifts and stay with him or at least check on him more often."

The little squirrel nodded. "Let's search the house for medicine. Although, not knowing for sure what ails him, we'll have to exercise caution."

The voices faded. As sleep carried him deeper, dreams mixed with reality, the past mingled with the present. His grandparents and his father returned to life and instructed a younger Seth in his carpentry skills. Meg drifted in, cooling his brow with her gentle hand and drifting away again.

At times, someone sang or read from the Bible. Those were the peaceful moments, with visions of blue sky and flowering trees springing from a lush carpet of green. At other times, he wrestled with an unknown enemy, writhing under its hot breath while slimy tentacles wrapped around his legs and arms. Strangers poured foul-tasting liquids down his throat, holding him with bands of iron. Violent rocking convinced him they'd put him on a ship in the middle of a storm.

Finally, they tossed him overboard, like Jonah, where he could repent of his waywardness or give up and drown in the dark, green deep.

～

SATURDAY MORNING, JULY 16, 1864
MARIETTA, GEORGIA

*P*ushing aside the cheerful green curtains of the bedroom, Lydia rejoiced to see sunshine drenching the backyard. After four days of gray clouds and rain, she wouldn't complain about the heat. Not yet anyway. She stretched to remove the kinks from her muscles, the result of sharing a bed with Millie last night after several hours tending to Seth in the cellar.

Seth. She had to stop thinking of him that way. It wasn't proper, her granny would say. Lydia snorted as she doused her face in the tepid water from the ceramic pitcher. Neither was it proper to spend hours tending a man who wasn't her husband, as she had this week.

To maintain propriety, Lydia, Olivia, and Emily had divided most of Seth's care between them. The unmarried women filled in from time to time for short periods, while Edith commandeered the kitchen and Ada served as chief housekeeper, each with her assigned assistants. Ada's husband, J.D., and Edith's Isaac lifted anything heavy and helped to occupy the three children between their school lessons with Rose and Celeste. In the space of a few days, the fifteen occupants of the Morgan house had coalesced into a team as efficient as any she'd ever seen.

Lydia slipped on her dress and shoes, then hurried downstairs to the dining room and peeked in. Empty. She pivoted to the back door and crossed the yard to the kitchen, where Edith stood at the threshold, a biscuit in one hand and a cup of chicory coffee in the other.

Lydia turned up her nose. "How do you drink that stuff when it's already hot enough to roast pigs in the kitchen?"

Edith smiled. "It cools me down and gives a little flavor to the water."

"I'd rather have a cool glass of buttermilk," Lydia said. "I think I'll take my breakfast to the cellar so Olivia can come on out." She loaded a plate with johnny cakes and ham and covered it with a second plate. Dropping two forks into a quart jar, she turned back to Edith. "I guess there's still water in the bucket down there?"

The other woman nodded. "There ought to be. Tell Olivia to check on Wade when she goes to the house. He had a fitful night. I hope he's not sickenin'."

Lydia tucked the jar into the crook of her elbow when she reached the cellar so she could pull open the door. Olivia stood nearby and assisted with the food. Setting aside the breakfast items, the women kept their voices low.

"How is the sergeant?"

"I think he's turned the corner. Fever broke sometime during the night, and he's sleeping easy now."

Lydia blew out a breath. "Thank You, Jesus. Maybe he'll be able to head out in a day or two. He needs to be gone before Captain Griffin comes back here. By the way, Edith says for you to check on your son. He didn't rest well last night. I hope he's not taking sick."

Olivia picked up the basket of soiled linens and utensils from her night's watch. "So do I. I'll see if Uncle Isaac can come down later and help the sergeant bathe and dress. Now you go ahead and eat your breakfast before it gets cold."

Lydia did as Olivia said. After eating her portion of the johnnycakes, she set aside the rest for Seth, hoping he'd have a good appetite when he woke. For an hour or more, she prowled around the dark room, straightening jars and rearranging items, checking her patient from time to time. After she ran out of tasks, she ventured close to his makeshift bed and found him watching her.

"You're awake." She reached forward to touch his brow. "No fever. How do you feel?"

A wry grin tilted his mouth. "Like I tangled with a mountain lion. You say I had a fever? My head feels like mush. How long was I sick?"

"Let's see." She thought back. "Nearly four days."

He worked his mouth, and Lydia grabbed the cup of water she'd poured earlier. Slipping behind him, she pushed him to a half-sitting position and held the cup to his lips. His hand covered hers so he could control the flow. Lydia's breath caught with awareness at their closeness. She could only pray he didn't notice the trembling of her hands or the increased rhythm of her heart. What would he think?

After several sips, he removed his hands from hers, allowing her to move away. He sighed. "Thank you, Mrs. Gibson. I appreciate the care you've given me."

Did she hear a warning note in his voice? Had she somehow communicated her attraction to him? Had she showed more interest than the care of someone nursing a sick friend?

Keeping her back to him, she strove for a calm response. "It wasn't just me, Sergeant Morgan." She used the formal address as he had. "Olivia and Emily also took turns seeing to your care. Edith thought only the married or widowed women should attend you, although the single ladies have visited and helped at times."

He offered no comment, and she turned to see why. He lay still, eyes closed, and hands folded over his chest. On careful observation, though, she noticed his brow puckered over his eyes and one finger twitched in agitation. The rise and fall of his chest indicated rapid breathing instead of the relaxed measure of sleep.

Her own breath increased, and her face flamed as she considered what that meant. Anger. She'd witnessed it enough in the past with Cal. At least Seth appeared to be working to control it, but she wouldn't stay close enough to see whether he did. Even in his weakened state, he could probably send her flying across the room with one swipe.

Destined to wait here until someone relieved her, she forced her shaky legs to carry her to the far side of the room. She'd stay out of his reach until she could figure out why she'd aroused his anger.

~

Seth struggled to rein in the yearning that came alive at Lydia's touch. Her softness and tender care had awakened long-dormant feelings, along with the memory of being loved and loving in return. Where was the icy anger that had driven him for the past year and a half? Had his illness weakened his focus of finding Meg's killer?

He ordered thoughts of Meg. Beautiful, sweet, and lively, Meg had driven him to distraction since her sixteenth birthday. No, not that.

*Remember how you found her, pale and still, the life drained away from her and the babe just beginning to round her belly.*

*Remember the fiend who'd overpowered her, the description from the neighbors.*

The man had played on Meg's sympathies to get inside the house, then he'd taken her life.

His breathing slowed, his body cooled, and Seth dared to open his eyes. Hearing no movement, he searched the space as far as he could see from his horizontal viewpoint. The place looked deserted. Inch by inch, he scooted himself into a sitting position against the wall. Still, he saw no one.

Where had she gone? Surely, he would've heard the cellar door close if she'd abandoned him. She must be hiding somewhere, but why? Had his response to her touch been so obvious that he'd embarrassed her? But she was a widow, no innocent miss. Even a plain little wren must've received her share of interest from the men in her area. And not so plain as he'd first thought. In the lantern light, he noted the most remarkable green eyes ringed by dark lashes and thick hair the color of freshly planed Carolina ash.

The rumbling of his stomach reminded him of his situation. After three days without solid food, he needed to fill it as often as he could and get out of here. He'd already decided his best plan was to make his way back to Robby's house and finish recuperating there. By sliding up the wall, he gained his feet.

He spotted the overturned crate the women had used as a table and aimed for it. The crate slid as his foot touched it and, instead of sitting, he grabbed the nearest shelf to keep his balance. Glass jars rattled. A basket of bolts tumbled to the floor, and a tin cup tipped over, cascading nails to the shelves below. Seth clutched the upright post and stood motionless, afraid further movement would result in true disaster.

"What in heaven's name are you doing?" The wren flew out of her hiding place and landed at his side.

He took refuge in teasing. "I was aiming for the crate, but it ran away. I don't know whether that was because of my ugliness or fear it'd be crushed if I sat on it."

Lydia shook her head, but a smile played about her lips. "Stay here, and I'll get the rocker J.D. brought down from the attic." She rushed into the aisle and dragged an old cane rocking chair close to the shelf, nudging the crate out of the way. She placed her hands on his arms and guided him into the seat. Her instinct to tend the helpless must have overcome her wariness.

While her attention centered on the chair, Seth's eyes strayed from her dark blond hair to the slender shoulders and the slight gap at the neck of her dress. Refusing to allow that track again, he squeezed his eyes closed. It must be a result of the fever. It had weakened his senses along with his body. He counted himself a gentleman, one who'd never abuse a woman, not even in the secret corners of his mind.

As soon as he plopped onto the woven seat, she stepped back, and their eyes connected like magnets seeking north. She whirled away to conceal the color spreading upwards from her décolletage. Had she read his thoughts? Probably. She was a widow, after all. And he was a widower, but he maintained what he'd told Robby on their journey home. He wasn't in the market for a wife.

# CHAPTER 7

*L*ydia's face burned. Though it had been a few years since her first experience as a wife, she recognized the sensations of desire. Cal had destroyed those romantic feelings long before he'd taken himself off to war. She'd considered such awareness gone forever. How could it return now? Why with this man? Nature was cruel indeed to awaken those passions in the middle of war for a man who'd rejoin the battle in a matter of days. She'd never see him again. She both dreaded and wished for the time of his departure.

For now, however, she had to control her emotions while she helped him recover from his illness. Pushing aside her hesitation, she kept up a running monologue about the current occupants of his house. Convinced he paid her prattle little attention, she got through the morning. Her relief was palpable when Rose and Celeste arrived with his dinner. But her face burned when she noticed Seth's face light up at their entrance. How shameful for her to spurn his attention and then feel slighted when he turned it on another woman.

She hoped nothing would delay his leaving.

~

SATURDAY AFTERNOON, JULY 16, 1864
MARIETTA, GEORGIA

Seth stretched his legs, marking the perimeter of the root cellar. He'd lost three days, according to his ministering angels. Now he chafed at having to wait until sunset to leave.

One of the brunette sisters passed him his haversack, reciting a list of the food she'd packed. "But you should eat again here before you set out." She pointed to the plate he'd set aside when they entered the cellar. He'd learned she was the singer, the one easily touched by the pain of others. He ran through the words to find her name—compassionate, warm like cherry wood—Charlotte? No, Celeste.

Seth flashed a grin. "No wonder those Yankee guards don't bother you gals. You fill them with food and show off your pretty smiles, and they lose what little wits they have."

Celeste blushed, but her sister's eyes narrowed as if she could discern his motives simply by staring. He'd called her the mouse, but recalled her name was Rose, like the rosewood color of her hair, a shade lighter than Celeste's.

Rose cleared her throat to get his attention. "Your uniform is packed at the bottom of the sack, clean and mended. You should leave it there and wear your civilian clothes until you reach North Carolina."

Seth turned to her with surprise, abandoning his play of provocation. "Yes, ma'am. I will heed your wise advice."

Celeste released the coat and hat she held. "I found the hat and jacket you wanted in your room. You ought to smudge them with dirt, though, to make it harder to see them in the dark. It's a pity to spoil the coat, but I daresay the dirt will brush out."

Rose didn't give him time to respond. "Someone will let you know when it's safe for you to leave. C'mon, Celeste. We need to help with supper."

The younger woman cast a regretful look his way but obediently followed her sister out. Seth chuckled under his breath, feeling better than he had in months. He'd always teased his sisters mercilessly, but they'd given as good as they got. Having this band of women flutter around him reminded him of those youthful years. Too bad he had to leave so soon, but he couldn't take the chance of being discovered by those Yankee guards.

Seth took advantage of the time alone to retrieve the weapons hidden beneath the shelving—a revolver held secure on the underside of the bottom board and an ancient blunderbuss buried in the floorboard beneath the six-shelf unit. Thanks to his father's foresight, he could remove the board without pushing aside the shelves.

He stashed both weapons in the knapsack with his clean uniform. They weighed it down and created bulges that would let any observer know its contents, but he wasn't planning to let anyone close enough to question him.

The soft thud of the cellar door warned him of another visitor. Ever on his guard, he stayed in his sheltered position, waiting in case it was someone other than one of his angels.

"Hello?"

The voice belonged to a woman, but not one of those he'd met. He knew there were others in the house. He'd heard about them during those one-sided conversations while he was sick. The women liked to talk while they attended him, even when he wasn't coherent enough to reply. He waited for the voice to speak again.

"Is someone here? I saw Rose and Celeste leaving."

A rough answer might serve him best. He stepped around the six-foot-high shelving. "Who are you?"

The girl jumped and whirled to face him. She stared open-mouthed, raking him with her brazen gaze. "Who are you?"

"I asked you first." He crossed his arms over his chest and assumed a hostile stance. Something about her approach bothered him. Best to take the offensive position.

She recovered and tossed her head with a show of arrogance. "I'm Phoebe Wilson, a neighbor of Rose and Celeste's. My family's staying in the house next door. Why are you hiding down here?"

He was tempted to exert his authority, but perhaps it was best to keep Miss Phoebe Wilson in the dark. If the other women hadn't seen fit to include her in the secret of his presence, they must have good reason. "I'm just passing through on my way to Alabama. The ladies kindly allowed me to rest here a while before continuing my journey."

It was the truth. Well, except the part about Alabama, but his direction was best kept close to his chest.

Miss Wilson directed her gaze around the cellar. Did she plan to challenge him, or was she more interested in the room's contents?

Finally, she looked his way again. "Well, I guess that's all right, as long as you're not planning to stay."

Seth scoffed. "Why would I want to stay?"

The girl couldn't be above eighteen, but she struck him as a schemer. The sooner she made her way out, the better.

She speared him with a suspicious glare but ignored his question. "Well, then, I wish you a pleasant journey." Without waiting for a response, she flounced away.

He waited until she left to return to his task, but his sense of urgency increased. He'd be ready to leave as soon as he got the all-clear signal from someone upstairs.

*L*ydia moved the food around her plate, hoping nobody noticed how little she ate. Her thoughts kept returning to her last visit with Seth. She couldn't figure out what she'd done to rile him. She was glad he'd be leaving tonight. It would keep her and the other women from getting in trouble for helping him.

At Olivia's signal, those who wanted to bid Seth farewell carried their plates to the kitchen. Rose and Celeste crossed to the cellar and left the door open for Lydia and Olivia to follow. Emily had said her goodbyes when she took him his supper.

Seth rose from his pallet as the four faced him together. "Is it time?" He reached out and brushed Celeste's arm as she stood closest to him.

Celeste blushed and sidestepped out of his reach. "Not yet," she said.

Lydia tensed. Was something brewing between those two?

Celeste continued. "The sun won't set for another hour, but the wind is blowing in some clouds, so we thought we'd best come on down. Here's the watch we found upstairs."

Olivia retrieved a packet from her apron pocket. "I found a small piece of oiled cloth to wrap the letters in. Emily and I appreciate your offer to get them to our husbands. And please tell anyone from our area what's happened."

"I won't forget." Seth's gaze swept across them as he slid the package inside his coat. He repeated the message. "Federals are sending workers from Roswell and New Manchester north on trains, destination unknown."

Lydia pressed a knotted piece of cloth into his hand. "A few coins we collected in case you need to purchase something." She snatched her hand back and looked away before her crazy emotions betrayed her. What would he think of the delicate hankie with her initials stitched in the corner? She'd hesitated about using something so personal—one of a set given to her as a wedding gift. But he'd likely not even notice. Men didn't fuss over sentimental things the way women did.

Seth cleared his throat and bounced the tiny bundle in his palm, attempting to lighten the somber atmosphere. "Too bad there's no horse I could buy to make the trip go faster."

Lydia forced a smile at the poor jest, knowing both armies confiscated any animal that could pull a load.

"I'm not eager to return to the fighting," he said. "But I have a mission to accomplish, and we need to bring this war to an end."

"Amen to that." Rose led the women in a brief prayer for his safety, and they filed out the door.

Edith waited on the back porch as they left the cellar. "I thought I'd enjoy a brief rest here before going in," she said, sitting on the top step. "Having both Shiloh and Dorcas help makes the work go faster, especially when they have other tasks they want to get started on." She indicated the space beside her. "Come sit with me awhile."

Lydia glanced back to see Rose close the cellar door. Edith must want to hold watch over their stowaway, to be sure nothing hindered his departure. Olivia and Celeste joined Edith while Rose and Lydia roamed around the yard, watching the sun ease toward the horizon. Few words were exchanged, only occasional random comments about the weather and provisions they planned to take with them when they left town.

At last, Edith hefted her frame, using Olivia's shoulder for support. The older woman swiped at her skirt to knock away the dirt. "These old bones will get stove up if I sit here too long. I think I'll find something softer inside."

Lydia hastened to follow. Sweeping her gaze across the yard in a silent farewell, she noticed movement near the house next door. "Uh-oh. This could be trouble."

The other women looked up to watch Phoebe making her

way to them. "Let's all go inside," Olivia said. "Someone may need to bring Phoebe along as well."

Lydia fell into line behind Olivia, hoping Rose and Celeste would take care of their young neighbor. Voices from the parlor caught her attention as she lingered in the hallway, and Lydia felt her heart drop as she heard Edith's greeting.

"Why, Captain Griffin, what a surprise. I'm sorry you're not in time for supper, but there's a bit of cornbread left, if you'd like a bite."

"No, thank you. I ate before I came over," he said. "When I got back in town, I heard some of the mill workers and their families had been sent north, and I wondered whether you folks had gone with them or were still here." He nodded to the others behind Edith. "Evening, ladies."

Olivia said her hello, then pivoted away, whispering to Lydia. "I'd better have them bring Phoebe inside."

By the time Lydia offered her welcome to the captain, Olivia was back, followed by Rose and Celeste and a reluctant Phoebe. Celeste eased by the captain to join Millie and Shiloh on the settee while Phoebe directed her attention to the children, who chattered about the pictures they were drawing.

Lydia wandered to the corner to stand beside the dormant fireplace, trying to watch the dynamics of the group without being obvious.

Rose approached Captain Griffin, presenting her hand and a warm hello. Did he notice her stiff posture? Maybe not, if his smile was any sign. He was well and truly caught. Poor Yankee.

"Olivia tells me we could be leaving soon," Rose said. "Do you know when that might be?"

Judging by the captain's expression, it took him a moment to comprehend her question. He opened his mouth to reply, but a shout rang out from the front porch.

"Hold, thief! Come back with that horse!" Pounding from galloping hooves fell away while the thud of boots running along the porch followed. Indistinct words abused the air and warned of trouble.

~

*S*eth pressed his knees deeper in the gelding's flanks and leaned over the pommel, absorbing the vibration from the hooves striking the ground. Holding the reins loosely, he whispered encouragement near the animal's ear, urging the mount to fly down the road away from town. Cool air rushed against his face and cleared his mind.

Exhilaration was powerful medicine.

The houses sped by, giving way to darkened fields and woods. The moon had diminished to a mere sliver of light, but stars among the patchy clouds were enough to guide him.

In less than an hour, his friends' house appeared in the distance. Earlier in the week, this trip had taken him half the night. A fast mount certainly made a difference, even when he had to keep checking the road behind to be sure nobody followed. Even if the soldiers had had other mounts near his home, it would've taken them several minutes to mount up. He ought to be in the clear.

Anxiety rendered him as winded as the horse beneath him when Seth slowed their speed and patted the dun's neck. "Good boy. You've earned yourself a rest."

Someone at the Roland homestead noted his arrival long before Seth reined in. A long shadow moved from the porch, lifting a weapon in warning. "Who's there?"

Not Robby's voice, but his older brother's.

"Seth Morgan," he called. "Zeke, it's Seth. Put down your weapon."

He was close enough now to see his friend's expression. "Seth, where in the name of all that's holy did you get a horse?" He gripped the bridle as Seth dismounted.

"You got room in the barn for him? Feed?"

Zeke scoffed. "He might find enough feed to keep from starving, and there's plenty of room, what with nearly all the animals gone. But how—?"

"I'll explain everything, soon's I get this sweet goer settled. Go on up to the house and warn your ma I might need to stay here a day or two."

Zeke sauntered back to the house while Seth led the horse into the barn and lit a lantern. Removing the saddle, he noted the USA stamp embossed in the leather. He'd have to figure out what to do with that. He gave the lathered horse a good rubdown and scooped together enough feed to satisfy his innocent accomplice.

When he joined the family in the house, Seth found them all gathered in the parlor, waiting to hear his story. He collapsed in a chair and took a minute to collect himself.

Mrs. Roland stood next to him. "Can I get you anything to eat or drink, Seth?"

"No, ma'am. I ate not long ago. I need to tell y'all what's transpired since I was here last week." He launched into his story of encountering the women in his house and his illness.

"How did you come by the horse?" Robby asked. "I can't imagine how one escaped the army's attention."

Seth grinned. "It was the strangest thing. When I slipped out of the cellar at sunset, I saw this beautiful horse on the side of the house. He was ground-tied and munchin' on the grass, which was standin' pretty high. I eased over to pet him, and he just gave me this look, as if to say, 'What are you waiting for? Here I am.' So, I climbed on his back. I first thought to sneak off into the woods behind the house, but the trees had grown too dense for the horse to get through. Figuring we had to make a run for it, I turned his head to the front and spurred him into a gallop." He slapped his hand on his thigh, remembering the wild ride. "Man, he could fly! It was like he knew we had to get out of there fast."

Zeke frowned in thought. "But where did he come from?"

"The best I can figure is he belonged to the Yankee captain who dropped by the house a time or two to check on the Roswell folks. I did hear some shoutin' as we rode past the front porch, but they didn't shoot at me, and I figure they gave up tryin' to follow."

"Do you think they'll come looking for you here?" Mrs. Roland's weathered face wrinkled with worry.

"I don't think so, at least not for a day or two." Seth looked from Robby to Zeke. "I plan to head back to my unit before then. Seein' as you don't have much feed here, Zeke, I'll take the mount with me. That way, nobody can trace him to you and accuse you of helping me."

Mrs. Roland slid closer to her younger son. "I reckon that means you'll be leaving too."

Robby shrugged, downplaying any reason for anxiety. "We would've had to leave in a few more days anyhow. It's better to travel together, and now we'll have a horse to take the load off our feet."

His mother saw through his attempt at levity. "A horse that belongs to the Federal army. It's rare enough for anyone to have an animal the armies ain't confiscated, but a Federal army horse..." She wagged her head in worry. "I'm afeared it may bring you more trouble."

Seth shifted his gaze from one family member to another. "I'm sorry, I didn't think it all the way through before I grabbed the mount. All I saw was a way to get out of there quick."

Zeke stood up and stretched his arms above his head. "Why don't we call it a night and get some shut-eye? Maybe things'll look better in the mornin' and we can come up with a good plan."

The others rose, and Seth made his way to the front door. "I think I'll sleep in the barn. It'd be best for someone to be there in case unwelcome visitors come calling."

Outside, he ambled down the steps and stood in the yard between the house and the barn. Pain built between his eyes and covered the top of his head. Rubbing his face, he stumbled out a prayer. "Lord, I messed up. What a predicament I've got us in. I need some help and direction. Please let me know how to go on from here."

# CHAPTER 8

*L*ydia's head ached from trying to figure a way out of their predicament. Lying in the darkness, she relived those terrible moments when everyone rushed out of the house to investigate the source of those sounds.

Captain Griffin had sprinted down the steps to meet Private Langley in the middle of the street. The younger man had already headed back to the house, dragging his feet, arms hanging at his side. Corporal Jones stood several yards down the road, looking away from the house, his rifle on his shoulder. Whoever the thief was, he was long gone.

Captain Griffin turned to Private Langley. "What happened here?"

The soldier raised his head and stood at attention, obviously expecting a reprimand. "He got your horse, sir."

Captain Griffin strode forward in outrage. "Do I understand that someone *stole* my horse? No, not *my* horse, mind you, the *army's* horse, while two Union guards sat on their..." He glanced at the women crowding behind him. "While you sat on this porch?"

"Yessir."

People from the nearby houses emerged, bending over the porch rails to listen. Everyone followed the scowling corporal's progress as he stomped back the way he'd come.

When he reached Captain Griffin, he explained. "I couldn't get off a clean shot, sir, not with him riding through the yards and into the trees. As the senior guard here, I take full responsibility. I should've kept the horse within sight 'stead of letting him graze beside the house."

The captain ran a hand down his face. After a moment, he turned to the group behind him. "Do any of you know who would dare to steal an army mount?"

No one uttered a word until Phoebe Wilson pushed her way forward. "It must've been that Rebel soldier what was hiding in the cellar."

Lydia gasped, twisting around to face the accuser. How did she know about Seth? What made her think he would be the thief? Would he have been so brazen, so bold as to steal a military mount?

Horrified expressions mirrored Lydia's. Nobody dared to offer another explanation or to question the accusation. Through the fog of disbelief, Lydia heard Captain Griffin order everyone inside the house. Olivia touched Lydia's hand and urged her toward the front door. As the civilians filed inside, the officer promised to deal with the guards after he discovered what had taken place under their noses.

He shut the door and faced the household members. For a moment, he merely looked from one to the other with lowered brows, working his jaw side to side. He inhaled sharply, and his countenance eased somewhat. His voice sounded normal, albeit strained.

Lydia's breath grew shallow as the officer questioned the children.

"Do you know anything about a man, a soldier from the other army, hiding here anywhere?"

*Smart man, asking the children. Thank goodness they knew nothing.*

The captain dismissed them, then he pointed to Phoebe and Dorcas. "Please tell me your names again as I've forgotten them in the days I've been away."

Each girl gave her name, and he asked them the same question. Like the children, Dorcas swore she didn't know about the man in the cellar.

He waited for her to leave the room before turning his expectant gaze on Phoebe. "So, what do you know, Miss Phoebe Wilson?"

The girl licked her lips, the one sign of awareness that she may have caused herself as much trouble as the others. Lydia had seen enough of the girl's behavior toward the Carrigan sisters to form an opinion. Jealousy could drive people to do strange things.

Phoebe pointed to Rose and Celeste. "I saw them two coming out of the cellar just before supper today. They looked guilty, like they's hiding something, so I snuck back after they went in the house. I went down in the cellar to see what was down there and saw that man and where he'd been sleeping on a pallet."

Captain Griffin kept his eyes on the girl. "And he had on a Confederate uniform?"

Phoebe hesitated, as if she debated on whether to lie. "Well, no. But why else would he be hiding down there?"

The captain shrugged. "He could be a deserter from either army, or just a no-account thief looking for a place to rest. He could have gone in there after Miss Carrigan and her sister left, after seeing them come out, like you did."

"No! I tell you, they was hiding him. There was a blanket and a pillow and...and a stack of dirty plates near the door."

Lydia rolled her eyes and shifted uneasily. How had the girl gotten in without anyone knowing? Had Seth seen her?

Captain Griffin waved Phoebe away. Hands on his hips, he glanced around the room. His frown promised he'd get to the truth.

When he motioned to Millie and Shiloh, Lydia pushed her way forward, defying him to protect her stepdaughter. "Millie had nothing to do with this."

Olivia and Rose joined her, sharing the blame and trying to explain why they'd acted as they did.

"All of you were in on this?" His gaze moved from one face to another.

Lydia's breath quickened. Would he now report their actions to his superiors? She dared not say more.

At last he stalked to the door, opened it, and left them. How would they go on now?

∼

SUNDAY MORNING, JULY 17, 1864
THE ROLAND FARM

"Maybe it was a mistake to drag your family into this," Seth said.

He and Zeke strolled beside the creek that meandered through Roland property on its way to join Sope Creek to the south. Did that stream know where it was headed, how it would be swallowed by the bigger creeks? Then it would unite with even more streams to join the Chattahoochee River and make its way to the Gulf of Mexico. Every drop raced with the others to a place where there were no more individual drops, only a great expanse of water.

Did the same thing happen to the men in these armies opposing each other? Did they cease to be men and become part of a mighty force, a giant power either for good or evil?

Zeke was not so philosophical. "What's done is done, Seth.

Nobody knows what'll happen from one day to the next. We'll muddle through somehow."

"I was thinking to leave the horse's saddle here."

His friend stopped short and faced him. "Why would you do that? We ain't got no horse, and I sure ain't gonna return it to the Federals. Their idea of a reward would be to ship me to Elmira or some other prison."

How would Seth's friend take his next daring suggestion?

"I wouldn't want it to be on your property, if they were to come looking. Maybe you could hide it for a couple of weeks. I'm thinking they'll soon head to Atlanta to try to cut off our communications."

"And what am I gonna do with it then?"

"I don't know. Toss it in the woods or take it to my house. With nobody at the house, they won't have any idea where it came from or how it got there."

Zeke grunted, not impressed. "We'll see. Maybe I can think of something else after you leave. Do you plan to ride that horse at all?

"Naturally, and it'll be easier for Robby and me both to ride without a saddle."

"You're gonna ride bareback?"

Seth smirked and elbowed Zeke. "My great granddaddy was Cherokee. I rode bareback long before I ever used a saddle."

"I hope you plan to teach Robby how to do that, and I want to watch when you do."

"Let's go, then. He can practice while we figure out how to carry our stuff without hampering our ride. The sooner we leave, the better it'll be for everyone."

# CHAPTER 9

Tuesday morning, July 19, 1864
Hall County, Georgia

*S*eth gazed across the gully a few yards from the campsite at the sunrise, finding the streaks of pink and orange against the blue pleasing to his artistic eye. Maybe one day he'd figure out how to capture those hues in wood, for furniture or artwork, whenever he got back to civilian life.

*May it please the Lord to make it happen soon.* He bowed his head on that brief prayer and recalled the minister's admonition at Meg's gravesite: "Our times are in His hands...a time to live, a time to die...a time for war and a time for peace." In Seth's opinion, the time for peace was long overdue.

He tramped back to the campsite and shook Robby awake none too gently. The boy would sleep all day if Seth let him, which his mama probably had during his time at home. Their leave-taking had been difficult, heaping guilt on Seth for his folly. Two or three more days mightn't have made much difference, but he couldn't—he wouldn't—put those good folks in any more danger on account of his foolishness.

Robby opened one eye. "Couldn't you've waited five more minutes and let me finish my dream?"

Seth's snort of derision answered. "What was it this time, a mountain of food or a beautiful lass that held your attention?"

"Both, and more than one woman—"

"It's good I woke you up then. One woman's trouble enough. Every time you add another, you multiply your problems."

Robby grumbled as he packed up his belongings. "And you would know, I imagine, after being tended by three or more women last week."

Seth paused in gathering the sacks and gaped at his friend. "Robby, I was out-of-my-mind sick. They said my fever raged for nearly three days. I wasn't trying to decide which woman to court." He tossed the blanket over the gelding's back to protect it from the ropes they'd used to string the knapsacks. "Besides, two of them were married, and one was a widow. They didn't let the single women do anything but bring me food. And I told you, I'm not looking for a wife."

"That's what you keep saying." Robby picked up his kepi. "How far do you reckon we are from the pickets we ran into coming over, and how do you plan to explain how you came by this horse?"

Looking up from securing the ropes, Seth pointed back the way they'd come. "Remember when we veered off the road a mile or so before we stopped yesterday? I believe that'll loop around just south of Gainesville, so we'll miss the pickets. It's a couple miles longer, but we're making better time with Mercury here." He stroked the horse's neck and offered him a carrot from their dwindling stores.

"Mercury? Ain't that the name of one of the planets that goes around the sun?"

"Yep, and it's also the name of one of the Roman gods people worshipped in ancient times. Supposedly, he had wings and served as the messenger god because he was fast.

This old boy is fast, too, but that's not why I decided on the name."

Robby fastened his knapsack and slipped it over his arm. "Why then?"

"Have you ever seen liquid mercury? It's about the same color as this old boy, a dull gray, and it slips around fast so you can hardly catch it. I'm hoping we can be just as slippery and avoid anything that would slow us down." Seth hoisted himself onto Mercury's back and grinned down at Robby. "Besides, he needed a name. We couldn't keep calling him Horse. Are you riding or walking today?"

"I'm riding so we can find somewhere to get breakfast quick. I'm hungry as a horse. No offense, Mercury." Robby accepted the hand Seth held out to mount behind him. "Maybe he'll go faster, looking for his feed. I don't think any of us are fond of riding double."

"You might as well enjoy riding while you can. I hope to be at the Spalding place around noon and get some of Miss Dottie's biscuits."

Robby jerked in surprise. "What? You're going to stop at that old man's house, the one what stole our rifles?"

"Yep, and I plan to trade him Mercury here and my pa's old blunderbuss in return for our weapons."

"You'd better be careful, or he'll keep all those things and send us away empty-handed again."

"He won't catch me asleep again, and we'll eat outside where we can keep an eye on everything."

"But why give him the horse? Ain't that like casting your pearls before swine?"

Seth chuckled at Robby's mangled metaphor. "Think about it. The Spaldings have a big meadow near their house where Mercury could eat his fill every day, as opposed to what your folks have at home. And if the Federals should happen to recognize Mercury..." He lifted his hands, palms up.

Robby sputtered in disbelief. "Seth, you're setting up the old man to get back at him? I never figured you to be so spiteful."

"Not at all. I just think Mr. Spalding would do a better job of arguing and haggling with the Federals than Zeke would. And I really doubt they'll ever find the horse, with Mercury being so far from where he disappeared. Either way, Spalding gets a good horse for the time being, and tracing him back to us would be nigh impossible."

"That means we'll be back to walking again until we get to Greenville."

"Not the whole way. Remember Moses makes his run to the Georgia border 'most every day. We can stop at the same houses as we did last week, although I hope we get a better reception since they should recognize us. Then once we get to Greenville, we'll board the train and ride in style back to Virginia."

Robby grunted. "Probably stuck in the baggage car again. But at least it ain't walking."

~

TUESDAY AFTERNOON, JULY 19, 1864
LOUISVILLE, KENTUCKY

*A*fter two days of riding in rail cars, Lydia looked forward to sitting in a room that didn't move. She'd be glad never to see the inside of a rail car again.

The women spilled out of the iron monster, following the directions of the provost guards across the tracks and onto the loading platform protruding from the brick building. They hastened through the depot and out the door facing town.

Dark clouds obscured the sun, threatening rain and making the late afternoon feel like evening. Lydia stumbled as she gazed at this strange environment, swept along by the flow of humanity surging around her. An unpleasant odor lingered in the air, barely lifted by the warm breeze chasing the clouds and sprinkling the women with drops of rain as they waited for the street to clear of traffic.

Millie took a step ahead, gaping at the cluster of buildings looming across the street. "What in the world is that place?"

A wooden fence enclosed the entire block. As the women watched, a gate opened, and two men emerged from the barricaded structure. Between them they carried a cloth-covered litter, which they loaded onto a waiting wagon.

"Hospital, maybe," Rose said. "But not for the town's residents, not with that tall fence around it. Could be a sanitarium, I suppose."

They crossed to the other side and passed a large iron gate with a prominent sign: "Union Army Prison." Lydia shuddered at the implication. Although considered prisoners, the group from Georgia had received decent treatment up to this time. Could that monstrous facility be the end of their journey?

Rose leaned close to Millie, who expressed the same horrified thought. "Relax. We're not going there. See, the guards are crossing the street again."

Their destination, however, appeared to be within sight of the Union prison. A newly constructed building sat square in the block facing the prison gate. No banner or marker graced the entrance. The guards led them into a lobby area then turned down a hallway, passing several doors. A quick look inside one room revealed another group of women lounging on cots or sitting around a table. Oil lamps created shadows in the dark areas.

Windows at the end of the hall offered little illumination for the stairs leading to the second floor. The guards stopped at the top to give instructions to the women huddled below. "You can choose which room you want. Each of them has a dozen beds, a couple of tables and several chairs, and a clothespress.

Your men and boys will be in rooms on the first floor since there're not as many of them."

The guard explained about the kitchen and other facilities available at the refugee house, which were not impressive at all. "Two water closets on each floor," he said, "but the water hasn't yet been established for this building."

The women stared at him in confusion. "There's no water?"

"Only a well in the backyard. We hope to have the gas lines in working order before the weather turns cold."

Following Olivia, who peppered the guard with questions, their group took a room near the far end of the hall. "The guard said Wade and John Mark might be able to visit us if we take this room, so they can continue their lessons," Olivia told them. "They'll be sleeping directly below us. It's not ideal, but at least they'll be close enough that we can care for them if they get sick."

Each woman dropped her baggage beside a bed, not bothering with any blankets for the moment. Once Lydia helped Millie get settled, she stretched out on a cot. While others fell into exhausted slumber, Lydia couldn't get her brain to settle. Scenes from the past fortnight played through her memory, compelling her to make sense of all that'd happened. Could she have done anything differently?

Everything hinged on the moment she heard the Voice telling her to leave. What if she'd left immediately, without notifying her supervisor? Perhaps she and Millie could have found someone to carry them farther south. Such thinking didn't help. Only God knew how that would've turned out. He surely knew how the sense of duty had been drilled into her from an early age and had expected her to act exactly as she had.

Meeting Olivia Spencer and the Wynns confirmed her actions had been right. Their strong faith bolstered her own, and already she leaned on them for wisdom in dealing with

Millie. Without their gracious influence, she probably would've reacted differently to the revelation that her own nephew had been the one to seduce her stepdaughter. Lydia still hadn't come to terms with that bit of news. Millie had promised to explain if they ever got a chance to speak in private.

Where was Troy now? No one in their group had seen him since their arrival in Marietta, and he hadn't been on their train to Louisville. Perhaps the army had sent him to another prison facility. Maybe he'd taken the oath of allegiance to the Union and been set free. She'd been too focused on Millie to give him much thought, but she ought to try to find out.

Voices near the door caught her attention, and she rolled onto her side to see who else couldn't sleep. Rose stood there with Phoebe and Janie Wilson, speaking softly so as not to awaken the others. Seeing Phoebe raised Lydia's hackles, but she waited until the Wilsons left to slip off her bed and pad in stocking feet to the door.

Rose lifted her head as Lydia reached her side. "Is anything wrong?"

"No," Rose said, but her eyes gave lie to the answer. She cleared her throat and explained. "Phoebe will stay in this room with us. Janie's room was full, and she didn't want to be separated from the younger girls. Since we have an extra bed, it seemed only right she should stay with us so we can look out for her."

Lydia's arms went around her friend. "You're a better woman than I am, Rose. I would have a hard time agreeing to that after what she pulled in Marietta. But maybe that's why she needs to be near you, to give her an example to follow, someone besides her mother."

"Janie's a good mother. She just has her hands full right now."

"We'll pray Phoebe will straighten up soon so she can help Janie more."

Rose nodded. "As for good examples, I'd say she has a room full of them right here."

~

SUNDAY MORNING, JULY 24, 1864
PETERSBURG, VIRGINIA

*M*aking his way to the field hospital, Seth spotted a familiar figure and shifted the package in his hand to salute Lieutenant George Right Smith. Noting Smith's wan complexion, he was surprised when the man stopped to chat a moment.

Seth had met the lieutenant before the war when he'd accompanied his father to deliver several pieces of furniture to Smith's cousin in Gordon County.

Smith acknowledged the salute, maintaining a balance between formal and informal conduct. "Sergeant Morgan, I heard you had an eventful trip to the home place recently." He raised his brows and quirked one side of his mouth.

Seth grinned. "It wasn't my finest hour, sir. I can only blame my lapse on confusion due to a recent illness."

"On the contrary," Smith said. "I consider it a brilliant joke to, um, appropriate a Union mount and leave it three counties away from the scene."

Scowling, Seth said, "Private Roland talks too much." He motioned to the package he carried. "Say, does this hospital also serve the men from the Thirty-fifth? I have a couple of letters to deliver, one for Doctor Spencer."

The lieutenant nodded. "I know the doctor, just saw him, as a matter of fact. He's still making morning rounds, so you ought to be able to catch him. Before you go, though, tell me, how did things in Georgia seem to you?"

"Not good. The Federals have Marietta tied up tight. I saw

their tents off toward Roswell, so I expect they've destroyed everything between there and Chattanooga. I know they burned the mills around Roswell 'cause I met some of the mill workers the army sent there. One of 'em was Doctor Spencer's wife."

Smith heaved a mighty sigh. "There won't be much left of the South, I guess, once this war is over. Now I doubt the wisdom of pursuing our rights on the battlefield. We should've done our fighting with words in the courthouse."

His comment triggered a thought. "Lieutenant, would you be acquainted with my cousin, Mansfield Peacock from Forsythe County? I've been trying to find him but don't know which unit he's in."

"Hmm. Unusual name. You might check the Georgia Forty-third. I hear they picked up a few new men."

This was excellent news. The object of his search could be nearby.

Seth saluted. "Good to see you, sir. I hope we might do business again once we get back home."

A few minutes later, Seth located the doctor. He would have known the man, even without asking the nurse, by his serious demeanor as he lifted a sheet over the face of a young private. The doctor's hand rested on the soldier's covered head for a moment, then trailed slowly across the chest in a silent benediction. When he turned around, he blinked back the threatening tears and squared his shoulders. It took him a few seconds to notice Seth.

"Sergeant, did you need me?"

Seth offered a hasty salute. "Captain Spencer, sir. I have a letter for you. From your family in Georgia."

The doctor's eyes widened then dropped to the package in Seth's hands. "Would you mind if we stepped outside before you make that delivery? I need to wash up a bit."

"As you wish, sir." He backed into the aisle so the doctor

could walk ahead of him. Following him to the backyard of the house, he chose a seat in the shade of a spreading oak tree while the doctor washed.

"My apologies," the doctor said. "I didn't ask your name." He sat beside Seth.

"Seth Morgan, sir, of the Eighteenth. I'm from Marietta, which is where I met the operatives sent there from the Roswell and Sweetwater mills. Including your wife."

Doctor Spencer's eyes left the letters to search Seth's face. "My wife is in Marietta?"

"She was a few days ago, along with all the mill workers. The Federals took them to Marietta where they were planning to put them on a train going north. I expect they've left Marietta by now. Rumor was they'd be sent to Nashville or even farther into Union territory."

The doctor leaned forward. "Is my son with her? And what of her aunt and uncle?"

"The whole family is together," Seth said. "At least the Yankees allowed them that much. I only met your wife and a few of the other women."

"How did Olivia look?" the doctor asked. "Was she holding up all right?"

Seth scratched behind his ear. "She appeared fine to me. I'm sure nobody was happy with the situation, but they seemed to be making the best of it." Seth stood and pointed to the packet. "There's also a letter in there for Martin Anderson from Roswell. He's in the Thirty-fifth, too, but I don't know how to find him."

Doctor Spencer stood and gripped Seth's hand. "I'll see he gets it somehow. Thank you for bringing these. I imagine you know how much it means to get news from home."

"Yes, sir, that I do. If you should need to contact me for anything, I'm in the Eighteenth, Company A."

"Thank you, Sergeant Morgan, and I will extend the same

offer to you. Although I hope you won't need my professional services. God be with you and keep you safe."

Seth turned back at the door to see the doctor open his reading glasses and tear into the letter. It felt good to be able to brighten someone's day amid all these troubles.

# CHAPTER 10

*I*saac Wynn adjusted the reading glasses on his nose and cleared his throat.

"Psalm three. 'LORD, how are they increased that trouble me. Many are they that rise up against me. Many there be which say of my soul, there is no help for him in God. Selah. But Thou, O LORD, art a shield for me, my glory, and the lifter up of mine head. I cried unto the LORD with my voice, and He heard me out of his holy hill. Selah. I laid me down and slept. I awaked: for the LORD sustained me.'"

Closing the Bible, he removed the glasses and addressed the group gathered for the prayer meeting. "The Lord has kept us through this war and brought us to a place of safety, though it may not be what we would have chosen. He's given us new friends to help us through our situation. We can trust Him to be with us always and keep us in the palm of His hand."

Lydia soaked up the words. She easily understood the simple message of hope and encouragement from this man who lived out his faith every day. Whether the reason was his clear language or their current circumstances, her mind didn't wander as it had in church back home. She hung on each word and tucked them away in her heart.

When the closing prayer ended, Isaac nodded to Rose, who'd asked if she could say a word to the women.

"There's a new guard here at the refuge house, Sergeant Edwin Pierce," she said. "You should be careful around him. He's the reason Celeste and I met Captain Griffin in Roswell, and I guess why the captain felt responsible for us."

Emily shifted in her chair. "What happened?"

"The day after the Federals arrived, Celeste and I ran into a group of rowdy soldiers on our way to the town square," Rose said. "Sergeant Pierce was the leader, and it was clear their intent wasn't honorable. Captain Griffin was riding by and stopped them before they could do more than scare us."

Lydia's jaw dropped. "And this sergeant is one of our guards? How in the world did he get assigned here if he's like that?"

Rose shook her head. "I suppose the Union leadership doesn't know what kind of man he is."

Ada Anderson huffed. "Or they don't care."

Millie darted a glance at Lydia. "Maybe he has friends in high positions who help him."

Memories surfaced of the day Millie warded off the soldier in their home. Would they never be free from worrying about men's unwelcome advances?

Rose lifted her hands. "Whatever the case may be, he's already threatened me and Celeste too. Somehow, he knew the captain was still watching out for us in Marietta. Sergeant Pierce seems to think causing us trouble will get back at Captain Griffin for thwarting his plans."

Olivia heaved a sigh. "If he's that vindictive, we should all be on our guard. He might decide to use any of us or the children if it serves his purpose."

Lydia's experience with men didn't inspire trust in most of the species. From the looks on the other faces, she wasn't the only one. "It might be a good idea to avoid being alone when we leave our rooms."

"Good point." Rose said.

With children falling ill and more people arriving daily, they had enough to worry about. How would they avoid unscrupulous guards?

~

WEDNESDAY EVENING, JULY 27, 1864
BAILEY'S CREEK, HENRICO COUNTY, VIRGINIA

*S*eth wedged his rifle in the trench beside him and tried to settle down for the night. After a trying day, he wanted nothing more than a few hours of sleep. And maybe a good, hot meal, but it was best not to think on something so unlikely.

The Yankees had resumed their assault on Richmond and captured four Confederate cannons, which the South could ill afford to lose. Their movements had prompted General Lee to send reinforcements from Petersburg to protect the capital. Among those troops, Colonel Joseph Armstrong led the Eighteenth as part of General Kershaw's brigade. Though a few of his fellows griped about the change in location, Seth figured he could sleep here as well as he could any place that wasn't home. He used every opportunity to scan the faces around him, looking for the low-down skunk who'd torn his world apart.

Seth pulled his kepi over his eyes and willed sleep to come, trying to ignore the gnawing in his belly. What he wouldn't give for a thick wedge of cornbread slathered with butter. His mind presented an image so real, he opened his eyes to see whether someone held that slice under his nose. Nothing was there.

He sniffed the air, hoping to find a lingering aroma, but the only odors he could detect were those of men too long without a bath and the slightly more pleasant stench of a few horses corralled nearby. Unable to stop the stomach's rumbling, Seth retrieved the pack of jerky hidden in his knapsack. He broke off a couple inches of the stiff beef and popped it in his mouth. He carefully rewrapped the remainder and stuffed it into his coat pocket.

When his fingers found the scalloped edge of a handkerchief, he paused. Who knew the feel of a soft scrap of cotton could conjure a host of thoughts and feelings? Closing his eyes, Seth saw the troubled green eyes and pink lips parted in surprise. Heard the breathy gasp of awareness, felt the trembling hands on his arms. He searched for the woman taste, but the fantasy evaporated as reality intruded. He hadn't kissed her, after all, but heaven help him, he'd wanted to. The salty jerky in his mouth was a poor substitute.

He hadn't kissed her. What had stopped him? Though she'd seemed skittish, he was sure he'd recognized the same hunger in her manner. No clueless miss there, the widow recognized the signs of desire. He could've persuaded her to share a kiss, so what had stopped him?

Ah, yes. He'd stopped because he had a prior commitment. Revenge on the monster who'd killed Meg. He couldn't commit to another woman. Not yet, maybe not ever.

But the soft fabric between his fingers released a faint whiff of lavender, and his mind whispered her name as he drifted off to sleep. *Lydia.*

SATURDAY, JULY 30, 1864

LOUISVILLE, KENTUCKY

*L*ydia's nose was to blame. The aroma of fresh baked bread wafting from the store down the street drew her as surely as music had tempted children to follow the pied piper of Hamlin to their doom. No good could come from it, but she yielded to the temptation anyway. She was hungry. Her feet hurt from walking all over town in search of a paying job. A number of the children they traveled with were ill, and she and the other ladies had asked if they could seek employment to pay for medicine and other incidentals that were sure to come up. But she couldn't function without sustenance. All valid arguments against the one reason she shouldn't give in. No money.

Perhaps she'd just look in the window or stand near the door so she could breathe in the sweet smells whenever it opened. Before the war, she and Granny McNeil had jokingly agreed they gained weight merely from smelling the cakes and puddings at Christmastime. Maybe it would prove true. Lydia crossed her arms over her middle to pull her dress closer. She needed no mirror to know her clothes hung loose and her face looked as washed-out as the worn shirtwaist.

Edging closer to the temptation, she jumped when the door opened to allow a stout Union officer to exit. "Oh, pardon me, miss," he said, sweeping off his kepi with a bow. His other hand clutched a sack with its bottom marked by oil stains seeping from the precious horde within.

He stepped aside and held the door open for her to enter. "If this is your destination, you've come to the right place. Nobody can outdo Watford's Bakery. The hard part is deciding what to try first."

In the face of his kindness, Lydia couldn't simply stand there. His fine manners inspired a regal nod and whispered word of thanks as he bowed and went on his way.

Lydia stood in the middle of the floor, transfixed by the displays of more confections than she'd seen in her lifetime. As if the sight was too much, she closed her eyes and inhaled the marvelous mixture of vanilla and lemon offset by the yeasty tang of sourdough. Jerked out of her fantasy world by the fierce rumbling of her stomach, she opened her eyes to find she wasn't alone. An elderly man regarded her with twinkling brown eyes. He watched her from the other side of the counter, which reached to his chin, though Lydia gauged it to be waist-high on her.

"Oh, excuse me." She turned for the door.

"No, don't leave, Miss." His face disappeared behind the glass shelves as he swept to the end of the counter. When he came into the aisle, she noticed he sat on a rolling chair, his legs covered by a blanket.

"Would you like to try something? We have dozens of varieties to tempt you." He gestured toward the display with a pair of tongs.

"Yes. No," Lydia said, torn between staying and leaving. "I'm sorry, I have no money. I just couldn't resist stepping in to admire everything. It smelled so lovely. I'm sorry. I'll go now."

"Please don't leave without sampling one of our specialties, free of charge." He reached into the closest case and transferred something onto a napkin.

She shook her head in vigorous denial. "I couldn't."

"Please?" He extended a large sweet roll toward her, the scent of cinnamon drifting her way while rich icing dripped onto the napkin. "Now one of us will have to eat this, and Mrs. Watford will be most unhappy if I spoil my dinner with another sweet."

Three hours later, Lydia recounted the story to her friends at the refuge house. "In the end, he was so persuasive that he convinced me he would be severely disappointed if I didn't try something."

"And then he offered you the job?" Millie asked. Like the others sitting at the table, Millie savored a bite from the cookies Mrs. Watford had pressed Lydia to take with her. She'd called them "three-day-old cookies" and said she'd have to throw them out if Lydia didn't take them.

"Not exactly," Lydia said. "He took me in the back to meet his wife, and she explained how they needed someone to help. Both have health issues, and when I explained our plan to earn money for the children's medicine, she clapped her hands and said it was an answer to prayer."

The other women exchanged looks all around while Edith slapped one hand on the table. "Ain't that just like the Lord, bringing two parties together to help each other out?"

Lydia nodded. "It is, as I'm learning. I'll only go a couple days a week to start, but Mrs. Watford expects to need me more as the weather turns cooler."

Millie's expression clouded. "But that'll be about the time my baby is due."

"I told her about the baby, and she said we'll work it out when that time comes."

Olivia squeezed Lydia's arm. "This is great news. With several of us working and pooling our funds, we should make enough money to purchase medicine. Added to our prayers, I expect they'll recover in time to join the local school when it starts up again."

Lydia's grin stretched wide. "I have an idea Mrs. Watford might send more treats when they're available. Those will probably do as much good as medicine."

~

Thursday, August 18, 1864
Richmond, Virginia

*S*eth tucked the package close to his body. The precious contents could mean the difference between life and death for his fellow soldiers. The Yankees' stranglehold on the Richmond-Petersburg area had hampered the Confederates in bringing in much-needed medicines. In the face of such dire necessity, a few local civilians risked their lives to venture into enemy territory on occasion to procure supplies for hospitals. Never knowing who watched their movements, the shadowy heroes never delivered the goods in person but passed their treasures through several hands to their final destination.

Today's delivery fell to Seth as he threaded his way to visit Robby, who recuperated in the infirmary. The boy had been shot at Cedarville. The minié ball had damaged muscle and drenched his sleeve with blood, but it passed clean through his upper arm before blasting a tree. Seth imagined how Robby would use the scar to his advantage when they returned to civilian life.

His first errand, however, was to deliver the medicine. Seth found Doctor Spencer at his desk, writing notes in a journal. He waited for the man's pen to pause before he rapped on the open door.

"Package for you, Doctor." Seth placed the bundle on the desk.

Doctor Spencer's eyes lit with interest. He pulled the package closer for a brief examination, then carefully placed it in the bottom desk drawer. "Thank you, Sergeant. I assure you it will be administered with care. If you know the person involved in obtaining this precious commodity, please pass along my heartfelt appreciation."

"I wish I did, but it seems secrecy is the order of the day." He tapped the doorframe and gestured toward the rooms where the ill and injured lay. "I guess I'll check on Private Roland and see if I can aggravate him out of his leisure."

"Before you go, Sergeant, I have something to show you." The doctor pulled a worn newspaper from the top desk drawer. "Another person who will remain unnamed brought this in the other day." The fold of the tabloid revealed a single column of print, which the doctor pointed out as he extended the paper.

Seth glanced at the top of the page. *July 21, 1864. The Louisville Democrat.* The month-old paper would be passed around to the officers and perhaps make its way through the lower ranks. Seth's eyes moved to the item indicated by the doctor.

*The train which arrived from Nashville last evening brought up from the South 249 women and children, who are sent by order of General Sherman, to be transferred north of the Ohio River, there to remain during the war. We understand there are now at Nashville, 1500 women and children, who are in a destitute condition, and who are to be sent to this place to be sent North. A number of them were engaged in the manufactories at Sweetwater at the time that place was captured by our forces.*

Seth returned the paper. "It appears your wife may be somewhere north of the Ohio River, unless she's among those still in Nashville."

Spencer tossed the paper on the desk. "Maybe, but one of the Yankees I treated from the Deep Bottom fight told me there's a refugee house in Louisville near the Army prison. His family wrote him about it, so that might be a good place to start my search. I don't know where the Army would put them in Nashville, but I'll try to find out. At least I know the general direction. Just thought you might want to know they're no longer at your house."

"I wish you well, Doctor." Seth retraced his steps to the door. "Let me know if I can assist. I'd better go see Robby now." He hurried away, thinking about the mill operatives. It seemed Lydia was in Louisville. Keeping a dainty handkerchief in his breast pocket held no significance. The scrap of cotton came in handy at times. Since he could well owe the ladies who were at his house his life, thinking of them was natural. He wished them well, but it was unlikely he would see any of them again.

He moseyed around the ward, speaking a word to the men he knew until he reached Robby's cot. The feverish complexion had receded, leaving a pasty color so common among these companions. A cocky smile bloomed when Robby spotted Seth, and he called out in jest. "Mama couldn't come to see about me, so she sent Seth. Anybody need a bedtime story?"

Good-natured chuckles issued from several of his fellows, and Seth joined in. "No story for you, Roland. I'm sure you've concocted a few of your own to tell the ladies about your injury." Knowing he hated it, Seth ruffled Robby's hair. "You seem to be feeling better. Ready to go out and face those Yanks again?"

Robby's face lost what little color it had, but he bluffed his answer. "Soon as Doc says I can go. With my fever down, I imagine he'll need to make room for others soon enough. You heard anything from home?"

Seth shook his head. "No, but I never get my hopes up. I sent a letter to my mother's friend in Savannah to ask if Mama and the girls had gone there. I told her to let your family know you're doin' well, if she can get word to them."

Their talk turned to old times at home, avoiding the war. When Robby's eyelids fluttered, Seth moved to leave. "You get some rest now. I'll check back later."

Robby caught Seth's hand with a firm grip. "Before you go, I need to tell you. I believe I saw your quarry just before I got hit. That's why I looked away from the line of Yanks and didn't duck in time. I was watching him."

Seth's breath backed up in his chest. "You only met my cousin once, though. At my wedding. Would you recognize him now?"

"I think so. He resembles you. I couldn't see his whole face, but it sure looked like him."

"Which unit?"

"Thirty-fifth. You could check their roster. Can't be too many Peacocks on it." Robby waved a hand to send Seth on his way.

"I will." Seth jutted his jaw and headed for the door.

# CHAPTER 11

*L*ydia called her farewells to the Watfords and juggled her packages to close the door behind her. When her boss had asked her to make a couple of deliveries after she left the bakery each day, she'd been glad to comply. Her first stop took her to the haberdasher's, a few blocks away. The last one was at the Union Army Prison for the officer who'd held the bakery door open for her that first day. Major Sullivan allowed himself a weekly treat of fried pies, but his duties sometimes kept him from getting to the bakery before it closed. Mrs. Watford came up with the idea of delivering the pies to him, and Lydia's proximity to the prison made it a practical solution.

The prospect had appealed to Lydia because it provided her a way to make discreet inquiries about Troy. Major Sullivan had promised to question the prisoners who came through the prison on their way to the holding facilities farther north. His initial inquiries didn't turn up anything useful, but he'd promised to send letters to his counterparts at the other prisons with each departing unit. Lydia knew better than to get her hopes up, but she prayed for any ray of light pointing to her nephew's whereabouts.

A sentry noted her approach this day and called for the major. By the time she reached the gate, held partially opened by the guard, she could see Major Sullivan hurrying toward her. She secured the bag of bread for the refugee home in the crook of her arm.

"Good evening to you, Mrs. Gibson. I trust you've had a pleasant day at the bakery." The major doffed his kepi and relieved her of the bag. He pressed a coin into her hand.

Lydia drew back. "What's this? You've already paid Mrs. Watford."

"Yes, ma'am, I have, but that good woman told me about you folks staying in the house over there and how you're working to help the sick children. This small coin is for that cause."

"Why, that's awfully kind of you." Lydia slipped the coin into her skirt pocket. "You'll be pleased to know all the children are recovering, and now our funds are going toward getting them ready for school. We had to leave most of our belongings back in Georgia, you know, so they need clothes for the cooler weather."

The man leaned against the gate post, apparently in no hurry to return to his duties. He bounced the package in his hands and ignored the soldiers who loitered nearby, pretending a lack of interest in their conversation. He tilted his head. "Do any of those children belong to you, Mrs. Gibson?"

When Lydia blanched, he rushed to withdraw the question. "I'm sorry if my question was insensitive, ma'am. I was given to understand you're a widow and thought you might have young children."

"You just caught me by surprise, is all. I am a widow, my

husband being among those lost at Chickamauga last year. I have only my stepdaughter, who's sixteen and...and in the family way. The nephew I've been asking about is the baby's father, so you can imagine why I'm desperate to locate him."

"Ah, I see." A conciliatory smile stretched his thin lips. "Forgive me if I overstep, but I can't imagine you're much older than sixteen yourself."

Did he make the remark as an apology for probing into her history or to hint at a personal interest in her? Either way, she'd no intention to advance the subject. She brought the interview back to her primary concern. "I don't suppose you have any information on my nephew?"

He shook his head. "I regret to say none of my inquiries have yet to bear fruit. Speaking of fruit, I suppose I should take these marvelous pies inside where the boys and I can enjoy them. I thank you for bringing them, and I wish you a pleasant farewell."

"Good day."

He tipped his kepi with a smile, leaving Lydia to mull over the nature of his questions.

~

WEDNESDAY, OCTOBER 19, 1864
CEDAR CREEK, VIRGINIA

*S*eth pondered his next move as the column of soldiers snaked around hills, hugging the creek below. Barely visible in the darkness, the water meandered through the valley with a whispering voice, as if it also kept its passage a secret.

The scent of damp loam resurrected memories of fishing trips from Seth's youth when he'd dug in the rich dirt for wiggly worms to use for bait. The slightest zephyr swept across his cheek, reminding him of the passing season. Another summer would soon be gone, and still the war persisted. Like his search for justice, it gave no evidence of ending.

He fought to keep his mind on the impending battle and off finding the monstrous cousin who'd ravaged Seth's wife and wrecked his world. He couldn't afford to divide his attention between the two. Lack of focus led to calamity.

"A double-minded man is unstable in all his ways." Seth felt sure the scripture applied to something else, but its warning fit.

The midnight march took little more than an hour, though they'd been forced to follow a narrow trail that snaked through the pines for part of the way. Seth figured the Eighteenth stood smack-dab in the middle of the battalion, with several companies in the front and others to the rear. Fog drifted low, obscuring their movement and muffling their footsteps. Straining to see into the predawn shadows, he concentrated on the men ahead of him.

The troops halted where the rocky bluff gave way to an open field and spread around the rim, noiseless, waiting for the signal. Seth marveled that the men sleeping in the tents below didn't waken to the tension in the air. Like a coiled rattler, the quiet issued an ominous warning of danger.

A flag waved, bayonets lifted, and the Confederate forces surged forward. They fell on the unsuspecting Yanks like vultures on a carcass. By mid-morning, the attacking forces had captured more than a dozen cannons. The guns swiveled to send fire back the way they'd come, blasting rows of tents, animals, and men as they scattered. Order erupted into chaos. As the blue receded, the gray advanced into the abandoned Union camp.

Euphoric with victory, the ravenous Rebels abandoned the battle and plundered the vacated tents. Restraint forgotten, they fell on the spoils like drunken men.

Seth might have joined them, at least for a handful of food, but a familiar face grabbed his attention. A face he'd known from childhood, tolerated then but despised now. The face he'd pummeled in his dreams for a year and a half. His anger exploded.

"Mansfield Peacock!"

He roared the name, the absurdity of the combination fueling his wrath rather than the humor of former years. He'd defended Manny as a boy against bullies, but today he'd call him out and make him pay for his deeds.

Seth bellowed again as the figure paused. The sound faltered, swallowed up in the melee of scavengers fighting over canteens and knapsacks. He slogged through the haphazard maze to confront his enemy, losing sight of him as Mansfield ran through the maelstrom. Someone darted inside a tent. Seth followed, fingers tightening on the barrel of his rifle, ready to light into the hated relative. He ducked into the tent and blinked hard to see in the dim interior. He opened his mouth to shout again, but his growl sputtered into a whimper. Pain spiraled in his head, and darkness enveloped him.

When he awoke, the pain held him immobile. He kept his eyes closed and concentrated on the noise around him, waiting for memory to return. Voices and footsteps came closer. Not the frenzied hurry of assault or retreat, but the calm movement of searching. He worked his dry mouth to call out but produced only a guttural barking of pain. The darkness threatened to pull him under again, so he lay in silence. His comrades would find him eventually.

His patience paid off when he heard steps pause nearby. Words floated over him as rough hands grabbed his feet and shoulders. Unable to protest the treatment, he retreated to the painless depths again.

MONDAY, OCTOBER 24, 1864

*M*illie crushed Lydia's hand in a painful grip and grunted with effort. Lydia dabbed the girl's brow with a cool cloth and murmured encouragement.

From her place at Millie's feet, Edith guided the process with calm assurances. "Hold on a minute. Now, one more push."

After fourteen hours of labor, the final push ushered Millie's protesting baby girl into the world. Millie fell back against the pillows and shared a shaky smile with the women who attended her.

Lydia felt as if she'd labored right along with her step-daughter, sleeping an hour or two at a time whenever Millie fell into exhausted sleep or one of the attendants insisted she lie down. Her first experience with childbirth left her equally drained and elated.

Olivia helped Lydia clean and bundle the squalling infant while Edith and Ada tended to Millie. As Lydia handed the sweet bundle to Millie, Rose and Emily joined Celeste at the door. Knowing they'd hurried from their various jobs in town, she waved them closer. "Come meet my granddaughter. I think she's gonna be a singer. She's got the lungs for it."

Emily admired the new arrival, then slipped away to tend her own children. With some coaxing and encouragement, Millie nursed the babe enough to calm her down before they both slept from exhaustion. With their charges resting, Ada, Edith and Olivia slipped out of the room to find their own beds.

Lydia lifted the baby and sank onto the straight-back chair, rocking back and forth, softly humming a disjointed melody. Celeste and Rose lingered nearby.

Celeste cradled the downy head, clearly enthralled. "Rose has to go back to the Turner house tonight, but I've arranged to spend the night here. I'm sure the rest of you ladies are exhausted, so you must let me help however I can."

Swallowing against the lump of emotion in her throat, Lydia nodded. "Thank you. I'm so glad to have y'all here to help because this is as new to me as it is to Millie. I was the youngest in my family, and my brothers and sisters rarely visited with young children."

"Celeste and I often watched smaller children from the church," Rose said, "so we have experience with changing nappies, but it's been a while."

Lydia sniffed back the building moisture, shoving down the melancholy that hovered beneath her practical nature. Fatigue weakened her defenses. "I always wanted a passel of young'uns, probably because I spent much of my childhood alone. Ma died from influenza only a year after the accident that took Pa, and I went to live with Granny McNeil. It was just the two of us from the time I was ten until I married Cal. When Granny passed a few months afterward, I became an orphan for sure."

Lydia remembered these sisters had experienced similar losses. Their gentle empathy invited confidence.

Once started, she couldn't seem to stop her confession. "I loved Millie from the time I became her stepmother, but I desperately wanted my own child as well." Her chest heaved with a sigh of resignation. "That didn't happen, and now I can see why. With this war, Cal gone, and the changes in Millie, I doubt I could've handled having a little one to watch out for."

Celeste rubbed Lydia's shoulder. "Our Lord sees so much that we can't. Sometimes His answers, or His silence, may seem harsh, but He has our best in mind."

Swiping a finger across her cheek to banish the tears, Lydia smiled. "But now God has given us this tiny miracle, and my heart is about to burst with joy."

Rose and Celeste slipped away while Lydia gazed at the

infant whose hand clutched her finger. She tugged the baby's blanket to cover the tiny feet, content to hold her close.

~

MONDAY, OCTOBER 24, 1864
EASTERN KENTUCKY

*U*nfamiliar voices penetrated Seth's foggy brain. Where was he?

"It's a miracle we even found him, rolled up in that blanket like he was. Whoever walloped him on the head didn't want him to be found, I expect."

"If he doesn't wake up soon..."

The voice faded. The person must've walked away.

Seth struggled to open his eyes, to see where he was. Listening was easier, but silence now replaced the voices. Were they all in his head? His nose detected the pungent odors of camphor and alcohol, reminding him of the field hospital he'd visited. But why was he sleeping in the hospital? He wasn't sick. Was he?

Though the darkness beckoned, his need to know outpaced the pull of oblivion. He concentrated on lifting his eyelids and squinted against the brightness. Sunlight filtered through gaps in the tent canvas. Dust motes danced in the beam. This was not Doctor Spencer's facility.

Moving his head brought on nausea. As soon as someone got close enough, he'd ask his questions. If he could remember them. He waited, saving his energy for the moment.

The trickle of liquid blessed his parched lips and roused him from slumber. A soft voice murmured praise while strong arms supported his head. Even the water that missed his mouth and dampened his neck revived him. Opening his eyes, Seth met the gaze of three unknown faces, watching him with concern. Two doctors and a nurse, he guessed. The nurse eased away, taking the cup with her.

He swallowed to prime his voice. "Where...?"

The younger doctor replaced the nurse at Seth's side. "You're in the Union army's prisoner hospital unit in Eastern Kentucky." The doctor reached for his wrist and held it while consulting his watch. Then he leaned over Seth to examine his head. His cool fingers pulled at Seth's eyelids while commanding him to look first left, then right, then up and down. He joined the other doctor at the foot of the bed, jotting notes in a journal while they conferred in low tones.

Seth rushed to get his questions asked before they went away. "What day's it?"

The older doctor answered, watching Seth like a teacher with a ruler. "Monday, the twenty-fourth of October. What do you remember of the battle? Was it at Cedar Creek?"

Seth searched his memory. Raising his eyebrows set his head to pounding, so he lowered them in a scowl. "Cedar Creek. Marched...at night. Caught Yanks...in tents. They ran."

He paused, remembering the confusion as men started grabbing items, stuffing their pockets. "Saw Manny. Followed him inside."

The doctor scribbled more notes in the book. "That's all?"

"Yeah. I think...someone came behind me...hit me."

"It certainly appears that way. You've got quite a goose egg on your head, and you've been in a coma for several days. I'm Doctor Marsh. Doctor Blackwell here studies head injuries, so he'll continue to observe you until you're moved. Since you don't seem to have any other injuries, you won't be needing me. The nurses will check on you each day and see you get some food." He scribbled in the notebook again and handed it to Doctor Blackwell.

The nurse followed Doctor Marsh down the aisle as Doctor Blackwell opened the book and walked to Seth's other side.

"Now, let's see how bad that knock on the head was. Tell me your name, rank, and hometown."

"Seth Morgan." He paused, concerned when the other information took longer to pull up than it should have. "Se... sergeant, I believe. Is that my coat there?" He motioned to the garment draped over the bed near his knees.

Doctor Blackwell snatched the coat. "Must be. Will that help you remember?"

Seth examined the garment gingerly, his arms weakened from days of inactivity. He found the chevrons on the sleeve, then plunged two fingers into the pocket, pulling out a wad of fabric. Unfolding the handkerchief, he withdrew a dark blue square that represented his new rank and showed it to the doctor. "First Sergeant, just awarded before the march." He returned the badge to the handkerchief, pausing to caress Lydia's initials in the corner before stuffing it back into his coat.

The doctor smirked but made no comment as he wrote in the journal again. "And your hometown?"

"Marietta, Georgia." So far from there, wherever he was now. Virginia? "Doctor Blackwell, where did you say we are?"

"Eastern Kentucky, not far from the last battle in Virginia."

What was it about Kentucky he needed to remember? Something from a while back. Fatigue pulled at his mind, and he closed his eyes. "Can I rest now?"

"I'd advise you to wait until Miss Davis brings your soup, but we can finish our conversation later." He snapped the book closed and perched the pencil behind his ear. "And I'd caution you to remember the owner of that handkerchief you carry. No dallying with my nurse, especially if you've a wife waiting."

Before Seth could answer, he walked away.

"Wife?" The word worked into his brain. No siree. No dallying. No wife. No worries.

# CHAPTER 12

*L*ydia urged Edith out the door to join those waiting for her. "You're sure you'll be all right while we go to church?"

"Don't you worry. We'll be fine. After all, there's three of us and just one baby." She gestured to the bed where Millie nursed the baby and Dorcas hovered like a banty hen over her chicks.

Edith smiled at the picture they made. "It's done that girl a world of good to help with the baby."

Lydia laughed. "And us too. Having her here while you and Olivia work at the hospital is a godsend. At least she knows what she's doing. Now go on. Major Griffin will wonder what's keeping you."

Noah Griffin, the officer who'd helped them in Marietta, had arrived at their door the previous day. Rose had corresponded with him a few times, and it was clear to everyone that the major intended to court her. While most of their group

114

attended church, followed by a meal at the major's cousin's house, Lydia and Dorcas traded off doing chores and watching over the new mother and babe. Babies could be quite demanding, Lydia learned, but the joy they brought made up for the extra work and lack of sleep.

Washing soiled nappies could not be postponed, not even on Sunday. Finished with hanging clean baby clothes on the line outside, Lydia found Dorcas in the kitchen. "If you don't need me for anything else, I think I'll take a short walk while Millie and Amy sleep. It may be the last warm day we have for a while."

"You just go on, Miss Lydia. I'm done here and thinking I'll go up and take myself a rest." She made a shooing motion, and Lydia smiled to see how lively the girl had grown since joining them. The relative freedom allowed in this house combined with the support of friends had released the sunny nature Dorcas had once kept hidden.

Lydia stepped onto the front porch and found Sergeant Pierce there, reclining on a chair with all his weight balanced on the back legs. She raised her brows at his juvenile pose, and he shifted to sit upright. He regarded her with narrowed eyes. If he intended to intimidate her with that look, it wasn't working.

"Where do you think you're going?"

The question hung in the air without benefit of a proper address. Rather than taking offense, Lydia swallowed a laugh. He didn't know her name. Some latent tendency to mischief prompted her attitude.

"Just taking a short walk over to the prison." Though she hadn't planned to go there, it might be the one place he couldn't refuse her. "I have business with Major Sullivan."

She could see the questions floating through his mind. Figuring he would assume the worst possible reason for her visit, she waited until he made the accusation.

"I thought all the doxies lived at the house down the road.

Your group is supposedly the good bunch, but then most women can be bought at a price."

The accusation stung. Had her price been security or the promise of family? Was that why she'd agreed to marry Cal? The possibility of that truth made her strike out.

"My, how cynical you are, Sergeant." Lydia splayed a hand at her throat in mock surprise. "Did your mother have a price?"

He shot out of the chair like a hornet from a stirred nest, righteous indignation awkwardly displayed. "You leave my mother out of it. Go on and try to sweeten up the major. You'll find he ain't so easy to take to the likes of you." His sneer made Lydia reckless.

"Oh, he's sweetened up all right." She moved a few more steps toward the road and dared to taunt him again. "We have a nice arrangement, and he positively lives for my visits."

The door to the refugee house shut with a satisfying bang as Lydia continued across the street. She waited until she reached the gate to the prison to glance back, glad to see the porch deserted. The satisfaction of her verbal sparring drained away. How foolhardy she'd become.

The guard in the "pigeon roost" at the wall called out a greeting. "Afternoon, Miz Gibson. Major Sullivan ain't about today. Had to carry out some orders from the governor, you know. But the rest of us would welcome you with any of those pies."

Lydia smiled. "No pies today, Corporal Mills. The bakery's closed on Sunday, so I guess you'll have to wait."

The guard's attention swung to the depot at the blast of a train whistle. He peered through a pair of field glasses. "Guess that's another load of prisoners. We're even getting a few from Virginia these days. Don't know why they ain't being sent to Maryland or New York."

Lydia's pulse picked up at the news of incoming prisoners.

Could she question those men about Troy? "I guess I'll get on my way then. See you in a few days."

She scurried across the street to the depot before the guard could answer. Her investigation wouldn't wait. Maybe one of the prisoners would know something about her nephew.

~

*S*eth shuffled along with the group of prisoners being herded through the depot. He didn't bother to look up, didn't need to. Just let the crowd push him along to the next room, the next station, the next war—which would be surviving the prison camp. Now there was a cheerful thought. His shoulders slumped, and his beard dragged against the rough fabric of his coat. The longer hair might keep his ears and neck warm through winter in a colder climate. With November underway, the cold would descend soon enough.

Eighteen days had passed since he'd marched in the darkness with the Eighteenth. The victory Seth witnessed had turned into a defeat when the Rebels failed to pursue. The Union had sent reinforcements to push back the assault.

He'd pieced together snatches of conversation he heard while in the hospital and on the train. The Southern loss was significant, putting the District of Columbia beyond Confederate reach. Thousands reported killed or wounded on both sides at Cedar Creek, plus hundreds missing or taken prisoner. The South limped along like a bird with an injured wing— flying was out of the question.

Seth didn't mourn the loss of the battle as much as he did the loss of his quarry and the opportunity to avenge Meg's death. He'd been so close, but Manny had gained the upper hand, and Seth had no idea whether his cousin had survived the counterattack by the Federals. Thoughts of finding the fiend again consumed him, anger smoldering like a banked fire.

Since that fateful day at Cedar Creek, he'd become a dangerous man to deal with, likely to erupt at the least provocation. That whack on the head must've knocked something loose in his brain. His volatile attitude needed taming, but he possessed neither the will nor the desire to tackle it. God help him, he was spiraling out of control and helpless to stop it.

Seth failed to note that his fellow prisoners had stopped to wait for traffic to pass on the street. He bumped into the man in front of him, who turned on him with a scowl. Unrepentant, Seth scowled back.

The hulking giant faced him. "Watch it, Morgan. You're no match for me, and I don't fancy being on burial detail today."

Seth pulled himself to his full height and stuck his face closer to the giant's. He raised his eyes past the double chin. How did this man know Seth's name, and how in the world had the Yanks captured someone his size?

Seth relied on his anger to carry out his bluff. He'd surely suffer a few more knocks for his folly. "Yeah? You suddenly turning yellow, or is that your natural color, Gargantua?"

The giant grabbed Seth's neck but sputtered when he heard the name. "Gar-who? Are you cussing me, Morgan? I'll teach you—"

"Here now!" A guard pushed his bayonet between the men. "No fighting on my watch. I'm too close to handing you over to Major Sullivan and being rid of you sorry excuses for soldiers. With such lack of discipline, no wonder the South is getting its butt kicked."

~

*L*ydia wasn't sure whether it was hearing Major Sullivan's name or the taunt about the South getting licked that caught her attention. She'd approached a guard to get permission to question the prisoners about her nephew. The Union man regarded her with suspicion, but she'd learned the magic of mentioning Major Sullivan's name.

She'd given her usual speech and started questioning the prisoners with a guard always near enough to prevent any questionable action. She'd approached half a dozen prisoners when the altercation between two of them captured everyone's attention. Following the movement of the guard, she watched him step between the men.

*A real David and Goliath clash. And this David doesn't know when to stop.*

The shorter combatant leaned against the guard to poke his finger in Goliath's face, not backing down yet. She couldn't hear his words, but another voice interrupted, demanding attention. "Sergeant Morgan. Calm down."

Like a sleepwalker suddenly waking, the antagonist straightened his arm and snapped a salute. The night-and-day transformation shocked the onlookers, and the guard moved Goliath several yards away.

Lydia's gaze swung to the man who'd issued the command, noting the superior rank of his Confederate uniform, then ricocheted back to the one she'd dubbed David. She eased closer to examine his face, warning herself it might not be Seth. Hair crept over his collar, but the color seemed right. A thick beard covered more of his face, making it hard to determine whether it could be the same man she'd met four months ago. She couldn't let the opportunity slip. She had to know.

"Seth?"

Both men whipped around to face her while others nearby stared with curiosity.

His eyes roamed over her features, seeking her identity just as hers sought his. Encouraged by his flaring nostrils and twitching lips, she pressed closer. "Seth Morgan of Marietta?"

"Lydia, uh, Miz Gibson?" The whisper of her given name gained volume with the more formal address.

Lydia's smiled stretched the limits of her mouth. "I can't believe it's really you."

He glanced back at the depot, took in the buildings across the street, before his scrutiny swept her from head to toe. Again, he gave the impression of someone waking from sleep.

"What are you doing here? I thought y'all went to Nashville...are the other women with you?"

Lydia hid her disappointment, puzzled by the question. Did he look for someone in particular? "All of us came here together."

Seth thumped the arm of the captain beside him, the one who'd bellowed his name. "They're here, Captain." Seth's mouth quirked in either a grimace or a smile, Lydia wasn't sure which. Maybe it was meant to be a smile, but he was out of practice. From the looks of him, he'd suffered much since she'd last seen him.

The captain speared a sharp look at her and gestured with his head to the group realigning around them. Traffic on the street had cleared, and the guards motioned them to cross. Oddly enough, the Union men didn't interfere with the trio lagging behind.

In a low voice the captain questioned Seth. "Who is here, Sergeant?"

Seth gave him a puzzled look but lowered his voice in answer. "The women who stayed at my house in Marietta. Your wife and the others. Lydia's one of 'em."

The captain straightened his spine and stared at Lydia. "My wife. Do you know where Olivia is, Miss?"

Lydia jerked her head back to meet the dark eyes of the officer. "Oh, my, it *is* you, Doctor Spencer. It's been a few years since we met. Yes, Olivia is here. Well, they've all gone to have dinner at...at a local residence, but they should be back soon."

*T*hey paused near the gate, waiting as the men ahead were processed into the prison. Seth peered at Lydia, wondering about her strange statement: *They've all gone to dinner at a local residence.* Weren't the women prisoners, just like he and the good doctor were? Did females get special treatment? Or did they play up to the guards for special favors?

He sent a scorching look toward Lydia, but she focused on Evan Spencer, explaining about somebody working for a Mr. Turner, who turned out to be someone's cousin and invited the group to his house for a meal after church. Seth calmed down enough to listen.

"I believe we can arrange for you to see Olivia and Wade while you're here. The guards let another family do that a couple months ago. We get along with them fairly well. A couple of the women take in washing for the soldiers, and Major Sullivan knows me."

Seth glared as the doctor thanked Lydia for promising to help him get a visit with his family. Did the woman have no shame? When the doctor walked away, she directed her attention to Seth. Before she could speak, though, he pounced. "How well does this major know you, Miz Gibson?

Her eyes widened at his tone. Seth might've taken the color rising in her cheeks for embarrassment until he noticed the furious glint in her eyes. Over the last four months, he'd imagined her in all manner of emotions—but not angry. From her expression, he figured her anger met or exceeded his. He backed up a step as she advanced.

"Not that it's any of your business, Sergeant Morgan, but I deliver from the bakery where I work. Major Sullivan has a weakness for fruit pies, and he has a standing order for a dozen of them each week."

The guard at the gate spoke from behind Seth. "You'll need

to move on now, Miz Gibson, so we can get these boys taken care of."

Though the words sounded polite, Seth recognized the steel beneath them—and the reference to taking care of the prisoners.

Lydia flashed a smile at the guard. "Of course, Corporal. Just one moment more, and I'll be gone." Her smile faded when she looked at Seth. "I just need to know one thing from you, Seth Morgan. Are you the one who stole Major Griffin's horse the day you left Marietta?"

Surprise knocked Seth off-kilter, but he recovered in a blink. Perversely not wanting to give her a straight answer, he folded his arms over his chest. "What if I was? War changes the normal way of doing things, you know."

"Well, it sure changes men, I know that," she said in a low rasp. "But Major Griffin is here in Louisville, and he's prone to visit the refugee house just like he did your house in Marietta. I suggest you watch your mouth when he's around, 'cause losing that horse riled him something awful. And then he found out we'd helped a Confederate soldier."

Seth snarled, unmoved. "What do I care about a Union man, and why does he hang around y'all, anyway?"

The provost guard grabbed Seth's arm and pulled him inside the compound. "All right, Johnny Reb, get yourself on this side of the gate. Miz Gibson, I expect we'll see you again soon." The man nodded her way as if they were leaving a pleasant excursion.

Seth glowered but didn't resist the guard's grip.

She looked back at the guard. "I expect so. Good luck with that one." She nodded toward Seth as he glared at her. "He's got the attitude of a Georgia rattler."

Seth twisted around to call back. He would not let that woman have the last word. "You'd best beware yourself, Lydia Gibson. I have more to say to you."

~

MONDAY, NOVEMBER 7, 1864
LOUISVILLE, KENTUCKY

*F*or a man who had more to say, as he'd claimed the day before, he didn't act inclined to share it with Lydia today. How had he managed to get himself included in the Spencer family reunion? Maybe the good doctor told the guards Seth needed constant medical care. His erratic behavior bore it out.

Lydia and Olivia had met with Major Sullivan that morning to arrange the meeting. In his typical good humor, the major agreed to their request. Most prisoners passed through Louisville on their way to another facility unless they took the Oath of Allegiance. As Lydia and Olivia left the prison compound, Corporal Mills bent to whisper near Lydia's ear.

"Your request coming today was a good thing for Major Sullivan. He was in an awful mood yesterday after assisting with Governor Burbridge's prisoner executions."

The confession sobered Lydia. Sometimes she forgot about the madness outside their little circle.

Isaac Wynn helped Lydia carry a small table from the refuge house to the backyard. Plentiful sunshine balanced the cooler temperature for the outdoor meeting. Besides Olivia and her family, Dorcas and Millie had joined the small gathering to serve the rare treats Lydia had begged from the bakery. The rest of their group tended to their jobs in town, but Wade took a day off from school to spend time with his father.

Lydia held baby Amy and blessed the Lord for providing another mild day so they could meet in the fenced area behind the refuge house. She'd been wandering around the yard to keep the baby content when she came face to face with Seth.

His frown firmly in place, he gestured toward the infant.

"You never said you had a baby. How did...that is, weren't you...?"

Lydia could see the questions forming in his mind, questions he wouldn't dare ask a woman not related to him. The man was clearly all to sea about babies. She seized the opportunity to tease him. Perhaps it would lighten his mood. "Do you think she looks like me?" She moved the blanket aside an inch, holding the baby next to her face for his inspection.

He merely stared.

"She is a little small for her age, I suppose. I guess it's too early to tell whether she'll look like her ma or her pa."

Lydia almost missed the glint of pain in his eyes as he started to walk away. "Seth, please. I'm sorry to be so mean-spirited. This is my granddaughter. Didn't I tell you about my stepdaughter when we were in Marietta? That she was in the family way?"

"I don't remember that you did. Where is she, the child's mother?"

Lydia gestured to the bench where Millie and Dorcas sat, watching Doctor Spencer interact with his family. "She's the beautiful blonde over there."

"But she's just a child herself." He looked from Millie to Lydia. "And you are much too young to be a grandmother."

Her face warming with pleasure, Lydia patted the baby's bottom. "Millie turned seventeen last month. This wee one is only two weeks old, born here in Louisville. Although I was teasing you earlier, it's possible she could look like me when she's older. Her father is my nephew."

He blinked. "Then you're her aunt. I think that title suits you better."

"Why, I hadn't considered that. I've been wondering what Amy should call me, and maybe you've hit on the answer." She tossed him a bright smile. "I think I much prefer Aunt Lydia to Granny."

"My mother's father remarried when his first wife died," Seth said, "and everyone in the family called her Aunt Carrie, even all the grandchildren who came along later."

He glanced over at the family huddled together across the yard. "I'm glad Doc's able to be with his family. I feel real bad that he was captured and stuck with me."

"What do you mean? Was he with you when you were taken?"

"No." Seth shifted his weight from one foot to another. "I got distracted in the battle when I saw the man who murdered my wife."

Lydia gasped. "You found him? What happened?"

He turned at an angle, directing his gaze to the guards posted near the gate. "We took the Yankees by surprise. The assault would've been a big success, but our men stopped to strip the tents. The whole dang regiment went crazy, looting what the Yanks had abandoned."

Seth paused as if reliving the entire scene. Lydia waited for him to continue.

"I saw Manny, his arms full of plunder. I hollered out and started toward him, but he weaved around the camp, so it took me a minute to reach him. He must've doubled back somehow. As soon as I ducked in the tent where I thought he went, he clobbered me over the head with something, his pistol or a pan, I guess. Something heavy enough to knock me unconscious for days."

"And Doctor Spencer found you?"

A crooked smile accompanied his grunt of chagrin. "No, darlin', the Yankees found me, probably saved my sorry hide."

Lydia wondered if he heard the term of endearment he'd used. Though surprised, she didn't take it to heart. Her pa and granny both had scattered such words like chicken feed.

"But Doctor Spencer?" she asked.

Seth's brows lowered, disapproval rich in his voice. "He

shouldn't have been on the field at all. He went out during a lull in the fighting to help rescue a certain general who'd been wounded. Everyone with him was captured. When the Yanks learned he was a doctor, they brought him to the field hospital where I was. Having him there saved my sanity, and he's kept me out of trouble more than once, as you witnessed yesterday."

"I admit it shocked me to find him here yesterday, even more than seeing you. Now I believe it's like Olivia said. God had it planned all along so they could see each other, especially now when she's had such a shock."

"What kind of shock?"

"At the dinner they attended yesterday, Mr. Turner's stepfather turned out to be Olivia's father. The one who sent her and her sister away when they were children. Having Doctor Spencer show up here helped her find her balance, I imagine."

"He does have a way of helping a body make sense of things. He seems to know just what to say."

Lydia bounced the baby, whose fussing was gaining momentum. Millie hurried her way. "I think she's hungry again," Lydia said, passing the infant to Millie but catching her arm to hold her. "Millie, you never got to meet Sergeant Morgan when we were in Marietta. Seth, this beautiful girl is my stepdaughter."

Millie's eyes widened as she looked from Lydia to Seth. She smiled. "So you're the one who stole Major Griffin's horse. Someday I'd like to hear how you accomplished that, but right now I've got to feed the little one. Nice to meet you at last, Sergeant."

Seth barely had time to acknowledge the introduction before Millie rushed the whimpering child toward the house. He slanted a grin Lydia's way. "Something tells me you've got your hands full there."

Lydia chuckled. "Don't I know it. We've had to keep the boys away since she was barely twelve." Her smile dimmed. "I guess

I wasn't vigilant enough, but I never expected her and Troy to get together. They always argued when he visited."

Seth's eyes roamed over her, skimming quickly downward before returning to her face. "I'd say that was a sure sign they were bound to end up together. Striking flint creates fire, you know."

# CHAPTER 13

$S$eth wished the words unsaid, though he knew the truth of them. The fire singed him every time he interacted with this woman. With the war still on and his quest for vengeance stymied for the moment, he had nothing to offer beyond a few words of friendship.

Doctor Spencer rescued him. "Seth, come over here and meet my family."

How did the man do that? While Seth felt he'd dragged the doctor down, hindering him like the fabled albatross, Evan always stepped in whenever Seth floundered.

"Lydia, you and Dorcas come too." Olivia's genial voice slashed at Seth's lifeline. He needed to get shed of the distracting woman.

The three stood on the fringes of the family group, waiting to be included in the conversation. Olivia drew the one called Dorcas to her side. "Sergeant Morgan, this is Dorcas, who came to us while we were in Marietta. Besides the food we used from your house, we appropriated some of the clothes for Dorcas and Millie, who were in need at the time. We plan to reimburse you for those things whenever we get back to Georgia."

Seth waved away her comments. "Considering all you women did for me while I was sick, don't even think of it. You're welcome to whatever you took."

Evan took charge. "Seth, I understand you didn't get to meet Olivia's aunt and uncle at that time."

The older man reached across to shake Seth's hand. "Isaac Wynn and my wife Edith." He looped an arm around the other young woman, teasing her fondly. "This is my niece Shiloh, whose name suits her. She's shy and speaks low, but we'd be lost without her."

"It's good to meet you all," Seth said. "I did hear about everyone during the time the ladies tended me, which makes me think this young man must be Wade." He stretched out his hand to ruffle Wade's hair, but the boy hid between the doctor and Olivia.

"Wade, this is the man who took our letters and your pictures to your pa," Olivia said. "Would you like to thank him?"

The boy mumbled his thanks before he remembered something else. "Are you the one who stole Major Griffin's horse, sir?" His voice held a note of awe.

"Shh. Let's keep that our secret, all right?" Seth cocked his head toward the guards. "We don't want the Yankees to know about that."

Wade covered his mouth and nodded vigorously.

Evan chuckled and slapped Seth's back. "I've heard several tales about that escapade. One day you'll have to tell us what happened."

Seth wagged his head. "It was a dumb thing to do. I can only plead foggy thinking after my illness."

"Not that I blame you, Sergeant Morgan, but it created quite an uproar when the guards couldn't even take a shot at you." Olivia's aunt smiled. "Major Griffin was exceptionally upset with them for not watching the animal more closely."

"I can imagine. Speaking of the major, Lydia said he was here in Louisville. I suppose I should stay on my side of the street." Seth tipped his head toward the prison. *Not that I'll be given much choice.*

"That would be a wise course of action." Isaac Wynn winked. "Of course, that young man's attention doesn't stray far from Miss Carrigan, so he may not even notice you."

"Which Miss Carrigan would that be, sir? If I recall, there were two of them."

Beside him, Lydia stiffened, but she supplied the answer. "Rose, the elder sister, is the one who's captured the major's eye. They exchanged a few letters before he came to Louisville."

"Ah, the prickly one." He murmured under his breath, apparently not low enough.

Lydia cast him a look of jaundiced inquiry. He stepped back and turned so she alone would hear him while the others resumed their conversation.

"A rose has thorns, and Miss Rose Carrigan struck me as prickly, so her name fit. It helped me remember which name went with each person."

Lydia regarded him warily. "Although I can see your point with Rose, it's not very complimentary. She's as pleasant as her name most of the time. I don't think I want to know how you remembered the rest of us."

No, she probably wouldn't appreciate the fact that he'd considered her small and nondescript, like a brown wren. Maybe he should try to come up with a more pleasing description. Women were funny about those things. Besides, he was revising his opinion of the little wren. Lydia Gibson had depths and appeal beyond the surface.

❦

*L*ydia dropped her gaze from Seth's penetrating stare. She didn't care for the calculating gleam in those brown eyes, and she remembered her primary task. "I have a favor to ask of you, as I do of all the prisoners I meet. You know I mentioned my nephew is the father of Millie's baby? Well, I'm trying to locate him."

"Which regiment was he assigned to?" Seth asked.

"He isn't in the military at all. He escaped the conscription by hiding and moving from place to place. Troy argued against secession and refused to be put in the position of killing someone he loved. He had a brother in each army. He got caught, however, when he followed our wagon train from New Manchester to Marietta. The soldiers marked him as a spy, but Major Tompkins put him with the men from the mill until we reached Marietta. We have no idea what happened to him after that."

Seth bit the end of his index finger as he thought about it. "What about that Major Griffin? Wouldn't he know, since he helped get y'all settled and have a place to stay?"

"He only helped us because we ended up with the group from Roswell with the Carrigan sisters. I've enlisted help from the guards at the prison to ask around and let me know if they find out anything. They allow me to pass the word on to prisoners coming through Louisville, but so far nobody has heard of him."

"Someone should ask the commander who took y'all to Marietta. Didn't you say it was Tompkins? Maybe he'd know what happened to your nephew."

Surprise hitched Lydia's breath. "Now, why didn't I think of that? He should at least know where they placed Troy in Marietta. But...who could ask him about that?"

Seth shrugged. "I'd say start with Major Griffin. He'd probably do anything to elevate his standing with Miss Carrigan if he's as smitten as y'all believe. A man likes to be thought a hero."

"Thank you for the suggestion, Sergeant Morgan. I will certainly do that as soon as I see him again." She swatted Seth on the arm. "As for you, I believe you're not half as bad as you make yourself out to be."

He glanced around in dramatic fashion. "Shh. Don't let it get out. I need my reputation as a rounder to hold my own in prison. And to help me find Meg's killer."

The friendly banter deflated like a pricked balloon. Perhaps Lydia could help Seth by encouraging him to talk about his all-consuming mission. "How? Do you know who it was? You weren't there when it happened, were you?"

Seth rubbed a hand across the back of his neck. "I was in another town, delivering a piece of furniture. The neighbors saw him go into the house with Meg, but they didn't see him leave. Of all the days for it to snow." He glanced beyond her, maybe back into the memory. "The weather slowed me down, else I might have gotten there in time."

Lydia stepped closer, not daring to touch him. "But how can you be sure it was the same man? Was there something different about him? You wouldn't want to accuse the wrong person."

He lifted haunted eyes to her face. "Oh, I'm sure who the man was. The neighbors said he even called a greeting to them before they went into their home. They knew him. Meg knew him. Otherwise, she wouldn't have allowed him inside the house. He's my cousin."

"Your kin? How awful."

"We were never close. He lived near Decatur, but our families got together a couple times each year. For some reason, Manny decided he had to best me at everything. Sometimes he did, and sometimes he didn't. When Meg and I announced our plans to marry, he tried to change her mind. Every time he visited, he'd try to find a way to get her alone, but she outwitted him."

"Smart girl."

"Yeah, she was." Seth grinned with pride, and Lydia's heart did a little flip. What a lucky girl Meg had been to have someone love her so much.

"But she had a tender heart and felt sorry for Manny. From the look of things at the house, she invited him inside to warm by the fire and have a hot drink. He took advantage of her kindness."

Lydia struggled to understand. "He just...killed her...for no reason, but to take her away from you?"

Seth gazed into the distance. "He wanted to have whatever I had. It looked like he'd grabbed her in the parlor. There was a stain on the rug where a drink spilled, and the furniture was upset. Knowing Meg, I'm sure she fought back, but he was stronger. He must've put one of the sofa pillows over her face and held it there until she succumbed. She died from lack of air."

Lydia was unaware of the tears coursing her cheeks until Seth wipe them away with his thumb. "That poor girl. She must have been terrified. I'm so sorry. Sorry for your loss, and sorry for asking you to talk about it."

"No, it's all right." Seth heaved a breath and dropped his hand to grip hers. "Somehow, telling it relieved some of the burden. Doc said I should talk about it sometimes. He offered to listen, but I just couldn't."

Mention of Doctor Spencer jerked Lydia back to reality. Here they stood, holding hands in the yard of the refugee house. Guards leaned against the fence, observing the Southerners with lax regard, knowing that little could pass beyond the yard. The Spencer family enjoyed being together for the small space of time allowed.

She and Seth stood caught up in the turmoil of memories,

both fettered by guilt. Lydia shuddered, left cold by her own recollection of pain, knowing what she'd endured paled compared to what Meg had suffered.

But in death, Meg had obtained freedom while Lydia remained bound by guilt.

~

TUESDAY MORNING, NOVEMBER 8, 1864
UNION ARMY PRISON, LOUISVILLE, KENTUCKY

*S*eth fought the demons of memories in his dream. He saw Meg as he'd found her that day, pale face against dark hair, her lips parted in a silent plea, her clothing ripped and twisted. Rising behind her, Mansfield Peacock loomed like a monster, leering and salivating. As always, Seth stood frozen while he watched the horror unfold...until he awoke in a cold sweat.

Knowing he wouldn't sleep again for hours, he sat up and tried to redirect his mind. He reached for his coat and pulled out the handkerchief that had become his talisman. Holding it called forth images of those days in Marietta. He sniffed the cloth, but the delicate fragrance had faded, overwhelmed by odors of medicines and smoke from his companions.

What had the scent been? Some kind of flower...lavender, perhaps? That would suit Lydia. Something calm and soothing...well, most of the time. He grinned in the darkness, thinking of the way they'd sparred yesterday. His words about flint creating sparks rang true for him and Lydia as much as for her stepdaughter and the nephew. Had she told him the nephew's name? He couldn't recall.

Near dawn, Evan Spencer scooted over near Seth. "Trouble sleeping?"

Seth shrugged. "Only when I have nightmares. It's hard to

get back to sleep afterwards, so I've learned to wait a while and try again. How about you?"

Evan grinned. "I've not had so much sleep since I left Campbell County. If I'd known prison life was so easy, I'd've gotten myself captured months ago."

Seth had learned the hospital staff stayed as busy as troops on the move, and that went for folks on both sides of the war. It could be as dangerous on the operating table as in the trenches simply because of lack of sleep. And so far, Seth had been fed as well by the Yanks as he had in his own unit, due to the scarcity of provisions in the South. Not that he considered switching sides.

Evan lowered his voice, his words meant only for Seth's ears. "Do you know what today is?"

"November something, I think. The eighth? Is it important?"

"Election day for the Union. Though Lincoln is expected to prevail, his opponent is General McClellan, and Kentucky is divided as to their favorite. The real problem could be their governor, Burbridge. He has a vested interest in the outcome, and it's rumored he may try to interfere to assure Lincoln's re-election."

"What's that got to do with us?"

Evan glanced at the other prisoners in the room. Nobody paid them any notice. "Back in July, Burbridge issued an order about guerilla activity in the state. Anytime an unarmed citizen is killed, he takes men from this prison and executes them in retaliation. In fact, the day we arrived, he had two men taken from here to another town and executed for the death of a Union soldier."

Seth bit back the oath burning his lips. "So much for the ease of prison life. Does such happen often?"

"Half a dozen times since he issued the order in July."

"Those aren't good odds, Doc," Seth said. Knowing the

doctor shared the information for a purpose, he braced himself. "What are you thinking?"

"We should take the loyalty oath if it's offered us. I don't know what happens afterward, whether we can go back home, but at least it should provide us a measure of protection while we're in Kentucky. My wife's father lives in Frankfort, maybe a hundred miles due east of here. He runs a store and supplies the army with some of their goods. I think Olivia would like to consider staying there a while to see if they can restore their relationship."

Seth clapped his friend on the shoulder. "Then you should take the oath and stay with your family. As a doctor, you'd be welcome anywhere. Truth be told, there may not be anything worth going back to in Georgia, even when this thing is over."

Evan studied his hands, hesitating to speak. "What will you do?"

"I don't know. I'm loath to give up the hunt for Mansfield, but sometimes I wonder if finding him is an impossible task. If only I could be sure of what happened to him at Cedar Creek."

"Seth, you've got to let go of your anger. It won't bring your wife back, you know."

Seth clenched his jaw, curled his fists at his sides.

Evan pushed on. "What would Meg want? Would she be happy to have you chasing after the man, eating yourself up with the need for vengeance? What's it been, two years? Your anger has taken more of a toll on you than the war, especially since Cedar Creek."

Seth had no answer. He respected Evan, knew what he said made sense, but he wasn't sure if he could give up his quest.

Evan stood, his lecture at an end. "This war we've been fighting is winding down, mark my word. It's about time you surrendered your will to God and let Him finish your personal war. Start thinking about the future instead of the past."

~

*L*ydia cuddled Amy, her heart conflicted with joy and sorrow. Worry wormed its way into her thoughts. What would the future hold for this child, born outside of marriage? While the war lingered, their circumstances shielded her from public scorn. Nobody at the refugee house questioned Amy's parentage. Probably most assumed her father and mother had married back home, just like they assumed Troy fought with the Confederacy.

It would be a different story, however, when the war ended and Lydia and Millie went back to Campbell County. Folks there would know Millie hadn't married before their journey north. So long as she got married before they returned, it would be all right. Amy could claim legitimacy.

That was why Lydia had to locate Troy. Millie still nursed her hurt at his indifference when she defended him, and now with the baby, she was too busy to investigate. Lydia had the time and the tenacity to do the searching in Millie's place. When she found him, if he protested she'd use every trick and threat in her arsenal to convince him to marry Millie.

Lydia couldn't consider what their marriage would mean to her own relationship with Amy. It would work out somehow. As Granny McNeil would say, "Don't fret. Everything will come out right in the end."

A growing racket from the street caught her attention. She laid the baby in her makeshift crib fashioned from an abandoned bureau drawer and kept her hand on the tiny shoulder until the babe settled with a puffy sigh. By the time Lydia reached the window to look out, Millie and Shiloh had rushed into the room, nattering about increased activity at the prison.

"Miz Edith said they're doubling the guards all over town. She's sending the men in my place to get the children from school. Do you think there'll be trouble?" Worry created lines in Shiloh's brow.

Lydia had never known the girl to speak more than a few words. Millie suffered no hesitation, having formed a bond with the Wynns' niece. "Heaven only knows. The Kentucky governor is determined to keep the opposition away from the voting polls. He even arrested the lieutenant governor and a judge, had them deported to Virginia."

Placing an arm around Shiloh, Lydia strove to calm them all. "The voting has nothing to do with us. We're out there on two counts, being female and being Southerners. We should be fine as long as we stay inside and off the streets."

Millie, however, stirred the pot of doubt again. "But those suffragists keep fighting for women to get the right to vote and get more education like the men can. I'd like to go to one of their meetings and see what it's like."

"Honey, those women have been working on that for years and haven't made much headway," Lydia said. "I reckon they never will as long as men are the ones voting on their proposals."

"What they have to do is convince the men to vote for it." Millie flashed a mischievous smile at them. "You know, use their charms to persuade their husbands and...others."

Lydia stared at her stepdaughter. She'd seen Millie in an array of attitudes, everything from sullen self-pity to outright defiance, though her normal outlook was sunny and playful, but she'd not witnessed such boldness before.

She remembered Seth's comment from the other day. "You've got your hands full there," he'd said, indicating Millie. Perhaps she needed to step up her search for Troy. What if she couldn't find him?

# CHAPTER 14

Seth paced the empty room. The other prisoners, including Doctor Spencer, lingered over their dinners. Seth had bolted down his meal and retreated to find some privacy and figure out his next step. Taking the oath would effectively shut down his search for Manny but would allow him more time to get to know Lydia. If he stayed in Louisville. If that was what he wanted.

Maybe she wouldn't want to spend time with him, much less pursue anything permanent. If he read her correctly, Lydia hadn't found marriage especially fulfilling. Perhaps she'd rather stay single and find contentment in helping her stepdaughter raise the baby.

And really, Seth wasn't sure he could face another close relationship. Losing Meg had nearly destroyed him. He couldn't endure going through that again. And if he did commit to someone, what would he do if Manny found him and took another woman he loved away from him?

Impatience urged him forward. He had to get out of there, continue his search for Manny. Every day could take his quarry farther away.

*Or it could bring him closer.*

He brushed the thought away.

What if he couldn't find him?

*Let him come to you.*

Where were these crazy thoughts coming from? He needed to talk with Evan, get some perspective on this situation. Swinging around, he started for the door but paused at the sight of Evan's open Bible on the bed.

*You'll find the answers you seek in there.*

He stood motionless for minutes, his breath growing shallow. His parents had instilled a thirst for knowledge and said you could find the answers in that Book. It called to him, and he put out his hand to touch it but drew back. He didn't want to read about vengeance belonging to the Lord. He needed the satisfaction of watching Mansfield Peacock suffer and die.

But he wanted answers too. How long had Meg struggled before the life left her? Had Manny prolonged her anguish with his cruelty before she died, or had he waited until after to brutalize her body, knowing it would enrage Seth?

If Seth had his way, he'd make sure Manny suffered as much pain as he'd inflicted. Unless he discovered Manny was already dead, he would not be deterred. Somehow, he'd find his quarry again. May heaven have mercy on both their souls.

His loyalty lay with his dead wife.

~

FRIDAY MORNING, NOVEMBER 11, 1864
LOUISVILLE, KENTUCKY

*L*ydia waited near the docks, feeling useless while Evan Spencer took a tearful leave of his family. The weather had turned cooler, and she stuffed her hands into her skirt pockets, wishing she'd pulled out the extra petticoat from her bags. A playful breeze tugged at the ends of the shawl she'd knotted above her waist.

Her heart ached for Olivia, knowing how this separation affected her. There would be no oath of loyalty to the Union yet. The doctor's Hippocratic oath overrode it, he'd said, along with his conviction that God had directed him to minister to the sick prisoners he'd face at Camp Chase. His reluctance to leave must bow to his mission.

Unlike Doctor Spencer, Seth seemed to chafe at the delay. He shifted from one foot to the next while the group of prisoners waited to board the barge that would carry them up the Ohio River.

Lydia hadn't planned to come see them off, but Olivia needed the support. Her uncle had developed a serious cough, and Edith wouldn't leave him. J.D. accompanied the women and Wade to the wharf as they followed the band of prisoners flanked by guards. During their walk, Lydia rehearsed her speech to the prisoners. She planned to enlist their help in seeking news about her nephew. Doctor Spencer and Seth knew about him, but she couldn't remember whether she'd told them his name.

Seeing her chance, she touched J.D.'s hand to get his attention. "I'm going to remind them to ask around for my nephew while they're there."

The old man's frown multiplied the wrinkles on his face. "What good will that do? You got a message for him or think he'll be able to come here?"

"Olivia gave her husband paper to write letters. He can serve as messenger in case they learn anything. I just need Troy to know where we are so he can find us whenever he's able to come this way."

At J.D.'s nod, she stepped toward the group of men and found herself nose to shoulder with Seth Morgan.

His eyes raked her once, but he didn't touch her. "Where do you think you're going?" he asked, his voice gruff and demanding.

Lydia took a deep breath to calm her reaction to his sudden appearance. "To remind Doctor Spencer and the others to ask after my nephew. They need to know his name and what to tell him."

He folded his arms across his chest. "Tell me. I'll pass the message along for you. What's his name?"

"Troy McNeil."

"And your message?"

Lydia mimicked his stance. "I want him to know that Millie and I are in Louisville, and he has a daughter who needs the protection of his name. He should come to find us and wed Millie at his first opportunity."

"Message received." He gestured with his chin. "Now go back over there with Mr. Anderson until Miz Spencer is ready to leave."

Lydia's temper reared. "Who do you think you are, Seth Morgan, to tell me what to do? I think I have enough sense to know how to behave."

"Why did you come here in the first place? Mr. Anderson could have delivered your message as well as protect Olivia and Wade. There was no need for you to see us off."

"Olivia asked me to come with her. Believe me, it had nothing to do with seeing you or any of the others. I respect Doctor Spencer, but Olivia's still upset about his decision, and she needs a friend who can listen."

Seth huffed and swiped a hand across his mouth. "All right. Sorry I laid into you like that. I guess I'm upset about the doctor's decision myself. I feel like he's going on account of me. He has this notion that it's his duty to keep me from doing something crazy."

Lydia softened. "He said he believes God has a mission for him there. I don't think he'd sacrifice everything just to save your worthless hide." She modulated her voice and smiled to be sure he recognized her teasing.

He slanted a lopsided smirk and tugged her toward a post. He placed her against it, hiding her from public view, while he remained in full view of the guards, though their attention centered on activity at the barge.

"You drive me crazy, woman, do you know that? Ever since that day in the cellar..."

His gaze slipped to her mouth. "Just one," he whispered as if to himself. He dipped his head to brush her lips with his in a featherlight kiss.

Lydia felt the sizzle clear down to her toes.

Dazed, she didn't resist as he leaned forward again, but he stopped when someone roared his name.

Doctor Spencer shot a playful look Lydia's way as he hauled Seth backward. "I'll save you from this uncouth rake, ma'am, so he won't bother you anymore. Your companions are waiting."

Olivia, Wade, and J.D. waited for her a few yards away. Lydia's blush climbed to the roots of her hair.

Doctor Spencer pushed Seth toward the men lining up at the barge. "And you, my friend, are holding up the parade." The guard nodded to the doctor, who'd garnered respect even among his captors.

Seth looked over his shoulder as they stood at the back of the line. "You'll write?"

Lydia nodded. "If you will."

He stared until the guard jostled him onto the gangplank. Lydia whirled about to find Olivia at her elbow. The other woman hugged her. "They'll watch out for each other."

~

MONDAY, NOVEMBER 14, 1864
CAMP CHASE, OHIO

*T*he vision stayed with Seth—Lydia and Olivia walking arm in arm away from the river, Wade on one side and Mr. Anderson on the other. The picture of friends caring for each other. Friends found in the middle of war's turmoil. It comforted him to know God had put them together to support one another.

He needed that vision to carry him through the first few days at Camp Chase. After the relaxed treatment in Louisville, Seth regretted deciding to continue his quest for revenge. Cold rain turned the dirt walkways to mud between the rows of wooden structures that housed prisoners. The roofs of those structures—not worthy to be called houses—leaked, prompting the inmates to find creative ways of dealing with the wet conditions. Competition for the bottom bunks could be intense. With a tiny kitchen at the rear of each shanty, prisoners ate and slept inside the close confines, along with a dozen of their companions.

Eating, however, required one to block out the stench of human waste in the camp long enough to satisfy the gnawing in his belly. It was days after his arrival before Seth attained that level of urgency.

Doctor Spencer's accommodations proved slightly better, since he was placed near the infirmary, but he rarely had leisure to do more than sleep a few hours at a time. An outbreak of smallpox had raged a few weeks prior to their arrival, and his services were always in demand. Seth worried his friend would become ill while he tended others.

Seth hadn't foreseen the benefit of searching for Lydia's nephew. Questioning each person about her relative gave him the opportunity to strike up conversations he might have avoided. He could also slip in questions regarding Mansfield, giving the impression he asked for family members. Though he'd yet to turn up anything positive on either man, he bided his time, feeling certain he was on the right track.

Walking the muddy paths earlier that week, Seth heard the same conversations repeated among the men about the upcoming Thanksgiving observance and the graveyard thefts of deceased prisoners. With the weather turning colder, he waited until the warmer hours of the afternoon to continue the inquiries of his fellow prisoners. As he neared the row of barracks designated for the sick, he found Evan leaning against the sunny side of the building. The doc looked up as he approached and lifted a hand in greeting.

"Afternoon, Seth. The guards haven't put you to work digging more privies yet?"

The doctor's flavor of humor never failed to amuse him. "Not yet, but maybe soon, judging by the level of stink. If that's their method of punishment, I promise to be a model prisoner."

"Just don't go picking on those big boys from Alabama. I don't have many bandages left. Any luck in your pole-cat hunting?"

"Nah." He kicked a stone down the length of the building and set his back next to Evan. "I tell myself it's like starting a garden. You've got to put the seed in the ground and water it, but if you dig around too much, you'll just stop it from growing. I can't afford to raise suspicions. One day something will come up. After all, who could forget a name like Mansfield Peacock?"

Evan's chuckle ended in a groan as he spotted two men helping a third toward the hospital. "Just when I think we'll have a slow night, they start coming in again. What about Mrs. Gibson's nephew?"

"Nothing there either." Mention of Lydia Gibson conjured up distracting thoughts. Best turn the conversation to another topic. "Hey, what's the talk I hear about bodies being dug up from the gravesite? Any truth to that?"

"I'm afraid so. I read in the newspaper about a doctor named Flowers being arrested on charges of grave robbing."

"But why would he do that?"

"To have free cadavers for students to train with, or maybe for research on a particular organ or disease."

Seth shuddered. "I reckon that makes sense, but I wouldn't want to answer for disturbing the dead." Both men studied the activity of the camp in silence until Evan announced he should get back to work.

"Yeah, me too," Seth said, grinning. "I wouldn't want to be arrested for being idle. It might inspire the guards to find ways to keep me in my place."

~

WEDNESDAY, NOVEMBER 16, 1864
LOUISVILLE, KENTUCKY

*L*ydia surrendered the last of her bags to Major Griffin and took her place next to Millie on the wagon seat. Peeping between the folds of the blankets in Millie's arms, Lydia verified the baby slept on despite the activity. With Rose and Celeste leaving on the morrow to visit the major's family in Indiana, Celeste's employer, Mrs. Coker, had invited Lydia and Millie to stay at her house, at least for the winter months. The older lady had been aghast at the lack of heat in the refugee house and insisted they live with her until better accommodations could be found. The women would fill in as cook's helper and housemaid in Celeste's absence while Mrs. Coker enjoyed her role as adopted great-grandmother to Amy.

Celeste had confided her prediction to Lydia yesterday. "I

fully expect the major to ask Rose to marry him while we're there with his family."

Lydia was happy for her friend, but the subject of marriage made her uncomfortable. "I can't believe we're going to enjoy that big ole house of Mrs. Coker's. It'll seem strange after being crowded in the refugee house." She brought up the one reservation she had about the move. "What about Mrs. Coker's grandson? I heard he came home ill? Will he be all right with us being there?"

"Lieutenant Hart?" Celeste shrugged, but Lydia caught the slightest note of concern in her voice. "He's not been out of his room since he appeared that night. Mrs. Coker's longtime manservant, Herbert, takes care of him and won't let the rest of us help. Mrs. Coker says he practically raised the lieutenant, so naturally Herbert feels protective of him. I don't think he'll give you any problem."

When they arrived at the house, Rose and Celeste helped with the baggage while Major Griffin tended to the horse and wagon. Celeste showed Lydia and Millie to their rooms.

After the company shared tea and scones, Rose and Celeste made their round of hugs and goodbyes to a chorus of prayers for a safe journey. Lydia blinked back tears. So many of their group had left town, some only for a few weeks, but several moves were permanent. Olivia and her family had gone to spend time in Frankfort with her father and his wife and children from his second marriage. Luke Turner, who employed Emily, had invited the Andersons to celebrate Thanksgiving with him and his daughter.

As the shelter became more crowded, the former mill workers seemed to be regarded the same as other displaced civilians seeking a place to start over. Many on their floor had moved out, or planned to, declaring they'd not spend winter in the unheated building. Their places didn't stay empty long. New refugees continued to pour into the city.

Lydia gave thanks to be out of the refugee house, if only for the winter, but she'd miss her friends.

How did Seth and Doctor Spencer fare? She'd heard rumors that Camp Chase was overcrowded and riddled with disease. She understood why Olivia had dared to argue with Doctor Spencer over his decision to go there. Lydia prayed the men would soon be released and kept safe until that time.

At least they didn't have to face the enemy at the point of a musket.

# CHAPTER 15

TUESDAY, DECEMBER 27, 1864
CAMP CHASE, OHIO

*S*eth's pleasant dream floated away and burst like a soap bubble. With something poking his ribs and a low growl in his ears, he opened his eyes slowly to determine the origin of danger. With his rifle aimed at Seth's mid-section, a young guard snarled. "I said get moving, you yellow-bellied lowlife."

Seth rolled off his bunk without using his hands, which he'd raised. It was lucky the guard had caught Seth asleep. Otherwise, an argument might have ensued and ultimately landed Seth in the tank. He couldn't afford that, not now. Just yesterday, he'd met somebody who remembered hearing of a prisoner named McNeil. He needed to follow up on that lead today.

The guard tossed a coat at him, then motioned to his hat by the door.

The bunkhouse was empty. Strange that nobody else had sought shelter from the rain that had lulled him to sleep. He thrust open the door and found the reason. The patter of rain had yielded to the silent fall of snow. While the guards laughed at the spectacle, Seth's Southern compatriots frolicked like children at a picnic

Seth's steps slowed as he navigated the slippery surface, but the guard nudged him forward. "Where're we going, Corporal?" He decided elevating the private's rank couldn't hurt.

"Over to the infirmary. Get a move on. I ain't got all day."

The guard's Southern accent bled through his words, though he tried to disguise it. Pockets of Union sympathizers dotted all the Confederate states, but this was the first time Seth had met one in the Federal military. And why should they go to the infirmary?

"Is Doctor Spencer all—?"

"You'll soon learn everything you need to know. Keep walking."

Controlling his impulse to force an answer, Seth walked as fast as he could while keeping his balance. As they approached the building, Doctor Spencer pushed open the door to his quarters and beckoned them inside. Was he still asleep and dreaming? Another nudge from the guard convinced Seth he was awake.

Evan pointed to a couple of chairs while he propped on the corner of his desk-cum-laboratory. "Before we get to proper introductions, let me explain why I asked the private to bring you here, Seth."

"Let me guess. You had a premonition I'd get into trouble today, and you wanted to save your bandages."

The doc gave him that doctor-to-patient look, raised eyebrows and all. "A couple of guards came to me this morning with minor injuries related to their duties. When I heard the other guard call this man's name, it caught my interest because he already seemed vaguely familiar to me." He switched his attention to the guard. "I believe I set the arm you broke a few years back while you visited relatives in New Manchester, Georgia."

The private's eyes widened. "I didn't think you'd remember. That was six or seven years ago."

"I probably wouldn't have remembered except your aunt has everyone in the Confederate army looking for you."

"What? Why?"

Seth gawked at Evan, then at the guard. "This is Troy McNeil, Lydia's nephew?"

While the doctor nodded, the guard spun to face Seth. "How do you know Aunt Lydia? And who are you anyway?"

Evan cleared his throat. "Troy, this is Seth Morgan. Your aunt was in the group that stayed in his house in Marietta, along with my wife and family."

Troy's glare bounced from Seth to Evan. He still clutched the rifle, but the business end of it pointed at the floor. Still, Seth didn't relax his vigilance.

"How'd they end up in his house?" Troy faced Evan. "And how did they meet him there if he's Confederate? It looked to me like the town was overrun with the Union army when I was there."

"I know you have a lot of questions. Give us time to explain, and you'll see." Evan motioned to Seth.

"When I heard the Federals were moving into North Georgia," Seth said, "I applied for a furlough. It finally got approved in July, and I headed home. Unbeknownst to me, the Union had housed refugee workers in Marietta."

"I know about that," Troy said. "When the soldiers with those wagons found me nearby, they thought I was a spy. Luckily, some of the folks spoke up for me before they could string me up. Major Tompkins took their word and put me with the single men until we got to Marietta."

"As I understand it," Seth said, "the army ran out of room for them, so they started putting the mill workers in aban-

151

doned houses until they could put them on trains heading north."

"I still don't see how—"

"I snuck into town at night and hid in my root cellar. I fell asleep, and when I woke up, I found three women going through my family's stores of canned goods. One of the women was Evan's wife." He inclined his head toward the doctor. "One was from Roswell, and the other one was your Aunt Lydia."

Troy lowered his eyes. "Who else was with 'em?"

Evan took up the tale. "My son and my wife's aunt and uncle. Her cousin Shiloh. Two sisters and another family from Roswell. Millie was with Lydia, of course."

"How's Millie doing?" Troy asked the doctor. "Do you know?"

"She seemed fine when we saw them in Louisville back in November. We also got to meet your beautiful little daughter."

The surprise and confusion on Troy's face hit Seth like a punch in the gut. "Daughter?" he asked. "Whoa. Who told you I have a daughter?"

∼

TUESDAY, DECEMBER 27, 1864
LOUISVILLE, KENTUCKY

The baby squeals and masculine laughter coming from the next room delighted Lydia.

Millie shook her head in amazement. "I never thought I'd see my daughter so taken with a man in Union blue."

Little Amy gurgled at Major Noah Griffin as he tickled her belly. The officer had convinced Rose to marry him during their visit to his family in Indiana. He'd offered to tend the baby while the women cleaned up after supper to give the cook a break.

"Or the day my straitlaced husband would be so delighted with a baby?" Rose asked. Tears glimmered even as she forced a smile. "I guess he's storing up all the pleasure he can before he leaves tomorrow."

Lydia reached for the bowl Rose handed her and plunged it into the soapy water. "I'd say he's practicing for the day he'll have one of his own to spoil." She smiled, trying to draw her friend's thoughts away from the impending separation and danger to her new husband. Lydia's pain over her own childless state had diminished with Amy's arrival, and she could anticipate being an adoptive aunt to her friends' future children.

"I hope that may be the Lord's will, but not until this hated war is over."

Millie put away the plate she'd dried and slipped an arm around Rose. "We're all praying for peace, as well as for Major Griffin's safety. Surely the end must be near, from the news we've heard. With the Federals in control of Georgia and the Carolinas, seems to me the Confederacy's doomed."

Handing the last clean dish to Millie, Lydia tried a more practical approach. "Will Lieutenant Hart and the major's friend Captain Bradley also return to the battle?"

Rose dabbed her eyes with a handkerchief and stuffed it back in her sleeve. "Cooper Bradley plans to meet Noah at Luke's so they can ride together until they join their companies. I imagine Lieutenant Hart will have to face down Mrs. Coker and Herbert before he goes back. The doctor warned him not to rush his convalescence."

"The lieutenant's company is in Virginia, where the fight seems to be centered. He should wait as long as he can." Millie draped the drying cloth over the sink's edge. "At least it's not so heavy in Georgia and Alabama right now, from what I hear."

Millie's attempt to comfort Rose fell short. "I know," she said, "but it only takes one bullet to destroy a man's life."

"Enough of this gloomy talk." Lydia motioned them all out

of the kitchen. "Let's join the fun in the parlor. Celeste will soon return from her errand, and Noah will whisk you back to Luke's house. Will you go to the market with us tomorrow?"

Rose nodded. "Yes, thank you. Shopping should keep me from sinking in the doldrums."

Cold air rushed into the hallway as Lieutenant Hart held the front door for Celeste to precede him inside. Their rosy faces testified to the dropping temperatures. Celeste bubbled about the possibility of snow while the lieutenant groused about Herbert refusing his help to tend the carriage horses.

Lieutenant Hart pulled a packet of papers from his overcoat and handed it to his grandmother. "I picked up the mail at the post office this afternoon but forgot to give it to you."

He settled beside Mrs. Coker as she sifted through the letters. The old woman raised her face and extended an envelope toward Lydia. "Letter for you, Lydia. You have a relative, perhaps, in Ohio?"

Startled, Lydia struggled to control her blush and avoided the questioning glances sent her way. "Not a relative, just a friend who assisted us in Marietta. Sergeant Morgan was here in Louisville briefly and promised to ask after my nephew."

She lowered her gaze to the envelope, surprised Seth had answered her first letter so soon. Could he already have news of Troy? Her nephew had a lot to answer for, and he would not blow off her concern with his charming ways. The evidence of his guilt gurgled in Millie's arms, and Aunt Lydia intended to set matters right.

～

TUESDAY, DECEMBER 27, 1864
CAMP CHASE, OHIO

*S*eth gestured to Evan. "I guess you'd better explain it to him."

The doctor gathered himself and choked off a laugh. "With my son being only five, I'd not planned on such a conversation for a few years. How old are you, Troy? Didn't your Pa ever talk to you about—"

"Yeah, yeah, I know how babies are made, but..." His anxious eyes shifted to Seth and back to Evan. "Don't it take more than one time?"

Seth barked a harsh laugh and stalked to the window.

While Evan explained a few details to the young man, Seth gazed at the white landscape beyond the glass. Falling snow no longer obscured the view, but the white stuff covered the blighted ground like a fleece, disguising the ugliness beneath—and increasing the danger if you didn't know where to avoid the ruts and holes. Like some people—namely, Mansfield Peacock—who pretended to be all that was good but hid evil under a cloak of innocence.

As the conversation behind him continued, Seth marveled at Evan's patience. That must be why they called the people doctors treated *patients*, because the doctors needed patience to deal with them. Seth had certainly tried the Evan's lately. Regret at the way he'd changed in the last two years seeped into his soul. His parents would be disappointed in him, as would Meg.

Visions of gentle hands touching his brow and administering medicines danced across the snowy background. He shivered at the whisper of skirts brushing his legs, the subtle scent of lavender so real. The woman who filled his thoughts these days wasn't Meg.

"Lydia."

Seth started. Had he spoken her name aloud?

Troy stood behind him with a questioning look. "Doc says

you have Aunt Lydia's direction. Can you help me write a letter?"

"Why me?" Seth turned to glare at Evan.

"Because you have nothing better to do," the doctor said, "while I have more patients than I can handle."

Seth's humor broke through his irritation. "You have more patience than any man I know." He scrubbed his face, tugged his beard, and directed a stern look at the young guard. "How do you propose we do that without drawing everyone's attention? I have the address back in the barrack, but I'm out of paper."

Troy hitched a shoulder. "With me being a Southerner, I wouldn't want to give anyone reason to question my loyalty to the Union. I suppose I could collect what we need and drag you here again tomorrow." He turned to the doctor "Would you be good with that?"

"I don't have a lock on the door, so you can just walk in." Evan hit Seth with a playful punch. "Seth could develop a cough or a rash so you can say he needs medical attention. I'll leave it to you to figure that out."

"I guess you'd better escort me back to my hotel then, Private McNeil," Seth said. "Maybe Doc can find some coffee to offer us tomorrow. You need only scoop a cup of snow off the roof..." He shot his friend a teasing grin.

"You just brace yourself for the cold walk over and be glad to get out of the wind while you figure out how to tell Mrs. Gibson you found her nephew."

∾

FRIDAY, DECEMBER 30, 1864
LOUISVILLE, KENTUCKY

*L*ydia pulled her coat tighter and braved the blustery weather. Leaving the warmth of the bakery these days reminded her of the time she'd plunged into the creek the year she turned seven. Her brother Ellis, nearly sixteen, had grabbed her doll and run. It was retribution for telling their mother he'd kissed their neighbor. Lydia had chased Ellis down the hill toward the stream swollen with spring rains. When he splashed across the creek, she followed but tripped over a submerged boulder and landed face-down in the icy current.

Twenty years later she still shivered at the memory.

Her head bent against the wind, she crossed Tenth Street and noticed a ragtag group entering the prison gate. Lydia slowed her steps and clutched a bag of baked goods against her chest. The aroma of apples and cinnamon drifted under her nose, tempting even when someone wasn't hungry. It wouldn't do to torment those starving prisoners with the smell of food they'd be denied.

She waited until the last man disappeared behind the wall, bouncing on her toes to keep warm. She mentally gauged the distance across the courtyard and followed when they should have entered the nearest building. At the gate, a guard she didn't recognize blocked her way. "Move along, lady. This is a federal prison. No visitors allowed."

Lydia straightened her posture. "You might want to ask Major Sullivan before you send me away. He's expecting his fried pies and won't be happy if he doesn't get them." She lifted the bag slightly.

The man regarded Lydia with cynicism.

Lydia tried another tack. "I've not seen you here before. Where's Sergeant Dunn?"

Before he could answer, the lanky sergeant called across the yard as he hastened to the gate. "Hey, thanks, Pearson, I didn't think I could—Mrs. Gibson! I plumb forgot it was Friday." His gaze swung from her to the guard barring her entry. "Sorry to keep you waiting out here in the cold. I'll be right back with your money."

He sprinted back the way he'd come.

Lydia stamped her feet and tucked her hands under her arms, eager to be out of the weather. When the wind shifted and snuck under her bonnet, she turned her head away. A line of prisoners shambled across the yard beyond the guard. She marveled at their disregard of the cold, though she deemed their clothing inadequate. Perhaps they'd grown used to it. Her thoughts spiraled to Seth and Doctor Spencer, even farther north and probably enduring colder conditions. How would they fare in that environment? Would they be able to continue looking for Troy? Seth's letter hadn't given her much hope.

One soldier lifted his head and speared her with a pointed gaze.

Lydia sucked in her breath. How had Seth landed back in Louisville? But no, it wasn't Seth. This man's beard was darker and much fuller than Seth's would be even if he'd let it grow unhindered since she last saw him. Still, the resemblance was uncanny.

Sergeant Dunn loped into view, and Lydia turned his way. She accepted the money he pressed in her hands but tugged on his gloved fingers. "Sergeant Dunn, who is that man? That prisoner just going into the barracks."

Dunn shrugged. "One of the new prisoners just arrived. Somebody you know?"

The other guard followed the direction they looked and huffed indignantly. "Him? That's one crazy man, ma'am. If you're smart, you'll avoid him."

The prisoner entered the building, but Lydia continued to watch. She had to know why he looked so much like Seth. Perhaps he was a close relative.

"What's his name?" she asked the new guard.

He barked a harsh laugh. "From his name, you'd think he'd be a perfect gentleman, but you'd be wrong. That's Mansfield Peacock. Mad Manny, the guards call him." His face hardened. "You know him?"

Lydia shook her head. "I've heard something of him. Sergeant Dunn, you remember Seth Morgan, don't you? He was here a few months ago along with Doctor Spencer."

The sergeant put a finger to his chin. "I remember the doctor for sure, helped him when he treated some of the—oh, yeah!" He grinned at the memory. "Morgan was the one what jumped on Bear at the train station. Now I recall. A feisty one he was—if somebody crossed him. But otherwise he kept to himself."

"That man, your new prisoner, looks an awful lot like Seth. He said he had a relative with a name like that, but I didn't know they looked so much alike."

Lydia rifled through her memories, trying to recall what Seth had said about his cousin. Pearson said the guards called him Mad Manny. A shiver racked Lydia, but the cold was inside her now. "Sergeant Dunn, I believe that's the man who killed Seth Morgan's wife."

# CHAPTER 16

Seth's hands shook as he read Lydia's letter. Manny was in Louisville? His thoughts swirled. Of all the dumb luck. How long would the Yanks hold him there before sending him off? What if Manny took the oath and headed back to Georgia? Seth would lose his best opportunity.

The date on the letter read January seventh, nearly two weeks before. Lydia had received the second letter he'd sent along with messages from Troy. He'd warned her not to do anything rash, like take the train to Ohio to confront her nephew. Troy's assurances that he'd find them as soon as he could get away should persuade her and Millie to stay in Louisville.

Only now, with Manny there, Lydia could be in danger. No, Manny didn't have any idea Lydia even knew Seth, much less meant anything to him.

That thought stilled him.

*Did* Lydia mean something to him? But how could she

160

when they barely knew each other? Even if it was true, he'd not given her any indication, and certainly nobody else knew how he felt about her when he'd just discovered it himself.

The memory of pulling her behind a post at the Louisville train station surfaced. He'd kissed her. Had anyone taken notice? He tried to recall who'd been there. Evan's family, Mr. Anderson, the other prisoners, the guards. Had any of those guards stayed behind in Louisville, and would they have cause to blab about what they'd seen?

He cursed himself for an idiot. Why had he put her in such a situation, leaving her open to ridicule or gossip or danger? He stuffed the letter in his pocket and paced the length of Doctor Spencer's office, pondering what he should do.

Four steps up, four steps back. Could he make the journey back to Louisville before Manny left there? The train would be the quickest way, but for that he'd need money and safe passage. Should he ask about taking the oath or take his chances on escaping? Nah, he might escape, but then he risked being captured again and losing his advantage of catching up to Manny.

The door opened on a snowy blast and revealed a haggard Doc. Seth abandoned his contemplation as he took in the doctor's stooped shoulders and dragging steps. He acknowledged Seth's presence with a weary nod, then dropped into the chair at his desk and rested his head on folded arms atop the scattered papers.

Crossing to the meager fire he'd stoked when he arrived earlier, Seth poured a cup of the simmering coffee from the battered pot. He set it on the desk with enough force to let Evan know it was there. "McNeil said you'd been up all night. What happened to your helper?"

He answered without lifting his head. "Fisher's been down with a fever for three days. He's recovered now but still weak. New prisoners brought dysentery with 'em."

"How thoughtful of them." Seth nudged the cup closer to Evan's hand. "You think you can drink this witches' brew, or would you rather take a nap?"

Evan peeked around his fingers. "At the moment, I think a nap is out of the question." He raised his head and gripped the cup with both hands. A few sips brought color to his face. He leaned against the chair and eyed Seth warily. "What brings you here today?"

"We gotta keep you going, or we're all doomed to die in this purgatory. That's why the guards let me visit so often." He ambled over to the window, deliberating on whether to include Evan in his decision. It might be best to make his move without consultation, but he figured he owed it to his friend to get his opinion.

"I had a letter from Lydia, probably written before Troy's letter made it to her."

"What did she say?"

Seth withdrew the paper from his pocket. He held it out, but Evan didn't take it. His gaze bore into Seth's, waiting for an explanation.

"She saw Mansfield Peacock at the Louisville prison."

Evan frowned. "I thought she didn't know him. How could she recognize him?"

"Because he looks like me. When we were young'uns, folks thought we were twins or at least brothers. Manny learned how to use that likeness to his advantage and my disadvantage. He'd sneak to the store and buy things on Pa's account or get some misbehavior blamed on me. People in town finally figured out the difference between us. That was when he turned real ugly."

"Hmm. He started striking out at your family?"

Seth nodded. "But he knew how to prey on people's sympathies, especially women."

"Like your wife. I see." Evan's brow puckered. "But your

cousin doesn't know Lydia, does he? So, she shouldn't be in any danger from him."

"But she makes deliveries to the prison every week. So long as nobody connects her to me in Manny's hearing, she'll be safe."

"Lydia Gibson strikes me as a sensible woman." Evan took another sip of coffee. "I don't think she'll put herself in harm's way, especially since she's aware of the man's past."

"Yeah, you're right, I'm sure. It's just hard to know he's there and I'm here."

"You're not thinking of going back to Louisville, are you? I don't think that's advisable, and probably not possible with the way circumstances stand."

Seth sidled toward the door. "You never know, Doc. Don't they say where there's a will, there's a way? I'll think on it some more and let you know."

~

Monday, January 23, 1865
Louisville, Kentucky

*C*louds scuttled across a blue sky on the warmest day in Louisville since Christmas. Lydia took advantage of the pleasant weather to be outside while the rest of Mrs. Coker's household was either resting or writing letters. She needed the time alone to sort out her thoughts.

More than a week had passed since the last letter from Seth had arrived. Glad that nobody else knew the contents, Lydia had postponed telling Millie about Troy serving in the Union army at Camp Chase. She was half afraid the girl would insist on joining him immediately.

Conversely, Millie might tell Lydia to mind her own business. Although she knew Lydia had asked Sergeant Morgan and Doctor Spencer to inquire about Troy, she never asked if they'd found him. Probably, she thought they never would. Lydia suspected her stepdaughter nursed a bruised heart at his indifference, even after Millie's defense of him last July. She'd devoted herself to caring for Amy and assisting with whatever chores needed to be done.

"Lord, what am I to do about this?" Her whispered prayer issued from a troubled heart. How she wished Edith and Isaac Wynn hadn't left Louisville. Those old saints always had wise counsel to offer in any situation. But they'd moved to Frankfort with Olivia, reuniting with Edith's brother and Olivia's father, Jonas Richardson, after years apart.

Lydia's steps took her to Luke Turner's house, where Rose worked with young Victoria to help her prepare for school. As Lydia hesitated near the gate, Rose emerged from the house and strolled down the walk. When she spotted Lydia, she waved happily and called out. "I was just wishing for someone to walk with me on this beautiful day, and here you are. Where are you bound?"

"Honestly, I had no destination in mind. I didn't even plan to come here, but I'm glad to happen by as you're leaving."

Rose closed the gate and peered around her bonnet. "Something troubling you? If you care to share, I'm willing to listen."

Lydia dodged the question. "Do you have an errand to run? I can share as we walk."

"I have a letter to post to Noah, but there's no hurry." She laughed. "It's not as if he's waiting around with nothing to do but read my letters, and he gets one every day or so."

"Let's walk over to the post office then, and I'll unload all my troubles." They set their feet in motion as Lydia gathered her thoughts. "Actually, a letter is what I'm contending with. I received one from Sergeant Morgan the other day."

"Oh? He's still at Camp Chase with Doctor Spencer, I presume?"

"Yes. You remember I'd asked them to see if anyone knew of my nephew's whereabouts. Well, he wrote to say he found Troy there at Camp Chase."

Rose beamed as she faced Lydia. "That's wonderful...isn't it?"

"Yes, in many ways. At least I know he's alive and well. In fact, Troy wrote a short letter himself and explained how he'd come through Louisville ahead of us. They sent him on to Camp Chase, but he's taken the oath and joined the Union army."

"Oh, my." Rose peered at her. "Does that upset you?"

"Not at all. He's a guard, so he won't be shootin' at anyone. He tried making his way north last year, but circumstances worked against him. Instead, he floated from his home in Alabama to ours, always moving so the Confederate Army wouldn't find him and force him to join them."

Their steps slowed, and Rose waited for her to continue.

"The trouble is I haven't told Millie yet. I intend to tell her, but I'm worried about how she'll take the news. She's changed so much these last few months."

Rose touched Lydia's sleeve. "She's had to navigate troublesome waters, what with her pregnancy, leaving the only home she'd known, and having the baby in a strange place. I guess anyone would change in those circumstances."

"You're right for certain, but I'm worried she may insist on going straight to Ohio to join Troy, even though he and Seth both advised against it. Troy promised he'd look for a place where they could live, but he doesn't want her to make the trip until it's safe to travel."

"Surely, she'll do as he asks." Rose faced Lydia as they stopped at the post office. Taking her friend's hand, she tugged her to the side of the building. "Let's put this in the Lord's hands right now, and you know I'll be praying for y'all later too."

They stood in the shadow of the post office, and Rose prayed for wisdom and His direction—and always for an end to the war in this new year.

~

THURSDAY, JANUARY 26, 1865
CAMP CHASE, OHIO

Seth took a roundabout route to the doctor's office and slipped in without knocking, nodding to Evan and Troy as he closed the door. Evan poured coffee into three cups on his desk. Troy leaned his rifle against the far wall.

"I'd say it looks like snow clouds out there," Seth said. "You'd best build up that fire." He stalked to the fireplace to warm his gloveless hands. Turning to Troy, he speared the younger man with a pointed look. "You have news we need to hear?"

"I reckon you might want to hear about it before you go trying to skedaddle back to Kentucky and get yourself killed. I was cleaning up near the commander's office and overheard him discussing his recent orders. General Grant plans to start releasing prisoners again as early as next week."

Seth glanced at Evan. "He's sure the Federals have all but won the war, then."

"The Union's locked down all but Virginia," Evan said. "It's just a matter of time before Richmond falls as well. The South is out of food and low on men to put on the front lines. In this weather, sickness kills as many as the enemy does, on both sides." He leaned against his desk and crossed his arms. His posture spoke of bone-deep weariness.

Seth turned to Troy. "So, when do you expect this to affect us here?"

Troy grinned. "What you really want to ask is how soon can you get on your way to Louisville, right?"

A lift of hands, palms up, acknowledged the truth of those words. "And what about you? Will the Army let you take a furlough and head that way?"

"I have a plan. It might work, and it might not, but it's worth a try." Troy's grin was beginning to irritate Seth, but he clamped his mouth shut.

Evan joined them at the fireplace, keeping his voice low. "With another doctor here and finally well enough to tend to things, I won't be needed as much. Knowing they'll be releasing a good number of prisoners, perhaps General Richardson can be convinced to let me go in the first wave. Troy's going to ask to accompany us to Kentucky to be sure you"—he poked Seth in the chest—"my half-crazed patient, will stay in line and not attack anyone along the way."

Seth ran shaky fingers across his chin. Conditions in the camp were wearing him down, especially since he knew Manny could slip away from him, again. "I'm willing to go along with you. Tell me what I need to do."

Evan draped his arm across Seth's shoulders. "Nothing, my friend, except be ready to leave at a moment's notice. And don't get into any trouble before we leave."

"Who, me?" Seth laid a hand across his chest. "I've been a model of good behavior, I'll have you know."

Evan snorted, and Troy laughed outright, clapping Seth on the shoulder. "As much as I hate to admit it, your reputation may work to our advantage here. The commander's been expecting you to go on a tear ever since you arrived. He'll be glad to see the last of you."

Seth gave him an irreverent smile. "Dang! I wondered why all your fellow blue coats avoided me."

"There's nothing scarier than a crazy man who doesn't fear

anyone." Troy pinned him with a serious eye. "I'll have to warn Aunt Lydia to tread softly around you."

"Nah, I never direct my anger at women. They know how to hurt you without fighting."

<<>>

SUNDAY, JANUARY 29, 1865
LOUISVILLE, KENTUCKY

"*H*old still, Amy. I'll be finished in a minute." Millie blew a stray hank of hair out of her eyes. "By the time I get her dressed, I'll be a mess myself. Why does she keep fighting me whenever I change her clothes?"

Lydia leaned over the bed and whistled softly to draw the baby's attention.

Amy's eyes widened and searched all around for the source of the sound.

Lydia chuckled and answered Millie's question between whistles. "She's getting more active and ready to explore her world, I expect. She thinks she has no need of clothes, isn't that right, sweetheart?"

"Well, I hope she'll behave herself in church. I don't want to have those icy stares directed at me again." Millie lifted Amy and handed her to Lydia. "Will you hold her while I repair my own clothes and hair? I won't be long."

"Of course, I'll hold this sweet girl. Come to Aunt Lydia, sweeting." She kissed the baby's brow. "I'm sure she'll be fine as long as we take a bit of food and something to capture her attention. I'll go on downstairs with her and wait for you there."

The rest of the household waited in the parlor. Mrs. Coker stood as Lydia entered. "We've decided that you and I will take the child in the carriage, Lydia, since the weather has turned so cold. Gideon will escort the younger women on foot. Despite the weather, Hattie insists she'll ride outside with Herbert."

Lydia's face flushed at being included with the older people, but she only nodded. "That's fine. I'm sure Millie will approve."

Lieutenant Hart smiled. "I'm glad Grandmother and Herbert have deemed me healthy enough to make the half-mile journey on foot. Strolling with two lovely ladies will make it that much more pleasant."

Millie hurried into the room as Herbert advised them the carriage waited at the gate. The lieutenant held the door for the women to precede him outside, where a weak winter sun worked to melt the recent snow.

Pointing to another carriage sloshing through the dirty ice, Lydia shook her head at the lieutenant. "Y'all will probably arrive at the church before we do. At least you can keep close to the houses and avoid the melt. I'm not so sure about the wheels on the carriage."

She handed the baby to Mrs. Coker inside the coach, then took Lieutenant Hart's hand as she set her foot on the first step. He leaned close to her ear. "You only get to ride today because of the baby, you know. Next time I shall carry her and let you walk." He winked, then shut the door and rejoined the other ladies.

With no time to respond as the carriage moved into the street, Lydia merely chuckled as she sat beside Mrs. Coker. "Your grandson can be quite charming when he wishes, I see. We'll have to watch him around all the young women."

The elderly lady stopped fussing with the baby's blanket to regard Lydia. "Yes, I have, and shall continue to do so. And that includes you, my dear. From what Millie tells me, you're younger than Gideon, though you hide behind being a widow and her stepmother. Don't give up on marriage yet. There are a few good men left in this world."

Lydia focused on her hands, pulling the kid gloves more securely over her fingers. "I know there are, ma'am. I just don't attract their interest, especially when so many younger women are around. Honestly, I'd rather be alone than endure another marriage like the one I had with Cal."

The older woman gave a brisk nod. "I can't fault you there, my girl. You hold out for whatever God has planned for you. Just remember you're worthy of love and honor too."

"Even though my husband called me a shrew?" Lydia forced a hollow laugh. "I truly believe he joined the army to get away from me. Which means I'm responsible in some measure for his death."

Her companion's delicate snort surprised Lydia. "I've yet to meet the man who didn't require some wifely prodding from time to time. I don't think you should take his complaints to heart. He made his own decision, and if he couldn't stand the prompting of a woman who looked out for his welfare, I doubt he took kindly to taking rough orders from his officers. Do not add that burden to your shoulders. Ah, here we are."

Lydia accepted the baby as Mrs. Coker prepared to exit the coach, but her mind focused on the woman's words. Had she overblown the meaning of Cal's criticism? Could he be at least partially to blame for the state of their marriage?

She joined the others filing into the church and sat with Millie near the aisle. Most of the heads in Lydia's view sported the new style of smaller hats with their trailing ribbons and bits of lace. Perhaps she could convert her old bonnet into one of those.

Wheezing notes from the pump organ at the front redirected her attention. Lydia sang the hymns from memory, enjoying the harmonies and letting the words cleanse her spirit. Did these congregants know that Mrs. Coker's guests were displaced Southerners? Did they accept them or merely tolerate them? But Kentucky was a divided state, so perhaps some of them held with the Confederacy.

Her focus shifted to the pulpit, where the pastor introduced a visiting minister. Lydia's musings had caused her to miss hearing the visitor's name and credentials.

Reverend Holland beamed at the taller man. "I'm delighted to have him bring this morning's message. I believe his sermon is what we all need to hear today."

The stranger opened his Bible but swept his gaze around the room. His first words shivered along Lydia's spine. "Isaiah one, verse eighteen. Come now, and let us reason together, saith the Lord, though your sins be as scarlet, they shall be as white as snow."

The familiar words rang with the authority of truth. But the voice. It sounded like the voice she heard months ago. *Pack and leave.* The words of warning then had prepared her to get ready to move. The words of comfort and healing now gave her peace, settled her spirit.

Lydia could only stare at the man as he continued preaching. Did she only imagine that the stranger's eyes twinkled in her direction?

# CHAPTER 17

*S*eth turned away from the domestic scene playing out across the room. Awkward in the home of Olivia Spencer's father, he could read the looks of longing between Evan and his bride. It reminded him of his own loss, so he directed his gaze elsewhere.

Young Wade Spencer alternated between playing a game of pickup sticks and running back to lean on his father's knee. Troy McNeil conversed quietly with Edith and Isaac Wynn, introduced to Seth as Olivia's aunt and uncle. Olivia's auburn hair matched that of his host, Jonas Richardson, who'd recently reunited with his daughter after years apart.

Although any family connection between Jonas and the commander at Camp Chase was too distant to count, Evan's pointed use of the Richardson name might have helped to sway the general's decision. He secured train fare to Frankfort for Seth, Evan, and Troy, along with a letter of commendation for Evan's services.

A wire from the general preceded their arrival, so a hack transported them to the home where they now lounged—a luxury they no longer took for granted.

Seth and the other men stood as Mrs. Richardson bustled into the room. She waved them back into their chairs. "Oh, sit down, please. If you stand every time I rise or enter, you'll look like Wade's Jack-in-the-box."

She sat beside her husband. "Supper will be ready shortly, and bedrooms are being prepared for you gentlemen."

Her amiable nature eased Seth's discomfort in this house of strangers. Though they were Unionists, Jonas and Caroline Richardson treated him with respect. With Evan as their son-in-law and Olivia's Aunt Edith being Jonas's sister, the current household included as many Southerners as Northerners, if one could call Kentucky part of the North. The state supplied soldiers for both sides. Seth suspected years of turbulence would continue even after the war ended, not only here but across the South.

"Sergeant Morgan, what did you do before the war?" Mrs. Richardson asked.

Seth offered her what he hoped was a smile. His social graces squealed with disuse. "Like my father, I was a carpenter. We had a decent business that kept our family clothed and fed."

Olivia spoke up. "You are much too modest, Sergeant. Remember, I saw some of your handiwork in your home, and those pieces were as fine as any I've ever seen."

Jonas Richardson perked up. "So, it was your house where the people from New Manchester stayed in Marietta?"

"Yes, sir, and mighty glad I am they were put there, else I might not be sitting here now."

"Ah, yes, Olivia told us how you took a fever during that time."

Evan draped an arm around his wife. "And that's why I had

to take care of you, Seth, at Camp Chase. I couldn't let my wife's first patient succumb to the rigors of camp life."

"We were very grateful to you for allowing us to plunder the food and clothes your family left behind." Edith patted her husband's hand. "Isaac couldn't get enough of the pickled pears."

Seth grimaced. "I'm glad somebody likes 'em. You noticed they were hidden behind some old furniture? My brother and I did that to keep from having to eat them again."

The group chuckled, and Seth felt his wariness slip away. Perhaps it wouldn't be too bad when the war ended. Perhaps people could set aside their political differences and accept each other at face value. He hoped so, for the sake of his family. He wouldn't think of plans for himself beyond the next few days. If he caught up to Manny, heaven alone knew where Seth's future would find him. He itched to hurry the process. He hated waiting.

~

FRIDAY, FEBRUARY 3, 1865
LOUISVILLE, KENTUCKY

*W*aiting at the corner for several vehicles to pass, Lydia let her gaze drift around the familiar area. She'd stopped at the refuge house to see whether Dorcas and Samuel Hawkins had set a wedding date. The genial young man had convinced Dorcas of his admiration and planned to go West with his bride in the spring. Though Lydia rejoiced at Dorcas's bright outlook, she'd miss her. So many friends had come and gone. At least Lydia would have a few weeks more to visit, and Dorcas had learned to read and write well enough to manage some correspondence after they relocated.

Shouts across the road drew Lydia's attention to the train

depot. A group of men halted at the road's edge while a wagon driver yelled and cursed them for daring to step in front of his team. With blankets draped around their head and shoulders, it was clear the prisoners had failed to wait for the vehicle to pass before attempting to cross. The wagon clattered by as she followed the men's progress toward the Union prison, herded by guards on all sides.

The contrast of tattered and soiled garments with the tidy blue uniforms roused her sympathy. Even the blankets provided by the Union army did little to protect the men from the cold.

Lydia burrowed deeper inside the fur-lined cloak Mrs. Coker had pressed upon her, thankful for its warmth and not minding its worn condition at all.

Just as she turned away and stepped into the street, one man's blanket slipped from his grasp and fell to his waist before he could catch it. In a moment, he pulled it over his head again as he continued with the ragtag band. Lydia reached the other side of the street before the vision triggered a memory. Fear made her look back. The men had reached the prison gate, and she was too far away now to see them clearly.

*It couldn't have been Cal. It was only someone who resembled him from a distance.*

She forced her feet to move, willed her heart to return to its normal rhythm. Surely, her imagination had conjured up his likeness because of what Millie had shared the night before.

The girl had vacillated between bouts of quiet contemplation and grumpiness the previous afternoon. At first, Lydia had thought it might be related to her time of the month, but Millie had explained. "I guess it's just being here, not able to get out much." She'd shrugged and turned away, so Lydia withdrew to give her some space, having learned that the harder she pushed Millie, the more she resisted.

After she'd put Amy down for the night, however, Millie

crept to Lydia's room and sat at the foot of her bed. In the lantern's light, her face glistened with tears. She pulled away when Lydia reached to comfort her, shaking her head and sniffing into a handkerchief.

"I have something to show you. Something I found this morning." She opened her fist to reveal a tattered piece of paper. "It was folded into a tiny square and pinned inside the pink bonnet amongst the baby clothes set aside by my mother. As you know, she gave me strict instructions about not touching those things until I needed them. I thought it was because she didn't want me to play with them and risk soiling them when I was younger."

Millie lifted her eyes to Lydia as she extended the paper. "It seems there was another reason."

Lydia unfolded the creased paper with great care and moved closer to the lantern to examine it. A glance at the signature confirmed Millie's mother had penned the message. Lydia recognized the handwriting from the recipes she'd found in Polly's apron pocket years ago, recipes she'd referred to often. Lydia read silently.

*October 20, 1852*
*My dearest Millicent Ann, today you are five years old, and I*
*fear I may not live to see you turn six. The doctor says my*
*lungs will never improve, so I must set my house in order.*
*He has no idea how hard that will be, but I begin by writing*
*to you, my heart, though it pains me to do so. To put it*
*plainly, you should know that Cal Gibson is not your father.*

Lydia caught her breath and sent a sidelong glance toward Millie. The girl stared down at her hands, twisting a worn ribbon between her fingers.

*If you've waited until you have a child of your own, as I*

*instructed, you will know what a hard man Cal is, so maybe you will understand why I ran away early in our marriage. I went to visit my Aunt Myrtle in Alabama, telling Cal and others that she was very ill and I had to help her out for a while. I stayed there all winter, using the bad weather as an excuse to keep from returning home. I was so unhappy with Cal, I let temptation in the door with a young man who showed me kindness.*

*In early March, Cal fetched me home, and I knew I had to stay with him because I was in the family way. I never told Cal. He treats you tolerably, which tells me that he thinks you are his child.*

*Now, I must confess my sin to him and to your real daddy or else take the secret to my grave. I don't know which would be the best thing to do. But I wanted you to know, when you are old enough to understand. Your real father has his own family now, but if you should get in a desperate way and need someone, you can find him in Randolph County, Alabama. His name is Ellis McNeil.*

Lydia stuffed a fist in her mouth to keep from crying out. Ellis!

Her brother was Millie's true father, which made Millie her niece. And Troy, the son of Lydia's brother John, would be Millie's cousin.

~

SATURDAY, FEBRUARY 4, 1865
LOUISVILLE, KENTUCKY

*a* cheery fire warmed Mrs. Coker's parlor. Lydia and Celeste worked on outfits for Amy while Lieutenant Hart read from the newspaper to his grandmother. The sound of his voice blended with Millie's humming to the baby.

A knock on the door interrupted their domestic gathering. Besides the gray skies threatening to drop icy rain or snow, it was much too early in the day for social calls. Lydia glanced from one face to another around the room, but nobody seemed to know who it might be.

In the hallway, Herbert's firm steps covered the distance, and he opened the door.

"Why, Miss Rose, er, Mrs. Griffin, I beg your pardon." Herbert said. "May I take your cloak and yours as well, gentlemen?"

Lieutenant Hart advanced to the parlor door, prepared to intercept the visitors.

Lydia put away her knitting, as did Mrs. Coker, while Millie tucked the sleeping Amy in the cradle beside her chair.

Celeste hurried after the lieutenant to greet her sister. "Rose? Is anything wrong?"

"No, dear." Rose clasped Celeste's extended hands at the threshold. "I just accompanied these gentlemen to show them the way here. You remember Sergeant Morgan from Marietta?"

"Oh..." Celeste's answer faded as Lydia's heartbeat pounded in her ears. Seth was here? Her anxious gaze found his before she noticed the Union soldier standing behind him.

"Seth?" Lydia squeaked. "And you brought Troy with you?"

Lydia scrambled to her feet and rushed to embrace her nephew. "Troy Harrison McNeil, I ought to strangle you for worrying us so. And here you've been with the Federal army all this time."

Troy hugged her briefly, but his gaze drifted beyond her. While introductions went on around them, Millie and Troy stared at each other with twin expressions of anxiety.

Lydia took Troy's arm and pulled him farther into the room. "Come over here and meet your daughter."

Troy jerked as Lydia pointed to the cradle. He looked from Millie to the sleeping baby and back to Millie again. He cleared his throat. "Millicent."

Millie lifted her chin. "Hello, Troy. How are you?"

Confident her nephew would behave himself, Lydia released her hold and stepped backwards. Right into Seth's arms. "Oh, pardon me."

He steadied her and eased his hands away. He nodded, but his dark eyes roamed her face, some question there she couldn't read. Both turned toward the other occupants.

Rose explained how Jonas Richardson had arrived with Seth and Troy the previous night.

"I plied Jonas with numerous questions about our friends in Frankfort," Rose said, "So I can pass the answers to the rest of our Marietta company."

Lydia tried to focus on Rose's explanations, but Seth's nearness distracted her. She needed to escape. "I'll ask Hattie to bring tea and coffee for everyone, shall I?" Lydia spoke to the room at large and hurried toward the kitchen without waiting for an answer.

She found Hattie and Herbert already loading the tea cart, so she continued into the pantry. Leaning against the doorjamb, she took several deep breaths to calm her racing heart.

Why did it surprise her that Seth had come? If he'd joined the Confederate Army to hunt down his cousin, nothing would keep him from that goal. Avenging Meg's death was his priority. How often had she heard it and read it in his letters? His loyalty was commendable, and yet she wondered what it would cost him.

"Lydia? Are you in here?" Celeste's voice came from the kitchen.

"In the pantry. I was looking for..." Lydia paused, surveying the shelves, and grabbed a jar of honey. "This will serve, I believe."

"But Hattie already put honey on the tray." Celeste took the jar from Lydia and replaced it. "Now, tell me what's wrong. Are you worried that Troy won't take up his responsibilities? If so, you can breathe easy. He's already in love with our little Amy, and he looks at Millie like he's scared she'll disappear."

Lydia forced a smile. "That's good. It would break my heart if he spurned them. Then I'd have to break his head."

Celeste laughed and motioned toward the parlor. "Come on then. Everyone's getting along fine, and I think Sergeant Morgan wanted to speak with you. He said we should drop the title and just call him Seth." She looped her arm through Lydia's and tugged her to the other room. "He's still rather handsome, don't you think? Though he's thinner than when we were in Marietta. He has a certain appeal..." Her voice drifted away.

Lydia pulled back to look her friend fully in the face. "Have you formed an attachment to him? I thought maybe you had when we were in Marietta."

Celeste chuckled. "No, silly, he's not for me. But I think there's an attraction between the two of you that might bear exploring."

Lydia wanted to protest, but they'd reached the entrance to the parlor. She would set Celeste straight later. Right after she figured out what she was going to do about her reaction to Seth's sudden arrival.

# CHAPTER 18

*S*eth drank in the sight of Lydia and Celeste arm in arm across the room. The dark-haired younger woman should have outshone the older one, but it was Lydia who held his attention. Flirty smiles and coquettish behavior worked fine for the younger set. He preferred the strength and stability of a mature woman, one who knew how to partner with a man and make him want to be better than he was. He hadn't been looking for another woman in his life, but Lydia Gibson had slipped past his defenses with her quiet ways.

He set his coffee cup on the tray and eased away from the group clustered around the elderly woman near the fireplace. Celeste whispered something to Lydia before facing him. "She didn't run away after all, you see. Merely became distracted with checking the items in the pantry." She looked over Seth's shoulder. "Oh, it looks like Millie might need me."

Lydia gave a slight shake of her head and met Seth's eyes. "Not very good at dissembling, is she? I'm sorry to have deserted you in a houseful of strangers."

"Not at all." Seth led her to a settee pushed against the far wall. The heat from the fire wouldn't reach them there, but

Lydia snagged the knitted blanket draped across the sofa back as she sank into the cushions. "I'm well acquainted with Troy," he said, "and Mrs. Griffin gave us a detailed history of the others last night, with a few additions from Luke Turner."

"Rose has a gift for storytelling. I wouldn't be surprised to find she's kept a journal of our wanderings. How did you happen to be at the Turner house?"

Seth sat beside her. "Quite round-about. Mrs. Griffin could add some tales from our sojourn at Camp Chase to her records. When we left the camp, Troy secured train tickets to Frankfort, where Doctor Spencer's family is staying. Jonas Richardson planned to deliver some goods to Luke, so he offered to bring us with him."

"Ah, I see. Between the Turners and Mrs. Coker, our band of Southerners has practically become established residents of Louisville." Her hand fluttered at her throat as she broached the topic uppermost in his mind. "I take it you haven't yet been to the prison here?"

"No. I wanted to release my promise to you and see that Troy didn't renege on his."

Lydia looked past his shoulder to observe the young couple who sat apart from the others. "He didn't want to come here?"

Seth kept his voice low. "Let's just say he wasn't sure of his welcome. It surprised him to hear about the baby. I think the guilt of stranding her in such a condition sat heavily on him."

"But surely, he must've realized the risk." She stopped and pressed her lips together. "Or he didn't give it a thought at the time. I hate to think ill of my brother's son, but it appears he's lacking in either good sense or good manners." Shooting one last killing glance in Troy's direction, she sniffed and turned back to Seth. "I apologize. Evidently, a lack of manners must be a family trait."

Seth rubbed his nose. "As for going to the prison...I've done a good deal of soul searching these last few weeks. Or maybe

Doc Spencer's lectures finally sank in, along with scriptures one man in camp quoted." He slanted a crooked grin her way. "It seems his Pa encouraged memorizing verses at the dinner table."

"My Granny McNeil would approve. She said those would always come back to you when you needed them."

"Wise woman. Anyway, I've decided I'll be satisfied if I can get proper justice for Meg. You know, have Manny stand trial for what he did. The problem is, I've carried this burden so long, I'm not sure how I'll act when I face him. I wonder if you'd consider going to the prison with me."

"But why?"

He played with the fringe of the blanket she'd tossed over her lap. "To vouch for my story. Persuade the officer in charge to hear me out. To keep me from acting on my worst impulse to attack Manny on the spot."

Raising his eyes to her face, he blurted the truth he'd been avoiding. "Only the thought of sparing you would stay my hand. I know we haven't spent much time together, but you've been on my mind every day since I left Marietta. Meeting you again here, sharing our correspondence, it seems like Providence wants us together. If I can control my anger at Manny and not mess things up, I think we could make a go of it. That is, if you'd be agreeable."

"Just what are you asking, Seth?"

He blinked and swallowed, surprised at his own conclusion. "I hadn't planned on this, certainly not so soon, but with everything that's happened, I believe we're meant to be together. I guess I'm asking you to marry me."

*L*ydia was certain she'd misheard. But she replayed the words in her head and came to the same conclusion.

Seth dropped his gaze, his face flushed. "I see I've shocked you. Forgive me. Pa always said I was prone to rush my fences." He started to rise, but Lydia stayed him with her hand.

"Wait. Please. I'll go with you to the prison, of course, but as for the other..." Her thoughts whirled. "I haven't given a thought to anything beyond each day as it comes. Being here, with the war still going on, I'm not sure what the future will look like. For all of us, I mean."

She nodded toward Millie and Troy, who ignored the rest of the company, intent on their conversation. From their serious expressions, Lydia surmised they discussed possibilities for their relationship. Their future. Across the room, Mrs. Coker and Rose focused on baby Amy, cooing happily in the old lady's lap.

"For the last few years," Lydia said, "my main concern has been taking care of Millie and now the baby. Although I prayed for Troy to come and make amends, I haven't considered what all that might look like. I never thought to marry again. My experience with marriage does not recommend it."

Seth brushed his thumb over her hand. "I'm sorry to hear that."

"Miz Coker has been so good to give us a place here," Lydia said, "but we can't stay forever. Rose lives for the day Noah will return, and I suspect Celeste and Lieutenant Hart may announce their own plans soon."

"And where does that leave you, Lydia? I believe I could make a decent living, even here in Louisville. Luke said he could put a carpenter to work any time, so I have some prospects." He patted the space between them. "Think on it as long as you like. I won't press you."

Standing in the doorway, Herbert rang a little bell to catch everyone's attention. "Hattie says luncheon is now ready."

Remarks about the swift passing of time drifted around the room. Had they really been visiting for so long?

Seth stood and offered Lydia his hand. He continued holding it as they followed the others to the dining room. She kept her eyes ahead. "When did you plan to go to the prison?"

"This afternoon, if possible. I'd rather not delay the task any longer."

Lydia nodded. "That's fine. We can leave when the meal is over."

Seth pressed her hand as he pulled out her chair. "Thank you. I'll let Troy know. Perhaps he can be persuaded to part from his little family for a while."

After the meal, five of them piled into the carriage to go to the prison. Rose and Lydia carried gifts of gloves and socks made from scraps they'd collected for the prisoners and refugees. Troy and Gideon Hart accompanied them, purportedly to protect the women, but Lydia sensed Seth's relief to have a couple of Union men at his side. With sunshine peeking through the scattering clouds, she could pretend their errand didn't involve the weighty issues of truth and justice.

A guard spotted them and alerted the man at the gate. They must have thought it strange to see two women and a civilian approach with two of their soldiers. She glanced at Seth, glad Jonas had provided him with clothes from the store in Frankfort. Showing up here in Confederate gray wouldn't have helped his cause.

The gatekeeper saluted Lieutenant Hart. "Good day, sir. May I ask your errand?"

"These ladies have articles of clothing for prisoners who may need them." He flicked a finger toward the women, who set their bags on the ground for inspection. "And this gentleman is here to inquire about one of your prisoners."

Lydia pushed forward, thankful the guard was one who knew her. "Sergeant Dunn, do you remember the day I was here and saw a man I thought I recognized?"

The sergeant scratched his chin. "Yes ma'am, I believe it was 'bout a month ago, wasn't it?"

Seth stepped beside Lydia. "Are those prisoners still here?"

"All but a few what was healthy enough to leave when they took the oath." Sergeant Dunn stared at Seth. "You've been here before, ain't you?"

Troy tugged Lydia behind him and saluted. "Private Troy McNeil, Sergeant. I'm attached to Camp Chase, where Mr. Morgan here took the oath. My superior tasked me with bringing him to Kentucky when I left on furlough. Mr. Morgan has a charge to bring against Mansfield Peacock, the prisoner in question."

"Well, I ain't never had anything like this happen before. I'll have to see if Major Sullivan will see you folks." He turned to the guard on the wall. "Marshall, come down here a minute."

While the other guard scrambled to obey, Lieutenant Hart exerted his authority. "Perhaps I should accompany you, Sergeant, to lend countenance to your explanation."

Lydia huddled next to Rose to whisper. "I believe he's come in handy. Maybe we won't have to mention Major Griffin's name at all."

~

Seth paced away from the women. Lydia's mention of Major Griffin reminded him of his foolishness in taking the officer's horse. And here he was, relying on the word of more Union men to help with the task he'd set himself. His pride smarted, but he recalled the verse about pride going before a downfall. The Good Lord sure had ways of teaching a body about humility.

Troy occupied the ladies with stories of his travels while evading the Confederate conscription. The young man's manner had lightened considerably since reuniting with Millie. Seth was glad the couple had come to an agreement, but he wondered how it would affect Lydia.

A group of men approached the gate. In the lead, Lieutenant Hart and Major Sullivan wore identical expressions of concern. Sergeant Dunn followed, one end of a rope in his hand and the other end wound around the wrists of a ragged prisoner.

The prisoner's beard obscured much of his face, while the top of his bare head revealed tufts of new growth after close cropping. His feet dragged until the sergeant drew beside the major and clipped him in the side.

With a brief acknowledgment of the women, Major Sullivan shot a piercing look in Seth's direction. "Is this the man you're looking for?"

The words barely left his mouth before the prisoner looked up and glared at the band clustered outside the gate. When his eyes connected with Seth's, he pointed a bony finger and screamed. "That's him! That's the man who killed my Meggie."

Caught by surprise, the accusation stunned Seth. After several heartbeats, the paralysis gave way to a violent rage. He leaped to attack his accuser, but the Federals blocked his advance.

Lieutenant Hart clamped Seth's arms to his sides in a bear hug. "This is not the way, man. Think! Let your friends speak for you, not your anger."

Lydia's white face swam into view, and he recalled why he'd wanted her there.

# CHAPTER 19

*L*ydia stumbled back at the fierce screeching, fearful of the wild look in the prisoner's eyes. His hair had been shorn since she saw him last month, splintering the resemblance between him and Seth. His stooped posture made him seem older, though Seth had indicated their ages were close. Had prison done this to him, or was it the result of a failing mind?

Like her companions, Lydia regarded the two, each accusing the other of the same crime. The matter of justice lay squarely on Major Sullivan's shoulders. They would have to persuade him of Seth's innocence and Mansfield's guilt. But how?

The commander barked an order to Sergeant Dunn, who turned and tugged the rope, prodding his prisoner to follow. Resisting, the man pulled in the other direction, pointing at Seth and yelling profanities. "Don't think your society friends will save you this time, Seth Morgan. This ain't Marietta, where you get everything you want. Meg was meant to be mine, d'you hear? Mine!"

Another guard jumped to Dunn's assistance, and they

hauled the prisoner back to his quarters. Waiting until the noise drifted away, Major Sullivan scrutinized the group before him. He pinned Lydia with his sharp eye. "Miz Gibson? What business do you have with this man?" He tipped his head toward Seth.

Lydia took a step in Seth's direction. "We met Mr. Morgan when we were placed in his house before coming to Louisville. Mrs. Griffin here"—she glanced at Rose—"met her husband there. You may remember Major Griffin of the Seventh Pennsylvania Cavalry. He rescued Rose when Sergeant Pierce abducted her."

Rose clasped Lydia's hand as she joined her. "We discovered Seth hiding in his own basement in Marietta because of the Union guards posted there. He generously offered us use of anything in his house before he left and returned to his post in Virginia."

"He told me about his wife's murder while we were there." Lydia said. "We saw the pictures the family left behind. My stepdaughter has some of his wife's clothing."

Troy flanked Lydia on the other side. "Major, Mrs. Gibson here is my aunt. She helped to hide me from the Confederate conscription before the Union army arrived in Georgia. You can rely on her to tell you the truth."

The major's eyes twinkled at Lydia. "I have no doubt of it, son. But how do I know what he told her was true?" After a moment, he addressed Gideon. "Lieutenant Hart, I will remand Mr. Morgan to your care for the immediate future. I trust you and the private here"—he nodded to Troy—"will see that he stays in town until I can hold a proper hearing. Let's say, on Wednesday."

Gideon and Troy responded with a proper salute.

Sullivan looked at Seth. "As for you, I suggest you find any proof you have to verify your story and be ready to present it to me then. I'd like to settle this matter without calling on my superiors. Good day to you all." He saluted the men and retraced his steps to his office.

Lydia's shoulders slumped. "Well, that's a turn of events I hadn't expected."

Seth grasped her hands. "Neither did I, although I should have. Manny always looks for a way to wiggle out of a predicament."

"But to accuse you of committing the very crime he's guilty of?" Rose wagged her head. "It's the outside of enough."

Gideon swatted Seth on the shoulder. "I guess this means you'll be staying with us for the time being, Morgan." He faced Troy. "McNeil, let's take Lydia to the house, then you, Seth, and I can meet with Luke when we escort Mrs. Griffin to the Turner residence."

Lydia accepted Troy's help into the carriage. "But what's to be done about evidence to acquit Seth of his cousin's accusations? With the way things stand, we'll be hard pressed to prove anything."

"That's what I want to discuss with Luke." Gideon offered his hand to assist Rose. "I believe he has some legal training. Perhaps he'll have an idea or a connection to help. I'll also ask Herbert and grandmother. I daresay we'll figure out something before Wednesday."

~

WEDNESDAY, FEBRUARY 8, 1865
LOUISVILLE, KENTUCKY

Seth glared at Manny as he entered the room with two soldiers. The blackguard had the temerity to grin as he sat at a table between his escorts. Manny expected to get out of this. What did he have up his sleeve that Seth didn't know about?

Behind Seth, the rustle of fabric told him Lydia, Celeste, and Rose had arrived. Each of them had given a statement to Major Sullivan earlier in the week but insisted on being present for the hearing. From the corner of his eye, Seth recognized Luke Turner as he took a seat with the ladies.

Major Sullivan presided from a desk at the front. He peered over his reading glasses to observe the attendees. "I have read all the testimonies presented to me and confess I am confounded as to what the truth is." He held up the papers. "These statements were given individually by the women from Georgia, and they agree as to meeting Mr. Morgan in Marietta. He left the premises a few days later to return to his unit in Virginia."

Laying the papers down, he sighed. "While I believe these testimonies, I cannot say I find in them any conclusive evidence that Mr. Morgan's word is true. On the other hand, Mr. Peacock claims he's the rightful owner of the house in Marietta."

"What? That's a lie!" Seth started from his chair, but Gideon restrained him.

Major Sullivan directed a glare in Seth's direction. "And he has certain property to vouch for his testimony. Sergeant Dunn?"

The sergeant threw a look of regret toward the onlookers as he pushed back from the table and passed an envelope to the major. Seth couldn't imagine what it might contain, but any proof Manny offered had to be stolen. He held his breath as the commander opened the envelope and poked his fingers inside to withdraw two rings.

Seth's chest collapsed with horror. "Meg's rings." He stared at Manny, anger building as the truth dawned. "You stole Meg's rings? I thought Mother removed them when the women laid her out." Anger overrode his grief as he surged from his chair. "You sorry, no account, thieving—"

Major Sullivan's raised voice countered Seth's. "And a man's matching band." Sullivan displayed the larger ring beside its mates.

Whispers and gasps rose all around him. Seth froze and blinked in confusion. How in heaven's name did Manny get his ring?

Gideon pushed Seth back into the chair and glared at him. "So help me, mister, if you've duped these women into believing you're something you're not, I'll see you hanged myself."

"I swear to you I've told the truth."

"Then, think. How did he come to have yours *and* your wife's rings?"

Closing his eyes to shut out Manny's triumphant grin, Seth struggled for control. *Lord, help me. How did this happen?*

A vision spread before him. The battlefield at Cedar Creek. Yanks running and Johnny Rebs falling on the spoils. Manny darting inside a tent when Seth followed him. Then complete darkness.

Seth opened his eyes. "I was following him at Cedar Creek. He struck me from behind. I was out cold until I woke up in the hospital. He must've taken it then."

Gideon released Seth as Luke Turner stood and addressed the commander. "Major, could I have a word with Mr. Morgan?"

The major waved his hand to grant permission, and Luke strolled to Seth's side. "Rose has reminded me that sometimes newlyweds have a message inscribed inside their rings. Would this be the case with yours?"

Seth considered. "We did, but how will that help?"

"Do you remember what they said?"

"Our date—"

"Shh. Write it down here." Luke supplied one of his business cards and a pencil. He turned to address the commander.

"Major, I believe we may be able to prove those rings were stolen."

"And how would that bear out the truth?"

"I think we can all surmise that Mrs. Morgan's rings were removed at her death, either by a member of her family or by the person who murdered her."

"That seems to be a matter of agreement. But what of the man's ring? Wouldn't it be in the possession of her rightful husband?"

"True, it would. Unless someone stole it. But a simple test should prove who is the owner of that ring. There's an inscription inside each of the bands. Simply have each of these men write or describe the inscription so you can compare it to what's etched in the metal."

Major Sullivan's brows lowered, and his lips twisted. Eventually he nodded. "That might work, at least for our purposes. Mr. Morgan, Mr. Peacock, you will do as Mr. Turner has said."

Since Seth had already written the information, he handed the card to Luke and turned to his cousin.

Manny's grin faded. A guard poked him in the side to urge compliance. Manny mumbled something, and the guard wrote it on a tablet.

The major received both items and placed them side by side on the table. Picking up the larger ring, he squinted to read the tiny etching, then passed it to Sergeant Dunn, who examined it and passed it to Lieutenant Hart. The three men exchanged glances, and Gideon handed the ring to Major Sullivan, who dropped both rings back in the envelope, stood, and strode over to the prisoner.

"Mansfield Peacock, you will remain in this facility until I may turn you over to the authorities in Georgia to be tried for the murder of Mrs. Morgan."

The soldiers yanked Manny to his feet. He resisted, but they restrained him and dragged him from the room while he cursed the Union army and everyone in it.

The commander crossed to Seth's side and handed him the envelope. "I believe these belong to you, Mr. Morgan."

Seth heaved a relieved sigh and extended his hand. "Thank you, Major Sullivan. Luke, Gideon," he said, moving to shake hands with each of them. "Thank you. All of you. God brought y'all my way when I needed help most." He included the women, his gaze touching briefly on his quiet champions, calm Celeste and feisty Rose, then lingered on Lydia's misty eyes and quivering smile.

Luke herded them all toward the door. "I guess you can go wherever you like now, Seth, but I have an idea where you can set up a shop, if you're inclined to stay here."

Out in the winter sunshine, the friends ambled toward the prison gate. When a guard called her name, Lydia spun to answer.

"Miz Gibson, someone here wants to speak to you."

"Yes, who is it?"

The young man hurried closer and lowered his voice. "Says he's your husband, ma'am. Says his name is Cal Gibson." A moment later, someone yelled her name.

Lydia whirled and looked beyond the guard. Disbelief gave way to stark fear.

And then, Lydia slumped. Seth caught her in his arms as she fainted.

~

Lydia's ears filled with a buzzing that rose and fell intermittently. How did bees get inside the house in winter? No, not in the house. By the swaying, she must be in a carriage. The sound grew fainter and transformed into voices. Whispers.

"I think she's coming around now."

"Such a great shock…"

"What about Millie? How do you think she'll take the news?"

"Shh. One crisis at a time, please."

Mention of Millie penetrated the fog around Lydia's brain. Why was Celeste concerned about Millie? Blinking fiercely in the low light of the carriage, she struggled to sit up.

"Hey, take it slow now," Rose said. "There's no need to push yourself after the shock you've had."

"What happened?"

Her friends exchanged worried glances. Lydia combed through her memories. Riding in Luke's carriage to the prison. Seth presenting his case to Major Sullivan. The rings proving him innocent. Leaving the prison compound, someone calling her name.

And there it was. She'd looked into a face she thought she'd never see again.

"Cal's alive. He was at the prison. He called my name." Familiar dread suffused Lydia's body. "Did he see me swoon?"

The ribbons on Rose's bonnet danced as she shook her head. "When you fainted, we rushed you away before he got close. Seth and Luke stayed to question him. Gideon will go back for them, and they'll talk to you before giving him any information as to your whereabouts."

"Thank God. I need time to think."

"What about Millie?" Celeste asked. "Will she want to see him?"

"She deserves to know he's alive, but beyond that, I couldn't say."

When they arrived at Mrs. Coker's house, Celeste and Rose lent their support on either side, though Lydia told them she didn't require assistance.

Herbert greeted them at the door, saying Mrs. Coker and

Millie were resting upstairs. Celeste offered to make tea and put together a small collation from the pantry.

Lydia sank into the rocking chair without removing her outer garments.

Rose surrendered her cloak and hat to Herbert, then tugged at her gloves. "Come now, Lydia. Let me have your things so Herbert can put them away."

She pulled the ribbons beneath her chin, trying to dispel the litany in her head. *What will I do now? Oh, what will I do?*

Giving up her cloak, she shivered and crossed her arms.

Rose pushed an ottoman closer to sit nearby. She clasped Lydia's hands between her own, chafing them. "I just realized you've not worn a wedding ring since I've known you."

"I sold it last winter to purchase...something, I don't remember what." She frowned at the finger where only a faint indentation indicated the missing ring. "I never wore it except on Sunday anyway, so it didn't make sense to keep it."

"I heard horror stories about people losing a finger or more to mill machinery, and not only from wearing a ring. It made me really cautious."

Celeste brought in the tea tray and placed it on the low table near Rose. "Here we are. Now eat some of these scones before the men arrive, else you may miss out on them." She poured tea and passed plates around.

Lydia's cup rattled against the saucer as Millie entered the room. "I thought I heard your voices down here. How did the meeting go?"

Rose answered with a quick glance at Lydia. "Seth was cleared, at least as far as the Union army is concerned."

Millie regarded each one. "Then what's wrong? You don't seem very happy about it."

Celeste cleared her throat. "Something else happened as we were leaving. Something that affects you and Lydia."

"I don't understand. What could affect only us?"

Lydia smoothed her skirts, wondering how best to deliver the revelation. "As we were leaving, a guard called my name, said someone wanted to speak to me, claiming I was his wife."

"His wife?" Millie scoffed at the idea. "Why would someone want to...Lydia?" She ended on a tremulous note.

Celeste sprang to Millie's side and drew her to the settee.

Taking a deep breath to calm herself, Lydia answered. "It seems Cal survived Chickamauga after all."

Millie leaned near and took Lydia's hands. "What will you do? You can't go back to him. You know how he is."

"He has legal authority over us, you and me, and now Amy, unless you marry Troy."

"Well, you can set your mind at ease on that. Troy and I have arranged for Reverend Holland to conduct the ceremony on Saturday. He'll have to return to Ohio alone, but at least we'll be married."

That was good news anyway. Millie and Amy would escape living under Cal's thumb. Lydia had no illusions that her life would be any different from the way it had been in Georgia.

# CHAPTER 20

*S*eth stared at the ragged man with the angry face. This is the man Lydia had married? No wonder she hadn't planned on marrying again.

Seth raked him from head to toe with one glance. Cal Gibson was little more than skin and bones, dirty and bedraggled, a testament to prison life. But Seth could've overlooked his appearance, even scrounged up a modicum of pity, having endured the same himself. It was the malevolence in the man's eyes that chilled his blood.

Luke folded his arms and studied the sorry specimen with cool regard. The prisoner glared at them and shuffled closer, heedless of the weapons trained on him by two guards.

"Where'd she go? Where'd that stinkin' Union man take my wife?"

Luke spoke first. "Don't worry, she's safe with friends. She needs time to recover from the shock of seeing you. She'd thought you dead."

A racking cough prevented Gibson from speaking. He spat a stream of dark phlegm to the side, barely missing the guard's boot. He wiped a sleeve across his mouth and sneered. "Well, I ain't dead, and Lydia's my lawful wife. I thought it was her when I seen her t'other day. When I heard the guard say her name, I knew for certain. You need to get her back here."

How in the world had Lydia tolerated this man? Had he been like this before the war? "You know this prison's no place for a woman," Seth said. "Once you get out of here, y'all can discuss your fu—what to do." He choked on the idea of Lydia having a future with this creature.

Cal glowered at him. "You're a Southerner. What're you doing running free with these Yanks?" He gestured to Luke and Gideon who'd returned and joined them.

"Not that it's any of your business, but I took the oath and count these men my friends."

"The oath! You're a traitor then and not fit to—"

Seth surged, but Gideon clamped him on the shoulder to keep him in place. "Where have you been, Gibson? You were reported missing at Chickamauga over a year ago. No word of your being taken prisoner or reporting back to your unit. How do you account for that?"

Seth's estimation of Gideon Hart notched upward. When had he gleaned all that information?

Cal grinned and preened as if he'd been decorated a hero. "When the Federals captured me, I was wearing a captain's uniform that I took off a dead man. Gave my name as Jimmy Calhoun. I was up at Rock Island in Illinois till they sent us all down here to be processed." He stressed the last word with a sneer.

Seth glimpsed Major Sullivan making his way toward them. "I suppose you didn't take the oath?"

Gibson stifled another coughing spell. "No, and I ain't gonna take it. I'll stay here until the South claims victory over the Northern invaders."

"That's not likely to happen," the major said, interrupting with a frown. "Sergeant, this man has no business jawing with visitors. Take him back to his quarters." He waited until the guards hustled Gibson away before addressing the other three. "What's going on here? I thought you men left."

Seth held his peace, trying to corral his errant thoughts. Complications had thrown a wrench into his plans. What legal options did Lydia have to get away from that madman? Would she seek a way to end the marriage? Did she want to? Perhaps he'd misread her feelings, misinterpreted her kindness toward him for interest? She'd never given him an answer about the future.

Once again, he'd proved himself an utter fool.

While Gideon and Luke explained the situation to Major Sullivan, Seth stood frozen. Only his fists moved, clenching and stretching over and over. His life had been good before the war, before a few dozen government men, men he'd never met, had dared to interfere. Without the war, Manny never would have approached Meg alone at the house and overpowered her. Seth wouldn't have joined the army to hunt Manny down. Lydia wouldn't have come to his house and insinuated herself into his heart.

Luke slapped Seth on the shoulder and urged him toward the gate. "Come on, Morgan. Let's take this meeting somewhere more private. Hart, you with us?"

Gideon grinned. "As long as you have something stronger to drink than what my grandmother keeps. I don't know if we're celebrating or plotting, but either way, I'm with you."

~

THURSDAY, FEBRUARY 9, 1865

*L*ydia observed Lieutenant Hart's careful movements at the breakfast table. His reddish eyebrows created a pucker in the pale skin above his nose while he concentrated on cutting the biscuit barely visible under the river of gravy on his plate.

Mrs. Coker grunted at her grandson. "I don't know why men's brains only work when plied with drink. Seems to me it renders the rest of them helpless afterward."

Lydia lifted her napkin to cover her smile. The old woman had the right of it. The night before, all the women had been on their way to bed when Gideon arrived. They'd paused to hear the grand plans he, Seth, and Luke had concocted for dealing with Cal Gibson. Taking up Lydia's defense, none of them felt friendly toward Cal. Gideon's rambling explanations failed to make sense, however, and Herbert had convinced the lieutenant to sleep off the effects of his indulgence.

Setting down her teacup, Lydia asked a question she'd failed to ask before. "Lieutenant, did my nephew join you men in your discussion last night?"

Gideon regarded her with confusion. "Certainly. Didn't I say so? His description of your husband's behavior spurred our determination to protect you and Miss Gibson."

"While I appreciate your concern, I doubt there's anything you can do to thwart Cal on my behalf." She held up her hand when he started to protest. "As for Millie and the baby, the only course of action I can see is for her and Troy to marry as soon as possible."

Gideon confirmed the idea with a nod. "I believe that's your nephew's intention."

"Lydia, I told you yesterday about our plans." Millie's brows knit in confusion. "Are you afraid one of us will back out?"

"No, dear. I'm sure you both intend to honor your commitment. But nothing seems certain these days."

"I know. It's only that you can't mean to go with Cal when he's released from prison," Millie argued. "Where would you go? What could he do, with the mill gone—and likely everything else—back home?"

Lydia looked away. "I've heard there's a mill over in Indiana. He might find a position there. However, I will not be leaving, at least not immediately. I'll tell him he can send for me when he's settled with a job and housing. That'll give me time to decide what's best for me." She patted Millie's hand. "As long as you and Amy are safe, that's what matters."

"I don't think you have to concern yourself about Mr. Gibson leaving prison anytime soon." Gideon laid aside his fork. "He told us he'd never take the oath, that he'd stay in prison until the war ends."

Millie snorted in disgust. "That sounds like him, stubborn and mean as an old mule."

She pushed away from the table and started collecting the dishes on a tray to carry to the kitchen. Celeste and Lydia did likewise while Gideon abandoned his place to help his grand-mother shuffle toward the parlor.

Celeste touched Lydia's hand as Millie passed by. "She told me about the letter from her mother. I can't imagine how you both must be feeling, but you know I'm praying and willing to listen if you want to talk."

"Thank you. You can see it hasn't softened her opinion of Cal. I'm afraid my complaints against him took root in her heart. I never should've said anything. At least he provided for us while he worked at the mill. That should count for something."

Though now that Lydia had a taste of her freedom again, she couldn't imagine returning to life with Cal Gibson.

# CHAPTER 21

*S*eth followed Luke into the workshop behind Turner and Richardson's Mercantile. Light streamed through the windows on either side of the room, exposing dust particles dancing in the air. The scents of wood, turpentine, and paint permeated the space, and Seth sighed. He'd missed this. The feel of wood under his hands. The rasp of a saw, the ring of hammer on nails. Applying his skills to create something useful and beautiful.

"These tools came with the shop," Luke said. "I expect some will need to be replaced. J.D. started a few small projects before he took sick, but he's self-taught, so he didn't know what else to ask for."

Seth examined the implements on the table. "A good cleaning will improve most of them. So long as nothing's broken, I can make do."

"No, Seth. You'll make a list of what's needed and give it to me. I'll get it ordered right away. I'm eager to make this venture profitable, as I'm sure you are. Soon as the war ends, the town is going to need a range of goods, and I expect good furniture will be among them. You're giving me the chance to get a head start on that."

"I appreciate the opportunity to do something I enjoy."

"I'll leave you to start that list." Luke pointed to the paper and pencil at the end of the table, then headed toward the door. "I expect someone from my house will bring us a meal around noon. Other than that, you should be able to work in peace."

Seth started at the far end of the room, wiping away the dust and cobwebs. He inspected all the items and made notes on their condition. He found a generous supply of lumber and nails, which would get him started. An unfinished chair lay on its side. It looked like the old man who'd been here only worked on one project at a time, the way Pa had. Seth liked to keep a couple of designs going. He might have to double that now, not only to provide items for Luke's shop, but to keep his mind off a certain female.

Troy visited Millie every day and returned with news. It wouldn't do for Seth to put in an appearance, not until Lydia's situation changed.

He'd been working for hours when a rumble in his belly reminded him of the time. He read over his list to be sure he hadn't missed anything, stuffed the paper in his pocket, and grabbed his hat. Maybe Luke expected him to take his meal upstairs. He reached for the door, but it creaked open before he got a hand on it. Head bent, Lydia concentrated on the package in her hands as she eased past the door. Aromas of roast beef and warm bread teased his nose, and Seth instinctively placed his hands over hers to prevent a collision.

She gasped and raised her head. Solemn green eyes met his. Her lips parted on a delicate breath. For a moment, he simply drank in her presence.

Lydia bit her bottom lip when Seth didn't move. "I, um, brought you a repast. But you're on your way out?"

"Just going to find Luke. I thought he might expect me to go up to the store. For the noon meal, I mean." He focused on their hands and tugged gently. "Here, let me take that."

Lydia surrendered the box and followed him to the cleared table. "Rose and Emily came by the bakery and persuaded me to come with them. They're upstairs."

Seth concentrated on emptying the box, barely registering its contents. "There's enough here for two. Will you join me?"

A blush bloomed on her cheeks. "I don't know if I should, although I think that's what Rose intended. She said we should talk."

Seth pulled out two plates and grinned. "We've been outmaneuvered. Might as well wave the flag of surrender."

Lydia's answering chuckle was rueful. "I guess that's what comes from having an officer's wife for a friend." She removed her bonnet, then stepped toward him and held out her hand for a plate.

A spark of mischief prompted him to pull back the plate before she grasped it. Her look of surprise made him snicker like a boy. The game had to stop there, though. Lydia wasn't free to offer her affections.

Seth stifled his groan. He couldn't understand the cruelty of Providence to present him with a woman he thought he could love, only to have her hateful husband come roaring back from the dead.

$\sim$

*L*ydia pretended she didn't hear Seth's hum of regret or notice the way his smile faded. Cal's arrival in Louisville had sent all their possibilities spiraling out of control, just when they'd thought things might settle down.

Turning to the generous array of food, she selected items at random. She'd come at Rose's insistence to explain her plan to

Seth. Their friends agreed he needed to hear it from her, even if it went contrary to his wishes. Time in prayer had solidified her resolve. She would do what was right and trust God with the outcome.

They sat at a small table, and Seth said grace. Lydia took a few bites, watching Seth covertly. He'd gone quiet, keeping his eyes on his plate. She cast about for a way to start the conversation. Straightforward might be best.

"Seth, I want you to know my decision."

"You don't owe me an explanation."

"Yes, I do. I plan to speak with a lawyer friend of Mrs. Coker's. He should be able to advise me on my legal rights. But Cal mustn't know. He'd find a way to upset my plans and keep me tied to him."

"Can't say I blame him for that. I'd do the same, I expect."

Lydia snorted. "But not for the same reason. Cal would do it just to exercise his power over me, to make me squirm and beg. He's not an agreeable person."

Seth's fist pounded the table. "Then why did you ever marry the bounder, Lydia? Or once you discovered how he was, why didn't you leave?"

Shock stole the words from her mind as he pushed up from the table and stalked away. He ran his hand through his hair, his posture communicating his frustration. She was astounded that he'd come to care so much in such a short time.

He blew out an apology. "I'm sorry—"

"No, it's all right. I've asked myself that question so many times." A full confession was in order. "I was nearly nineteen when we married. Cal's first wife had died eight months before, but she'd been sick a while. He was all smiles and charm while we were courting, but more than that, he had Millie, and I was ready to have my own family."

"Did nobody else ever court you?"

Lydia lowered her gaze to the table where she'd been dragging her fork through the gravy. "I was a quiet child, the youngest. I ended up living with my grandmother after my parents passed on and my brothers moved away. I worked in the mill to provide for the two of us, but it wasn't much. Granny knew she was nearing the end of life, and she urged me to accept Cal's proposal. She died right after we married."

"Lydia, you don't have to say any more."

"I want you to know. You need to know everything. It turns out Cal wanted a son, and he knew I came from a large family. I hadn't had any serious suitors, so he figured I'd be easy to convince. He said he was willing to take care of Granny, too, so that was a big factor for me. He probably knew she wouldn't last long."

Lydia paused to take a sip of water. "Unfortunately, I couldn't give him what he wanted, or at least it seemed the fault was mine. Month after month I prayed, but nothing. I felt like such a failure, and Cal blamed me too. Now that I know he's not Millie's father—"

"What? You mean to say—" He stopped when she held up her hand.

"A few weeks ago, Millie found a letter from her mother. In it Polly confessed she'd left Cal for a while early in their marriage and got involved with another. When she learned she was with child, she returned to Cal."

"So, perhaps he's the one who couldn't produce children."

Lydia shrugged. "Anyway, to cover the hurt, I focused my attention on Millie, maybe even influenced her bad opinion of Cal with my complaining. Soon as the war started, he signed up, eager to get away from us and the mill. Ready to see new places and new faces, he said. And honestly, I was relieved to have him go."

*S*tuffing his hands in his pockets, Seth forced himself to keep his distance. He ached for the pain she'd endured for so long. She might condemn herself to be brave for untold years in the future unless she could find a way out. If Troy and Millie moved away, that would leave her to deal with Gibson alone.

Seth twisted away before he realized she was speaking again.

"I assume Cal will insist I go with him when he's released from prison. Lieutenant Hart said he scoffed at the notion of taking the oath, so maybe I'll have time to come up with a better plan. Until then, here's what I'll do. There's a cotton mill or two over in Indiana. Cal has no other skills, so I'll insist he go alone to find a position to support us. Mrs. Coker thinks I might be able to claim he abandoned me, depending on how long he's gone."

Seth caught the gleam of tears as she lifted her head.

"Does it make me a heartless shrew to let him think I'll go back with him while I'm scheming to get free?"

"No. It means you've decided to take care of yourself rather than suffer his poor treatment any longer."

They lapsed into silence for several moments.

Lydia stood and gathered the remnants from their meal. "I suppose I should get these dishes back upstairs. I imagine Rose and Emily must be ready to go."

Seth put out his hand to check her movement but stopped short of touching her. That would be a mistake, considering the situation. "Leave it. I'll take them with me when I finish up here."

"Thank you, and thanks for letting me explain. If things were different..." Her voice trailed to a whisper.

Seth nodded. "Whatever happens, I'll be here. I'll support

your decision even if I don't like it." He tried to smile but felt the result was closer to a nervous tic.

"You're a good man, Seth Morgan. You deserve better than what life has given you these last few years. I pray you'll be rewarded." She donned her bonnet and slipped out the door.

Waves of regret, strangely mixed with pleasure, assaulted his mind. After several minutes of trying to sort those feelings, he gave up. Work would be the best therapy. Distract his mind with design measurements and keep his hands busy. His list for Luke could wait until later.

~

*L*ydia checked the list she held against the items in the box going to the prison. She closed the container and reached for her cloak. The bakery door opened, sending a gust of cold air into the room as she buttoned the garment. "Right on time. I guess army life did you a heap of good."

Troy grinned at her teasing. "Now, Aunt Lydia, I wasn't that bad. Besides, I knew if I didn't get here when I said, you'd just go traipsing off by yourself like the stubborn woman you are. I couldn't risk that."

"And who do you think escorted me to the prison before you showed up? Nobody, that's who, and I've not come to harm these past six months."

"Yeah, but you didn't have a hostile husband inside the prison then." He took the box from her as she put on her gloves.

She pulled down the shade on the window to show the store was closed and called back to her employers. "Mr. Watford, Miz Minnie, my nephew's here, so I'm leaving now."

The old man rolled his wheeled chair from the partition separating the kitchen from the storefront. "All right, Mrs.

Gibson. I'll lock the door. You take good care of her now, young man."

Troy and Lydia leaned into the wind and spoke little as they traversed the city streets toward the prison. A few flakes of snow swirled in the aura of lights shining from the store windows. Lydia laughed as one of the icy pieces landed on her nose, already numb from the falling temperature. The scent of spiced apples wafting from the box Troy carried made her stomach rumble and wish their errand was already over.

"Hattie promised a hearty stew for supper," she said. "I'll be ready to eat my share as soon as we get to the house."

Troy jostled the box. "Me too, especially after smelling these pies." He sidled closer to Lydia as they passed the train depot, where a group of men materialized from the growing darkness. Nobody dawdled in the cold street. The men hurried on.

Reaching the corner of Tenth, Lydia and Troy waited for a wagon to pass before crossing to the prison. "Do you think Cal knows you're the one who delivers the baked goods to Major Sullivan?" Troy asked.

She spoke around her scarf. "Probably. I'd imagine he heard the guard call my name the other day. They had no reason not to tell him who I was. They probably thought it a funny coincidence that both our names were Gibson."

Sergeant Dunn must have been watching for her. He stepped in front of the gate and spoke in a low voice. "I'm real sorry, ma'am, about the way you discovered Mr. Gibson here. I couldn't imagine that you was married to him. He's such a..." He paused and worked his jaw. "Well, suffice it to say, you deserve better than what I've seen of him. 'Course, the war does awful things to a man. Why, I've seen—"

Lydia raised her hand. "It's all right, Sergeant. You couldn't have known. Now if you'll have someone take this box up to the major, I'll be truly grateful to get on my way home."

The guard whistled and motioned for another guard to join

them. When the soldier scrambled down, Dunn thrust the box in his hands. "Take this to the major and be quick about it."

Lydia smiled her thanks. "By the way, Sergeant Dunn, this is my nephew, Troy. Remember, I'd asked everyone to let me know if they saw him?"

"Oh, yeah, we thought he might be a prisoner, but here he is a member of the Union army." He shifted his rifle and thrust out his right hand. "Good to meet you, Private. I guess you surprised everyone when you showed up, huh?"

Troy nodded and accepted the welcome. "That I did. Well, our job is done. We should get on to the house."

Lydia stopped him. "I must wait for the payment. Major Sullivan will send it down in a moment."

A heavy sigh answered her. Troy had good reason to want to hurry. Besides the promise of a hot meal and spending time with Millie and Amy, Troy never had gotten on well with Cal. Truth to tell, hardly anybody got along well with Cal, but he'd been especially belligerent toward Troy.

The truth dawned on her with startling clarity. Polly must have confessed her adultery to Cal before she died, as she'd suggested she might in Millie's letter. If she'd told him the name of her lover, Cal would resent anyone named McNeil. Had Cal married Lydia as punishment or as an effort to prove he could sire a child as well as Ellis?

Either way, he'd not wooed and wed her for anything resembling fondness. No wonder she'd never been able to make him happy. Her marriage had been doomed from the start.

The young soldier returned with payment for the pies and passed it to Lydia. With a final word to Sergeant Dunn, she and Troy hastened away. She hoped she never had to lay eyes on Cal Gibson again.

# CHAPTER 22

Seth prepared himself for the shock of seeing Lydia after several weeks apart. Twenty-six days, but it seemed like months. Even with the rigorous pace he'd set himself to turn out furniture, he couldn't banish thoughts of her. How often he'd started to rush over to the Coker house to see how she fared, but he controlled the impulse, ruthlessly reminding himself she wasn't available. Being together only courted heartache.

On Sunday, Rose had reported that Herbert was still the only male present to protect the ladies at Mrs. Coker's, since Lieutenant Hart had left the prior Wednesday to return to Virginia. The way Rose had cut her eyes toward Seth told him she expected him to act on the information and offer whatever assistance he could. He'd resisted for two days, only giving in today because images of imminent danger kept disrupting his sleep.

Now he stood at the door, rehearsing what he might say whenever he worked up the nerve to knock. He stared at the brass lion's head fixed to the burnished oak standing between him and a houseful of females. With the sunshine blocked by the portico columns and the wind whistling its way around them, Seth shivered. He wondered if Daniel had been as nervous facing real lions in a pit. Not that he was afraid, only unsure of what he'd say while he was there.

At last, he raised his hand to grip the ring hanging from the fixture, only to find the door swinging inward and his fist closing on air.

Herbert's gaze raked him with more levity than he'd guess the man possessed. "Mr. Morgan, what a pleasant surprise. The ladies are in the parlor." He shut the door and waited for Seth to surrender his coat and hat.

"Thank you, Herbert. I trust everyone is well?" Seth gave up his hat and tucked his gloves in a pocket before removing the overcoat.

Herbert's eyebrows rose to meet his hairline. "Certainly, sir. See for yourself."

Seth tugged his jacket in place. "Thank you." He stepped to the parlor door as Herbert pushed it open. "Good afternoon, ladies."

All eyes turned his way while his gaze swept the room until he found Lydia. A tentative smile accompanied the blush of her cheeks. Her knees, where the baby had been bouncing, went still until a fussy demand set them in motion again. While the other women greeted him warmly, she merely nodded and resumed the playful song he'd interrupted.

Seth bowed to all the ladies and took a seat near Mrs. Coker, deferring to her position as the eldest and hostess.

Celeste glanced up from her stitching. "We haven't seen you for an age, Mr. Morgan."

"Now, Miss Carrigan," he chided, "I thought we all agreed first names suited for friends such as we are, except for those who've earned greater respect, such as Mrs. Coker."

The older woman chuckled. "As friends and peers of Gideon, I suppose you could all call me Grandmother, but that might raise questions better left alone."

Seth nodded toward Lydia, who had shifted Amy so the child could face the room. He turned back to their hostess. "What do you plan for the baby to call you? Is there a name you prefer?"

To his surprise, Mrs. Coker blushed and glanced toward the wee one. "I've started using the name my nieces and nephews called me years ago, before my children came along. I'd almost forgotten, but it just slipped out one day when I was holding her."

Millie reached over from her chair to pat the woman's hand. "Well? What is it? We should know so Amy isn't confused by hearing different names."

"It's Lottie. My oldest nephew couldn't say Charlotte, so he called me Aunt Lottie."

"I think it fits you," Seth said. "Would you object to us using it as well?"

Laying aside her knitting, Mrs. Coker glanced from him to each of the other women. "I'm agreeable to the suggestion. Now, speaking of the wee one, I believe it's my turn to hold her for a while." She peered at Seth with thinly veiled humor. "Unless you'd like to take her? I do believe she misses Gideon and her papa. Babies always seem to be enamored of men."

Aware his face must have broadcast his fear and surprise, Seth balked. The wise old woman had thrown down a challenge. Unwilling to be deemed a coward, he rose to the occasion. He tamped down his nervousness and took the half-dozen steps to Lydia. She also stood.

Sharing a private smile with his green-eyed goddess, he reached out to the gurgling child. The baby broke into a toothless grin and held out her chubby arms. His hands brushed Lydia's in the exchange, sending sparks through his body and threatening his equilibrium. He grasped Amy as he and Lydia both spun away.

It had been a mistake to come here. Holding the child and touching Lydia only increased his sense of loss.

~

MONDAY, APRIL 10, 1865

*L*ouisville buzzed with the news even before the papers could print it. Lee surrendered in Virginia. After years of countless deaths and destruction, the South lost its bid for independence.

Lydia had sensed the loss coming for a while. Her chief concern centered around the prisoners held by the Union army. What would happen to them? Would Cal be released even though he refused to take an oath of allegiance? Would Seth's cousin be turned loose to prey on other innocent women?

What would happen to the thousands of displaced Southerners who had left or been driven from their homes? She thought Seth might remain in Louisville, and Troy had promised to return for Millie as soon as he could arrange it. Lydia's future remained uncertain.

Mrs. Coker's lawyer friend hadn't been encouraging when Lydia consulted him. Although sympathetic to her problem, he warned that women seldom won in divorce suits. He recounted cases where women were denied a divorce even when their husbands had beaten them to the point of serious injury.

"You might fare better in Indiana," he'd said, "but you'd have to reside there for a year before bringing your case against your husband. Of course, if you live with him during that year, you would essentially cancel your plea of abandonment. Since judges are men, they tend to empathize with the man's arguments more than the woman's accusations."

With Edith and Isaac Wynn removed to Frankfort, Lydia didn't know where to turn for spiritual advice. Mrs. Coker—Aunt Lottie—promised to support whatever decision she made, though Lydia could tell she wasn't keen on the idea of Lydia reuniting with Cal. At least Lydia knew she was welcome to stay there if necessary. Celeste often remarked how the older woman had transformed from a persnickety complainer to an indulgent benefactor. Her loyalty to the younger women kept her from offering objective counsel.

Lydia took advantage of the warmer weather to venture over to the Turner house. She found Rose preparing to take the girls—Emily's Sarah Grace and Luke's Victoria—for a walk to the nearby park.

"No school today?" Lydia tried to mask her disappointment. She'd hoped to have the privacy she needed for a serious discussion.

Rose shook her head. "In honor of Lee's surrender, school dismissed early. Emily's reached the miserable point with the coming baby, and the girls are anxious over it. I thought an hour in the park might help everyone."

"Where's John Mark?"

Rose opened the door and warned the girls to stay close. "He went with Luke to the store. With half the household out of the way, maybe Emily can rest awhile."

They set a brisk pace to keep up with the youngsters, who danced ahead until they reached the corner. Each woman took a girl's hand to cross the road. Rose reminded them to "walk like young ladies rather than rapscallion boys."

Lydia laughed at Rose's admonition. "You're good with them. I'm sure Luke and Emily appreciate having you near at times like this."

"I hope so. It was awkward at first, after Noah left, but we've settled into a routine."

"Do you think Noah will get to come home soon, now that the Union has claimed victory?"

A soft sigh conveyed Rose's longing. "I hope so, but Luke says it may take them a while to secure areas farther west. Of course, some soldiers will need to stay for much longer to help restore and rebuild. Noah promised to resign his commission as soon as the fighting stopped."

"And then you'll be moving to his home in Indiana, I suppose." Lydia mourned the idea. "I'm happy for you, but you'll be sorely missed here. It's hard to lose friends."

"You know we'll come back to visit. I believe Celeste will remain here, and I can't stay away from my sister too long."

The girls ran up to present each woman with a bunch of wildflowers they'd collected. Rose and Lydia responded with appropriate delight before the girls scampered off to find more.

Rose wrinkled her nose at the questionable scent but tucked the stems into her waistband. "What about you? How will the war's end affect your situation?"

"That's what I'm struggling with, Rose. I'd hoped to get your perspective. Though young, you've been blessed with wisdom some elders don't possess. The result of being a preacher's daughter, I suppose."

"I'm honored by your confidence, but I don't have any answers other than what comes from the Bible."

Lydia nodded. "Exactly why I sought you out. I remember someone in my past, perhaps my pastor, saying that God hates divorce. But didn't He allow it? I was reading in Leviticus last week—"

"Without falling asleep?" Rose laughed. "I'm sorry. I shouldn't have said that."

"It can get rather tedious, but I suppose all those names and rules were really important to the people at that time."

"Yes, Da liked to say God pays great attention to details, and Leviticus is the proof. But go on. What was it you read?"

"There were certain allowances made for divorce, though it seems God wasn't happy about it."

"You're right. God meant for marriage to last a lifetime. The Apostle Paul likened it to the relationship between Christ and the Church. I don't know the details of your marriage, my friend, but I've gathered you were unhappy. Having your husband reappear when you'd thought him dead must have been a great shock." Rose's brow puckered. "However, he's still your husband in the eyes of the law. First Corinthians says the believing wife sanctifies the unbelieving husband, but if the unbeliever leaves, the believing spouse is free."

"Cal left for the war, but I think it was the excuse he was looking for. I wonder if that's truly a case of abandonment. And what if he wants to reunite? Am I obligated to take him back?"

Rose grasped Lydia's hands. "I don't know. All I know is we must petition heaven for an answer."

~

FRIDAY, APRIL 14, 1865

Swinging the walking cane he'd crafted from a broken branch of the hickory tree behind the shop, Seth strode the three blocks between Luke's store and Watford's bakery. The cane lent him an air of elegance, boosting the confidence he needed for his current errand. He could claim an innocent motive in escorting Lydia to the prison. After all, he'd protect her against any threat directed her way. But in his heart, he admitted he sought her company for his own protection.

He desperately needed her beside him when he confronted Manny. But this time, he hoped her presence would provide the impetus he needed to keep to his plan. Otherwise, he might convince himself, for the one hundredth time, that Manny should beg his forgiveness. The minister's sermon last Sunday, combined with Seth's continuous restless nights, had pointed out that the process must begin with him.

"If your brother has ought against you"—the words rang again through his mind—"go to him and be reconciled with your brother."

Memories he'd long forgotten surfaced in his dreams. Manny being the last one chosen for a children's game. Manny struggling with arithmetic problems that seemed simple to Seth. Manny, the lonely single child of his parents, watching Seth and his siblings tease and embrace each other. Seth didn't shoulder the blame for his cousin's actions, especially as an adult, but he saw where he could've been more sympathetic over the years.

And so, he planned to apologize and ask Manny's forgiveness. Having Lydia along to provide support would make it easier.

He reached the bakery and peeked in the window. Lydia didn't look up as she filled a box with cookies for the customer standing at the counter. Seth waited until the man turned to leave, setting the tiny bell to ringing when he opened the door.

Slipping in without an announcement, he admired her while she worked with her back to him. A few strands of tawny-brown hair had escaped the chignon and floated at the nape of her neck. The apron covering her dress, tied in the back with a perky bow, accentuated her figure.

He looked away to quell his imagination. Either he made a noise or Lydia sensed his presence, because she turned abruptly with wide eyes.

"Seth? I didn't hear you come in. What are you doing here? Not that I'm unhappy to see you. I just didn't expect anyone so late in the day." She rambled, obviously unsettled by his sudden appearance.

He took a step forward. "I'm sorry if I startled you. I know you usually take a package to the prison on Fridays, and I thought I'd accompany you. If you don't mind." He stopped. He sounded as flustered as she had.

"Oh. That's very thoughtful of you." She glanced at the clock on the counter. "It is time to close. Give me a minute to pack the pies and gather my things."

She disappeared behind the partition, then returned with a container in her hands, a cloak over one arm, and a hat dangling from her fingers by the ribbons. "Miz Watford already boxed up the pies, so they're ready to go." The older woman followed Lydia into the room and greeted Seth with reserved curiosity.

Setting the items on the counter, Lydia donned the bonnet first. Seth moved forward to help with her cloak but held back. Sometimes the ingrained etiquette was best suspended to squelch inappropriate feelings.

With all in place, Lydia picked up the package and bid her employer good evening. Seth held the door and offered to carry the box, but Lydia insisted she'd keep it. Perhaps she thought it wise to have something to place between them.

~

*L*ydia clutched the box and held it waist high. A poor barrier indeed, but it reminded her she was still tied to another man.

Seth revealed his intention to mend the breach with his cousin. Lydia listened with growing respect as they covered the thawing ground. Could she be so generous with Cal? The thought frightened her.

As soon as they reached the gate, the guard gripped Seth's arm. "Mr. Morgan, glad you received our message and got here so quick."

Seth regarded him with surprise. "What message? Where did you send it?"

"To Mr. Turner's store, sir. We'd heard you was working for him. Don't know how the messenger missed you, but glad I am you're here now." The soldier tugged him inside the compound, and Lydia trailed behind.

Seth resisted the pull and asked again, "What message, Private?"

"It's that Peacock fellow. Major Sullivan said you ought to be alerted, seeing's how he's related to you, even though there ain't no love lost betwixt the two of you."

Seth glanced at Lydia, pressing his lips together. "What about my cousin?"

The youngster halted at the tone of authority. "He had some kind of fit and attacked one of the guards, I was told. Another guard had to wrestle him to the ground. Broke his arm in the tussle."

"He broke Manny's arm. Is that all?"

"No, sir. The prisoner broke the guard's arm, trying to get his knife. The guard ended up ripping open the prisoner's gut." He glanced at Lydia and murmured apologies but rushed on as he urged Seth forward again. "Doc says he's in a bad way, likely won't make it to morning. Major thought you should know."

Seth paled and turned to Lydia. "I have to see him. Will you go with me, or would you prefer to wait here?"

The private lowered his voice. "Probably best you wait at the gate, ma'am. I'll get someone to stay with you." He pulled back his lips and released a shrill whistle. At the summons, another guard trotted over to join them. "Perkins, keep the lady company while I escort Mr. Morgan here to Ward Number Two."

Perkins nodded and urged Lydia closer to the fence. Her reticle bounced against the box in her hands. Recalled to her original errand, she halted. "I need someone to take this box to Major Sullivan."

"I'll see if I can catch somebody walking that way, ma'am."

He twisted around to survey the area. "Looks like that's the major coming over here now."

Lydia looked beyond the soldier's lanky frame and breathed a sigh of relief. Major Sullivan indeed had headed in their direction but stopped to confer with a subordinate. When he reached them, he offered Lydia a tired smile. "Ah, Mrs. Gibson, you are the one bright spot in my day, in fact, in my week. And not just because of the sweets you bring. After looking at all these sorry mugs, I'm reminded of what a blessing God gave us when he created females."

Despite the blood heating her face, Lydia smiled at the officer's praise. "Such flummery, Major. I'm no young miss to have my head turned by your flowery words, but I thank you anyhow. Now I'm past ready to hand over this burden to you."

He accepted the box and handed over his coins, then looked sharply at the guard. "Perkins? I thought Crawford was at the gate today. Where is he?"

Lydia spoke before Perkins could answer. "If Crawford is the guard who was here earlier, he took Mr. Morgan to see his injured relative. He said you'd sent someone to fetch Seth as you don't expect Mr. Peacock to survive long."

"Ah, good." He wagged his head. "Can't understand what came over that man, to attack a guard in plain view of everyone. Especially as he might soon be released, thanks to Lee's surrender."

"That may have been the very thing to cause it, Major, if I may say so. Some of these people," she said, sweeping her hand toward the refugee house and the prison grounds, "won't have anything to return to. By all accounts and what I witnessed on the way to Louisville, almost everything's destroyed."

"You may be right. And with your friend's charge of murder against him, I guess Peacock figured he'd simply move to another prison." He shifted the box to tuck it under his arm.

"Mrs. Gibson, I need to ask you about that man who claims to be your husband."

Alarm shot from her head clear to her feet. "What about him?"

"Well, first off, is he your husband?"

"He is, or he was. He left me and my stepdaughter to fend for ourselves when he joined the Confederate Army in sixty-one. I received only two or three letters, and he spent less than a week with us when he came home on furlough. Then I heard he went missing at Chickamauga and was presumed dead."

She paused to take a breath. "Seeing him here was quite a shock, and I'm not too keen on a reunion. The lawyer I spoke to said I don't have much chance of a divorce, but I don't have to go back to him. I guess that would give Cal reason to divorce me for abandonment."

Major Sullivan rubbed his nose and pulled at his graying beard. "You aiming to stay in Louisville then?"

Lydia nodded. "At least for a while, until my stepdaughter joins her husband when he's reassigned. I don't know where they plan to settle."

"Your stepdaughter?" His gaze sharpened. "That would be Mr. Gibson's daughter?"

Lydia sagged. "Yes." *Legally anyway.*

"I don't reckon I ought to ask you about taking care of the man."

"What do you mean, take care of him? Is he injured?"

"Not injured, but powerful sick. Doc says he's got lung sickness and fever. We've isolated him to keep it from spreading, but it'd be better to move him out. The local hospital's overflowing and doesn't want to take in prisoners. I was hoping maybe you could see fit to tend him. It probably wouldn't be for long. He was already sick when he arrived here."

Lydia recalled her conversation with Rose. Could this be the answer she'd been seeking? Did God want her to help Cal in his time of need? If his time on earth was short, how could she refuse? She chewed her lower lip, torn between self-preservation and family responsibility. "I'm staying with friends. I can't put the other members of the household in danger of illness. There are elderly people and an infant to consider."

Major Sullivan pointed to the refugee house across the street. "You might see if there's a place over there you could use. It was originally meant to be a hospital. We've noticed a steady stream of folks leaving since the news came about Lee's surrender."

Turning to look in that direction, Lydia sighed in resignation. So much for moving forward with her life. Without even trying, Cal had exerted his authority and forced her back into her wifely role, making her twice the prisoner he'd ever been.

# CHAPTER 23

$S$eth followed the guard along the prison's brick pathways to the building on the south side marked Hospital Number Two. Seth wondered where Hospital Number One might be but didn't bother to ask. The soldier opened the door and gestured Seth down a dark corridor. "He's in the room at the end of the hall. I'll wait here for you."

"Much obliged."

He didn't blame the guard for staying behind. The metallic smell of blood, mixed with the pungent cleaning chemicals and the odors of human excrement, assailed his senses as the door closed behind him. *God, give me strength, not only to maintain my composure but to carry through with my mission.*

His journey down the hallway was torturous. Moans and desperate sounds of distress issued from every doorway. He glimpsed men lying on the floor with only blankets or thin mattresses for comfort, a couple of skinny women leaning over buckets of water to wash away the filth, and one man, presumably a doctor, dozing with his chin in one hand and the other holding a pen suspended over notes scattered across a small desk. Each room held countless men. He'd seen field hospitals in better shape.

Thankful he'd missed being part of this scene, he quickened his footsteps to the end of the hall and entered the room. A gray-haired woman held the hand of a young man on the right. She glanced up briefly, still whispering words of comfort to the prisoner. Seth searched the other faces, recognizing the raspy breaths of impending death. He found Manny curled on a cot with a stained blanket held to his belly.

*Gut wound.* That was why his time was short.

Seth laid his hat and cane across the foot of the bed. He moved close enough to notice the dried blood on Manny's hands. "It must have been some fight."

Seth didn't mean to speak so loudly. His words roused his cousin. A slight grin twisted Manny's face as his eyelids slid open. "It was."

For a moment, the scene transported Seth back to a fishing trip in Georgia with his family. He must have been twelve or thirteen. Manny, Seth, and their fathers had endured a cold rain on the last day, and Manny had landed a big bass after a mighty struggle. It was the only time Seth could remember seeing Manny truly happy.

"Sorry I missed it."

"I give him what-for, I did."

"Yeah, I heard." Seth paused, searching for words. "Manny, I need to tell you something right now. I need to ask you to forgive me for how I treated you when we were growing up. For not helping you when I could've."

Confusion puckered Manny's brow. "Help with what?"

Seth ran his hands through his hair. "So many things. Choosing you to be on my team, explaining arithmetic, including you in my circle of friends. I guess it boils down to this. I should have shown you love."

Manny swallowed audibly, gathered his breath. "Loved

Meg, you know. I didn't mean to hurt her. She..." He stopped to collect another gulp of air. "She fought me, and I fought back." Tears slid down his cheek.

Seth rested a hand lightly against the blanket-shrouded shoulder. "I'm sure Meg would forgive you, and I forgive you. But I need you to forgive me for all those years when I could've done more for you. Will you?"

A slight nod and more tears preceded the whisper. "Yeah. Jesus said we have to." The last words came out with a gurgle.

"Do you believe in Jesus? He died for you and wants to take you to heaven." Desperation drove Seth. He had to do whatever he could to make this right. Tears cascaded down his own face. "Manny, don't die yet. I need to know. Do you believe?"

Manny's head tipped forward, and his grip on the blanket slipped.

Seth leaned forward to listen for sounds of life. Shallow breaths said Manny still lived. But for how long?

∼

*L*ydia left instructions with the guard to tell Seth where she'd gone and crossed the street to the refugee house. Visiting the facility felt like stepping into the past. After spending several months in a proper home with friends who cared for one another, Lydia found the separated wards with their sparse furnishings cold and forbidding.

The one spark of encouragement swirled into her path as she entered, and the heavy front doors snapped shut behind her. "Dorcas. Oh, you are a welcome sight for my poor eyes."

Dorcas grasped her outstretched hands. "Why, Miss Lydia, I didn't 'spect to see you today. Didn't I send you word my Samuel couldn't leave until next month?"

"Yes, you did, although I imagine he's not happy with the

delay. He'll be counting the days till your wedding. Look at you. My dear, you're so beautiful."

Dorcas spun around to show off her dress of bright blues, reds, and yellows threaded in a flowered pattern. The colors enhanced her dark skin and sparkling brown eyes. "Samuel picked out the fabric, said I was born to wear pansy colors."

"He's right. They make you shine."

Dorcas reached for Lydia's hand again. "But you didn't come to look at my dress. What brings you back to the shelter?"

Lydia swallowed her bitterness. "I have to see if there's a place here where I can take care of my husband."

"Your husband? You done married without telling me?"

"No, no. It turns out my husband wasn't killed in the war after all. He was reported missing but in fact he was captured and sent to a prison in Illinois. That prison started releasing men a couple of months ago, but Cal refused the oath and ended up here. I suppose he was already sick when he arrived, and now the commander tells me it's lung inflammation."

"That's too bad. And jes' when you found him again. So they gonna move him here? Can't the doctors over there tend to him?"

Lydia shrugged, accepting her fate. "The disease spreads easily, and they don't want it to infect anyone else. Major Sullivan found out Cal was my husband and asked me to find a place where I could look out for him."

Lieutenant Goodwin rounded the corner from his office and stopped short at the sight of them. He nodded. "I thought I heard voices. Hello, Dorcas. Mrs. Gibson, I'm surprised to see you here."

"Lieutenant." Lydia rushed into an explanation. "I understand some of your tenants have moved out."

He tapped a pipe with one finger and pulled a match from his pocket. "Yes, three or four families started back to their homes while the weather holds. Most of them have a long journey ahead, going on foot, without any wagons or pack animals to spare around here."

He lit the match with his thumbnail and puffed on the mouthpiece. A speculative gleam lit his pale blue eyes. "What about you, ma'am? You planning to go back to Georgia?"

"No, at least not yet. I wonder if there might be a room here where I could tend to someone who's sick? It would need to be away from the other folks to keep from exposing them to the illness."

"Hmm." He exhaled a cloud of smoke while he considered the matter. "There's only one place set apart from the rest, the guards' sleeping quarters down the hall. With the place emptying out, I suppose I could arrange for the guard rotating off duty to bunk with the few men who're left. You want to look at it?

"Yes, please."

Lydia and Dorcas followed the lieutenant to the room at the end of the west hallway. He lifted a lantern off a hook at the door and lit it with another match. The light revealed two cots pushed against the far wall, a small table set between them. Lydia noted the blankets spread across each bed and a chamber pot beneath. A tall armoire had four drawers on one side and a space for hanging clothes on the other. A mirror hung above the washstand, which held a metal pitcher and bowl.

It would do. "Where's the other guard now? Will he have a lot of things to move? I hate to put him out."

"It happens he's a local boy. Goes home for supper and his off hours, so he won't mind. He only stays here when his sister visits, says he can't sleep with her yapping in the next room." Concern lined the lieutenant's face. "Not to be nosy, but I hope it's not your daughter or her baby who's sick."

"Thank you for asking. It's my husband, who surprised us all by showing up as a prisoner when we thought he was dead. Now I'll nurse him through his last days on earth, it seems."

His stunned look reflected Lydia's own feelings on the matter. Only Cal Gibson would pull such a Lazarus stunt, forcing them all to endure a reprise of his final departure.

$\sim$

*A*fter locating the doctor to arrange for Manny's burial, Seth and his escort returned to the main gate. Crimson streaks across the western horizon warned he'd left Lydia alone far longer than he intended. The women at Mrs. Coker's house would worry if he didn't deliver her there soon.

His alarm increased when he reached the gate to find her gone. "Where's Mrs. Gibson? Surely you didn't allow her to leave on her own."

The guard who'd been with her turned at Seth's demand. "No, sir, she only went across the street—"

"I'm here, Seth. Sorry to hold you up."

Both men spun at her call from the corner.

Her dash across the street quickened her breath, but she looked well otherwise. Seth's alarm faded, but he examined her covertly while she addressed the guard.

"Private Perkins, please let Major Sullivan know I've made arrangements with Lieutenant Goodwin at the refugee house. The lieutenant will show y'all where to put Mr. Gibson. I have to go to my friend's house and get my things, but I'll return as soon as I can."

Seth gaped. What was she talking about? Had someone coerced her into reuniting with that sorry excuse for a husband? What happened to her plan to encourage him to go across the river to look for work?

Before he could ask, Lydia took his arm. "We must hurry,

Seth. Millie will be worried." She set a quick pace, dragging him along with her.

"Lydia? What was all that about? You're planning to go back to the prison?"

Her lips tightened, belying the nonchalance of her shoulder shrug. "Cal is terribly sick, according to Major Sullivan. It's consumption plus lung fever, and he's afraid it'll run through the camp if Cal stays any longer. I won't endanger the others at Aunt Lottie's, so I've arranged to tend him in an isolated room at the refugee house."

Seth stepped in front of her and grasped her arms. "And what about you? You'll be putting yourself in danger, taking care of him every hour for who knows how many days. What if you get sick?"

"I will be careful. I've done this before, and I know how to protect myself."

"You've cared for someone with this disease before?"

"Granny McNeil. You may remember I told you she encouraged me to marry Cal because her time was short. I nursed her up until her death. Despite her pain, she remained concerned about me. She'd taken care of me for years. I couldn't abandon her."

"Of course, you couldn't. I understand that, but—"

"It's the same with Cal. Though I wasn't happy with him most of the time, he provided for me while he was at home. I didn't have to work in the mill after we married, at least not until he left to join the army. And he gave me Millie. Though I regret not having a child of my own, Millie filled an empty place in my heart. Considering those things, I can't abandon him now. Besides, it's my duty as his wife to take care of him when he's in need."

Seth released her, and they covered the remaining blocks to Mrs. Coker's house. He'd have to find a way to help Lydia. He wished Doc Spencer didn't live so far away. Perhaps Luke could recommend a doctor to offer his advice.

When Lydia explained the situation to the rest of the household, Millie reacted much as Seth had, trying to dissuade her stepmother from the course she'd agreed to. But Lydia would not be deterred.

In an hour's time, Seth escorted her back to the refugee house. He followed her into the building and down the hall to the room where Cal Gibson lay asleep on the first cot. While the doctor gave Lydia instructions, Seth introduced himself to Lieutenant Goodwin.

"I work with Luke Turner down at the mercantile, Lieutenant," Seth said. "I'd appreciate it if you'd contact me if she needs anything."

Goodwin eyed him with curiosity but nodded. "I know Turner. He employed some of the women who came here with that group from Georgia. Did Mrs. Gibson work for Turner?"

"No, she works at Watford's bakery. I'll let them know the situation."

"It wouldn't hurt to say a prayer as well." Goodwin nodded toward the room, concern etched on his face. "She's like to run herself down looking after him."

Seth gripped the lieutenant's shoulder. "You're right. I'll try to enlist more help in that area. Thank you for providing this room."

"Mrs. Gibson and her friends looked for ways to be useful, never gave me any trouble or complained." His gaze swung back to Seth. "I don't recall you being in the group. Do you hail from the same town as them?"

Surprised by the question, Seth blinked under the sudden scrutiny. "No, we met just before they were transported to Louisville. One of the women is married to my good friend Evan Spencer." *There. That should suffice for an explanation. No sense going into details.*

Goodwin directed his attention to the room as the doctor picked up his black bag to leave. "This building's a poor excuse for living quarters, and we lost our share of refugees to sickness. Maybe with the war winding down, we can all learn to love our neighbors again instead of fighting them."

When the lieutenant followed the doctor to the front door, Seth poked his head into the room to bid Lydia goodnight. She stood in the middle of the floor, head bowed, hands on her hips as if contemplating what to do.

He cleared his throat. "I'll be leaving now, unless there's something you need me to do before I go."

Troubled green eyes connected with his, but she shook her head. "No, nothing. Except pray. For me. For him. And don't despise me."

Though he longed to go to her, he stayed in the hall. "I could never despise you. And I'll pray for you both. If you need anything, let the lieutenant know, and he'll contact me."

"Thank you. Seth, I..."

"Shh. Get some sleep while you can. It's liable to be a long night."

# CHAPTER 24

*S*eth's prediction proved true. Lydia slept soundly until the sound of Cal's coughing and wheezing pulled her from the depths of a dream. She staggered to her feet and found the bucket of water on the table. She drenched a cloth, pressed the water from it, and laid it on his brow.

His fever persisted, and he thrashed in agitation. Deciding it must be time for more medicine, she was thankful for the moonlight streaming through the lone window. No need to light the lantern. She measured the prescribed amount of quinine. Murmuring soothing sounds, she lifted his head and pressed the cup between his lips. He swallowed the dose but flung the cup across the room and pushed her away.

Lydia toppled onto her backside.

Cal sat up and loomed over her. "Stop trying to kill me"—a vicious spate of coughing interrupted him—"with that foul stuff."

Lydia rolled to her feet and retrieved the cup. She muttered under her breath. "I'm trying to help you get better." She blinked back tears and rubbed the hip she'd landed on.

Cal peered in her direction. "Bella? Bella, I'm sorry. I didn't mean to hurt you. I thought it was the prison guard... But wait, didn't they shoot you?" He coughed again, but not so forcefully as before.

Lydia sighed, unsure if she should try to correct him. Whatever he'd been dreaming must have confused him. "Cal," she said. "It's Lydia. You're in Louisville, not Illinois. I'm taking care of you now, just like I took care of Granny McNeil." She hoped to calm him with her gentle explanation, but she remained on her own cot, out of his reach.

He latched onto the last name. "McNeil. He's the low-down skunk who violated Polly. Put a baby in her belly and sent her back to me so I'd think it was mine. She never told me, not until the day she died. I oughta go to Alabama and teach that coward a lesson."

His words slowed and slurred, proving the medicine must be working.

"Lie down and go to sleep now." Lydia waited until he slumped and settled on his side. She crept to the foot of the bed and gingerly pulled the blanket up to his shoulders.

Fatigue dragged her toward sleep, but she played his words over in her mind. Best not mention the name McNeil again. She wasn't sure if he understood where he was now. Maybe he'd sleep until morning, when she needed to apply the mustard plaster. She didn't want to get in the way of his hands again. He'd thought somebody got shot. Somebody named Bella.

Who was Bella?

~

SATURDAY, APRIL 15, 1865

*S*eth pounded the last nail into the joined panels, threw the hammer down, and shouldered the light wooden frame. Although he'd chased his cousin over the countryside for two years with the intention of killing him, he'd never given a thought to making Manny's coffin.

Now, he thanked the Almighty for turning things around. Compassion had replaced the poison of hate when he'd finally acknowledged his own guilt and sinful condition. Providing a decent burial for Manny would be his ultimate act of repentance.

He carried the coffin outside and lifted it into the bed of the wagon. Back inside the shop, he retrieved his coat and hat, then shut the door and climbed over the wagon wheel to take up the reins. "Let's go, Plowboy. This'll be the easiest trip you've made in years."

After he delivered the plain pine box and joined the prison funeral crew for a graveside service, he wanted to check on Lydia. Rose had assured him last night that she'd meet with Millie and Celeste to devise a plan for helping Lydia. One of them would make a trip to the refuge house each day, supplying food and anything else Lydia needed while she served as her husband's nurse. The women took care of those things better than he could, but he'd go by as often as his work allowed.

Seth found he could truly mourn his cousin's passing and wished he could be sure Manny had taken advantage of those last few moments to secure the eternal life offered him. Major Sullivan assigned two men to carry the body to the wagon and keep it steady on the short trip to the cemetery. The major accompanied them, said a few words over the grave, and led them in the Lord's Prayer.

Conversation lagged on the journey back to the prison,

each man keeping company with his own thoughts. As they neared the gate, Major Sullivan spoke.

"Don't suppose you've heard the news yet, Morgan, but you might want to be aware, in case folks get stirred up. President Lincoln was killed last night."

Seth jerked on the reins, shock vibrating through his body. Urging the horse onward again, he shot a look at the major. "What? How did that come to pass?"

"Got a telegram this morning. Some crazed actor attacked him while he was attending a theater performance."

"In full view of the whole theater?" Seth snorted. "I reckon he didn't get far after such a brazen attack."

"Curiously, he did. But the government will find him soon enough, I warrant. I'm just worried about how this will affect our chances of finally ending the war."

Seth rubbed the back of his neck. "I see your point. I won't claim to have any love for the man. Thought he might've done more to avoid a full-out war, but I'm sorry to hear he's been killed. Nobody deserves that."

Sullivan nodded. "It's a sad day when men turn against one another the way we have. I pray every day the Lord will show us the way to peace."

Pulling the wagon to a halt at the front gate of the prison, Seth jumped down while the others scrambled from their seats. "I thank you for all you've done here, Major. If there's anything I can do to return the favor, I hope you'll let me know." He offered his hand in farewell.

"You can count on it, Morgan. Just see you keep your nose clean and stay on guard for your friends." He tipped his head toward the building across the street. "Give Mrs. Gibson my regards when you see her."

Seth's ears warmed at the oblique suggestion, but he merely smiled and asked the guard to keep an eye on the wagon for a little while. Then he sprinted across the road to see how Lydia fared.

~

*L*ydia stood in the hallway with Dorcas, talking quietly while Cal slept. Heavy footsteps on the bare wooden floor interrupted their conversation. Lydia's heart sped up at the sight of Seth striding toward them. She stifled the urge to go to him but drank in his lanky form and the slight upward curve of his mouth as he drew closer.

He stopped an arm's length in front of her, his gaze focused on hers. "How are you and your, uh, patient?"

"We're managing. Seth, I want you to meet my good friend, Dorcas." She gestured to Dorcas and turned to smile at her. But Dorcas's ingrained response was to drop her gaze and dip into a slight curtsey.

Lydia held her breath as Seth's gaze bored into the girl. *Oh, dear. Will we always fall into old habits?*

Before she could think what to do, Seth offered Dorcas a crooked grin. "I believe we met when Doc Spencer and I were here last year."

Dorcas nodded, and Lydia released the breath she'd sucked in.

"As a matter of fact"—Lydia motioned to the three of them —"we were in the same place before that. Seth's the owner of the house where we met last summer."

Seth said, "I hope you're finding Louisville a more pleasant place to live than your previous home."

Dorcas's smile lit her face. "Yes, it's better, but I'll be leaving in two more weeks."

Lydia hugged the girl. "She's getting married, and they're moving West to settle. I'll miss her, but I'm glad she found someone who's *almost* worthy of her. She was a godsend when Amy was born and has turned out to be an excellent cook."

Dorcas waved away the praise. "Thanks to Mrs. Edith and Shiloh, who took time to teach me."

A noise from inside the room halted their conversation. Lydia peeked around the doorframe, but Cal slept on.

"I should get back to the kitchen now," Dorcas said. "I'll bring you a meal before sunset. And you send someone if you need me afore then, you hear?"

"All right, but I think we'll be fine. Thank you for looking out for me."

Dorcas nodded. "Nice to meet you again, Mr. Seth."

Seth performed a brief bow. "And you, Miss Dorcas. I wish you well on your marriage and your move."

As the young woman left, Seth poked his head into the patient's room before he reached for Lydia's hands. "How are you holding up?"

"Fine. Rose came by earlier and brought some food. She said Celeste would come tomorrow." His thumbs stroked the inside of her wrists and distracted her thoughts. She tugged her hands from his and folded her arms at her waist. "Dorcas is staying upstairs until the wedding, so she's dropped by a couple of times to see if I need anything. She offered to take my place for a few hours, but I'm afraid Cal might wake up and give her problems."

Seth tucked his hands in his back pockets.

"I'm glad they're watching out for you. I was over at the prison. The major gave me some concerning news I wanted to pass on. The President of the United States was assassinated last night. Such an event might cause the fighting to flare up again." He shrugged. "I guess it depends on who did it and why. Anyway, just be aware and don't take any chances."

Lydia's laugh held no humor. "I don't expect I'll be going out anytime soon, so I should be fine."

His gaze caressed her. "I'm sorry you must bear this burden alone. You know we're all praying for you and stand ready to help any way we can."

A spate of coughing in the room called Lydia to her duty. "I'd better get back in there."

Seth pursed his lips as if he'd say more but spun on his heel and marched down the hall. Lydia watched him for a moment, then squared her shoulders and turned.

Cal stood at the foot of his cot, steadying himself with a hand on the wall, his eyes glaring with accusation. He pointed his finger at her and demanded an answer. "Who in blazes was that?"

~

Seth retrieved the wagon and drove it back to the mews behind the row of businesses. He unhooked the wagon, released Plowboy from the traces, and rewarded him with an apple for his good behavior. Rather than go directly to the workshop, he climbed the stairs to the store.

The young clerk looked up from his books as Seth greeted him. "Hey, Frank. Where's Luke?"

"Gone to deliver that trinket box you made for the mayor's daughter. Probably stopped by his house for the meal, but he should be back soon."

"He might hear the news from the mayor then."

"What news is that?"

"Someone killed President Lincoln last night."

The clerk dropped his pencil. "You don't say. Who'd want to do a fool thing like that?"

Seth shrugged. "Some fancy actor who didn't like him, I reckon. I expect all the details will be in the newspaper when it comes out."

The front door opened, and Seth turned, expecting Luke to

come striding through. But it was John Mark Anderson, the boy whose room he'd shared when he first came to Louisville. He left the door standing open and barreled to a stop at the clerk's counter, heaving from a recent sprint.

"Hey, John Mark," Seth said. "What's your rush?"

"Ma's having the baby. Gerta sent me to fetch the doctor and to tell Mr. Luke."

Seth exchanged a glance with the clerk. "Did you already go for the doctor?"

"Yessir. He's on his way to the house."

Frank flipped the page in his account book. "Mayor might be bending Mr. Turner's ears with his political jabber. The man can make a speech out of nothing."

Seth figured the boy had done his duty, although Luke wasn't around to get the message. "Tell you what, John Mark. You go down to the workshop and start sanding the cedar chest I finished yesterday. I'll grab Plowboy and go after Luke. If we're not back by closing time, Frank can take you home. Right, Frank?"

The clerk nodded without looking up.

John Mark jumped at the chance to help with the woodworking. He grabbed a peppermint out of the glass jar and followed Seth down the stairs.

After giving the boy a few instructions, Seth headed to the mews. He wasn't sure how Plowboy would take to a saddle, so he hitched up the wagon again and set out for the mayor's farm on the outskirts of town. He'd only been there once but thought he could find it. When the road forked, he paused and pondered which way to go.

*When in doubt, go right.* The words echoed in his father's voice, although he didn't remember the occasion of hearing them. He glanced at the sun and figured he had time to spare, even if he had to retrace his path. He veered right.

A half mile later, he figured he should've gone left, so he

directed the horse in a wide semicircle. Movement in the trees made him pause. His gaze swept the ground and found flattened high grass on the side of the road. An inner voice prodded him to investigate.

His senses on alert, he stopped the horse and climbed over the wheel. Walking into the unknown without a weapon amounted to foolishness, so he surveyed the area for a sturdy branch. The three-foot pine limb would have to serve.

Pushing through a thicket where the track ended, he gave thanks for taking the wrong fork. Luke lay face down at the edge of a group of scraggly pines, blood seeping from a wound on his head.

~

*L*ydia collapsed on the cot and pulled the blanket up to her chin. Cal's cantankerous attitude had exhausted her more than the physical aspect of caring for him. She couldn't understand why he persisted in arguing. *You'd think he'd be thankful to have someone to tend to him.* Perhaps illness merely amplified a person's natural character. Lydia recalled how compliant and apologetic Granny had been during those last weeks, even while she grew sicker.

He'd used up his strength when he confronted her over Seth's visit. She'd said it was someone from the prison come to check on them—a variation of the truth that appeased Cal.

After consuming the broth Dorcas had left, Cal had pushed into a sitting position and instructed Lydia to sit and visit with him. Between coughing spells, he'd wanted to know everything that had transpired during the two last years. Lydia debated what to tell him about Millie and the baby. She didn't want to spark his anger by mentioning Troy or any other McNeil. She told every minor detail she could remember about the mill, the invasion of the Union army, and the trip that eventually landed them in Louisville.

He forced her hand. "You ain't said much about Millie. How is she?"

"She's held up well under these trying circumstances."

"Why hasn't she come to see me?" He crossed his arms like a petulant child, determined to get his way.

"Cal, you're very sick. If she should get sick, too, she'd risk passing it on to the people we're staying with."

"You might get sick."

"Yes, but I'm taking all the precautions I know of. I'll do my best to stay well so I won't pass it on. We don't know how this sickness spreads, but it seems to help to keep the sick ones away from as many people as possible."

"I want to see Millie."

"Cal, be reasonable."

He pointed at Lydia. "She needs to know the truth about her mother and who her father is."

*So that was it.* Lydia sighed. "She knows. Polly left a note, which Millie found and shared with me a few weeks ago. Polly had put it where she wouldn't find it until the right time."

"Where was that?" His brow puckered. "All I recollect Polly left her was a box of baby clothes." He cut accusing eyes at Lydia. "Are you saying Millie's expecting? Did one of them Yanks attack her?"

"No, that's not what happened. She was already in the family way long before the Federal Army came to town."

"Then it was somebody back home. Who was it?"

Lydia shook her head. "She never told me. I asked, but she refused to say." And that was the gospel truth. Millie had never explicitly told her Troy was Amy's father.

"Wild, just like her mama, I reckon. You should've put her out of the house."

Her patience was slipping. "You know I'd never turn her out, especially not when she needed me."

"What about you? Did you take up with some man while I was gone?"

Anger lit Lydia's fuse. "How dare you ask me such a question? Even if I were inclined to be sinful, who was there to take up with? Nobody was left in town except boys and old men."

"You seemed to be surrounded by men here. I saw 'em with you in the prison yard that day, remember?"

"Those are friends, men related to the women at the house where Millie and I stay. You can't judge every woman by what Polly did."

"No, I guess not." Cal's chest deflated, and his eyes slid shut. "Reckon it's like the chaplain at the prison said. I judge everybody by my own actions."

The medicine finally took effect, and he slumped down in the bed and slept.

Worn out from the conversation, Lydia stacked their dishes on the tray and set it outside the room. She had to grab any sleep she could while he was quiet. No telling what he'd be like on the morrow.

~

"*H*e'll be feeling the effects of it tomorrow." Gerta shook her head at Luke's obstinance.

Seth followed her down the stairs, leaving the family gathering in Emily's room. "Aw, you know he's got to take a peek at the baby, Gerta. Why don't you take a break and put your feet up? I'm sure you could do with a few minutes to rest yourself."

The housekeeper, who doted on Luke as much as his own mother, nodded her gray head. "I believe I'll do that. You tell 'em to call me if'n I'm needed." They parted ways at the foot of the staircase.

On his return to the house, Seth had been relieved to find the doctor still lingering in the kitchen after Emily delivered a healthy baby girl. The doctor helped him escort a groggy Luke into the house, then he bandaged and cleaned him up so Luke could totter up the stairs to view the new family member. Seth still hadn't recovered from the shock of finding Luke beaten and tossed off the road. He didn't know how he'd found the strength to lift his friend, who was a head taller and several pounds heavier than Seth.

While he'd wanted to question Luke about the attack, he figured that conversation would wait a few hours. Seth wandered into the parlor at the same time Frank delivered John Mark to the house. The boy nodded but continued straight to the kitchen to wash up, knowing Cook would have a plate set aside for him.

Seth chuckled. "I think the boy intends to make up for missing a few meals last year. He always heads to the kitchen."

He followed the boy and found John Mark seated at the kitchen table, cornbread crumbs dotting his chin. No sign of Cook, but a couple of pastries remained on the plate she'd left. Seth snagged one for himself. "Don't you want to go up and see your new sister?"

The boy groaned. "Ah, shucks. Another girl? That makes three girls and me the only boy since Wade moved with his family to Frankfort. We need to get more boys in this house."

Seth chuckled, guessing future children were a distinct possibility. He saluted John Mark with his half-eaten cookie. "All in good time, my boy, all in good time."

# CHAPTER 25

Sunday, April 16, 1865

*L*ydia woke to a strangely silent room. Burrowing beneath her blanket, she savored the peace and clung to the vestiges of a dream, but it was slipping away like fog in the sunlight. The crunch of wheels carried on a slight breeze through the window casement, and in the distance, church bells called the faithful to gather. A curious smell tickled her nose, and she frowned, trying to identify the familiar pungency.

Blinking to banish the darkness, she gasped at the sunlight slanting across the room's far corner. How long had she slept? She jerked upwards and recalled her location. Turning toward the other cot, she found Cal gazing her way. His hand lifted from the bed, beckoned to her.

Lydia slid from the bed, dragging the blanket over her shoulders. "What is it, Cal? How are you feeling?" From habit, she put her hand to his forehead to test for fever. Warm but not burning as before.

"Lydia," he rasped. "I'm dying."

"No," she said, but the word stuck in her throat. Visions of Granny McNeil's last day flooded her mind. The labored breathing, the unfocused gaze, the grayish pallor. How quickly he'd spiraled downward. She choked back sudden tears and grasped his icy hand. "What can I do for you?"

"Pray. I need...to pray. Repent?" The last word rose in a question. She took it to mean he wasn't sure if he'd used the right word. He must have attended church as a youngster, but he'd always found an excuse when they'd been together. She had no idea what he'd done during the war.

She sank to the floor, amazed by his question. "Yes, you must repent. Simply tell God you're sorry for your sins and ask Him to forgive you. My favorite scripture says He is faithful and will forgive us when we ask. Do you want to do that now?"

He nodded and closed his eyes. After several moments, she thought he might have fallen asleep, but he opened his eyes and squeezed her hand. Realizing his weakness, Lydia offered her help. "Why don't I pray, and if you agree with what I'm saying, you can just say amen at the end? Will that work?"

Another nod and a squeeze. He closed his eyes, and Lydia prayed words that would represent them both. "Lord God, I'm sorry for everything I've done against Your Word and Your law. You said Jesus died for our sins, and I ask You to forgive me of all my wrongdoing. Wash me and make me fit to enter Your kingdom in heaven. I thank You and believe it's done. Amen."

A long moment passed before Cal added his amen. Lydia's conscience pricked her. "And Cal, I need to ask you to forgive me for not being a better wife. I'm sorry for all my fussing and not being the Christian example you needed me to be. Please forgive me."

His lips lifted in a slight smile, and he nodded. Tears stood out in his eyes while he inhaled a slow breath to speak. "Forgive. Bad husband. Do you?"

"Of course, I do." She shifted as her legs cramped from her

odd position on the floor. "I need to see if Dorcas left something for you to eat."

Lydia slipped her fingers from Cal's as he nodded. Braced against the cot, she rose and tottered to the door. A covered dish had replaced the dirty dishes from yesterday. As she picked up the tray, steps in the hallway caught her attention. Celeste and Millie rounded the corner. Millie held a squirming bundle against her shoulder.

Lydia's jaw dropped. "What in heaven's name are you doing here?"

Millie's hold tightened as Amy poked her head around the blanket draped over her. A watery grin broke out as she spied Lydia.

"She wouldn't stop crying for you, so we thought we'd come by on our way to church."

Celeste took the tray from Lydia's hands, and Amy lunged for Lydia.

"Oh, sweet girl. I've missed you so much, but you shouldn't be here."

*Maybe Millie needs to say goodbye.* "If you want to speak to him, this is a good time."

All three women edged into the room. Celeste placed the tray at the foot of the cot, and Millie moved closer to the headboard. "Pa?"

Cal's eyes blinked, then opened wide. "Millie. You came."

Lydia moved closer so he could see Amy. "And she brought your granddaughter to see you. This is Amy."

The baby gazed at Cal as he focused on her. His faint whisper of the baby's name acknowledged her. He looked from Amy to Millie. "Pretty. Like you."

~

*T*he arrival of a new baby set the entire household at sixes and sevens. Seth's tiny apartment above the carriage house provided a haven for the males living in the Turner residence. John Mark had camped out on his worn sofa the night before. J.D. Anderson asked if he could hide out there for an afternoon nap, and Luke forced his battered body up the stairs an hour later.

The swelling in Luke's face had gone down, but the bruises would remain for a while. He groaned with every move, telling Seth, "This may be the only place available on the property for a moment of peace and sanity."

Seth led him to one of the chairs at the table and poured them both a cup of coffee. "It's all I have to offer right now. The bakery's closed on Sunday, and Cook seems to be preoccupied with restorative broths for you and Emily."

Luke nodded. "I know. Every time she sees me, she tries to pour something down my throat." He chuckled and then grimaced at the pain. "I'd forgotten how demanding a baby could be. Victoria's five, or nearly six, as she informs me, and the years have a way of eroding the memories. This was not a good time for what happened to me yesterday."

Seth lifted his cup in a salute. "I'd be glad to hear about it, if you've a desire to share." He sipped the bitter brew while Luke shifted in his chair. "However, you don't owe me any explanation. I'm just glad I found you when I did."

"So am I. I'm not sure there's any further danger, but I'd like you to know the story so you can help me keep an eye on the women."

Frowning, Seth sat forward. "Would the person who attacked you go after them?"

Luke snorted. "Possibly. When Noah was in Louisville late last year, before he and Rose married, one of Rose's questionable *admirers* had her kidnapped."

"Lydia mentioned something about that. Wasn't one of the guards at the refuge house involved?"

"Yeah. Edwin Pierce grew up in the same area as Noah and me. He was a bad influence, and the two of us gave Noah fits for a while. Even as a youth, Noah was serious and a strict follower of rules, so it was easy to rile him up. When Mother realized how badly I'd behaved, she took drastic action. We moved to Frankfort, near my grandfather Turner, and she took a job in Jonas's store."

"The man she eventually married."

"Right. The man who straightened me out in short order. Back in Indiana, though, Pierce accused Noah of defiling his sister Alice. Noah proved that a lie since he'd been away at school when the seduction happened. Pierce would not be persuaded, though, and he carried a grudge against Noah all those years."

Seth leaned back in his chair. "So, he kidnapped Rose to get back at Noah?"

"Yes, but not only for himself. One of our prominent citizens, Vernon Fordham, hired him to do it. Rose had refused Fordham's *carte blanche* offer. She even quit her position at the library to avoid seeing him. That's when she came to work here, as Victoria's governess. I guess Pierce and Fordham knew each other from previous exploits, and the lure of money, plus getting a strike at Noah, was an offer Pierce couldn't refuse."

"But why attack you, and why now?"

Luke shrugged. "I helped Noah bring them down, and Pierce knows it. He was court martialed and jailed, but Horace must have used his influence to get his time reduced."

"Are you sure it was this fellow Pierce? Did you see him? It looked to me like he hit you from behind."

"I heard a noise and turned my head enough to get a glimpse. I couldn't swear it was Pierce, but the height and coloring seemed right." Luke rubbed his nose. "I suppose I've accumulated a few enemies, but I get along with people on both sides of the conflict. Even in a town as diverse as Louisville."

Both men fell to contemplating the situation. Luke sighed at last. "All I know to do is keep our eyes and ears open, in case they try anything else."

"I'm good with that," Seth said. "As long as you don't expect me to move to the main house."

~

Wednesday, April 19, 1865

*L*ydia straightened the room where she'd spent the last few days and stuffed her scant belongings in the valise. With a last glance around, she closed the door and trudged down the hall. Lieutenant Goodwin looked up when she stopped at the office door.

"I cleaned up as best I could, Lieutenant. Dorcas helped me take the mattresses outside to air, and the bed linens are on the line."

He pushed to his feet. "You shouldn't've gone to all that trouble, Mrs. Gibson. I expect you're plumb worn out."

Lydia dredged up a tired smile. "That I am, but I appreciate you letting us stay here. I wouldn't dare leave you a mess to clean up. Now I need to go clean up myself and get back in time for the burial."

He started around the desk. "Do you need me to hitch up the wagon for you?"

"No. No, I'll be fine. It's only a few blocks, but I thank you for offering."

Lydia scurried down the hall and out the front door. Before

she reached the gate, someone called her name from a wagon turning the corner. Seth pulled the vehicle to a stop, handed the reins to Rose, and jumped to the ground.

"Hey, let me take that so you can climb up." He took her bag in one hand and offered the other for support.

When she settled on the seat, she grasped Rose's hand. "How did y'all know?"

"Mr. Morgan here is a forward thinker. He'd asked Major Sullivan to send word whenever he needed another coffin delivered. We just got the word, and we thought it might be for Mr. Gibson, so I asked to come with Seth so I could look in on you."

"Thank the Lord. Lieutenant Goodwin offered to hitch up the house wagon, but I'd rather not be more beholden to him than I am already. However, I wasn't looking forward to the walk."

Rose patted her hand. "Poor thing. I imagine you're nearly past going."

"That's the truth, and I must look a fright, although I'm about too tired to care."

On her other side, Seth leaned against her and whispered. "We'll take care of you."

His nearness suffused Lydia with warmth, but she dared not relax until she'd completed the business of this day. When they reached Mrs. Coker's house, everyone helped. Seth carried the hip bath upstairs, and Celeste heated water on the stove. Mrs. Coker directed Hattie to prepare a light meal. Rose watched Amy while Millie hustled Lydia into her room for the bath and a change of clothes.

"You'll feel much better after you wash and eat. At least, that's what you always told me." Millie pulled a face designed to resemble Lydia at her worst.

Lydia laughed. "When did you become so bossy?"

"I guess it comes with motherhood, although Troy declares I always ordered him around whenever he visited. I think we can manage a hair washing as long as you keep your bonnet on while we're outside, then you can dry it when we get back to the house."

"Yes, Mama." Lydia winked.

Millie soaped Lydia's hair and rinsed it with clear water. After handing Lydia the towels, she plucked a black dress from the wardrobe. "This is a loan from Aunt Lottie. She said it was useless to dye your dresses when she had several that would do. And Celeste found one for me among her clothes."

Lydia fingered the fine material. Though the style had been fashionable a decade before, the dress showed little wear. A few tucks indicated some altering.

"I measured it against your dark green, so it should fit reasonably well."

"My, you ladies were busy while I was away."

"Aunt Lottie said we should be ready for the inevitable. It helped to pass the time and keep us from worrying about you."

They assisted each other with dress buttons and pinned up Lydia's damp hair. At the top of the stairs, Lydia pulled Millie into a hug. "Thank you for taking care of this. I'm glad you took Amy to meet Cal. I think seeing you, getting your forgiveness for his lack of affection, helped him pass onto the other side."

Millie dashed away the dampness on her cheeks. "When I recited the Lord's Prayer like you taught me, I realized I couldn't ask for His forgiveness unless I was prepared to forgive others. I figured nobody ought to die wondering about that."

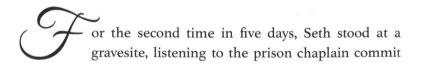

*F*or the second time in five days, Seth stood at a gravesite, listening to the prison chaplain commit the deceased to the earth. At least Lydia could rest easy about her late husband's soul. She'd witnessed the change in him, however short the time had been. Seth could only hope Manny had heeded his pleas and offered such a prayer in his heart before passing from this life.

The minister's voice droned in the stillness. Unlike many funerals, there was no weeping, only a collective relief that Cal hadn't lingered longer and increased the risk of illness to Lydia. She stood between Rose and Millie, who stroked the sleeping baby against her shoulder, with Celeste beside Rose. While the earth sprouted its springtime colors, the women had dressed in darker shades in deference to custom for the occasion.

At the chaplain's nod, Lydia scooped a handful of soil from the mound of earth and sprinkled it over the coffin. She dusted her hands, donned her gloves, and led the way to the carriage Mrs. Coker had insisted they take. Seth assisted each lady into the vehicle, then climbed on the coachman's bench and guided it back the way they'd come a half hour earlier.

He pondered Lydia's cool demeanor. He could excuse it as fatigue and respect for the deceased, but an uneasy feeling plagued him. Replaying their conversations over the last week, he soon arrived at the sticking point. Lydia's commitment to him went no farther than accompanying him to the prison when he'd first arrived. And that was before she'd discovered Cal Gibson alive. Had he misread her interest, perhaps presumed too much based on their exchanged letters? While thoughts of her had sustained him through the harsh months of prison life, Lydia's days had flourished with responsibilities. Family and friends surrounded her, depending on her to uphold her part in their little community.

Seth determined his best plan of action would be to give her time to sort through her feelings before he again broached the subject of marriage. Resigned, he predicted long hours of labor in the workshop to keep his mind off the woman. Perhaps he'd also throw his efforts into figuring out how he could help Luke protect the members of his household against further attacks. Altogether, those things should keep him well occupied for two or three days before his patience ran out.

He stopped the horse in front of Aunt Lottie's house and vaulted to the ground. The front door thudded open as he reached for the carriage handle to let the ladies disembark. Hearing his name, Seth's attention swung back to the house.

John Mark tumbled down the walkway, broadcasting his message. "Mr. Seth, you're needed right away. Pa says to come quick."

*Pa? When had the boy started calling Luke his pa?*

Abandoning the women to scramble down on their own, Seth grasped John Mark's shoulders. "What's happened?" Various scenarios floated through his mind. Fire. Theft. Abduction. Another beating. It must be dire to send the boy so far from home.

Rose and Celeste crowded behind Seth, alarm on their faces. In his peripheral vision, Lydia navigated the carriage steps and reached up to receive Amy from Millie's arms.

Turning to Rose, the boy shook his head. "I'm sorry, Miss Rose. Grandpa said it's a good news, bad news day."

"How's that? What's the good news?"

A broad grin lit his face. "Major Griffin's at the house." The smile wobbled. "Bad news is he's wounded. Mr. Seth needs to get us back there right away."

Celeste took charge. "Don't bother to change vehicles," she said to Seth. "Take Rose in the carriage. I'll get Herbert to help me with the wagon and follow you. John Mark can come with me. We'll swap at Luke's house and bring the carriage back, so you don't have to make an extra trip."

Seth confirmed her quick thinking, said goodbye to Lydia

and Millie, then swung onto the coach bench again as Rose climbed inside. All the way to the Turner house, conjecture about Noah's injuries swirled. Were the major's wounds from a military conflict, or had he fallen prey to the same enemy who'd attacked Luke? Whatever the case, Seth predicted a long night ahead.

# CHAPTER 26

Thursday, April 20, 1865

*A*fter a restless night filled with disturbing dreams, Lydia surrendered the fight at dawn. She dressed and crept downstairs, where the aroma of coffee led her into the kitchen. Herbert nursed a cup of the fragrant liquid while Hattie dropped biscuit dough onto a greased pan. Both offered a surprised greeting at Lydia's early arrival.

Lydia waved the older woman away when she moved toward the coffeepot. "I can pour for myself, Hattie. You just keep making those lovely biscuits so we can all enjoy them in a while."

Herbert examined her face with concern. "It's good to have you back, Miz Lydia, but we thought you might require a few days' rest to recover from the strain of the last week."

Lydia offered a weak smile. "Oddly enough, I found it difficult to rest in such luxurious surroundings. Herbert, did you and Celeste find out what happened to Major Griffin?"

"Only enough to learn he wasn't seriously injured in battle, ma'am. Mr. Seth helped me swap out the vehicles while Miss Celeste went inside to see if she was needed."

"Did I hear my name?" Celeste breezed into the room and went straight to the coffee. "That house was so full of people, I didn't want to add to their number. Rose promised they'd visit in a day or two so everyone can hear Noah's story. At least he verified the war is ending, with other Confederate generals laying down their arms."

Millie entered the kitchen in time to hear this last pronouncement. She bounced Amy on her hip. "You hear that, sweetness? The war will soon be over, and your daddy will be coming either to stay with us or take us to live with him."

Lydia's heart clenched. Their prayers for the war to end had been answered, but it would bring more changes. She wasn't sure if she was ready for them.

As if she'd read Lydia's mind, Hattie bent a stern look her way. "Now, don't anyone be in a hurry to leave us. Miz Coker was worryin' over that last night before goin' to bed." She set a platter of biscuits on the table and turned away.

Herbert patted his wife's arm. "There's plenty of room here, and having you all has brought new life back into us old folks."

"And a lot more work," Lydia said. She snatched two steaming biscuits and put one on Millie's plate. "More clothes and dishes to wash, more food to cook, more rooms to clean."

"And more laughs and love to go around," Hattie insisted. "I reckon we've become each other's family."

"None of us knows what the future holds," Celeste said, "but I daresay nothing will ever be as it was. The newspapers speculate the government will appoint new governors for all the states that joined the Confederacy. I don't think it would be wise to return to Georgia just yet."

"From what we saw on our way here," Lydia said, "it's gonna be a long time before the South recovers, with property and businesses destroyed everywhere. Not to mention the lives lost on both sides."

Amy interrupted the somber mood with her gurgling as she reached for Lydia's cup. "No, ma'am, no coffee for you. It's too hot."

"Ha," the baby repeated. All the adults exclaimed over her cleverness, and Amy beamed at their praise.

A thud and clatter on the stairs spurred everyone to action. Lydia arrived a step behind Celeste to find Mrs. Coker lying near the bottom step, one leg extended from her skirts at an odd angle. No moans or mild curses from the woman suggested her condition.

Lydia clutched her throat at the sight. *Oh, my Lord. She's broken her neck and died while we sat at her table drinking coffee.*

~

*S*eth set down his cup of cold coffee and laid aside the newspaper he'd been reading. He stood and started to toss the tepid brew but stopped. How many times over the last few years would he have been glad for such a treat? He moved to the mercantile stove and checked the temperature of the pot there, then added the warm liquid to his cup.

The war might be over, but its effects lingered on.

Reflecting on the articles he'd just read, he shook his head. Unfortunately, the craziness hadn't stopped. The United States government had enough to handle with trying to clean up the destruction, and now everything halted while the nation mourned the loss of President Lincoln.

The door to the mercantile swung open and drew his attention.

"Mornin'." Frank rubbed his hands together and hurried to the stove. "Cool out there today," he said as he poured coffee into his cup. "I heard y'all had another guest show up last night."

Seth raised his brows. "News travels fast."

"John Mark showed up early to borrow my fishing pole. Said he was gonna find someplace quiet. Too many people at home bossin' him around."

Seth grimaced. "I guess he's right about that. Boys his age don't like to be shut in with so many adults." He set aside his cup. "Well, I'd better head on down to the shop and start on that table Mr. Duncan ordered."

He grabbed his jacket and took long strides across the floor. He reached to flip the sign in the window so the *"Open"* side faced the street but stepped back in surprise when a face peered at him from the other side of the glass. Though a beard sprouted on a chin usually scraped clean and his frame showed the deprivations of hard times, there was no denying the face of Meg's brother staring back at him.

Seth jerked the door open with a shout. "Will Larsen, you rascal." He embraced the other man and urged him inside.

Will leaned into Seth's arms and gripped his shoulders. "I've found you," he said, his voice suspiciously close to a sob. "At last, at long last."

"What do you mean? No, never mind. Come over here and have some coffee to warm you up." Seth tossed his coat on the counter and guided Will to a chair near the stove. "Will, this here's Frank George, our clerk. Frank, this is my friend from home, Will Larsen. I think I'll visit with him a while before I go down to the workshop."

Seth pressed his lips together and motioned Frank to the other side of the store.

The clerk scrambled from his chair and nodded at the newcomer. "Nice to meet you, Larsen. You two sit and talk. I'll be at the counter if you should need me."

Will sank onto the cane-bottom chair, heaving a sigh. He stretched his hands toward the heat and suppressed a shiver.

Seth emptied the pot into a clean cup. "I'm afraid it's strong enough to talk back to you, but it's the real stuff. I can add honey and canned milk, if you like."

His friend waved off the offer. "No, this is fine." He sipped with caution, holding the cup with both hands.

Seth brought another chair closer and took stock of Will's condition. His coat and trousers were layered with dirt, rendering the color a deep brown rather than butternut. His shoes looked to be held together with twine. Had his golden hair darkened, or was that also courtesy of travel dust? None of that information answered his most pressing question

"Why did you come here instead of going home?" Seth regretted his outburst when Will turned smoldering eyes his way.

"What home? Mrs. Roland wrote to tell me the Yanks burned everything but the outhouse. Mama's in Brunswick with Aunt Ivy. Joe's gone. Meg's gone. You're the closest family member I got."

Seth gazed at his feet. "I didn't know about Joe or your house. I'm sorry, Will. You're welcome to stay here, of course. I'm amazed you found me."

A crooked smile lit Will's face. "You know how to make an impression on people, Seth, everywhere you go. Stealing a cavalry officer's horse, startin' fights, and convincin' folks you're crazy out of your mind. And yet you hook up with the strangest group."

"How's that? What strange group?"

"A Georgia doctor and his wife, who happens to be the daughter of a Yankee merchant in Frankfort."

Seth sat forward. "Wait. You met Doc Spencer and Jonas Richardson?"

"Nah, but I heard a feller tellin' about the doctor and his

wild patient at Camp Chase, who took the oath and got escorted by a guard to Frankfort. That man worked at the Richardson mercantile there. All I had to do was ask a few questions to find out you come to Louisville lookin' for a feller named Peacock." Will's smile dimmed, and his gaze bored into Seth's. "I need to know if you found him, Seth. Did you make that miserable good-for-nothing pay for killing my sister?"

~

MONDAY, MAY 1, 1865

*L*ydia ushered Gideon Hart into Mrs. Coker's room. He leaned over the bed and patted the wrinkled hand lying at the woman's side. "Well, Grandmother, I certainly didn't expect to return from the war and find you'd nearly killed yourself taking a tumble down the stairs."

Lydia hovered near the foot of the bed, ready to offer assistance. The doctor's firm instructions demanded Mrs. Coker not be left alone until he gave permission.

Lieutenant Hart had returned from Virginia only minutes earlier. When he'd heard of his grandmother's accident, he rushed up to her room to announce his arrival and see how she fared.

The old woman offered a weak chuckle. "I always told you I'd go out in high fashion, didn't I?"

"At least your sense of humor wasn't damaged," he said. "Although it seems you broke or bruised every other part."

Lydia smiled at the easy banter between them. She turned at the clatter of dishes near the door, where Celeste entered, carrying a tray laden with cups and a teapot. The officer jumped to assist her and set the tray atop a doily on a bedside table.

Celeste thanked him. "Hattie insisted I bring some

refreshment for Lieutenant Hart since he didn't wait for it in the parlor." She arranged the dishes and poured tea in the cups.

"Hmpf." Mrs. Coker grunted. "I hope she sent enough for all of us and some scones too. I could use a bit of sustenance myself. Not planning to stay in this bed forever, you know."

Lydia helped the woman sit up and set a platter across her lap. "Now, Aunt Lottie, remember what the doctor said. You must allow yourself time to heal."

Celeste added, "Yes, and Hattie has sent your favorite black-berry preserves and cinnamon cakes." She handed the plate to Lydia, who offered it to the woman in bed. "We're all doing our best to spoil you so you won't try to move about and risk another fall."

The lieutenant stood by the bedside, no doubt waiting for the women to be done with their ministrations so he could resume his visit.

Lydia tapped Celeste's arm. "Since Lieutenant Hart is here to help watch over our patient, perhaps I'll slip downstairs to check on Millie and Amy."

A slight blush dusted Celeste's cheeks as she nodded. "I ought to see if Hattie needs me." She took hesitant steps toward the door.

"No." Lydia put out a hand. "Stay in case the lieutenant should require help here."

The gentleman looked up and added his request. "Please stay, Miss Carrigan. I promise to behave myself. After all, Grandmother may be bedridden, but her eyes and ears seem in fine shape, and she'll keep me in line."

Mrs. Coker gave a raspy chortle. "If he acts up, I'll tell stories of his boyhood mishaps."

The lieutenant groaned, and Celeste smiled as she took the chair on the other side of the bed.

Lydia hadn't planned to play matchmaker, but it was clear

that those two had taken a fancy to each other. A little push might give one of them the courage to speak up.

She found Millie sitting on the parlor floor with Amy. The baby could sit up well enough to play with the rag doll and wooden spoons in her lap. Lydia lowered herself to the rug and leaned so Amy could see her. "Hello, my angel. Are you having a good day? I see you've already given Dolly her bath with your drool."

The child squealed and grinned in response. She flailed her arms and reached out.

"No, I can't pick you up now. Mommy wants you to sit and play a while, so you'll be ready for a nap." Lydia picked up the doll and bounced it in Amy's lap to redirect her attention.

Millie rested against the upholstered Queen Anne chair behind her. "How's Aunt Lottie?"

"Holding her own for now," Lydia said. "Of course, having the lieutenant here brightened her day considerably. I'm still pondering what the doctor said."

"Me too. I know she's old, but she's always been so spry. It's hard to believe a tumble down the stairs could be set her back."

"She's gonna be wantin' out of that bed before long, I'm afraid. We'll have our hands full keepin' her there."

Millie's eyes flickered with fear. "I've grown to love her, and I pray she recovers soon. But Lydia. If she dies, what'll we do? Where will we go?"

"Oh, I expect you and Amy will go wherever Troy goes." Lydia patted Millie's hand. "When he gets his orders, he should have a few days to come and collect y'all before he has to report to his new location."

Millie nodded. "Like Ruth in the pastor's sermon yesterday, we'll go where he goes and trust God to take care of us." She inhaled sharply. "You'll come with us, won't you? You know we both want you to."

Lydia shook her head. "No, dear. Y'all don't need a stepmother living with you when you start out. I'll stay here in Louisville with Aunt Lottie until I'm no longer useful."

"But if she dies, what will happen? If the house goes to Lieutenant Hart, he might decide to sell it. Then where would you be?"

"You worry too much, sweetie." Lydia pushed herself up and lifted Amy, who yawned widely and settled against Lydia's chest. Kissing the baby's forehead, she willed away the vision of a future without this little one nearby. "We should know by now that nothing is certain. We'll take life as it comes and trust God to see us through whatever happens."

She carried her sweet burden upstairs and laid her in the old-fashioned crib brought down from Mrs. Coker's attic. She fought back the tears and stiffened her spine. The verses she'd read in Jeremiah that morning settled into her heart. "Thus saith the Lord of hosts, the God of Israel, unto all that are carried away captives, whom I have caused to be carried away ... Build ye houses and dwell in them ... And seek the peace of the city whither I have caused you to be carried away captives ... and therefore ye shall have peace."

The words seemed directed to her. She'd stay and see what the future held. It wasn't as if she'd be completely alone. She had friends here. Good friends in Rose and Celeste. Emily and her family were just across town at Luke Tanner's house.

And Seth. He'd been a big help during the last few weeks. Despite the image he'd developed during his time as a prisoner, he'd always showed compassion toward women. His letters to her revealed humor and a deep sense of loyalty to those close to him.

Did he still want to marry her? When he'd suggested it in February, it had been too soon after his return to Louisville. Then events had spiraled out of control, from Seth's confrontation with his cousin to Cal's death. She hadn't seen Seth since

Cal's funeral. Was he so busy, or did he think she needed time to mourn?

She wouldn't find any answers sitting in the house. She'd have to find a way to ask if his offer was still available. Could she work up the courage to do what Ruth in the Bible had done? Seek him out and pressure him to renew his offer? She shrank at the thought of such boldness. Could she commit her life to another man for the sake of security? That had proven a mistake before.

One thought bolstered her. Seth was not Cal.

# CHAPTER 27

Thursday, May 3, 1865

*A* mighty sneeze rent the air behind Seth, causing him to look up from the dresser top he sanded. He laughed as Luke fished a handkerchief from his back pocket and covered his nose.

"I don't know how you can work with all this sawdust flying around." Luke blew his nose. "I think I'd have to find another occupation or else plug my nose and keep my eyes closed."

Seth removed his spectacles and waved them in the air. "I find these help protect my eyes. As for the dust, I reckon I've breathed it so long I don't pay it any attention." He traded his sandpaper for a rag and wiped his hands. "I'll sweep up this mess before I leave today. What brings you down here? Must be important to make you brave the flying bits of tinder."

Seth motioned to a couple of chairs, but Luke ignored them. Instead, he paced a few steps away to fiddle with the latch on a dresser drawer. "You were married back in Georgia, right? So, you know something about women."

A snort prefaced Seth's answer. "If you're implyin' I might

understand how they think, you are far off the mark, my friend."

"But you have experience with how they react, how...unpredictable they can be."

"What're you gettin' at, Luke? You got trouble brewin' on the home front? Do I need to make room for you in the carriage house?" He made light of the situation, but he worried about what might be coming. Will had moved into the small apartment with Seth until his friend could land a job and get his own room. They had to dance around each other in those limited quarters, but neither could afford another place.

"I hope not. Here's the thing. I had a note from...a friend back home, asking me to meet for a meal tomorrow at the hotel. To prevent any misunderstanding or ugly gossip getting back to Emily, I'd like you to accompany me." Luke stuffed his hands in his pockets. The jingle of coins betrayed his anxiety.

"All right." Seth studied Luke's face while he pondered the request. "You're not exactly looking forward to this meeting, are you?"

Luke pursed his lips and shook his head.

"Mind telling me why you think having me along will help?"

Luke paced away, then turned back. "It's a girl—a woman now—from my younger and wilder days. She's rather aggressive and—"

"Pretty?"

"Yeah."

"And you're afraid word will get back to Emily that you dined with a pretty young woman, a stranger to Louisville."

Luke clutched Seth's arm. "But if you're with me, nobody will know whether she's there to meet you or me. Safety in numbers. No fodder for the gossips. Plus, you can run interference for me if Florence gets pushy."

"Why didn't you ask Noah? Wouldn't he know this woman too? That way, it'd just be a reunion of old friends."

"But Noah has Rose to worry about and—"

"He turned you down."

"Yeah. As the only single man, you're the best choice."

"Frank's single." Seth couldn't hold back his grin.

Luke guffawed. "And about as discreet as a struttin' rooster at daybreak." He sobered. "So, you'll do it? I know I can trust you to do what's necessary."

Seth blew a huff of agreement. "Yeah, I'll be your nanny to keep the bullies at bay. Besides, my curiosity's stirred now. I'm eager to meet this gal who's got you shakin' in your boots."

"Just hold on to your suspenders. She might take a liking to you."

Friday, May 4, 1865

*L*ydia observed her reflection in the milliner's window. While it might look like she was admiring the hats displayed there, she wanted to be sure she presented a decent appearance. Showing up at the mercantile was unremarkable, but she'd never before tried to win a man's regard. The prospect worked on her nerves and tied her stomach in knots.

What if Seth had changed his mind? Or forgotten he'd ever suggested marriage? So much had happened since then. Lydia hadn't seen him in weeks. He was at work during her visits with Rose, and now, according to Rose, a friend of his had arrived and moved into the carriage house with him. If Lydia wanted to know Seth's feelings, she had to take the initiative.

So here she was. She hoped he'd be in the store and not in the workshop. Going there would be too forward. Rose had indicated Seth usually took his midday meal with the clerk, so he should be in the store. She drew in a deep breath and opened the door.

Various scents competed for her attention, the most prominent being tobacco and leather. A few people milled around, but no one noticed her entrance. A woman and a girl dug through the fabrics while a man in coveralls examined the tools on a rack of shelves. The clerk at the counter tallied the cost of items placed there by a young couple with a baby. He glanced up long enough to nod to Lydia and say, "Be with you soon."

Thankful for a moment to gather her courage, she wandered to the collection of threads and buttons. She selected a spool of white and one of pink to finish a dress for Amy. Moving farther to the back, she spied several small chests on a three-tiered table near the rear of the store. She traced their graceful lines and smooth finish, certain they were all products of Seth's workshop.

The back door opened, and Lydia's heart raced, then plummeted. It wasn't Seth. This man was taller and possibly younger, with wavy blond hair and brown eyes.

He smiled as he looked her way. "Hello. Do you need help with something? Not that I'm familiar with everything in here. But I could tote something for you if needed."

"Uh, no. I was just looking at these lovely chests. I only came for thread." Lydia opened her hand to reveal the spools she'd picked out. She turned back toward the front, then spun around. "Do you know if Mr. Morgan is around?"

Surprise lit the man's face. "Seth? No, he went with Mr. Turner to the hotel. That's why I'm here." He held out his hand. "I'm Will, by the way. Seth's brother-in-law."

Understanding dawned. "Oh." Lydia accepted his friendly gesture. "You're Meg's brother." She'd seen Meg's picture months ago in Marietta and remembered it well enough to make the connection.

Will's eyebrows rose, and his jaw clenched. He dropped her hand. "How did you know?"

Heat seeped into Lydia's face. It was a reasonable question, but it felt awkward to explain her relationship with Seth. "We, uh, that is, I was in the group of mill workers from New Manchester who were routed to Marietta before coming to Louisville. The Federals put us in Seth's house for a few days."

"Oh, you're one of the women who helped him when he got sick. Yeah, he told me about that. What's your name?"

"Lydia Gibson." She smiled, but her anxiety returned full force. What was she doing? How could she compete with the memory of beautiful Meg Morgan? Even if Seth could overlook her shortcomings, she doubted this young man would. She'd be compared to Meg and found wanting. Cal's frequent taunts rang in her ears. Plain. Persnickety.

She grasped her skirts and headed to the counter. "Well, it was nice to meet you, Will. I need to get back now. Perhaps I'll see you around later."

Thankful the other customers had left, Lydia pulled out her coins to pay for the thread.

"You want that in a bag?" the clerk asked.

"No, thank you." She snatched up the spools and scurried to the door.

~

Seth followed Luke into the opulent lobby of the Riverton Hotel on Market Street. He admired the gleaming wood floors and workmanship of the cherry staircase that rose behind the registration counter then divided and curved into two staircases at the landing. Bold lettering graced the arched doorway on either side of the lobby and identified the areas beyond: Smoking Room and Restaurant.

They crossed to the restaurant, where an employee in a blue-and-gold uniform greeted them.

"We're meeting a friend here," Luke said in a low voice. "Mrs. O'Brien. Has she been seated?"

The man covered his fleeting expression of surprise and picked up two menu cards. "Right this way." He started across the busy area, where businessmen in dark suits occupied the tables, along with a few military officers, their rigid posture as indicative as their blue coats.

Near the window, Seth's alert gaze found the lone female, who looked up as they drew near. Probably once a stunning beauty, Florence O'Brien's dark brown hair was pulled into a chignon and topped with a triangular beige hat covered with feathers and netting. Beige piping trimmed the collar and sleeves of a dark blue jacket.

Her eyes widened as the attendant snagged a third chair from an empty table and placed the menu cards in front of the empty chairs.

"I'll have your waiter bring another place setting immediately," he said, then darted away.

Luke clapped Seth on the shoulder and urged him forward. "Mrs. Florence O'Brien, may I introduce my friend Seth Morgan? Seth has recently relocated to Louisville and is my partner in supplying furniture in the area."

Seth hoped he didn't reveal his surprise at this introduction. Partner? The term signified a higher relationship than Seth had figured. Of course, Luke didn't want to blurt out Seth's recent occupation in the Confederate Army, but his accent would give him away soon enough. He executed a proper bow as Luke completed his duty. "Mrs. O'Brien is an old friend from my childhood home in Indiana."

Best to keep his mouth shut as long as possible. "Ma'am."

The woman tilted her head his way. "Mr. Morgan. Please, won't you both be seated?"

Luke chose the seat across from her, leaving Seth to take the one between them. The proper spot for a mediator—or a referee. He hoped this didn't turn ugly.

~

*L*ydia wandered down the street in a daze. How could she think Seth would be interested in her when his wife had been such a beauty? What had prompted him to even mention marriage to her? Pity for her lack of resources? She huffed. Oh, that was a fine basis for a lifelong sentence, wasn't it?

But he'd just returned from the prison camp, so perhaps his judgment had suffered from that experience. He'd been concerned about facing his cousin at last. Afraid he might not be able to control his rage and thereby bring more trouble down on his head.

While she wandered, mired in thought, her feet took her to the bakery where she sometimes worked. Her growling stomach reminded her of the time and her light breakfast. She opened the door. It had been weeks since she'd seen the Watfords, so a visit was in order. Besides, nothing soothed a bruised heart like a piece of cake.

Half an hour later, she left the bakery in a better frame of mind. The dear old couple had assuaged her feelings with friendship and laughter. They'd insisted she should come back to work whenever she could arrange it and then sent her off with a bagful of sweets that "would just go in the trash bin" if she didn't take them.

Since Cal's death, Lydia had avoided taking the route that led to Tenth and Broadway. Too many memories involving the prison and the refugee house. Besides, all the people she'd known in those places had moved on. From the bakery, she strolled down Market Street, which took her past various shops and businesses, now bustling with activity. Some people hurried to their appointments while others ambled along and enjoyed the mild weather.

She slowed as the Riverton Hotel loomed in her vision. Wasn't that where Will had said Seth and Luke had gone? Perhaps she'd see them as she passed and finagle a way to talk to Seth. Maybe then she could gauge Seth's reaction and determine whether he was still interested in a relationship.

~

*S*eth followed Luke's lead and ordered the daily special.

When the server left, Luke offered Mrs. O'Brien a tepid smile. "You're looking well, Florence. So, what brings you to our fair city?"

The woman's soft laughter parried. "Getting right to the point, Luke? What happened to the Turner charm? Have you forgotten how to use it?" Without giving him time to answer, she continued. "I have plans that require me to bring you up to date on certain matters."

"I fail to see how your plans could affect me. It's been years since we've seen each other. I thought your family moved away about the same time as Mother and I did."

The arrival of their food interrupted the conversation, but Florence answered as soon as the waiter left. "Our last meeting was rather strained, you may recall. After a while I gave up on the thought of ever seeing you again, but when certain changes took place and I learned you'd settled in Louisville, it became clear that I needed to arrange for this meeting."

Luke chewed over that information while they all made inroads on the meal. Seth savored the delicious food, thankful the days of privation had ended. With polite but discreet interest, he observed the interaction between his dinner partners, measuring the carefully contained tension at the table. If Luke had expected this woman to make overtures toward either of them, he seemed to be off the mark.

"You spoke of changes," Luke said. "What could have happened that would prompt you to seek me out?"

The coquette took a sip of her tea and smiled. "Are you sure you want to discuss this in front of Mr. Morgan?"

"Seth can be trusted with whatever you have to say, Florence. Let's stop dancing around the issue and get to it."

"Ah, dancing. That's what led to our relationship, wasn't it?"

Luke growled. "The issue, Florence."

"An appropriate word, issue. I believe that's a general term used in the Bible to designate children. The issue, Luke, is our child. Our son who has long believed his father was Joseph O'Brien."

A quick indrawn breath was the only sign of Luke's surprise. "What did you say?"

Florence leaned forward, gripping her utensils in both hands. "You left town before I could tell you, supposedly whisked away by your mother to remove you from bad influences. When my parents learned of my condition, they sent me to Aunt Maude in Bloomington. That's where I met Joseph. I married a man more than twice my age in order to legitimize my baby. My parents died before the war, then Joseph died in sixty-three, leaving me alone with a young son. I moved back home with Grandma Walker. She died in January, and the house went to Cousin Ernest."

Seth's sympathy was stirred, as was Luke's, judging by the frown and furrowed brow. He cleared his throat. "I'm sorry for your loss." Luke opened his mouth to say more, but Florence didn't let him continue.

"I don't need your pity, Luke. I am not destitute. I have money but no permanent home, and I've decided it's time to do what I want to do."

Luke cocked his head. "What is it you want to do?"

"I'm going to enroll in a school to become a nurse." She set her utensils down and smoothed the tablecloth. "I've already put the plan in motion. I'll be traveling to New York next month to begin. However, I cannot fulfill my duties as a parent when I will be in classes and studying at all hours. So, it's time for you to accept your responsibility as Nate's father. He will stay here with you until I finish my schooling."

If Luke's head was spinning as much as his, Seth pitied him. *I'm merely an observer of this news. Poor Luke is caught in the middle of it.*

⁓

*L*ydia had lingered near the hotel entrance as long as she dared. Even in her Sunday best, she wouldn't be brave enough to enter the fine hotel and take a chance on being escorted to the door by some proper personage. She shifted the package of sweets to her other hand and moved to the corner, ready to cross the street. A bank of windows followed the curve of the walkway and provided a view of the outside to the diners in the restaurant.

Lydia tried to disguise her interest in the occupants, but her gaze caught a sudden movement at a table near the window. An elegant woman stood, her attention on the man who bowed over her hand. The man then touched the woman's shoulder to usher her away from the table.

Unless Lydia was seeing things, the man was Seth Morgan.

She jerked her head away and stepped blindly off the curb into the path of a dray wagon.

# CHAPTER 28

$S$eth quickened his step to catch up with Luke as he exited the building. The scream of horses and shouts of a driver drew Seth's attention to the corner. The driver fought to bring his animals under control while a woman fell in the street.

Seth sprang into action without thinking. Luke sprinted beside him, his longer legs outpacing Seth's. Another man joined them as Luke approached the woman.

"Wait, don't move her yet," the third man said. A mop of black hair with liberal splashes of gray drifted over his ears, setting off a beardless chin and hawkish nose. His voice brooked no argument. "I'm a doctor. We need to be sure we won't injure her further."

From his seat atop the vehicle, the driver alternately cursed and pleaded innocence. "She just stepped right in front of me afore I could slow the horses."

A lanky boy stood by the far horse, holding the bridle and speaking in a soft voice to calm the creatures.

Seth hung back while Luke went to speak with the driver. The doctor ran his hands over the female's lower limbs up to her waist, then checked her arms before pushing aside the bonnet that hid her face. Seth's heart dropped when he recognized Lydia's flaxen hair framing a pale face. He must have said her name out loud because the doctor looked up.

"You know her?"

"Yes. She's my...a friend. From back in Georgia."

Luke shot him a questioning glance but turned to the doctor. "Can she be moved now? My gig is just up the street, and we know where she's staying."

The doctor narrowed his eyes as if debating whether to entrust Lydia to their care. "I think it would be best to take her to my office. It's around the corner. I'd like to keep an eye on her until she comes around."

All three of them reached for her, but Luke backed off when Seth shot him a look. The doctor must have read Seth's expression too. He helped lift her but allowed Seth to bear her weight. He adjusted his bowler. "Does she have any limitations that you're aware of? Her hearing or vision, perhaps?"

Seth shook his head.

They followed the doctor to a small house squeezed between two taller buildings. A placard on the door identified it as the office of Dr. Uriah B. Yates.

As they mounted the steps, Luke touched Seth's arm. "I think I'll go to the house and get one of the women. Lydia would probably rather have one of them here when she wakes up."

Seth nodded his agreement. "Good idea."

Luke reversed his direction while Seth trailed Dr. Yates through a small parlor and into the first room behind it. He lowered Lydia to the table in the middle of the room. She emitted a soft moan as she settled but didn't waken.

Seth loosened the ribbons of her bonnet and let them fall to the side. "Is it normal for her to still be unconscious?"

Dr. Yates looked up from the drawer where he rifled

through his medical instruments. "It's not unusual with a blow to the head. Hopefully, she'll wake up soon." He moved to Lydia's side and stretched out a hand to Seth. "Dr. Yates, by the way."

"Seth Morgan." He accepted the handshake but kept his eyes on Lydia.

The doctor lifted a listening device like one Seth had seen Evan Spencer use. He motioned to Lydia. "I'm going to do a more thorough examination now. You can wait in the outer room if you like."

Seth glared. "I'd rather stay."

"How do you think she'd feel about that?"

"I've asked her to marry me," he said, hoping that answer would satisfy.

Doctor Yates raised his eyebrows. "Did she accept?"

Seth crossed his arms. "She wanted to think about it. We've had a rough time since coming here, but I don't want her to wake up to a stranger."

The doctor huffed. "All right, you can stay. But if she wakes and says otherwise, you'll have to wait outside."

"Luke's gone to bring one of the women back. I'll stay around until they get here."

<<>>

*L*ydia couldn't make out the voices she heard. Were they in a cave or a tunnel? Someone touched her neck and lifted her head. Gentle hands probed her hair, pulling hair pins from their place. Sudden pain caused her to gasp.

"Lydia," a voice called. "I think she's waking up."

*Whose voice was that? She should recognize it.*

"Call her name again," another said.

"Lydia. Can you hear me?"

*Seth? It couldn't be. Why would he be in her bedroom?*

She struggled to open her eyes. "Seth?"

His face floated above her, and he squeezed her hand. "Yes, I'm here. Just take it easy now. Don't try to get up just yet." His hand held her shoulder in place when she tried to sit up. "You've had an injury."

"Where are we?"

"We're in a doctor's office," he said. "Fortunately, he was nearby when the accident happened, so we brought you here."

A clean-shaven face peered at her from the other side. His smile and gentle hazel eyes contrasted with the unruly mane springing in all directions. "Hello, Lydia. I'm Doctor Yates. You're going to be fine, but I'd like you to stay where you are for a few minutes more."

Seth still gripped one hand, for which she was grateful. She lifted her other hand to the pain above her eyes and found a bandage. "What happened?"

Seth exchanged a glance with the doctor, then slanted a grin her way. "You had a run-in with a delivery wagon."

Noise from another room caught his attention. "That'll be Luke and whoever he found at the house, I imagine. We figured you'd want another female with you." He cocked his head. "Sounds like Rose. I'll go out and let her come in." He offered an encouraging smile as he released Lydia's hand and slipped out of the room.

Lydia worried over his explanation. She directed her question to the physician. "I was hit by a wagon? How did that happen?"

The doctor patted her hand. "I didn't see it, but I'm glad I was nearby. Your friends might have moved you too soon and caused more damage. They seemed surprised to see you, though, so I suppose you were alone when you started across the street."

A timid knock on the door jamb announced Rose's arrival. "Hello. I'm Rose Griffin, a friend of Lydia's. May I come in?"

The doctor nodded, and Rose took up the place Seth had vacated. "Oh, Lydia. I'm glad to see you're awake. Is there anything I can do for you?"

"I guess that depends on what the doctor says. When will I be able to leave?"

He lifted each of her eyelids and peered inside. He pulled aside the bandage at her head and surveyed the area. "The swelling seems to be diminishing, so I don't think you'll suffer any ill effects from that. I didn't detect any broken ribs or other significant injuries. However, you might find a few bruises, and I expect you'll be quite sore for a day or two."

He drummed his fingers on the table. "I suppose you can go home now, if you feel up to it." He drew a packet from his pocket. "If the pain gets to be more than you can bear, mix a pinch of these powders in water and drink it. Also, a warm bath should ease the soreness."

Rose patted Lydia's hand. "We'll take care of that. Let me have the men come help you out to the carriage." She went to the doorway and called for Seth and Luke.

Doctor Yates helped Lydia sit up and swing her legs over the table side. "Sit there a minute before you try to stand, else we might be picking you up off the floor."

Lydia clutched his hand and closed her eyes as the dizziness hit her. "Whoa."

"Don't be alarmed. That's perfectly normal." He slid an arm around her waist. "I won't let you fall."

Swift steps crossed from the door. "She won't have to worry about falling. I'll carry her out to the buggy."

At Seth's strident tone, Lydia looked up. What had his dander up? "I'm sure I can walk as long as someone helps me."

"No need. It's only a short distance." He moved close, and the doctor scooted away. "Just put your arm around my neck."

Seth slid one hand beneath her legs and the other around her back. He smelled of bergamot and peppermint. Like he'd had some stick candy after a meal.

The scene at the restaurant came back. He'd been assisting another woman. "Who was she?"

"Who was who? What are you talking about?" Seth huffed as he lifted her off the table.

Lydia cringed. Had she said that out loud? The knock to her head must be worse than she thought.

<<>>

*S*eth hauled Lydia into his arms with more force than gentleness. His brain said he was being unreasonable. The doctor had merely been caring for her as a patient. He'd witnessed Evan display the same kind of tender aid to men in the prison camp. Those admonitions didn't appease the raw emotion that flooded him now. Seeing her in Yates's embrace had his nerves vibrating like a tuning fork on a piano string.

Then she whispered against his neck, sprinkling tingles down his spine so intense he had to tighten his hold to keep from dropping her. Those words, though. *Who was she?* He couldn't fathom their meaning.

He glanced into Lydia's face. "Who was who?"

She didn't answer but rested her face against his shirt. Though he strove for a normal pace, Seth had the sensation of slogging through mud. His fingers flexed involuntarily where they held her in place. He resisted the urge to rub his chin against the top of her head.

"Get the door, Luke," he said and slowed enough to allow it. Behind him, Seth could hear Rose and Luke speaking to the doctor, something about paying him. Chagrin pinched Seth's lips. He should have asked about the payment. After all, Lydia was his...his what?

He nearly stumbled through the gate. Carrying her like this reminded him of his long-ago wedding day when he'd lifted Meg over the threshold of their home. The pain that went with that memory had diminished over time.

Seth lifted Lydia onto the rear carriage seat and took his place beside her. He slid his arm along the bench top behind her but maintained a respectable distance. He wanted to ask her about what she'd said, but Luke and Rose arrived.

Luke picked up the reins. "You let me know if the pace is too much for you, Miz Lydia, or if you need to stop for any reason."

"Thank you. I'm sure I'll be fine." Contrary to her assurances, she sank against the cushions and soon leaned against Seth's side. "Oh, I'm sorry," she said, pushing to right herself again.

They'd left the busier streets of town and entered the tree-sheltered avenue that led to the Coker house. Seth pulled her closer and whispered into her hair. "It's all right. You'll soon be home."

She ceased resisting and remained close until they reached the Coker residence. As soon as Luke pulled the horses to a halt, Rose turned in her seat. "I'll go in and let everyone know what's happened. I'm sure you gentlemen need to get back to your work, so don't feel you have to linger. I'm happy to stay a while." She looked at Luke. "Perhaps you can have Noah come back for me when he's finished his meeting."

Luke nodded and helped Rose from the carriage. Seth shifted away from Lydia, climbed over the side, and reached back to lift her down.

Lydia wobbled, then found her balance and took a step away. "I believe I can walk now."

Seth took one of her hands in his and circled her waist with his other. "I'm sure you can, but I'll escort you just the same." He strove for a tone between wheedling and ordering, adding a slight smile. She relented and allowed him to guide her to the door.

Rose had a place ready for Lydia on the settee.

Celeste wheeled in the ancient teacart laden with teapot, cups, and saucers.

Millie stood near the fireplace, biting her lip and wringing her hands.

Seth ushered Lydia to her seat and straightened, reluctant to leave but suddenly awkward in the women's presence.

Rose tucked a pillow behind Lydia's back. "There you go, dear. Thank you, Seth, for taking such good care of her. I'll see you to the door."

Had Rose always been so commanding, or had she taken lessons from her military husband? Either way, Seth meekly followed and promised to call again later to see how Lydia fared. Nothing, he vowed, was going to keep him from doing everything he could to secure Lydia's commitment soon.

~

*L*ydia lay against the settee cushions and propped her feet on the ottoman Millie positioned closer. Celeste poured tea in cups while Rose removed her bonnet. The motion made Lydia sit up with a gasp. "My bonnet and reticule. Did someone get them?"

"I have them." Rose smiled. "But I'm afraid the cookies didn't fare as well. Luke picked up the bag and your reticule from the street. He swore the cookies had gone to crumbs, but I suspect some ended up in his belly."

The sweet aroma of cinnamon mixed with vanilla preceded Hattie, who held a tray of scones. "I just took these out of the oven, so you ladies help yourselves before Herbert and Lieutenant Hart return from the livery. I swear I don't know why both of them had to take one horse to get reshod." She waddled over to Lydia and patted her face. "How're you doin', sweet girl? It set us all in a dither, it did, when Miss Rose tol' us 'bout your mishap. You just set there and rest now, have your tea and sweets. I'll be in the kitchen fixin' supper should anyone need me." Hattie's last words floated behind her as she tottered to the back of the house.

The other women chuckled, and Celeste shook her head. "I hope I can get around as well as Hattie does when I get to be her age." She looked at Lydia. "Are you up to some tea and scones?"

"Just tea, thank you." She took the cup and lowered it to her lap, not fully trusting her hands to keep it steady.

After a minute of silence, Celeste set aside her dishes and faced Lydia. "Do you feel like telling us what happened?"

"I suppose." Lydia spoke toward her lap where she toyed with the teacup. "I went to the mercantile this morning. I wanted to pick up a spool of thread to finish Amy's dress. Also, I wanted to speak to Seth, but he wasn't there." Her face warmed as the blush spread from her neck.

Rose reached over and grasped her hand. "You don't owe us any explanations, Lydia." Her eyes sparkled when she smiled. "Although it's easy to see you two are drawn to each other."

Millie moved to the settee. "Does this have anything to do with our discussion the other day? About you staying here when Troy and I leave?"

Lydia nodded. "I thought it might be wise to question Seth about... When he first arrived in town a couple months ago"— she directed her words to Rose—"he said we ought to marry. It took me by surprise, so I put him off. Then Cal appeared."

"That did put you in a predicament." Rose sipped her tea.

"Seth was so kind and helpful, even providing the coffin to bury Cal. But he hasn't come around since then, so I thought he might've changed his mind. Anyway, when I got to the mercantile, Will said he'd gone with Luke to the hotel."

"Is that their normal practice?" Celeste looked to Rose for the answer.

"Not to my knowledge. They usually eat right there in the store, although sometimes Luke might come to the house. But I've interrupted you again, Lydia. Please go on."

Lydia swallowed and glanced at each eager face. These were her friends. She could share her feelings with them. "Seeing Will reminded me that Seth's late wife was young and beautiful. I just couldn't imagine Seth having an interest in me."

She held up her hand to stop their protests. "Please. I'm just saying what I was thinking. Anyway, I left and went by the bakery because I hadn't eaten. When I left there, I continued down Market Street. I happened to look in the window at the hotel, and I saw Seth in the restaurant there. He was with a woman."

Rose tilted her head. "But didn't Will tell you Seth was with Luke?"

Lydia nodded, but Rose paid little heed as she put forth another thought. "And Luke was with him when they witnessed your accident. So, what happened to the woman?"

~

Seth brooded.

Luke didn't seem inclined to talk until they guided the horses into the stables near the mercantile. Seth wouldn't have spoken then, but Luke forced it on him.

"Well, I think I can say that was the most eventful meal I've ever had."

Seth jabbed a finger in Luke's chest. "What did you say to Rose when you went back to the house?"

Luke heaved a sigh. "Only that Lydia was at the doctor's office and needed her."

"You didn't say anything to Emily?"

"I didn't have to, thank the good Lord. She was upstairs with the baby. Rose and Gertie happened to be in the parlor, so I asked Gertie to let Emily know where I'd gone and to get someone else to pick up the children after school. I figured Noah or J.D. could do that."

Seth frowned and poked Luke's chest again. "What are you going to tell her now?"

Luke scrunched his eyebrows and poked him back. "What are *you* going to do about Lydia?"

Seth reared back and lifted his hands. "Whoa. I don't think it's any of your business."

"Lydia's a friend of Emily and Rose. I don't think they'd take kindly to someone mistreating her, so that makes it my business."

"And Emily helped nurse me back to health when I was sick in Marietta, so I don't take kindly to anyone hurting her."

Luke blew out a breath. "We're both in a fine pickle, aren't we?"

"You said it."

The stable hand sauntered closer, looking as if he was afraid they might start throwing punches.

Seth climbed out of the carriage. "I've got work to do. Furniture to make and deliver, and I've already lost half a day." He headed toward the workshop. Seconds later, he heard Luke following him. Seth swung around. "You're not going home yet?"

Luke threw him a disgruntled look. "Yeah, I'm going, but I'm going on foot. Maybe I'll decide what to tell Em by the time I get there."

# CHAPTER 29

SATURDAY, MAY 6, 1865

*A*fter discussing her dilemma with her friends, and spending some time in prayer, Lydia decided to give up on approaching Seth. It wasn't the proper thing to do, and it went against the grain for Lydia, who'd been reared not to put herself forward.

Mrs. Coker caught wind of it, though, and sent word for Lydia to come to her room. "What's this I hear about you and Mr. Morgan?"

Lydia's face warmed. "What do you mean? There's nothing between me and him."

The older woman scowled. "Pshaw. Don't try to flummox me, girl. I knew he was taken with you soon as he came here the first time."

"I reckon he changed his mind. Men do that, you know, when they find someone younger and prettier."

"And has he found someone else?"

Lydia sighed. "It would seem so. I saw him with another woman at the hotel yesterday."

"Let me see if I understand. You saw him with a woman, and then you walked in front of a wagon that was barreling down the street." She slapped her hand on the bed. "Were you trying to get his attention?"

"No!" Lydia covered her flaming cheeks with her hands. "I never saw the wagon, not that I remember anyway. Seein' them surprised me. I guess I was trying to work it out in my mind and wasn't paying attention."

Mrs. Coker patted Lydia's knee. "I understand. The Lord knows I can appreciate how something like that can happen when you're not watching where you step. What I'm wondering is if you've decided you're ready to try marriage again. You've not been in favor of it for some time. Having to care for a husband you'd assumed to be dead must've been hard. Did that change your thinking?"

Lydia shook her head. "I don't know. Maybe. But I think it was more. After your fall, Millie and I started talking about her and Troy leaving. I think it would be wrong of me to go with them, and Louisville suits me fine. I ought to take charge of my own life, now that the war's over."

"I agree with you wholeheartedly. Times are changing, and while I don't agree with everything those suffragists preach, I can see why women need to be able to fend for themselves. The Lord blessed me with two good men, Gideon's grandfather for thirty years and Mr. Coker for twelve. Each of them made sure I would be cared for in my old age." Her voice trembled, and her eyes misted in memory.

Lydia stood to take her leave. "You're tired. I should go and let you rest." She adjusted the light blanket over Mrs. Coker's knees. "Can I get you anything before I go?"

"No, thank you, dear. I'll be praying the Lord will show you what to do."

"I appreciate that, and I know He will. After all, He led us all to you, didn't He?"

The gray head nodded. "He knew we needed each other."

"Yes, He did." Lydia left the door ajar in case Mrs. Coker might need to call for help. "I wonder if we might need one another even more in the future."

～

Seth poked his head through the back door of the mercantile to check for customers. Only an old man and a skinny youth wandered the aisles, so he figured it was safe for him to enter. Frank bent over his ledger at the front counter, mumbling to himself as his pencil scratched against the paper.

Seth threaded his way through the rows of merchandise. He ran his hand along a bolt of lavender cloth and straightened the bottles of Doctor Brown's Liniment for Achy Joints. Several smaller pieces of furniture he'd made were on display in the center and prompted a surge of pleasure. There was nothing like the feeling of creating something both beautiful and useful. He inspected the door fastenings on a jewelry chest while he waited for Frank to finish his ciphering.

Frank put down his pencil and looked around. "Hey, Seth. You need something?"

"Nah, I just wanted to get out of the workshop while the finish dries on that last piece for Colonel Houston's wife. Has Luke been around?"

"Not since early this morning. I expect he'll be along directly."

Seth wouldn't count on that, not with that O'Brien woman showing up at his house at noon. He might spend more time in the store later. He might need to until the other women at his house adjusted to his news.

Through the window, Seth watched the people enjoying the warmer weather as they strolled along. Behind him, Frank totaled an order and thanked his customer. The door rattled open and shut, and the old man clutched a worn cloth bag as he crossed the street.

Seth's mind drifted to Lydia. How long should he wait for her to recover before visiting? Seeing her lying in the street the day before had made his heart drop to his feet. What if she'd been killed? He'd already lost the woman he'd loved once. How would he survive losing another? Why had he waited so long to speak to her again?

Those questions might never be answered. They were only conjectural. The real question, the one he could answer, was what he was going to do about it.

He made up his mind and pivoted to the back of the store, nearly plowing into the youth who lingered near the kitchenware collection. "Pardon me." Seth steadied the boy, then turned back to shout in Frank's direction. "When Luke gets here, let him know the armoire is ready to be delivered to the mayor's house. I'm gonna finish up and take off early since I worked late last night."

His plans went by the wayside, however, when three visitors entered the workshop. John Mark Anderson proudly led his two companions—a boy who looked to be about ten and a tall military man to meet Seth. "Mr. Morgan, Pa said I should bring Nate to see where you make furniture. Nate's going to live with us while his ma goes to nursing school."

Seth extended a hand of welcome to the boy while he marveled at his close resemblance to Luke. Frances O'Brien hadn't been fabricating falsehoods about the boy's parentage. "Nice to meet you, Nate." The handshake was brief, and then John Mark nudged Nate over to the worktable. Seth called after them. "John Mark, you know the rules."

"Yes sir. We won't touch anything."

"At least not much," Seth said as he turned to the third visitor. He noted the left arm in a sling. Seth breathed in a measure of courage and held out his hand. "Major Griffin, I believe."

The other man's grip was firm. "I don't suppose you've been avoiding me, have you, Sergeant Morgan? I've been in Louisville two weeks now, staying on the same premises, and yet I had to come to where you work to meet you." Though he kept a straight face, the glint of humor shone in the major's eyes.

Seth shuffled his feet but offered a slight smile. "It's not easy to meet the man whose horse I stole on my way out of Marietta. I suppose I should offer some type of repayment."

"I believe I was guilty of commandeering your family home for the Union army, so I suppose we can call it even."

Conversation lagged as they watched the boys explore the shop. The major turned to Seth. "When I heard the boys clamoring to come see your workshop, I offered to bring them and get them out of the way."

"How're things going at the house—with Luke and the women?"

"Surprisingly well. Emily accepted the situation with grace and persuaded Cook and Gertie to do the same. Luke's solicitor arrived just as the boys and I left."

"Solicitor?"

"My cousin insisted that their agreement be legal and aboveboard. I expect I'll have to witness to their signatures when we return, which we should do now." He called John Mark and Nate to finish their tour.

"By the way, Sergeant," the major said, causing Seth to wince, "one day I'd like to hear all about your trip from Marietta to Virginia. I understand it's quite a tale."

Seth passed a hand over his face. "Not my finest hour, Major. But I believe God used it to set some things right."

Major Griffin grinned as he guided the boys out the door. "And, just so you know, that horse was one from the army corral. If I'd ridden my Hercules to the house that day, you never would've made it out of the yard. He's particular about who rides him."

Seth waved his guests on their way and surveyed the shop. The boys had respected the equipment and left everything in order. John Mark would make a fine carpenter if he continued to hone his skills, and Seth was happy to offer his instruction. Nate's addition to the household was bound to affect family interactions. Though he moved on the periphery of the Turner ménage, Seth was drawn to the young Anderson and resolved to help the boy if he could.

As Seth started to close the shop, his gaze snagged on the armoire destined for the mayor's house. Major Griffin's words echoed in his head. "Luke's solicitor arrived.... I expect I'll have to witness their signatures."

Seth groaned. So much for an early escape. Luke would never have time to deliver the mayor's order today. He'd probably forgotten all about it, with so much going on in his house. With a sigh of resignation, Seth went to fetch the wagon so he could make the delivery himself. Duty before pleasure, Pa always said. The trouble was that duty seldom left any time for pleasure.

~

SUNDAY, MAY 7, 1865

*L*ydia knelt on the folded towel at the edge of the flower bed and plunged her hands into the dark soil. Some might say she shouldn't tend this task on Sunday, calling it work. But it wasn't work to Lydia. It was a simple pleasure, one she hadn't been able to enjoy in several years.

She turned over the dirt and contemplated the pastor's sermon from a familiar verse in Proverbs. "Trust in the Lord with all thine heart and lean not unto thine own understanding." He'd paired it with another verse in James and admonished the congregation to commit every plan to God.

Lydia whispered her surrender as she carefully divided and reset plants. "Dear Lord, teach me to know what to do. I submit to Your will, whatever it may be."

An hour later, she brushed the loose dirt from her dress and rinsed her hands in the outside basin to join the rest of the household for tea. They had gathered in the parlor when Herbert ushered Noah and Rose inside.

Lieutenant Hart stood to greet them. "Major, Mrs. Griffin," he said, offering Noah a handshake. "Pleased to have you join us. How's your arm healing?"

Rose sat beside Lydia on the settee. "Have you heard about what happened to Seth?"

Lydia's hand trembled, and she returned her cup to the saucer. The liquid sloshed over the cup's rim. "Seth? What happened to him?"

All eyes turned to Noah as he explained. "It seems he was attacked late yesterday while making a delivery to the mayor's house."

Millie gasped. "What do you mean, attacked?"

"Why would anyone attack Seth?" Celeste's troubled gaze settled on Lydia.

Noah held up a hand. "All we know is that someone shot him after he left the mayor's house. It was on the same road where Luke was ambushed a couple of weeks ago. Fortunately, Doctor Yates had been there to tend a broken arm. He left the mayor's house a few minutes after Seth made his delivery and heard a gunshot. He found Seth slumped over in the wagon."

"Thank goodness he wasn't far behind," Rose said, "or Seth might have bled out. The doctor staunched the bleeding and took him to his office for further treatment."

"How bad is it?" Lydia asked.

"Not as bad as it could've been. Either the gunman was a bad shot or Seth shifted before the bullets hit him." Noah pointed one hand to his opposite side. "Doctor Yates removed two slugs from his right shoulder. We're praying there's no infection. He won't be able to work for a while."

Urgency pushed Lydia to her feet. "Do you think I could see him?"

The others exchanged varying expressions of surprise. Rose tugged at Lydia's hand. "I don't see why not. You can check with Doctor Yates."

Lydia withdrew her hand and started upstairs to retrieve her bonnet and shawl. "I just need to see for myself that he's all right." She looked back. "Would one of you gentlemen take me there?"

Lieutenant Hart accepted the charge.

A few minutes later when he halted the carriage in front of the doctor's office, he turned to Lydia. "Stay a moment, please. I want you to know what Grandmother and I discussed yesterday."

A frisson of alarm wrenched Lydia into the present. What could this mean? Her recent prayer of submission seemed to have loosed all kinds of possibilities. Seth's injury prompted her to set aside any expectations she might have in that regard, and now this.

"Lieutenant—"

"Please, won't you call me Gideon? I believe our close circumstances must render a less formal address. Besides, I appreciate the way you ladies have cared for Grandmother and hope we can all consider ourselves friends."

"Of course...Gideon." She shrugged. "It will take some getting used to. I will say, however, we're happy to do what we can for Aunt Lottie. She's been so good to us."

Gideon smiled. "I'm glad we're mutually satisfied on that score. In fact, I want you to know you're welcome to stay however long you need to. Grandmother wanted to be sure that you're able to stay in the house even after she passes."

He paused and seemed to choke back his emotions. "Of course, Herbert and Hattie are permanent residents, but I fear they'll not be far behind Grandmother in leaving this world."

Lydia had noticed the older couple's health had waned in the few months she'd known them.

"I expect I'll be assigned to a post some distance from here, either out West or farther to the south to help with reorganization. My immediate future lies with the army, so I don't expect to be in Louisville more than a week or two at a time. I'd consider it a great favor if you, and perhaps Celeste, would stay and occupy the house as long as it suits you."

"I'm stunned." Lydia pressed a hand to her heart. "And grateful." *Thank you, Father. You were making a way even before I brought my need to You.*

Gideon secured the horses and helped her from the carriage as she pondered the kind offer. Now she needn't bother with asking about Seth's plans. Strangely, the observation didn't relieve her as it should have. Especially since she'd failed to discover anything about the woman she'd seen him with the other day. Who could she be, and what did she mean to Seth? Did Lydia dare ask?

# CHAPTER 30

Seth gazed at Luke's serious face, struggling to understand what his friend had told him. "Do you mean the person who shot me thought I was you?"

Luke paced away from the bed where Seth sat propped up with pillows to cushion his wounded shoulder. Seth's shirt and coat had been discarded, leaving only an undershirt to cover his chest. The blue-striped blanket stretched over his legs up to his waist, where another pillow provided support for his injured arm.

"It makes sense, doesn't it?" Luke asked. "I'm just sorry I took so long to figure it out and we both took a beating."

"Explain your theory to me again, if you will. I don't know if it's the pain or the medicine Doc gave me, but I'm having a hard time wrapping my mind around your explanation."

"We found out one of our councilmen accepted a bribe to push for a street railway along Market Street. Mayor Tomppert's refusing to approve the measure because of the bribery involved. I support the mayor's decision on moral grounds, regardless of the effect that might have on my business."

Seth tipped his head against the wall behind him. "So, you

think our attacker was trying to scare you away from supporting the mayor?"

"He probably thought we were using the furniture delivery as a ruse to meet and plot ways to defeat the proposal. When I didn't give in after the first attack—because I never connected it to coming from the mayor's house—he tried a more drastic method and shot you, thinking I was in the company wagon." Luke scratched his chin. "What I can't figure out is how anyone knew about those deliveries."

Seth repositioned his arm on the pillow, thinking over the previous day's activities. "I was alone in the workshop most of the day. I put the final touches on the chest that Colonel Harrison ordered and left it to dry. When I asked Frank if he'd heard from you, he said he expected you back soon. Since I'd worked late the night before, I figured I'd leave early. I told Frank the armoire was ready to go to the mayor's house whenever you arrived."

Luke leaned against the wall near the door. "Were any customers in the store then? It was empty when I got there."

"There was an old man who left before I did. And a boy, maybe a little older than John Mark, looking at kitchen wares, which is odd. I nearly plowed into him on my way back to the shop. Do you think he was there to spy on you?"

Luke spat a mild oath. "You should've gone on and left the armoire for me to deliver."

"Then you'd be here in my place, I expect, and maybe in worse shape."

Sounds from the hallway indicated an end to their privacy. "I guess that'll be Doc Yates coming back," Luke said. "He should hire a nurse to help him out, like Doctor Scarborough has."

Seth peered through narrowed eyes. "Maybe Miz O'Brien could come work for him."

Luke shot him a sour look. "If you weren't already injured, you'd pay for that remark."

Voices drew closer, and Seth pulled up the blanket when he realized one of them belonged to a familiar female. "Hello?"

Lydia? What in the world was she doing there?

Lieutenant Hart peeked around the doorframe. "Anyone here? Ah, there you are. Hello, Luke. The doctor doesn't seem to be around, but Mrs. Gibson is determined to see how the patient is doing. Shall I let her come in?"

Lydia huffed as she entered. "Of course you'll let me in. It isn't as if I'm an innocent miss who might swoon at the sight of blood or bare arms." Her gaze traveled from one man to the next. She stepped to the foot of the bed, her gaze roaming Seth's face and upper body.

Luke and Gideon hung back, watching with amusement.

Seth grinned at her. "Well? Do I pass inspection, ma'am?"

She gave a curt nod. "You'll do. It's fortunate Doctor Yates found you right away."

"Yeah, he was an immediate answer to prayer."

"As he was for me last week, along with you and Luke, I'm told." Her voice hinted at tears, but she sniffed and gestured toward the bed. "Although I see you got a bed, whereas I only rated a table." She moved to the headboard and patted the pillows.

Seth raised his eyebrows suggestively, and Lydia blushed as if reading his thoughts. At least it wiped that scowl off her face. He lowered his voice. "I was the one who put you on the table, and I stayed beside you until you woke up."

Gideon made a guttural noise and sauntered closer. "Except for that patch on your shoulder, you seem none the worse for wear. Noah made it sound as if you were ready to stick your spoon in the wall."

"Not likely." Seth chuckled. "The ladies who came from

Marietta will testify I'm not easily killed, although you fellows in blue tried it a few times."

Luke poked Gideon. "Just don't ask Noah about the time Seth stole his horse."

Gideon's jaw dropped. "What? You stole a cavalry officer's mount?"

Seth dismissed the subject with a shake of his head. "Only took it across a couple counties. Left it with a good family." He covered his yawn and struggled to stay awake.

"Gentlemen"—Lydia gestured toward the door—"I think we should leave that conversation for another day. Our patient needs his rest."

She touched his arm, and Seth grasped her hand. "I hope y'all will come again when I'm better prepared for visitors." His words included them all, but his eyes lingered on Lydia.

~

*L*ydia stayed quiet on the drive back to Mrs. Coker's house. Gideon didn't seem inclined to speak either. The recent conversation had taken Lydia back to the days in Marietta. She'd felt the pull of attraction toward Seth from the start, though she'd denied it.

Living with Cal had left her with a sour attitude toward marriage. She'd resented the power he held over her and her lack of resources. Oddly enough, the Union army had set her free by shipping her north. Despite the refugees' struggle for the necessities during the first few months of their exile, she'd learned she could survive without a man controlling her life. She enjoyed being able to make her own decisions, as scary as it sometimes was.

So why did she keep gravitating toward Seth Morgan? It was more than their similar states of widowhood. From what she knew, his marriage had been a good one, cruelly destroyed by a vindictive relative. Her marriage had been...tolerable.

Thanks to the friends she'd made in Marietta and Louisville, she'd grown spiritually and learned to seek God's direction. Could this desire for Seth's company be His way of guiding her next steps? But she wasn't sure if Seth was so inclined, and there was the matter of the woman from the other day.

The carriage slowed to a stop, and Gideon set the brake and rounded the horses to help her descend. "I have another errand to attend, but please tell Hattie I'll be back in time for supper."

"Of course. Thank you so much for going with me, Lieu—Gideon."

He smiled at her lapse and opened the gate for her. "You're welcome, Lydia."

He returned to the carriage, and Lydia lifted her eyes heavenward. "And thank You, Father God, for providing good friends, a home, and all we need. I reckon we can trust You to take care of us no matter what happens in the world."

She entered the house to find Rose still there, chatting with Celeste and Millie as they watched Amy play with a rag doll on the blanketed floor. Lydia tossed her reticule on the hall table and followed it with her bonnet. "Rose, I'm happy you stayed, but where is your husband?"

"I'd forgotten he'd promised to take John Mark and Nate out to fly their kites today. When he looked at his watch the third time, I insisted he go ahead and come back for me when they were finished."

"Ah, I haven't seen John Mark in a while. Who is Nate? One of his friends from school?"

Celeste put a hand to her mouth as Rose lifted her brows. "You haven't heard about Nate and Florence O'Brien?"

Millie glanced at the others and then at Lydia. "You might want to sit down. Rose just told us, and it's quite the tale."

~

MONDAY, MAY 8, 1865

Seth jerked awake and hissed at the pain shooting through his shoulder. He'd slid from his sitting position in his sleep and must have rolled onto his wound. His throat felt as rough as the sandpaper he kept in his shop. The room had grown dark, with little light seeping through the clouded sky outside the lone window. The only sound he could make out was a clock ticking.

He worked his mouth and licked dry lips. "Doc?" His voice sounded more like a rutting pig's snort than a human call. He tried again. "Hello? Doc? Anyone?"

A woman's voice answered him. "I'm coming, Mr. Morgan."

Seth sifted through the females he knew but couldn't work out whose voice it was. Even when she entered his room, all smiles and cheeriness, he didn't recognize her.

"Here's some water for you. Sit up now. While you drink it, I'll fluff up your pillow."

Her dark brown hair was pulled tight into a chignon, and hazel eyes shone with secret amusement. A white apron covered her forest-green dress. A vague memory tugged at Seth, but he couldn't place her.

He took the glass of water but didn't drink. "Do I know you?"

"Not really. We only met last week, but I understand it was your idea for me to work with Doctor Yates." When he didn't respond, she went on. "Florence O'Brien. You came with Luke to the restaurant on Friday."

The memory crystallized, and Seth downed the water in the glass to postpone his answer. "Why do you say I suggested you work for the doctor?"

She shrugged. "That's what Luke said. Since I have a whole

month before I leave for New York, it seemed like a good idea. My main purpose in staying here so long was to give Nate a chance to get to know Luke and his family before I move."

"I see. I think." He handed her the empty glass and settled back against his pillows.

"Doctor Yates was called away, but he showed me where the medicine and dressings are kept. He also sent something to break your fast, if you feel up to eating."

"That sounds good, but I feel the urge to move around." He gave her a shooing motion. "If you, uh, could—"

"Oh, of course." She fled the room to allow him some privacy.

It took Seth a few minutes to make himself presentable. He managed his trousers and one arm in his shirt, but his weakened state wouldn't allow for boots. He dropped into the chair beside a small table.

Mrs. O'Brien's voice rang from the hallway. "Are you ready for these biscuits now?"

"I reckon I am."

She sailed into the room, a cloth-covered basket and a glass of milk in her hands. "I kept them warming at the back of the stove." She sat the items on the table and surveyed the room. "I'll just tidy up in here while you eat. Let me know if you need any help."

The woman stripped the linens off the bed and remade it with fresh sheets while Seth munched on a biscuit slathered with butter. He searched for something to say to cover the awkward silence. "How is Nate settling in with Luke's family?"

"He seems to like it so far. He's glad to have another boy his age there."

Seth gulped his milk. "He came with the major and John Mark to my workshop the other day. The two of them looked to be getting along fine."

"Nate makes friends easily. Even being the only child, he's

never acted spoiled." She launched into a humorous tale about the boy while she wiped the counter on the other side of the room. Another story followed while she moved closer to Seth. They were laughing at the boyish antics when another voice interrupted.

"Excuse me. I guess nobody heard me call from the front room."

Lydia stood in the doorway, her bonnet sporting fresh spring flowers and ribbons. It drew his eyes to the tendrils of hair framing her face. The lavender dress modestly displayed her curves.

Seth's heartbeat sped up at the sight of her. She held a basket with gloved hands. He frowned when the basket shook. Was she trembling?

His gaze moved back to her face, where rosy splotches contrasted with her natural paleness. Warning bells went off in his head as Mrs. O'Brien froze beside him. When had she placed her hand on his shoulder?

Lydia stared first at Seth and then at Mrs. O'Brien. "Seth. It looks like you're much improved today."

No words came to Seth's mind. What did you say to an angry woman?

~

*H*ow Lydia's voice kept from wavering, she'd never know. Perhaps the anger pushed aside her feelings of betrayal and embarrassment.

The woman—Lydia was sure it was the same one she'd seen in the restaurant the other day—dropped her hand from Seth's shoulder and picked up a dish from a side table. "I'm sorry I didn't hear you come in. Did you need to see Doctor Yates?"

"No." She turned from the woman and faced Seth. "I

brought a couple of Hattie's scones in case you hadn't eaten. I'll just leave them with you."

She strode to the side table and set them down. She squeaked when Seth clasped her wrist with his free hand.

"Don't leave." His voice rumbled, low and husky. "We need to talk."

He speared her with his stare and spoke louder as the other woman headed for the door. "Mrs. O'Brien, before you go, I'd like you to meet Lydia Gibson. Soon to be Lydia Morgan, I hope."

Mrs. O'Brien turned back and nodded with a congenial smile. "Nice to meet you, ma'am. Now, I'd better get back to work before the doctor arrives."

Lydia uttered a vague response before she rounded on Seth. "Mrs. O'Brien? As in Florence O'Brien, who brought her son to stay with the Turners?"

"The same."

"What were you doing with her at the hotel restaurant the other day?"

That question surprised him. "How did you know I was there?"

"I saw you."

Seth blinked. "I was there for Luke. He asked me to tag along so gossip wouldn't get back to Emily before he'd had a chance to explain."

"I didn't see Luke." Her pain lessened, but embarrassment made her hold onto the anger.

"If you saw us leaving, it must've been when he went to speak with the mayor at another table." Seth entwined his fingers with hers. "Look, if you don't believe me, you can ask Luke."

Lydia's anger fizzled. "I believe you. But why is she here? Rose said Florence O'Brien planned to go to school in New York. That's why she brought her son here."

"She doesn't leave for New York until next month. She wanted to see Nate settled in before she leaves." He lifted her hand to his lips. "I guess Luke mentioned her plans to Doctor Yates, and he offered her a job as nurse until she leaves."

"Oh. I see. I think." She couldn't think straight with him kissing her fingers.

Seth stood and tugged her closer. "You have no reason to be jealous."

She reared back, but he'd slipped his good arm around her waist so she couldn't flee. "Jealous? Why would I be jealous?"

"Because you've decided you're going to marry me after all, just as I said a few moments ago." He grinned.

Lydia shook her head. "When did you say that? You haven't mentioned getting married since you first came back from Camp Chase."

"Weren't you listening, woman? I told my nurse I hoped to change your name to Lydia Morgan."

She frowned, trying to reason away the rising hope. "I don't understand why you want to marry me, why you'd pick me over a younger woman, like Celeste."

"I could give you a hundred reasons, but who can explain why we care for one person over another? Except maybe the Lord sees what we need and puts a love in our heart for the one who fits us best."

That stubborn hope swelled. She had nothing of value to offer this man—no house, not even the promise of a family—only herself. "You never mentioned love before. Do you really think you love me?"

"No." He pulled her closer. "I know it. Lydia, I've loved before and never thought I would again, but I was drawn to you from the first time I saw you. I know your first marriage wasn't good, so I wanted to give you time to see how it could be different for us."

She touched his face, trying to take in his words. Love was

the element that had been missing from her first marriage. She and Cal had other reasons for marrying and never found a common purpose. "I think maybe it could. If we both work on it and let the Lord lead us."

"I won't rush you. It's been a year of upheaval. You can decide when you're ready to make that commitment." He laughed. "I don't even have a house to offer you right now, but I'm saving my earnings so we can look for land to build one. Or, if you prefer, we can head south and see whether anything's left for us in Georgia."

"That's a long journey to make when we don't know what we'll find."

"I know. But we'll go if it's where you want to make our home."

Lydia tilted her head. "I've come to realize home is not just a place. It's a feeling of belonging. Guess I had to lose my house to figure that out." She patted his chest. "My home will be wherever you are. We'll figure out where that will be later. Together."

~

SATURDAY, MAY 20, 1865

Seth tightened the last screw in the trunk and stepped back to admire it. Though it wasn't the fanciest item he'd ever made, he'd poured himself into the creation, and it reminded him of Lydia—beauty in simplicity. He draped a cloth over the trunk to protect it and to prevent anyone else from seeing it before he was ready.

A knock at the open door caused him to whirl around. He heaved a sigh to find Gideon there.

"Hey, Seth. I've been dispatched to transport you to your

fiancée's for supper. Celeste is with me, and your prospective nephew has returned from Camp Chase."

"Troy's back? Wonderful. Lydia will be happy." Seth locked the door and followed Gideon to the carriage where Celeste held the reins. "Hello, Miss Celeste. How are you this fine spring evening?"

The brunette smiled. "Spoken like a man in love. I'm well, Seth. Did Gideon mention our visitors?"

"He said Troy's back. Is there someone else?" Seth joined her on the bench as Gideon claimed the other side and guided the horses into the street.

"Oh, yes. Troy found Lydia's brother in the prison camp and brought him along."

"Really? That must have been a surprise."

Celeste nodded. "Hmm. Especially since this is the brother who happens to be Millie's natural father."

~

*L*ydia stifled her tears and Celeste clasped her hand. Her joy at having Troy and Ellis in Louisville dimmed with the news that Troy's next assignment would take Millie and Amy away.

"I'm sorry, Troy. I didn't mean to spill the beans." Ellis paced the floor. "It just slipped out when we started talking about how I'd get back home."

Troy pulled Millie close to him. "Now don't turn on the tears, Lydia, and ask me to leave Millie and Amy here. I promise I'll take good care of 'em. Besides, we won't be far from other family. We're like to have all kinds of company visit us by the end of summer."

Millie squeezed onto the settee beside Lydia and patted her hand. Before she could speak, Seth and Gideon entered the parlor. Their attention focused on the three women.

"Hey, what's wrong?" Seth took a chair near the settee and leaned toward Lydia. "Is someone hurt or sick?"

A tear slipped past Lydia's defenses, and Millie gave a shaky laugh. "Nothing so serious. Amy and I will be going back to Alabama with Troy in a couple of weeks."

Seth's countenance dropped. His disappointment would be for her as much as himself.

"At least you'll be here for the wedding, right?" Celeste glanced from Millie to Troy, who stared back.

Troy shrugged. "When is it?"

"Next Friday." All three women chorused.

"Yeah, we can wait for that." Troy glanced around when nobody said any more. "Uh, I guess I oughta ask. Who's gettin' married?"

Everyone laughed, but Gideon moved close to Celeste and squeezed her shoulder.

Seth stood and drew Lydia to her feet. She smiled up at him. It was a strange journey that had brought them together, but she had a feeling the adventure had only begun.

~

FRIDAY, MAY 26, 1865

*L*ydia grinned at Seth as he twirled her around the room. It might be the last time this group got together for a while, but she wouldn't be sad. She meant to enjoy every minute of this special day—special for all of them.

She tilted her head to where Mrs. Coker sat. "I believe Queen Charlotte is quite thrilled with the way our plans turned out."

Seth and J.D. had built a platform large enough for Mrs. Coker's chair, a stool for her feet, and a table to hold her refreshments. The doctor allowed her to leave her bed for short periods now, so everyone pitched in to make sure she didn't overtax herself.

Seth chuckled and pulled Lydia closer. "She played an important part in bringing about these marriages by providing jobs and housing for you ladies."

The elderly lady's fingers tapped out the tempo as she beamed at the dancing couples. Seth's brother-in-law, a musician before the war, provided the sweet strains of a waltz on the piano. Will smiled at the dancers as his fingers glided over the keys.

"He plays so well," Lydia said. "But it sounded like he tortured the poor instrument yesterday when he was tuning it."

"I'm glad he agreed to come. It's been good for him to get back to his music."

Across the floor, Troy spun Amy in a circle on his way to join Millie next to Mrs. Coker. Ada Anderson stood nearby, holding Emily's baby girl, and Amy went into Mrs. Coker's arms while Troy swept Millie into the dance.

Lydia squeezed Seth's hand. "I have a hunch Mrs. Anderson and Emily may be frequent visitors after Troy and Millie leave. That child will help fill the void left by Amy."

Seth guided her through the other swaying couples. Celeste and Gideon Hart would head West for his next assignment. Gideon had asked Seth to watch over his grandmother, so he and Lydia would occupy the master suite at Mrs. Coker's until Gideon and Celeste returned.

Rose and Noah Griffin planned to move to his home in Indiana next month. Olivia and Dr. Evan Spencer hadn't decided whether to settle in Louisville or in Frankfort where her father lived. Luke and Emily would stay here.

Seth danced her into the hallway and stopped out of sight of the others. "With all the recent marriages around here, I suspect Mrs. Coker may welcome more babies into her home before long. Perhaps even one for us."

Lydia's heart filled with hope. "Perhaps we will be so blessed, but if we are not, we can share in the joy of those around us. I am content to say with Solomon, 'I have found the one my soul loves.'" She cocked her head. "Do you know what Seth means?"

He shook his head. "Ma once told me, but I don't remember."

"Reverend Holland said it means 'appointed.' In the Bible Seth was given in the place of Abel. I believe God appointed you for me, Seth Morgan."

He kissed her knuckles, then leaned his forehead against hers. "I can't say I know the official meaning of your name, but I know what it means to me. A heart full of love. You put others ahead of yourself, and that's the proof of love. My lovely, loving Lydia."

## THE END

Did you enjoy this book? We hope so!
**Would you take a quick minute to leave a review where you
purchased the book?**
It doesn't have to be long. Just a sentence or two telling what
you liked about the story!

Receive a FREE ebook and get updates when new Wild Heart
books release: https://wildheartbooks.org/newsletter

Don't miss the next book in the Rescued Hearts of the Civil War Series!

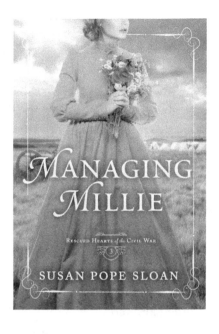

*Managing Millie*
*By Susan Pope Sloan*

JANUARY 24, 1864
CAMPBELL COUNTY, GEORGIA

Millie Gibson's whole world changed on account of a pan of dishwater.

She'd tossed it toward the rosebushes. And missed.

A hard freeze hit Georgia that night. The next morning, in her haste to return to the warm kitchen after visiting the outhouse, Millie skidded on the patch of ice beside the rosebushes. One ankle twisted, and her hands flew outward for balance. Her frantic movements only delayed her fall. Her bottom hit the ground. Hard.

She struggled to stand, but pain shot through her right leg. Her wrist was swelling too. She crawled the remaining several yards to the house, feeling the rocks and stubble through her thin skirt, and at last collapsed inside the door.

Her stepmother turned from feeding wood into the kitchen stove. "Oh, dear. What happened to you?"

Millie stifled the urge to cry. At sixteen, she should be able to avoid such a tumble—or at least endure the pain. She'd experienced her share of mishaps over the years, often earning her pa's scorn for her clumsiness.

Lydia helped her to a chair and ran her hands over Millie's arms and legs. "I don't think anything's broken," her step-mother said. "But you'll be out of work for a few days, the way that hand looks."

Millie groaned. They could ill afford the loss of her wages. Even before Pa had been reported missing, the funds from him had dried up. She and Lydia together made just enough to keep the two of them clothed and fed.

Lydia wrapped a cloth around a bit of ice from the yard and laid it on Millie's wrist. "Hold it there while I get another for your ankle." She clucked her tongue. "Child, when you take a tumble, you do it with your whole body."

"How well I know." Millie's backside ached. She raised her skirt to examine her bruised knees. At least no one would see those. Her wrist and ankle, though. She groaned. Why did she have to be so clumsy?

Thank goodness for Lydia. She'd tended Millie with loving care since her marriage to Pa, Millie's pa. She never scolded or criticized, only admonished her to slow down and be more careful. Unlike Pa, who would berate her for the smallest infraction.

Lydia returned with another cold compress. "Let me help you to bed, then I'll bring you a biscuit and a bowl of grits." She looped Millie's left arm over her shoulder, and they shuffled to Millie's small bedroom, which backed up to the kitchen.

Millie sat on the bed, and Lydia helped her swing her legs over the rumpled covers. Millie couldn't suppress the groan when her injured members came in contact with the mattress. Lydia adjusted the quilts so Millie could spread them without causing her more pain.

"We should put a pillow under that foot. Maybe one under your hand too. Granny McNeil always said to let the blood flow away from the injury. I'll bring a couple from my room."

Within minutes, Lydia had wrapped Millie's injured limbs, brought her a few bites of breakfast, and made her as comfortable as possible. She stood by the bed and surveyed Millie's situation. "It's a good thing this happened on Sunday. I'll have time to prepare a pot of soup, so you'll have plenty to eat while I'm at work tomorrow."

Remorse increased Millie's discomfort. "I'm sorry you'll miss church."

Lydia waved away her concern. "I'd debated whether to go anyway, with it bein' so cold. There could be other icy places along the way. I'll get that soup on the stove and see what else we might fix so you don't have to move around much."

"Thank you for taking such good care of me. I'm sorry to be so much trouble."

"Shut your mouth. It's no trouble to take care of someone you love. I thank God you aren't seriously injured."

Millie closed her eyes as Lydia left the room. *Thank You, God, for Lydia. What would I do without her?*

Pa's decision to marry Lydia eight years ago had been a blessing. He hadn't done it to give Millie a mother after Mama died, of course. His primary consideration had been his own comfort, having someone to cook and clean his house and warm his bed. He'd also wanted a son, but that hadn't happened. Lydia suffered Cal's scorn as well as her own disappointment for that failure.

His last visit home—over a year before—had ended in harsh words between him and Lydia. After that, months passed without any word on his whereabouts. Then his name was printed in the list of those presumed dead at Chickamauga. The preacher had read it from the *Macon Daily Telegraph* a few months ago and offered his condolences.

Beyond that, nobody mourned Cal Gibson's passing.

$\sim$

January 28, 1864
Whitfield County, Georgia

Troy McNeil shivered, but not from the frigid temperature but the sight of dozens of mounds that dotted the landscape below his position near Rocky Face. He'd heard rumors of recent skirmishes around Dalton, and this verified it. Fighting in the dead of winter.

A few miles behind him, more graves scarred the ground from last year's battle at Chickamauga. Scores of monuments to so many lost wagers, wavering hope, and shattered boasts of glory. Defeat dogged both sides.

A hawk soared overhead, its strident call interrupting Troy's silent vigil. Frustrated that his attempt to reach Union-held Knoxville had failed, he turned his steps toward the family home. Pa might not throw out a big welcome, but he wouldn't turn Troy away either. Ma and Old Liza would be glad to see him. He could avoid the rest of the family until spring. Maybe by next week he'd be able to sleep in the barn loft. That was, if he could avoid soldiers from both armies long enough.

He picked his way down the rocky terrain, his senses on alert for any movement that might mean a threat. Bears shouldn't be a problem this time of year, but wolves and bobcats could be on the prowl for easy prey. His greatest worry, though, walked on two legs and wore colors that blended with the winter gray. The dearth of green foliage increased his vulnerability, a man alone with no apparent means of defense.

Troy shifted the pack strapped to his back and pulled a strip of jerky from his pocket. A flock of geese honked as they flew overhead. He traced their movement as he tore off a bite.

"Hey, birds. You're goin' the wrong way. Winter's just gettin' started good." He kept his voice low by habit. You never knew when someone might be listening.

He tramped on, making note of familiar landmarks and the sun's slow descent across the cloudless sky. He should make it to the state line in a couple of days. He'd go by Aunt Lydia's first, though, and see how she fared. Her and Millie. A strange sensation coursed through his veins at thoughts of Millie. He tried to ignore it, recalling earlier visits to his aunt's house and the blond hoyden who was her stepdaughter.

During his first visit after Lydia's marriage, the girl had followed him around asking persistent questions. He'd thought it crazy that a nine-year-old female would want to help him set rabbit traps and hoe up the garden. No other female he knew did that.

Later, when he went through that terrible phase of his voice wobbling from low to high, Millie had laughed at him. "I declare, Troy, you ought to make up your mind whether to sing bass or soprano. And what's all this stuff on your chin? You're fuzzy as a peach."

She'd learned to jump out of reach and hide behind Lydia's skirt, knowing what her punishment would be if he caught her. He knew her ticklish spots.

Those memories brought a smile. As much as he'd hated her teasing, he loved to hear her laugh and watch her face light up. Her blue eyes glimmered like a lake under the summer when she flashed that jaunty grin. Ah, she was a beauty, all right.

His smile faded. Last time he'd seen her, she'd been all grown up, with womanly curves and graceful movement. Even now, the recollection sped up his heartbeat and made sweat dampen his hands inside their gloves. With ruthless effort, he remembered what she'd said.

"I started at the mill last month." She spoke with a mixture of pride and dread in her voice.

"Why?" He'd glanced to where Lydia pulled a pan of corn-bread from the stove and kept his voice low. "Are y'all needing the money? I can lend you what I have."

Millie placed a hand on his arm, and he felt a shock run clear down to his toes. "There's no reason I can't work. I've been blessed to stay at home and go to school till now, but Pa hasn't sent any money home in a few months. It's time I helped out."

Troy hated the idea of her going to the mill. He'd seen too many women worn down by the double labor of a job and home. In the few years Lydia had carried that burden, he could see how it dragged at her. But his funds wouldn't have made much difference. Lydia deserved better than what life had dealt her.

As it happened, he was at their house when the women came home with the news that Cal had been reported among the missing at Chickamauga. Millie's fate as a mill operative was sealed, at least until this war ended and Troy could return to a normal life. He couldn't reveal his feelings for her while he lived as a fugitive. By dodging the Confederate conscription, most folks in the South labeled him a coward and wouldn't think twice about turning him in.

A rumble announced a buckboard coming on the road. The driver wouldn't see Troy, who stayed inside the tree line. stopped on a slight rise where a group of evergreens ded some cover and a welcome shelter from the persistent wind. As the wagon came into sight, Troy took a hurried inventory.

A mule pulled the conveyance, his pace steady but slow. The driver sat hunched over so only a floppy hat and dun-colored coat were visible, along with the booted foot propped against the box. There didn't appear to be any other occupants. Inside the bed, boxes lay higgledy-piggledy on top of some ancient furniture, as if the owner had thrown everything in without a care for how it landed.

As Troy pondered whether to show himself, the wind gusted, and several items tumbled over the wagon's side. The driver glanced back, calling the mule to a halt. "Whoa, there." The stranger descended from the seat and limped to the back, grumbling at the delay.

Troy jerked to see the driver's boots covered by a dark skirt, and a long braid slipped from the hat. Without thought, he jumped from his hiding place and darted to the closest object in the road. He called a greeting as the woman noted his presence. "Looks like you're losing your load." He grabbed another parcel and carried it to the wagon.

Her wary stare gave way to a nod. "Much obliged, mister. I didn't see you back there."

Troy hoped his grin would put her at ease. "I just came over that hill about the time you passed. Saw your parcels bounce out and thought you might need some help. Where you headed?"

"Far south as I can git," she said. "Away from the guns and cannons. You from around here?"

"Pert near, a little farther down, west of Cartersville. I'm headed home for a visit. I'd appreciate a ride, if you wouldn't mind, as far as you care to go that way. I could hold down your wares."

Neither of them moved while she studied him.

"You got a name?"

"Troy McNeil. My folks live in Alabama, but I got kin in Campbell County. They'll put me up for a while. I expect they could find a place for you if you like to go that far, Missus."

"Mabel Tarvin." At last, she nodded and gestured to the wagon bed. "Hop on."

~

Campbell County, Georgia

Millie limped around the house, using the old cane Lydia found in the shed. The object must have evoked her stepmother's memories, as she'd run her fingers over the worn wood after she wiped away the dust.

"Cal wanted to give it away, but I convinced him one of us might need it one day. This cane, her Bible, and the old wheelbarrow are all I have left of Granny's things."

"Besides the house, you mean," Millie had said. Lydia never mentioned it, but the house, and the farm it sat on, had been part of Cal's attraction to Lydia. He'd hated paying rent on the tiny mill cottage. Ma's death gave him the opportunity to improve his living situation and get a younger wife, one he meant to control as he hadn't been able to control Millie's mother.

Lydia's smile didn't reach her eyes. "And the house. Clearing out her possessions was about the hardest thing I ever did."

"I remember Granny a little," Millie said. "She had the most remarkable laugh."

"That she did. It would tickle her to know that a young lady of sixteen would be the next one to use her cane."

Lydia had showed Millie how to hold it in her left hand. "It's ʼtunate your injuries are on the same side. It seems backʼds, but you should put it on the opposite hand of the hurt

She'd wavered at first but soon developed a rhythm so she could move between the rooms without much difficulty. After two days, she could even venture outside.

"Well, hello, Mr. Sun." She shaded her eyes as she stepped out the front door. She dropped into a rocking chair and leaned the cane against it. "Why did you let Mr. Frost trip me up the other day? I don't mind bein' away from the mill, but I don't like not bein' able to walk around without this stick."

"Who are you talking to, and why are you at home in the middle of the afternoon?"

Troy's voice came from the corner of the house as he sauntered into view and slipped the pack off his shoulders.

Millie's heart leaped, and she drank in the sight of him. His bare head revealed light-brown hair that drifted over his ears and melted into a reddish growth on his chin. Hazel eyes twinkled as he swiped the hair from his brow and stepped onto the porch.

"Troy McNeil, what are you doin' out here in the broad daylight where anyone can see you?" She hoped her scold would cover her joy at his presence—and remind him of the risk of being seen. Some people in this county would consider it their patriotic duty to report him to the Confederate Army.

"Who's gonna see me, Little Bit? Everybody's at work, either in the mill or on their farms. I just traipsed all over the road between here and Tennessee without seein' the first speck of Roswell Gray."

He settled in the other rocker with a sigh. "Ah, it's good to sit and rest."

"You've been to Tennessee and back? Then you didn't make it through the line to the Union camp." She shared his disappointment but secretly rejoiced that he wouldn't be so far away she might never see him again.

Troy gazed off into the distance. "No. I guess I left too late i the season. It started snowing, and I got turned around. A f folks let me stay in their barn or shed, but most were afraid to take a chance on somebody who didn't support the Confederacy."

She gestured to the coat draped over the rocker. "The coat your ma made didn't help?" Connie McNeil's clever idea had impressed Millie. With gray fabric on one side and blue on the other, Troy could reverse it anytime he found himself in a stronghold for either side.

"Not much. Everybody acted suspicious of a man traveling alone. Guess I'm lucky they didn't shoot me on sight." He stretched his arms overhead and turned her way. "Y'all got any food around here, or do I need to go trap us something to cook? And you never did say why you're layin' around the house today. Did you quit your job?"

"Whoa, one question at a time, please." She laughed at his puzzled expression. "We have food. There's a pot of potato soup on the stove, and no, you don't have to set any traps. I didn't quit the mill, but Lydia ordered me to stay home for a few days."

His brows lowered. "What'd you do?"

She flashed him a saucy smile. "I tried to skate on the ice out back last Sunday. My slippers didn't work so well as skates."

She waited for the crack of laughter to follow her flippant remark, but it never came. Troy gaped at her, his eyes skimming her body and finally landing on the low stool where her foot rested. He jerked his gaze back to her face.

"You broke your foot? You should be resting in bed." His face flushed crimson—the curse of a pale complexion, he'd always complained, letting everyone see his emotions.

She couldn't figure why he'd be angry or embarrassed.

"I, uh, I mean you shouldn't be up and around on it."

"It's not broken, only sprained. And I have Granny McNeil's cane to help me."

Troy blew out a breath. "That's good then." He looked away and appeared to collect himself, then smacked his hands on the arms of the rocker and pushed out of the chair. "Well, let's find some dinner. I expect Aunt Lydia will be home before long."

～

Troy prayed Lydia would be home soon. He didn't know how long he could be around Millie and act like nothing had changed since childhood. The difference in their ages had restrained a close relationship between them in years past. He'd brushed off her efforts to be his friend and treated her much the same as he did his younger cousins.

But she displayed all the signs of womanhood now. She wore her hair up, even at home, and she'd let down the hems of her skirts before she started working. He wouldn't even think about everything between those two points.

He stood rooted in place while she used the cane to get to her feet. It was rude not to help her, but he dared not touch her in his present state. She might chide him for his lack of chivalry, but better that than having her discover his feelings.

"Troy?" She paused in front of him and smirked.

Dear heavens. Could she discern his thoughts? He took refuge in ignorance. "What?"

"I thought you wanted to go inside and eat."

"Yeah, that's what I said."

"Well, move your big ol' self outta the way. You're standing in front of the door, and I can't get around you."

He fought to control the color seeping up his neck. "Oh, sorry. My mind wandered off there a bit." He pushed at the sturdy wooden door and gestured for her to precede him.

"Where did it go off to, some girl you met up in Tennessee?" Scorn filled her voice.

"No. Why would you say that?"

She shrugged. "You had a funny look on your face, c ain't never seen before. I just figured it had something with a girl. After all, you are nineteen now, and Lydia's always warned me about older boys."

"Men."

"What?"

"Fellows my age don't like to be called boys. We're men."

"If you say so."

Millie thumped her way over to the stove and added a couple of sticks to the fire.

Troy followed at a safe distance. He'd been here often enough to know where they kept everything, and he hated to have Millie wait on him in her condition.

"Why don't you sit on the sofa and let me tend to this? You can just yell out what I should do."

Her eyes went wide. "I can manage well enough." She bypassed the sofa on her way to the kitchen. "Lydia put the bowls on a shelf I can reach. I'm going to fry up a batch of corn-bread because it's faster and easier than puttin' it in the oven. It'll be ready in a few minutes."

He jumped away when she came too close. He needed to get out of here. "Uh, I believe I left my pack on the porch. I'll get it and set a trap over at the tree line."

"But the food will be..."

He didn't hear the rest as he rushed out the front door, grabbed his pack, and beat a hasty retreat across the side yard. Streaks of pink in the west reminded him to hurry through his task. Folks would be heading home from the mill in minutes. Though most of them lived in the company cottages closer to work, a few still maintained their small farms on the outskirts. Lydia's home hadn't functioned as a farm for more than a decade, and Cal had sold off small sections now and then to supplement their income.

Setting rabbit traps also gave him a chance to check on something he'd noticed while they'd lounged on the porch. He couldn't say he remembered seeing a figure, but a movement among the trees had triggered his instincts. He'd honed his senses to detect danger so long, he was afraid he would never be at ease again.

Keeping his eyes and ears alert, Troy laid traps without conscious thought to the familiar task. He found a slight impression on the ground where a ring of pine trees created a ragged square. This was the place ten-year-old Millie used to claim for her "house" and swept clean so she could designate each room and dare him to mess it up. It would also make a temporary resting place for anyone who wanted to watch the farmhouse. Beyond that possible footprint, he detected no cause for concern. No need to imagine trouble where none existed.

As he started back to the house, a lone figure approached from the direction of town. He studied the stride for a moment to be sure. "Thank God." The words slipped past his lips as the sway of skirts danced around the woman's feet.

Lydia was home.

# ABOUT THE AUTHOR

Born into a family of storytellers, **Susan Pope Sloan** published her first articles in high school and continued writing sporadically for decades. Retirement provided the time to focus on writing and indulge her avid interest in history. Her Civil War series begins (and ultimately ends) in her home state of Georgia with references to lesser-known events of that period. She and husband Ricky live near Columbus where she participates in Word Weavers, ACFW, and Toastmasters.

# AUTHOR'S NOTE

I owe a huge debt of thanks to Mary Deborah Petite for her excellent scholarly work in *The Women Will Howl* (McFarland & Company, Inc., Publishers, 2008). Her book was my primary source of information, especially for the timeline of events related to the workers' journey from North Georgia to Louisville, Kentucky.

Information on in-state travel and other conditions in *The War-time Journal of a Georgia Girl, 1864-1865*. Also *Red Clay to Richmond: Trail of the 35th Georgia Infantry Regiment, C.S.A.* and the Civil War Index provided movements of the 35th Georgia Infantry.

For weather, the National Weather Service website is valuable, and always Wikipedia is an excellent place to begin research on people and places.

Here are a few more websites I used:

www.roadsidegeorgia.com

https://en.wikipedia.org/wiki/
18th_Georgia_Volunteer_Infantry

https://tribupedia.com/louisville-military-prison-tribute/

https://confederateshop.com/archives/10956

https://elkinsdepot.com/blog/camp-chase-west-virginia-song-tells-civil-war-history/
http://38thalabama.com/camp-chase.html
https://www.mycivilwar.com/pow/oh-camp-chase.html
Divorce in the 19th Century | Blog | Author Shirleen Davies
American Civil War Prisoners of War History (thomaslegion.net)

Civil War Index - Civil War Battles from the Official Records - Volume 32, Chapter 44

A Reasonable Captivity: Soldier Experiences in Camp Chase – The Gettysburg Compiler

I tried to stay as true to the timeline as I could, but sources vary on what happened when. Also, I could only speculate on some particulars, such as how the women obtained water at the refugee house, how they prepared meals, how many stayed in one room, etc.

Few, if any, of the women from Roswell could read and write. The workers in New Manchester had more opportunities for schooling.

If you love historical romance, check out the other Wild Heart books!

*Marisol ~ Spanish Rose by Elva Cobb Martin*

***Escaping to the New World is her only option...Rescuing her will wrap the chains of the Inquisition around his neck.***

Marisol Valentin flees Spain after murdering the nobleman who molested her. She ends up for sale on the indentured servants' block at Charles Town harbor—dirty, angry, and with child. Her hopes are shattered, but she must find a refuge for herself and the child she carries. Can this new land offer her the grace, love, and security she craves? Or must she escape again to her only living relative in Cartagena?

Captain Ethan Becket, once a Charles Town minister, now the seas as a privateer, grieving his deceased wife. But wh takes captive a ship full of indentured servants, he's i by the woman whose manners seem much more refined than the average Spanish serving girl. Perfect to become governess for his young son. But when he sets out on a quest to find his captured sister, said to be in Cartagena, little does he expect his new Spanish governess to stow away on his ship with her six-month-old son. Yet her offer of help to free his sister is too tempting to pass up. And her beauty, both inside and out, is too attractive for his heart to protect itself against—until he learns she is a wanted murderess.

As their paths intertwine on a journey filled with danger, intrigue, and romance, only love and the grace of God can over-come the past and ignite a new beginning for Marisol and Ethan.

~

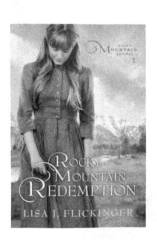

*Rocky Mountain Redemption by Lisa J. Flickinger*

*Rocky Mountain logging camp may be just the place to find* *lf.*

To escape the devastation caused by the breaking of her wedding engagement, Isabelle Franklin joins her aunt in the Rocky Mountains to feed a camp of lumberjacks cutting on the slopes of Cougar Ridge. If only she could out run the lingering nightmares.

Charles Bailey, camp foreman and Stony Creek's itinerant pastor, develops a reputation to match his new nickname — Preach. However, an inner battle ensues when the details of his rough history threaten to overcome the beliefs of his young faith.

Amid the hazards of camp life, the unlikely friendship growing between the two surprises Isabelle. She's drawn to Preach's brute strength and gentle nature as he leads the ragtag crew toiling for Pollitt's Lumber. But when the ghosts from her past return to haunt her, the choices she will make change the course of her life forever—and that of the man she's come to love.

~

*Lone Star Ranger by Renae Brumbaugh Green*

*Elizabeth Covington will get her man.*

And she has just a week to prove her brother isn't the murderer Texas Ranger Rett Smith accuses him of being. She'll show the good-looking lawman he's wrong, even if it means setting out on a risky race across Texas to catch the real killer.

Rett doesn't want to convict an innocent man. But he can't let the Boston beauty sway his senses to set a guilty man free. When Elizabeth follows him on a dangerous trek, the Ranger vows to keep her safe. But who will protect him from the woman whose conviction and courage leave him doubting everything—even his heart?

CPSIA information can be obtained
at www.ICGtesting.com
Printed in the USA
LVHW052304070623
749171LV00001B/104